THE

HOURGLASS

SEA

Part two of

The Dandelion

Farmer

1

By

MAT McCALL

O, wonder!

How many goodly creatures are there here!

How beauteous mankind is!

O brave new world.

That has such people in't!

THE TEMPEST, ACT V, SCENE 1.
WILLIAM SHAKESPEARE

That Mars is inhabited by beings of some sort of other we may consider as certain as it is uncertain what those beings may be.

PERCIVAL LOWELL

Dedication

For my Sister

Jennifer Compton

and all the little Comptons…

This story would never have been written without the love and

inspiration of

Nikki Jackson

With thanks also for the help and encouragement of

Nick Lambert

James Richardson-Brown

Ian Furey-King

Tom and Nimue Brown

Cover design by

Grace Jackson Photography

Special thanks

Sir John Sydeian and James Sydeian remain the copyright of James Richardson-Brown.

Some nights I dream of Mars.

Dreams of another Mars. A desolate, frozen world of saffron-hued sands and endless rock fields. There are no canals, no red forests or cerulean lakes, no swaying grasslands of crimson weed. No abandoned glass cities, monuments to a lost race.

Nothing.

In the silence, two tiny, deformed moons glitter as they tumble precariously through the cloudless mazarine of a merciless, airless sky.

A dry, cold place where nothing stirs but the dust devils created by the freezing winds.

A sterile lump of sandy red clay discarded by The Great Creator as he moved on to fashion another more perfect sphere.

A Mars upon which nothing has ever endured, nor ever shall.

A desolate stillborn world.

I often wake, chilled to the bone, weeping. On those nights, I seldom can return to sleep and so I take a strong cup of tea out with me to the veranda to smell the sweet scent of the jasmine and watch the first of the dawn's rays appear in the morning sky.

As the sun rises, I say a prayer to thank the Lord that it was only a dream.

A dream of another world, another place, another time. Maybe even, another Mars.

Edwin Ransom

Proem

Dear Reader.

I present to you the second folio of letters, diary entries, and transcribed journals attributed to members of the Flammarion Expedition and other interested parties.

As with the previous bundle, we have included as much material relevant to your understanding, not only of the occurrences that overtook the Expedition, but the broader political context that impacted upon those events, as well as memoirs, and statements taken some time after, that reflect upon those events.

By the 33rd of September in the Martian Year 26.

My grandfather Professor James Athanasius Flammarion, against all accepted wisdom, had assembled a team of adventurers and scientists to form an expedition to seek out and contact what he believed to be the last remaining vestiges of the Aresian, First Martian, civilisation.

While investigating an ancient Aresian Tomb discovered on my father's farmland, the Flammarion Expedition was ambushed by corsairs of the airship Wyndeyer. Caught helpless by the sudden assault, the expedition members were saved by the intercession of a gigantic sand kraken, disturbed and enraged by the gunfire.

My father and his good friend Adam Franklin had been diverted to the farmhouse to collect some of my father's possessions but had fallen into a trap laid by a villainous wretch called John Lloyd and had been forced to fight their way out.

Lloyd and the crew of the Wyndeyer were in the pay of the Zephyrian fuel magnate Eleuthère Du Maurier, whose reason for his continued pursuit and persecution of my father and grandfather were, as yet, unclear.

Captain James F. Ransom. Rtd.
London.

"The best laid schemes o' mice and men,

Gang aft agley,

An' lea'e us nought but grief an' pain,

For promis'd joy!"

TO A MOUSE
ROBERT BURNS

DAY FOUR

(Cont.)

<u>POLYPUS DEI</u>

Charity Bryant-Drake.
Notes to self.   33/9/26.
Cont.

In all my life, I have never known such fear.

Above us, the huge black and red galleon gave out a deafening bellow, like a clarion call from Hell itself, and threw open its gun ports. The Seren Bore lay helpless before it, like a floundering carp in the sights of a diving eagle.

We on the ground could only stand petrificated by sheer terror. ~~*And then*~~

I am at a loss to recount what occurred; it is almost beyond my ability to encapsulate in simple words.

The largest of the sand dunes that had piled up on the edge of Mr Ransom's farmland suddenly burst apart. Rust red tentacles, as thick as the stoutest tree trunks, flung upwards to seize the pirate's ship, tearing it from the sky.

In all its fearsome glory, the great crimson and black airship crumpled like a tin toy in the monster's grip. Sails ripped, rigging snapped, and screaming men plunged from its decks, flailing wildly as they fell to their inevitable deaths upon the ground.

For a moment, the pirate's balloon resisted, enough to keep the ship aloft, but the creature heaved at it, almost revealing itself entirely from its burrow. A sand kraken, of unimaginable size, eyes bigger than the wheels of a Hanson cab. Its rough, saffron-coloured body, vast beyond description, grappled pitilessly with its stricken prey.

The crew of the Seren Bore had, in that short time, recovered themselves enough to retaliate, mercilessly spewing gunfire into the belly of the pirate ship. The ship exploded from within (Mr Ransom tells me; it was probably the boilers that ruptured). The whole burning wreck crashed down into the writhing limbs of the kraken.

Unperturbed by the fire spewing from its prize, the monster wrapped its mighty tentacles, as gnarled as a thousand-year-old olive tree, about the shattered hulk, and began to drag it back to its lair.

The gunners upon the Seren Bore, seeing the creature as a menace they had to defend against, began to pour down a barrage upon it.

We on the ground all saw the creature pause. It paused as would an angry prattan beset by hounds. Its vast, lozenge-shaped amber eyes with their strange sha-shaped irises turned to the Seren Bore and narrowed. There was not an iota of fear in that glance. I believe that at that moment, it was deciding whether to destroy the Seren Bore, as one would swat an annoying insect.

I do not doubt that the monster could have launched the remains of the broken galleon at the Seren Bore as easily as Mr Ransom can throw a cricket ball and with equal accuracy.

Abruptly, above the deafening noise, a voice rang out. What I cannot explain is that at that moment, the voice seemed to be more inside my head than fighting its way through the hellish cacophony assailing my ears.

It was Aelita Fontenelli. Somehow, she had slipped past us into the midst of the pandemonium. She stood there, a tiny figure, surrounded by devastation, but her voice carried even over the roar of the guns. She commanded the gunners to cease, and they did. Strangely I cannot for the life of me quote the words of her passionate plea, but everyone felt the compulsion to obey her. In fact, for a moment, everything appeared to stop.

The eerie stillness was finally broken by a cavernous sound that resonated through the kraken. It lifted its vast head, exhaled a choking cloud of cinnamon coloured dust and began to flail its colossal appendages, whipping up an enormous whirlwind of sand.

Everyone became too distracted in their desperate attempts to pull respirators over their faces or cover their mouths with scarfs and kerchiefs, that by the time our eyes had cleared, as if by some great stage magician's trick with smoke and mirrors, the kraken was gone.

There was no time for consternation. Colonel Jahns appeared at the tomb side, blood-splattered and streaked with perspiration. He ordered us, unequivocally, back to the Seren Bore. Following his explicit orders, his soldiers hustled everyone to the ship. Patty and I tried desperately to hurry Dr Spender, who seemed utterly befuddled by the whole experience, but without a great deal of success. We had just managed to get him over the ledge of the tomb when he swooned. Luckily, one of the Colonel's men rushed to our aid, swept Dr Spender up into his sturdy arms, and ran for the ship. Patty and I clasped hands and ran after them.

The Captain had ordered the lowering of a loading platform to hoist the Expedition members back up to the safety of the ship.

We piled on, hanging for dear life to the ropes and cables that were the only barrier between the rapidly increasing drop and us.

As we raised into the air, we were all appalled to witness the destruction wrought in such a short time. The smouldering hulk of the pirate's airship lay shattered into several pieces across the sand dunes, shrouded in its ripped sails, and surrounded by a dozen unmoving bodies. Like some enormous red and black pseudopod, the ship's balloon lay further out, slowly deflating into death. Its frightful skull and crossbones emblem, with its jauntily worn top hat, now ripped through in such a manner it appeared as if it were screaming. Those of the pirates who could flee had fled, abandoning their dead comrades.

The pleasant pastoral scene we had arrived at was now a battlefield, strewn with burning wreckage and the grotesquely twisted bodies of the dead. The partial remains of the smaller dirigible that pursued me at Alba Kirk were now scattered in a wide arc through the field of dandelions. Around the tomb itself, several bodies lay crumpled where they had fallen in the red dirt.

The hoist operator announced to us, in almost an accusatory tone, that we had lost at least three or four crewmembers and one of the "darkies." He added some other remark that was lost to the rest of us under the noise of the hoist's steam-powered mechanism. Lost to our ears, but not to Patty's.

Angrier than I could have possibly imagined, she struck the crewman across the face with the flat of her hand and shouted at him that those "darkies" are better men than he, soldiers of the Republic in fact, and that man had died fighting to save our lives. Therefore, he should show them proper respect, or she would teach him some. I think under other circumstances that crewman, a huge burly brute with a dark ginger beard and cruelly piercing blue eyes, would have immediately hit her back, but, with all our eyes upon him, all he could do was blush and mumble something approximating an apology.

It was only when we had safely boarded the Seren Bore that it occurred to me to ask of the kraken. Harkett, the acting Purser, took Professor Flammarion and myself to the starboard side and gestured out into the sandy wilderness. At first, our eyes searched hopelessly until the Purser pointed out the tell-tale signs of movement that gave it away.

There it was, moving away at an astonishing speed. Someone handed us a spyglass, and we watched engrossed as the creature distorted itself, changing shape, colour, even texture, to blend in with the landscape it moved so effortlessly across.

For the first time in my life, I felt that I have no real understanding of this world I call home, the planet I was born on, a world that could spawn such a wondrous alien monster as that, can it ever be anything but hostile to our existence?

As those thoughts were coalescing in my mind, the creature stopped. Turning back towards us, it raised itself onto its great appendages, as if it were looking back to study us with those huge yellow agate-like eyes, and then, and I shall swear this to my dying day; it vanished.

I know that it most probably simply changed colour again and melded into the landscape, but I must believe the evidence of my own eyes; for I saw the kraken vanish into thin air.

Excerpt from;
Memoirs of Aelita, Lady Sydeian.
The Athenaeum of Harendrimar Tai.
Cont.

I confess to remembering little of what transpired thereafter. What remains embedded in my memory is that, for what was in truth only a mere split second, I stood in the direct gaze of the kraken. Its strange, shaped irises opened like vast golden agate whirlpools, transfixing me to the spot. At that moment, I knew her. It was as if our minds had touched. I can only describe the sensation as that of suddenly waking from a dream to find oneself standing at the top of a towering precipice over some bottomless abyss. I felt my very insides freeze. The breath stilled within me, my heart near stopped.

She was ancient. Powerful beyond comprehension. Undoubtedly capable of destroying us all if she so wished; however, she did not desire our deaths. A wave of compassion surged over me, tinctured with a melancholy so profound it erased my own trivial qualms, washing away my uncertainties. Within it were other emotions; empathy, yearning, even love, and the fearsome steadfastness of a mother defending her young, as if we friable little creatures were her progenies.

Suddenly strong arms seized my waist and hoisted me off my feet. It was Ursula. She swept me up like a child's doll and carried me away from that ossifying gaze. As if loosened from the terrific weight of some physical burden, my senses whirled, and darkness flooded my vision. The last thought that I can clearly

16

recall was my shock at the sight of Ursula's beautiful alabaster countenance, now partially shattered by some terrible trauma, revealing the spider's web matrix of intricate cogs and gears beneath.

The Field Journal of Octavius Spender, Dr
33rd of Sept 0026.
Cont.

Such an eventful and dreadful day.

The events of this day surpass almost any other single day in my life. I have seen, with my own two eyes, the wonders of the universe played out around me in a vast panorama. I have been privy to an awe-inspiring history so far surpassing the parsimonious conjectures of my fellow academics as to make their narrow notions laughable. Then, in but a few instants, to have found myself thrust into the midst of an appalling mêlée, in which all of our lives seemed momentarily forfeit. Until the intervention of...

The creature.

One has read as a child of such things, adventurous yarns, boy's own escapades, and, of course, some of the more lurid tales one finds in the pages of the yellow press, but nothing could prepare one for such a sight. To witness such an attack, from a manifestation of fables, was almost too much for my weakened constitution.

I awoke safe in my bunk aboard the ship.

Since then, I have had cause to do little else than to write this entry.

James came to check up on my condition a few moments ago, we spoke of the horrors of the assault upon us and the monster's intervention, for, mark me well on this; intervention it was.

As always, the pragmatic wielder of Occam's razor, James put it down to nothing more than a fortuitous coincidence; the sheltering creature, disturbed by the guns and clamour of the air buccaneer's cacophonous blast, arose to attack what it saw as an immediate threat. It was, to his thinking, merely the luck of the turn of a card that the buccaneer's ship lay between the enraged monster and the Seren Bore. I disagree wholeheartedly, but all is subjective interpretation only.

We agreed upon the remarkable size of the beast, to both our knowledge, it was bigger than any we had heard of, or even alluded to in Sydeian's seminar. Beyond that, there was little else I could, or would at this time, share with my old friend, lest he thinks me gone entirely insane.

I must now reflect upon what was revealed to me in that sepulchre that was not. I believe that in fact, it was some form of athenaeum, a repository of knowledge. I fear that if I should talk too unguardedly, my fellows will think I have lost my wits, babbling like some pious ascetic about mystical revelations. However, I genuinely doubt that what I experienced was mystical in any way. I believe what I saw was an actual record of real events transcribed directly into my mind by some higher technological means, which, even to a mind as educated as mine, appears almost mystical. A technology so in advance of our own understanding that I would be forced to use esoteric or religious terms to describe the experience of the interaction if I were tasked to explain it.

I believe Madam Fontenelli underwent a similar perception, and I have resolved to broach the subject with her as soon as both of us have recovered from this ordeal.

James has informed me that we are returning to Tharsis forthwith.

P.E.S. Seren Bore. 18.32/33/09/26

Ship's scrap log (excerpts from) Captain R. K. Llewellyn.

Ship attacked by ground forces as well as hostile airships.
Damage to ship minimal. Minor damage to balloon envelope.

Successful in driving off ground attackers. Both attacking crafts destroyed.

Two crew members killed.

Stubb, Peter. Motorman.

Flask, John. Stoker's Mate.

Three seriously injured.

Rokovoko, 'Harry' Haere. Steward's Mate.

Fedallah, Abdulla. Able Crewman.

Enderby, Samuel. Ordinary Crewman.

Several crew members have received minor injuries.

One of Colonel Jahns' Negro soldiers killed.

Expedition members all accounted for and unscathed.

Numerous casualties amongst the attackers.

Upon Professor Flammarion's orders, we did not give chase to those who fled the scene.

Colonel Jahns and I strongly advised that we should leave as soon as practically possible.

Departed location at 17.10. Under the cover of darkness.

Journal of Adam Franklin.

The sound of cannon fire reached our ears, long before we saw the devastation it had wrought. A ship, no doubt the *Wyndeyer* that the rogue I questioned named, lay shattered into a dozen smoking pieces upon the ground. Its crew either dead or fled. A dozen or more bodies lay crumpled in bloody heaps around the tomb. While we had contended with Lloyd and his henchmen to rescue a few books, the actual battle had happened here.

Edwin wanted to talk and wonder, but we would only have time for that once we were within the safety of the ship's gunwales. Upon our arrival, the crew swiftly lowered a platform, hoisting us up into the belly of the aerostat.

It was only then, as we stowed Edwin's possessions and secured the vehicle, that the story of what had transpired came out. Sergeant Rawlings was informed by his comrades that Sergeant Capon was killed defending the expedition members. For the short time I had known him, Harry Capon, had seemed a decent, jovial fellow, and I am aware, or at least the part of me that was once Sergeant Major Franklin is aware, of how hard it is to lose a close comrade you have served beside for years.

Rawlings is a good fellow, redoubtable, but I saw the slump in his shoulders at the news. He asked politely to be excused, and, with my condolences, I readily gave my permission.

Then, as Edwin and I made our way to the upper decks, we heard the stories of the kraken. At first, I thought they were jesting, having a little macabre black humour at our expense, but by the time we reached the wardroom and the company of other expedition team members, we had already gleaned enough to understand it was no joke.

The Professor's face was a grim mask, Jahns was subdued in his manner, Charity and Parthena were wrapped in each other's arms, Dr Spender was, we were informed, resting in his cabin, so was Aelita Fontenelli in hers.

Sir John arrived a short while after us. He said his flying apparatus had conked out on the way back to the ship, so he had had to land in one of Edwin's dandelion fields and carry the kit all the way back. He had run into a couple of "corsairs," as he called them, but they had been in no mind to cause him any trouble.

Inside me grows a sense of disquiet about Sir John Sydeian. I cannot put a finger on it, but the man uneases me.

The tale of the afternoon's events unfolded, told in the main as it was by Charity and Parthena. The events of the attack upon the ship, the Expedition and the terrible fate of the Wyndeyer became our main topic of conversation for the evening. Even the Professor talked about the events with wide-eyed incredulity. There was much debate as to the actual size of the monster; its tentacles alone must have been, at least, a hundred and fifty feet long, able to reach from the ground to the sails and rigging of the ship to rip them asunder.

Sydeian loudly proclaimed his frustration at not having encountered the monster himself.

For me, all this speculation was a relief, as neither Edwin nor I wished to be questioned too closely over our own little adventure. It sufficed to say; we had encountered some cutthroats and dealt with them quite severely. No one, not even Charity, enquired further.

The most intriguing news in the wardroom was that Mrs Fontenelli interceded for the defence of the creature, commanding the guns of the Seren Bore to cease. Later the Captain joined us to say that we were underway (to return directly to Tharsis). Charity questioned him as to why the gunners so readily obeyed Mrs Fontenelli's orders. As the noise of those guns, let alone the distance, would have surely deafened them to her words.

The Captain's explanation led to much dismay and raising of eyebrows. Apparently, the gunners did not hear Mrs Fontenelli's order at all, but, in an incredible coincidence, both Cogswaine guns simply jammed in the very same moment.

However, the others spent a lot of time marvelling over the opportune intercession of the kraken. I am left more perplexed by the incident of the steam rotation guns. Guns like that jam up, I know that. Every soldier who has ever worked with mechanised weaponry, no matter how well maintained, knows *full well they are prone to jam at the most inopportune moments, usually in the midst of battle. The Sergeant Major has a dozen anecdotal stories of his own, but "and there's the rub," as the Doctor likes to say, how could they jam at the very same instant? It is inconceivable to me. None of the speculations of the others, including Edwin and our renowned Professor, could make any sense of it.*

I was somewhat lost in my thoughts when into the wardroom came Aelita Fontenelli's automaton maid, ostensibly to take a salver of food to her mistress. Its exquisitely carved, impassive alabaster facemask had been partially shattered. The left cheek down to the jawline was gone, revealing the mechanisms underneath it, an intricate framework of cogs, gears and tiny pistons. A horologist's masterpiece, powered by the continual motion of its internal balanced springs, a clockwork automaton that winds itself, almost perpetually. Like Karl, no doubt, it takes some extra energy to maintain its cognitive processes, such as a gravity cell, a battery, built into its core. The intricate details of such things Edwin had regaled me with, at some great length, on our railplane journey. The damage to its face lent itself to a baleful beauty, though it brought clearly to my mind's eye the thoroughly unbeautiful face of John Lloyd.

Underneath this fleshy husk I too am mostly machine, not one as elegant or aesthetically pleasing as Ursula, but one born of an alien technology of an infinitely more complex nature. I cast a glance about the room, idly wondering if anyone of those present unknowingly shared my predicament. Maybe we are all machines, mechanised marionettes, trapped in some unreality, playing out some over mighty child's fantasy.

I have discovered that, though my constitution is far advanced of what it once was, if I imbibe enough good brandy, a lot of brandy, it does eventually have the desired soporific effect.

Edwin, who had been drinking almost as much as myself, was in no state to argue when I took him back to our cabin and put him to bed.

It took some time to settle him down as he insisted upon explaining to me all his ideas of how he could make Pyréolophore's in-cylinder compression engines far more efficient and less noisome. He had dreams of building new aerocraft, with faster, lighter, more powerful engines, all driven not by steam or electricity, but by botanical fuels made from his dandelions and sunflowers, of course. He had a head full of detailed inventions and designs, which he must have been musing on for decades. It was pointless trying to stifle a drunken man, especially one so lost in his enthusiastic ramblings, so I let him chatter on until he wore himself out and finally fell asleep.

I shall sleep here on the floor, propped up in the corner of the room, with my knees tight under my chin. With my back pressed against the bulkhead, I can feel the engine's rhythmic pulse carrying through me. A reassuring physical memory from when the Sergeant Major was a small child or that is what it feels like.

The Diary of Dr James Athanasius Flammarion.
33rd Sept. 26th.

We flee into the night, carrying our wounded and dead. All aboard are confused and frightened. I must admit I could never have imagined that that cad Du Maurier would go so far. Edwin was right to be fearful of such a tyrant. As soon as we return to Tharsis, I will contact Bogdanov and have that swine Du Maurier arrested. On my beloved Alexa's grave, I swear I shall pull every string, redeem every reciprocal favour owing to me, to bring that vile little popinjay to justice for this. I have never wished a man dead, nor shall I allow myself to do so, but, as God is my witness, I shall do whatever it takes to bring the wrath of the Law down upon his head, in full knowledge of the consequences for him.

I shall have to bury three of my crew, and I shall have to look their loved ones in the eyes and explain to them that they died because of some megalomaniac's obsession with an empty tomb. I have now three families to recompense and support in some way, for the loss of their fathers, for which I shall eternally carry the weight of responsibility.

As for the beast's intervention, I shall attribute that to the grace of the Almighty, as proof of His approval. Although I shall not openly put it in such terms to the expedition members, though as such events are almost beyond any coincidence imaginable, they have already flirted with the idea of heavenly intercession.

I did not wish to be drawn into a religious argument with either Jahns or Spender, especially in front of the others or the crew. The Lord moves in mysterious ways, and if he could move through the agent of Jonah's whale, then I must accept he can move through the avatar of a sand kraken. So be it.

We are making good time for Tharsis. I have requested Llewellyn to push the engines as hard as he can. The journey will be a little choppy, facing into the prevailing winds channelled between Alba and Olympus Mons, but we can waste no time. Two of the crew were severely injured in the attack. I fear it may be to a level beyond Mr Holly's capabilities, and that of the ship's sickbay resources, to attend to properly. In addition, I am concerned about the health of Octavius and Mrs Fontenelli, both of whom collapsed during the incursion.

Such distress, but what for? An empty crypt, devoid of anything other than a few engravings on the inside of its capstone.

THE REPUBLIC OF THARSIS BUREAU OF STATE
INTERNAL SECURITY
CRIMINAL INVESTIGATION DEPARTMENT
THARSIS DIVISION
Witness Statement

Interview statement taken from Prisoner 452, Henry Avery, aka "Long Harry" on the 43rd, October. 29. Tharsis Panopticon.

Convicted crewmember, "Rigger," of the aerostat The Wyndeyer.

No. I have no idea.

I must hav' got meself tangled in somethin' on the way down 'cos I wakes up wrapped in shreds of sailcloth, arse up'ards' in a sand dune.

No, by the time I got the sand outta me peepers and me gob, it was gone.

The place looked like the gateway to Hell. The Windy was just burning flotsam all over the place, and those bastards on the moocher's ship were shooting at everything' that moved.

When someone's firing a steam cannon at yous from above, yous don't hang around for a natter. As soon as the coast looked clear,

I legged it faster than a sailor on his wedding day.

The others?

Nah, you's need to disavow yourself of such ideas, matey. In situations like that there ain't no honour amongst no one, least yous wanna die helpin' some critter (1) who wouldn't hang back to piss on your if you's was on fire. It's everyone for himself. Yeah, sos I thanked God above and ran.

I ran for one of those big stands of sunflowers, lots of 'em on the edges of the field were knocked over, an' they were's a bastard to climb over, but when you got into the thick of 'em they were pretty good cover.

Nobody came after us, well's least not immediately. Their ship departed pretty smart like, and then those of us that were still around heard the Captain's whistle.

Dullahan had this old rozzer's pipe she used, I dunno why, as she had a screech on her that could crack glass. Anyhows, she's blowing this bloody thing as a signal the coast is clear. Sos out we trot. Back to her lovin' arms.

No! She was a vicious colleen. You need to be, to be a Captain.

She didn't get elected 'cos she had a pretty face or woz good in the sack. She certainly wasn't the first, an' I heard she wasn't much use at the other either. Preferred her own kind.

Nah, not women. Weirdies like herself.

There woz rumours that she kept an old hand-o'-glory, not for witchcraft yous understand, but for those more intimate moments.

She was pretty knocked about, covered in blood, but like me, she'd been thrown off the ship and landed in the dunes.

Twenty-three of us came back. I dunno, if others survived that, might hav' had the good sense to hav' just kept runnin.'

Dullahan? She may hav' been an evil-minded trasseno, but she always had a plan. She was a Rapparee (2) from a long line of them, cunnin' as a fox, always knew wot to do, like an instinct on her.

She took us back to the site to scavenge whatever we could carry, food, barkers, anythin'. We even found two of our own alive and well enough to follow on.

Nop. I did not have anythin' to do with that.

But, cos' you ask, yes. I believe that Dullahan did end some of those who were not already dead but were in no state to come with us. Did them a favour really. Either they'd die of their wounds, or the cold or someone would save 'em, nurse them back to helf and then hang 'em for pirates. Wot's the point of that? And the only way they'd save themselves from that'd be to snitch on us, and then we'd swing. Dullahan did us all a favour an' shot 'em herself. Dead men, an' all that.

Oh, aye, well as I told yous, she woz probably too tight to spend a bullet on them, anyways, as I said, she woz a Rapparee, they like to work with the blade.

We grabbed wot we could and got away from there quickly before either the Law turned up or that bloomin' thing came back to gorge itself on its kills. All that fresh meat was bound to attract somethin' hungry.

We headed up to the farmhouse on the property, but everyone there was dead too. Inside the house looked like a butcher's yard. There were some tough hands amongst those she sent with the 'Passenger.' All dead, and some hadn't even had ammunition wasted on 'em. Even the 'Passenger' was dead, an' he looked like he'd taken an awful lotta killin'.

Some of us were already worryin' what exactly that mad colleen had gotten us caught up in.

Dullahan blamed the little ginger sort that had done the original hiring. She said she knew where we could find him.

Nah, nothin' worth taking, so we just grabbed food and stuff and got outta there. Dullahan said we needed to head towards Tremorfa Township. Some of us wanted to bed down in the house, but she wouldn't hear of it.

Sos there we woz, in the pitch bloody dark, no lanterns, trudging along some old farm track in the middle of no wheres.

I have no idea, probably just after midnight.

A couple of the keen-eyed saw it coming at us over the top of the stands of vegetation. Just a light in the sky at first and then this merciless bastard is on us.

A rocketeer. Yes.

I have no idea, never came low enough to see and to tell yous the truth, I didn't stay around to bloody look.

He's up there about ten yards above us like the bloomin' demon king himself. He had some sort of rapid-fire gun, like a Maxim or some such, and he could see us easily in the darkness. He had this red beam of light that shone from his helmet. I swear we weren't too busy running not to put a few rounds into him, but it made not a jot of difference.

I don't know. Twenty minutes or so, maybe less, felt like a lifetime. I have never been hunted like that befores.

Have yous? Do you think you'd be waistin' time lookin' at that fancy bloody pocket jerry of yous?

Yes, hunted.

He hunted men down and blew 'em apart. Some stood their ground shootin' back, but they might as well have been pissin' in the wind. I caught two in the shoulder and back, but had armour on, som' old boilerplate that Tricky Tom had fashioned, I took it off his body back at the farmhouse, wasn't any use to him no more, but it saved my hide.

I got down in the undergrowth an' bloody well stayed there until he had his belly full of killing anyone that moved. Once he stopped, he just hung there in the air for a while waitin' for something. Like some nasty big-arsed bat. No, more like a moth.

He was probably waiting for people's nerves to break. Finally, a couple did, and that's when he used the fire thrower on them. Like a big jet of liquid fire, he sprayed out over them as they ran, then he proceeded to burn the whole area. Vegetation like that burns well, but it creates an awful lot of smoke very fast. I held me nerve until I could barely breathe and then I bolted.

Oh, I have no idea. He either didn't see us or just didn't care.

Only ten of us got out of those fields alive, one didn't make it to Tremorfa, but the rest of us did.

It was barely morning when Captain Dullahan and the eight of us got into the town,

We just wanted to find food and horses and get bloody well outta there as fast as we could.

Dullahan had other plans, in any case, as I said, she was always a chess move ahead of most peoples. She had the handle of the little ginger gink that got us into this mess in the first place, and he lived just outside of Tremorfa. She wanted us to go pay him a visit and avail ourselves of his hospitality for a few days.

(1) A common contemptuous term for someone with no personal connection to the speaker.
(2) An Irish Bandit.

"Greater love hath no one than this; that they lay down their life for another."

JOHN 15:13

HOLY BIBLE.

THE MARTIAN UNIFIED REDEMPTIONIST VERSION

(MURV)

DAY FIVE

<u>SACRIFICE</u>

The Diary of Eleanor Athaliah Ransom (Mrs).
34th September 26

I hardly rested at all last night.

I have never suffered the beleaguered existence of one who has fallen victim to a curse. Though my mother wholeheartedly believed in the power of such things, it seems to me to be the nonsense stuff of romantic novels and ancient plays, not reality. Nonetheless, I imagine that this is what in actuality to labour under such a terrible malediction feels like. For that is what Everheart's condolence cardis, a curse. Frankly more than this artless threat, I think there is a hex upon me, my household and, more terribly, my children.

My sleep is plagued with nightmares in which this fiend Everheart figures significantly. I have never set eyes upon the man, but I seem to be able to see him in my mind's eye in awful clarity. My sleeping imagination must have sketched him from the briefest of descriptions, imbuing him with a dreadful sense of menace. In those dreams, I found myself wresting my children from his bloody hands.

Startled wakefulness brought instant relief, but my fears are like wild animals chasing around in my head to the point where the idea of returning to sleep fills me with dreadful trepidations. And yet I have resolved, I shall not live in fear, for to do so, I believe is the only real power such imprecations have, they kill one's mind with the poison of anxiety and despondency. I will not allow it to contaminate my household, or myself and, should it come to it, I would fight, with tooth and nail, the Devil himself, should he attempt to harm my children.

I arose in the very earliest of hours to find myself checking door locks and window latches. Danny discovered me on his patrol. We withdrew to the kitchen to drink tea and talk quietly. He has grown so much this last year, quite becoming a handsome young man, worthy of the pride his father and mother have in him, but one of few words, as so many young men are. After a few pleasantries and with his deftly avoiding my questions about Milly, the daughter of Josiah Grote, Papa's vintner and occasional drinking companion, we fell into sipping our tea in silence. Silence as it was, though punctuated with Bowen's gentle snoring from her cot by the stove.

By the time Mrs Carstairs arrived to start the morning ritual of chores, Danny had left. Bowen was beginning to stir from her slumbers by the grate.

I withdrew to the morning room, where I found Karl awaiting me. We went over the plans for the day, especially those centred on our safety.

Perceptive in a manner unimaginable to those who have never lived, or worked closely besides, such an automaton, Karl is the rock upon which all our safety rests.

Lady N, Minnie and Neriah joined me to take a late breakfast, but fearing I would not make good company, I explained that my mind is so full of fears that it will not let me rest. Lady N and Minnie would hear nothing of it. Minnie took my hand and firmly instructed me to go back to bed, as I was far too weary to be up. I attempted to poo-poo her concerns, but it was of no use trying to argue with her.

So here I am, back in bed, writing this diary. Part of me wishes to write down every fear in detail as if putting them into words on the page would somehow purge them through the act of transcribing them. Still, such a list would, even upon semi-completion, be so frightfully insurmountable that I would quail before it.

I shall endeavour to rest a little. Minnie brought me a cup of Mrs Carstairs' sleeping draft, often celebrated throughout our family, which I know, through experience, is most potent, and she insisted that I drank it. I can indeed feel its puissance beginning to overwhelm my senses as I write, but I fear how my worries will manifest again in my dreams.

Oh, Edwin, how I miss you, and dear Papa. I fear I am too weak to defend my family on my own. Would that you were here, I could be so much stronger.

Excerpt from;
Diary of Aelita Fontenelli (Mrs).
Thursday, September, 34th. MY.26
Dear Diary.

In all those long empty days spent at home in contemplation of my circumstances. In all my fantasies of what exploits and trials freedom may present me with, and the dreams of what adventures I would pursue, I never suspected it would be all so terrifying.

Has the Lord, in His wisdom, seen to put me to the test in so many ways like Job, or am I, as Pandora was, beset by the myriad anguishes I have foolishly set loose upon myself?

Yesterday I killed a man. I shall never know his name or if he truly was a bad man or some poor lost soul forced into evil by circumstances. I shall forever, in my memory, see his face. It was an angry face, a grim face, though the face of an evil man? How could one ever know? I fear that face will haunt the darkness behind my eyelids for the rest of my lifetime. I committed a terrible mortal sin. For which there are many pale excuses, though there can be no true forgiveness. I wish I could speak to Father Ignacio to make my confession and seek my penitence. What penitence is a measure for such a mortal sin?

Worse still, if I cross-examine myself as to would I do it again, though my heart cries out against it; I know I would. More to save my companions than my own miserable life.

Then, there was the great beast. I know nothing of the woman who ran out to confront that ancient monster. She is entirely unknown to me.

Last night I could hardly sleep for dreams plagued by visions of the horror of yesterday's events. Yet when I finally did, I fell into an exhaustion-fuelled torpor. The dreams that came felt more like visions, memories almost, however, they were seemingly not mine.

I have a terrible mounting fear that I cannot even share with Ursula; I fear that when I confronted the great beast, our minds touched, in some unfathomable way. For want of a better word, some conjoining was made, and it is yet to be unmade. I saw through the eyes of the creature, I thought its thoughts and felt its emotions, sensations, and most predominantly, its intent. The aspect though, most disturbing to my sensibilities, is that the impression did not in any way feel alien to me.

My sensations of empathic awareness seem to be expanding into my waking world along with the awareness of myself, none of which brings me any comfort. I feel that I have always been cognizant of the duality at the core of my existence, like the flaw in a gemstone, only I am not made of stone. Now I am aware of the true nature of that dichotomy and how deep the fault runs, deep into the foundations of my existence. I am perplexed to the point of being at a loss to comprehend it.

Am I a woman? Assuredly so. My anatomy is the closest approximation to those others I have known. I grew up in a

Catholic Convent with all the communality that encompasses; however, I can hardly be a woman in delineations meaningful for Tellurian women. I have long wondered about that issue of female maturity that afflicts my good friends, nevertheless, has never visited upon me. Dr Hammond suggested that it is the reason for my failure to present Giovanni with a child.

Nevertheless, I believe it takes more than simple fertility to produce offspring. Some activities need to be engaged in, of which Giovanni has always shown little interest. At least where it concerns me.

Now I look in the mirror and find myself beholding a reflection that is totally unknown yet is so familiar. I can see Gethen's face in mine. Not, as I thought it, some mere familial resemblance, simply as a facet of myself, he is part of me, not as Tellurian brothers or sisters share aspects of their origins, he was in actuality, a living presence within me. This realisation brings with it some comprehension of the conflicting humours that have obstructed my maturation. Within the strictures of Tellurian concepts, I can be neither female nor male. I feel like an uncompleted work, a creature trapped in an incomplete metamorphosis. A dragonfly ensnared in its transformation, unable to remain one thing or become another.

Now, as I gaze upon my reflection, beyond the masquerade I have so striven to make acceptable to others, I can see the alien clearly, and that alien is me.

THE REPUBLIC OF THARSIS BUREAU OF STATE
INTERNAL SECURITY
CRIMINAL INVESTIGATION DEPARTMENT
THARSIS DIVISION
Witness Statement

Statement taken from Henry Williamson Carstairs, Butler to Professor Flammarion.

Date taken 39th September 0026.

Regarding events of the evening of Thursday 34th September 0026

The day had preceded into the afternoon with little events. Mrs Carstairs and I saw that our role was to retain the normality of household routine as much as possible, regardless of the situation.

As usual, Miss Peyton, the Nanny, schooled the children in their rooms until teatime when they were allowed to spend some time on the lawn. Though she supervised them, Karl, the Ransom's automaton, was present at all times.

Karl organised the men into regular patrols about the grounds and outside the house. It fell to me to oversee the provision within.

Mrs Eleanor had strictly forbidden weapons to be openly carried inside the house, especially where the children might see them. This created difficulties, although we managed to follow her wishes. To achieve this, I had arranged for small caches of weapons to be secreted about the house. Atop of cupboards or bookshelves mainly. All out of sight and reach of the children, but easily accessible to those stationed within.

As I said, Mrs Eleanor had been up all night, so Mrs Minerva Ransom decided to let her rest on into the afternoon.

It was just after 4 pm, and the children were returning into the house through the morning room doors. I was about to rouse Mrs Eleanor with a pot of tea when the first incident occurred.

There came a pounding on the front door. My eldest boy, Danaus, opened it to find Michael Hopeforth, the youngest of the Overseer's sons. He had been sent to inform us that a group of men on horses had been spotted circling the estate just the other side of the garden walls and the pond.

There is a body of water to the south-west of the property. It has always been referred to as "the Pond." Though, in wetter times it is, in fact, a small tree-lined lake.

Several of the men wanted to go out to chase the riders off. Nevertheless, Mr Ransom's automaton, Karl, forbade it, saying it was probably nothing, maybe a group of gentlemen out for an afternoon constitutional ride. On the other hand, it could be an attempt to draw some of us out of the

confines of the estate. Either way, he would not countenance any rash actions.

Mrs Eleanor, awakened by the commotion, came down to tell us to obey Karl's instructions. We redoubled the patrols, put all available men on guard duty and secured the house.

In the evening, Lady Niketa suggested that her dogs be let loose from the orangery to have free run of the ground floor. They would definitely raise the alarm if any intruder disturbed them.

I could not see the benefit of allowing those mutts free range, they were not guard dogs and of absolutely no deterrent value to anyone, but both Mrs Ransoms agreed. Therefore, once dinner had been served and cleared, and after making sure the dogs had been introduced to all the men we had stationed in the house, the animals were let loose to roam the ground floor.

Mrs Eleanor and Lady Niketa, Mrs Minerva, along with her niece, Miss Brownlow, were still up, reading to each other and talking in the drawing room at almost 11 pm. I had just been dismissed for the night and was crossing the floor of the front hall when the dogs started barking. They immediately gathered into a pack and rushed towards the morning room, yapping wildly. I seized a shotgun from behind the grandfather clock in the hall, and calling for assistance, hurried to investigate.

Upon Karl's instructions, we had left all gaslights on throughout the house, and no interior door on the ground floor was shut. Therefore, the door to the morning room was already swinging wide, as the dogs had stampeded through it, when I entered the room.

Two men, dressed in dark clothes, one with a scarf across the lower part of his face, the other wearing a dust mask, were standing just inside the doors onto the patio. Caught by surprise, suddenly beset upon by a pack of yapping lapdogs, and confronted by myself, they froze. Whether they were armed or not, I did not wait to discover, I levelled the shotgun and let them have both barrels.

One screamed as he fell to the floor, the other one, the chap wearing the scarf, pirouetted and fled out into the darkness. Before I could reload, Karl rushed past me into the room and pursued the other out onto the patio.

There were more gunshots outside. By the time I had reloaded and checked whether the intruder on the floor was alive or dead, Karl had returned through the windows. The intruder was not dead but severely injured. My aim must have been better than I anticipated. He was, without a doubt armed, as he had with him a large knife and a pistol.

I dragged him off the carpet so he would not stain it with his blood. We were securely binding the wounded man up with a tieback from the curtains when there came screaming from the drawing room. Karl and I ran across the hall, though someone slammed the door shut on us as we approached, Karl easily shouldered it open.

Never for so long as I shall live, will I ever forget the scene that we burst in upon.

The room was in utter chaos. The ladies were struggling with two men. Lady Niketa and Miss Neriah were grappling hand-to-hand with a large man wearing a sheepskin coat and wielding a cutlass. Both Mrs Ransoms were using a chair and a poker to fend off the assault of another man with a large machete.

Karl drew his pistol and shot the man wearing the sheepskin in the back. As the intruder staggered away, Karl shot him a second time in the head.

I ordered the man with the machete to put the weapon down; however, he only turned as if to throw the weapon at me. I levelled my shotgun at him, but it was Karl that shot him down.

I was about to express my relief when Miss Brownlow pointed behind me and screamed. Not being as young as I once was, I tried to spin around, but I was caught off balance. I believe I was pushed, sending me sprawling onto the chaise lounge.

It was the man we knew as Everheart. Tall, dressed all in black, like a cowboy, with that big drooping moustache. It must have been he that shut the door on us. He was standing behind Karl.

Karl was not fast enough either. Everheart fired three shots from a very big pistol into Karl's faceplate from only inches away, knocking Karl off his feet.

To my eternal shame, I was so shocked that I could not react in time. I heard the ladies screaming, then there were shots, and suddenly the room went deathly quiet.

It was like being in a slowed version of a zoetrope, everything seemed impossibly sluggish.

All of us except Everheart that is.

He smiled; it was the most chilling expression I have ever seen on a human face. He then nonchalantly holstered his gun, turned and walked out of the room into the hall.

As my wits returned to me, I realised Miss Brownlow was no longer screaming. She was standing in the middle of the room, howling like a wounded animal. The other three women were huddled together on the floor.

There were now gunshots and shouting coming from all over. As I stood up, Lady Niketa, whom I remember, was soaked in blood, screamed at me to protect the children.

Obeying immediately, I ran as fast as I could into the hall and up the stairs. I reached the nursery door and pounded upon it with all my might, shouting my name and theirs. Nanny opened the door and assured me the children were safe. I gave her the shotgun, and the pistol I had taken from the intruder and ran back down to the drawing room.

It was only then, as I entered the room again that I realised Mrs Eleanor was lying unmoving upon the floor between the other two ladies, her head cradled in the bosom of Lady Niketa. There was so much blood, and she was not moving. Mrs Minerva was clasping her hand, kissing it and calling her name repeatedly, but she was gone.

James Ransom.

I clearly remember the night my mother died. Though we were kept away from the horrors of the calamity that befell our family, we heard the screaming, the gunfire and the panicked shouting of the men.

Though Nanny tried desperately to keep us safe, we listened intently and stole peeks out from behind the shutters and curtains.

My bedroom window overlooked the garden on the morning room side and, desperate to catch even a glimpse of what was happening, I had, in the past, managed to rig the latch so that I could open them without a key. That night I had the shutters open enough to put my head up under the heavy drapes and peek over the windowsill.

Although it was late in the night, I witnessed the excitement of all the running about, the shouting and the sound and flare of the guns discharging in the dark. I believe my excitement entirely overcame my fear until I saw the man I have since come to know as Everheart.

We were only children, and the whole household had kept us shielded from what was going on, to the point of what I see now as blithe ignorance. I did not truly understand what was happening or why, but, as children are want to do, I had made it my business, at all opportunities, to eavesdrop and thus had on several occasions overheard a name, whispered in fearful tones; "Everheart."

Tabitha had thought it such a pretty name when I told her and resolved to give the name to the puppy, she was sure father would bring back with him from his adventures, but I had no such illusions after perceiving the fear in the voices of those that spoke of him.

When I saw the man in black walk out that night through the morning room doors, look back, and up at where I watched. I knew with absolute certainty as if by some terrible mesmeric art, it was he. He wore a mantle of evil about him as one would wear a limousine.

Then, even with all the pandemonium going on, he stopped and took the time to light a cigar. All while never taking his eyes off mine. The phosphorous flare of the closely held match lit up his face like a demonic mask, reflecting burning yellow in his eyes. Leaving me frozen to the spot, he tipped the brim of his hat as if bidding me a mannerly adieu, then turned and strode off into the darkness. I think I knew then that he had accomplished whatever terribly evil deed he had come to perpetrate.

Aunt Minnie told my sister and I the following morning that our mother was dead. Tabitha was too young to comprehend what that even meant, but I was not, and hence as the man of the house, or so I saw myself, I wanted to know, as an overly precocious child does, precisely what happened.

I kept up those childish demands until I had garnered the truth by the end of the day. Lady Niketa finally confirmed things to me; Everheart and his brutes had broken into the house, and after Everheart had shot Karl, he turned his gun on my mother. Aunt Minnie had tried to shield my mother by stepping between them, but mother moved her aside and stood her ground defiantly. Chin up and eye to eye with the murderous brute.

I always felt that my mother's sacrifice led to the sacrifice of our childhood. Though everything was done to protect us, spoil us a little even, life in my grandfather's household was never truly happy again. Not as it had been in those days. My mother had been a joyful soul, always laughing. She was creative; she loved to paint and sew and sing. Sometimes she would read to us for hours anything she found interesting or believed would aid us in our learning, she fired our imaginations and interests in the whole world of science, the arts, nature, and music. She loved the gardens and tended my grandmother's orangery with a level of loving care unmatched by the gardeners. Our mother had been the foundation stone of our little world.

It was not until I left to attend university that I realised how heavy the cloud of her death that hung over my family was.

As a child and young man, full of self-centred angst, I wished so many times that she had not been so courageous. Unable to understand how she could have abandoned us so? However, I am an old man now, a father and soon to be grandfather myself, and I have nothing but the most profound admiration for her bravery. I believe she feared that if it were not for her sacrifice, he, Everheart that is, would have killed us all, Tabitha and I, even our cousin little Minerva, who was but a babe in arms.

Of what I have learnt of that monster, I am sure she was right.

The Diary of Dr James Athanasius Flammarion.

34th Sept. 26th34th of Sept 0026.Thursday. Day 5

I am afflicted by insomnia, and the sleeping draft, provided by Mr Holly, furnished me no rest other than fitful dozing plagued by nightmares.

I seldom dream, let alone suffer the night-time attentions of the incubus of the mind. In the glare of the cabin's electric light, I am left with little memory of the images that stalked my dreams. Nevertheless, I am unable to shake their impact on my emotions.

Reviewing our situation, after some time to calm my anxiety; I cannot, I shall not allow the events of yesterday to derail our mission. I shall have the ship ready for departure from Tharsis as soon as practically possible. The weather will not hold for us if we defer for too long.

I shall visit my old friend Bogdanov myself and set Bravett to harry our quarry. Wilberforce will be my proxy in this, he is like an old hound, and once he gets the scent, he will never give up. He will scrutinise the intricacies of Du Maurier's business activities throughout the Tharsian Republic, with a fine-tooth comb, and bury the little Napoleon in vexatious litigation.

The Flammarion Expedition Journal of L. Edwin Ransom.
Day Five. 34th. 9th. 26.
Thursday.

I must admit to having spent most of the day nursing a frightful hangover. Hiding away in my cabin to avoid my expedition companions and the accusatory eyes of the crewmembers. I know I brought this upon us, and it is my responsibility to deal with it, but I feel so…

Damn it. I should have faced up to Du Maurier like a man, and should his henchmen have killed me, then that would have been done with it. Instead, I ran away like a coward and, forced others to fight my battles for me. Especially Adam, who has stood by my side in a way no man could with any reason ask a friend to do so.

We have not told the others of the events at my house. They had seen enough bloodshed to last a lifetime, and so we chose to keep our own counsel on that. Nonetheless, such a decision has left me with a dozen unanswered questions of my own.

While the others marvelled at the events they had witnessed, and I must say, even amid all this insanity, I would have loved to have seen the kraken, what a tale I would have been able to tell James and Tabitha. Unfortunately, however, I have been more preoccupied with the man-engine creature that Adam killed in my hallway. Sergeant Rawlings called it a "Golem." A Yiddish word for a mythological automaton of clay. I think it suited that creature well. In a conversation over dinner when I was young, my father ruminated on the tale. He believed it was an early form of android invented by ancient Jewish artificers, a clockwork man with a ceramic ironstone skin, alive yet not and hardly controllable.

The creature Adam killed in my hallway was...

What? A man-engine covered in human skin. Nonetheless, deeper inside it was living tissue. A brain or what little remained of it had resided inside that metal and bone casement, but...

The metal that lay beneath that flesh was of a kind I have only seen the likes of once before. Therefore, it drives me to distraction to contemplate it; the metal and the workmanship underneath that monstrosity's skin were the same as Adam's arm.

I cannot discuss it with him; how would one broach such a conversation?

Moreover, what if I did?

I say, old sport, are you some kind of man-engine under that... skin? In addition, if so, where does the machine end and the man begin?

I have never seen someone so fearless or move as fast or shoot so accurately.

Oh, Dear Lord, what if he is?

What if he is?

I stayed away from the others and from my friend until summoned to attend upon the Professor in his cabin.

Colonel Jahns was talking with the Professor when I arrived, he sat casually, his boots up on the corner of the Professor's desk, puffing on a cigar and sipping brandy as if oblivious to my presence. I could barely credit the Professor's tolerance for such disrespectful behaviour. The Professor poured me a large drink, and we exchanged small talk, something I have seldom experienced with him in all the years I have known him as both mentor and then father-in-law. It was awkward, almost excruciatingly so, much like the time I came to call on him to request his permission to court Nelly, even more so in the imposing presence of the Colonel.

After a few minutes, the Professor gladly dispensed with the confabulations of such social pleasantries and moved to the point. His tone became grave as his demeanour toughened.

Fixing me with his gaze over the rims of his pince-nez spectacles, he spoke calmly but in the most hardened of tones. "I have committed myself to see Du Maurier hang for this outrage." He then set out his plan of actions. I must admit it was impressive, though its aims were far out of the character of the man I believed I knew. It indeed held the Professor's level of ingenuity. He intended to pressure the High Sheriff of Alba to pursue criminal investigations against Du Maurier with utmost prejudice.

Meanwhile, he would pull as many strings as he could in the Governmental apparatus to bring about similar investigations by the Bureau of State Internal Security, while also setting Wilberforce Bravett to investigate all of Du Maurier's business dealings across the Republic. He envisaged that as soon as they catch the first whiff of criminality, they would seize Du Maurier's funds and property in Tharsis and insist upon our allies doing the same. Without access to his wealth and resources and with the forces of Law on his heels, Du Maurier will find himself short of friends, and a man like that when he runs short of friends rapidly learns just how numerous his enemies are.

I agreed, however, I wondered how we could be sure it would result in Du Maurier's demise.

The Professor smiled, stoked his pipe and lit it.

Colonel Jahns dropped his feet to the floor, gave a long exhalation, and sat forward. "Ah, there. Tharsis is a young Republic, my boy. And we cherish our freedoms, do we not?" I agreed readily. "But to keep those beloved freedoms, we have to maintain our vigilance. We build bulwarks and revetments, both physical and metaphorical, to keep out those forces that would threaten our freedoms, and so it falls to some of us to be the guardians upon those walls. The watchmen in the towers. Because of that, those who guard are privy to things ordinary people like yourself do not have any idea of." He poured himself another generous glass of the Professor's brandy. "There is in existence already, enough evidence to hang Eleuthère Du Maurier a dozen times over. All you have to do is ask the right questions of the right people."

"And they are?"

The Colonel fixed me with a cold gaze. "We, the Watchers on the Walls, as we like to think of ourselves, keep meticulous records. I chanced to take a look at Du Maurier's before I joined this Expedition."

"Why?"

"Because you concern the Professor, and what concerns the Professor is of concern to my superiors, and that, in turn, concerns me." He smiled smugly and casually returned his boots to the corner of the desk.

"Then of whom do we ask these pertinent questions, Colonel?"

"Ah there, that would be whosoever has that bundle of documents in their possession, of course."

I could not help but blurt out irritatedly, "And whom would that be?"

Jahns swigged his brandy and chuckled, "Why, me, of course."

I discovered that they were playing with me. The Professor had already perused the bundle of documents, but now together, we studied them in some detail. It was all there, a plethora of venality. Enough damning evidence to connect Du Maurier with sundry instances of vitiation of public officials, bribery, coercion, consorting with known rakes, felons and killers. However, all that paled into insignificance against the butcher's list of murders, attempted murders and disappearances suspected as assassinations, that he was implicated in. Even the death of my neighbour, Mr Hindecker, and the murder of Constable Nielsen. Everything Miss Bryant-Drake had suspected for years was right. And there, running throughout the litany, was another name I knew well, Du Maurier's bloody right hand; Lucius Everheart. Alternately described as an enforcer, a gunman and, most spine-

chillingly, a 'hatchet-man.' The paper trail directly linked him to a dozen or more killings and suspected of far more. I was a gasp.

"My God! Why murder an old recluse like Mr Hindecker?"

"Searching for that tomb, no doubt," answered the Colonel. Overcome, I sat down heavily.

"Ironic is it not?" The Colonel snorted. "All this nonsense for an empty tomb?"

"What did he hope to find, I wonder?" The Professor mused.

"Miss Bryant-Drake believes he is an obsessive collector of Aresian artefacts," I explained. "I should think an unspoilt tomb would be worth hundreds of thousands of pounds, if not millions."

"Hmm," the Professor tugged at his beard thoughtfully. "I wonder, though. Indeed, obsession and greed can ride such a man's soul. Nonetheless, I do wonder. Is he searching for something more than just baubles?"

Curious, I asked, "What do you mean, sir?"

"To quote Stephanou; 'The only things more valuable to a nation than gold...'"

"'...is technology. And the knowledge to use it.'" The Colonel concluded the quote.

"But the tomb is empty." I realised how naive that sounded as the words left my mouth.

"Ah there, yes indeed, but he did not know that," smiled the Colonel. "In fact; he still does not know that."

I shook my head in disbelief. That such information lay in the hands of the authorities, and yet Du Maurier and Everheart walk abroad freely, astounded me. Du Maurier had even attended the soirée to celebrate the completion of the Daedalus, in the presence of the President himself! He even approached my wife! I could not contain my utter confoundment.

The Colonel pulled a mocking expression at my outrage and explained. "Dear boy, if we arrested every wrong'un we knew of in Tharsis, then that little coming out party your lovely wife attended would have been a far less salubrious affair. These records did not come from the archives of the Police; they came from the Ministry of Internal Affairs. Even so, they are far from the complete picture. Du Maurier is indeed a treacherous man, but he is incautious, shambolic even in his methods compared to others of his ilk. Thus, his wide trail of facileness has often unwittingly led us to threats that are far more pernicious. In some way, his idiosyncratic behaviour and self-assuredness, let alone his ill temperament, has been of more use than half a dozen well-placed informants."

Sometimes I wish that my mind would not just blurt out of my mouth the thoughts that come into it. "He is a spy for the Zephyrians, is he not?"

With slow deliberation, the Colonel looked from me to the Professor and back. "Yes, most probably, amongst other things. He also has connections with known Utopian and Thylian agents still active within our borders as well as undesirables in Gorgonum and Sirenia. Some of them are indeed highly placed infiltrators for other national interests."

"Thus, Ranolph, he is more valuable to you alive and free than dangling on the end of a rope outside the gates of New Tyburn." The Professor struck a match and relit his pipe.

The Colonel nodded, "However, James, times change, circumstances change, and all things are fluid. Increasingly Du Maurier has called attention to himself. As he has done so, those valuable connections he once had, have distanced themselves from him by increments, until the gap between them and he, has become wide enough for them to feel comfortable. Without his connections, Du Maurier will become worthless to them and to us." He then grinned, "Well, no value running around at large, that is."

"Connections with people such as that monster Windlestraw Volpone and the traitor Rollo Lenox?"

"Volpone?" I queried, "That alone is quite a name to conjure with."

"Ah, there. Indeed, we think Volpone and your man Du Maurier may have shared a mistress. There is quite a hornet's nest to kick there."

"Really?" I sat back in amazement.

The Professor fixed the Colonel with a hard stare. "So, 'Grand Inquisitor,' have you decided Du Maurier's usefulness is at an end."

"If I were more of a man of business, James, I would liken it to cashing him in as one would a speculation that has reached its maturity. Though it would be best he is publicly denounced for his criminal activities, those who are distancing themselves from him

will be expecting that, but it will not stay their hand from attempting to silence him themselves."

"God's teeth, man! You talk like it would be a death sentence."

"Is that not what you want?" The old Colonel laughed humourlessly. "Remember, James, he has caused the death of one of my best men and three of your crew. Four, is it not? He has threatened your son-in-law, your daughter and your grandchildren, and the lives of everyone on this ship. I will lay my hands on him, for sure, and he will pay a heavy price for it." There was a glimpse of something genuinely disquieting behind that bluff exterior of the old war hero, something unreservedly merciless.

For a moment, I almost felt a pang of regret for the little Zephyrian, but I brushed it aside as one would an irritating fly.

The Professor faltered for a moment, "Yes... but... If it must be so, then it should be through the due course of the Law. After a trial. In God's good name, Ranolph, it is just not civilised!"

The Colonel laughed derisively. "Ah there, fear not, old boy. Justice will have her day, but I will lay good odds that that little Zephyrian fox would rather fancy his chances throwing himself on the mercy of the High Court than at the hands of his erstwhile associates."

Seizing upon his metaphor, I pointed out, "But surely he will flee, as soon as he gets a whiff of the hounds."

The Colonel chuckled again, "He will certainly try, my boy. He will certainly try, but there are more ways of catching a fox than simply running it to ground."

Time had marched on, and we broke our meeting for dinner.

I expected it to be a sombre occasion, as it was the first time we had gathered since yesterday's events, and so it was. Everyone filed in quietly, took their usual seats and conversation was kept to the barest minimum of polite discourse. Save for Sir John holding forth in his usual entertaining manner upon the subject of his suspicions that some lag had been availing themselves of his flight apparatus. That that "someone" had used half a tank of his fuel, and a good deal of his ammunition appeared to be the basis for his excuse for yesterday's tardiness. Sir John ventured various colourful speculative scenarios as to whom he thought might be responsible, until finally settling upon Parthena, who, taking the jest in good part, admitted playfully that it was indeed her; she had been chasing moonbeams in the darkness.

Only partly distracted by their repartee, I sat stewing in my own apprehension of Adam's imminent arrival. When he did arrive, I found myself flustered and unable to manage even the meekest of exchanges with him as he took his customary seat beside me. I dread to think what he must have thought of me.

I quickly became so uncomfortable that I spluttered through my gazpacho soup and was about to excuse myself when Mrs Fontenelli arrived.

Then the damnedest thing happened.

Parthena and Charity stood up and began to applaud her, Adam stood too, and suddenly we were all on our feet clapping untiringly. The automaton steward and her maid joined in, and even the Colonel drew to his feet.

Mrs Fontenelli appeared utterly discombobulated by the reception.

The Professor rang his glass with a spoon to bring the outpouring of emotion to a pause.

Once he had our attention, he began; "Thank you, ladies and gentlemen. We have all been terribly affected by the ghastly events of yesterday, and it has left us all somewhat traumatised. However, if it were not for the astounding bravery of Madam Fontenelli in confronting the beast, I fear we might all have perished." He paused for a chorus of 'hear hears' and 'bravos,' before addressing Mrs Fontenelli directly.

"Madam, I have no idea how you communicated with that monstrosity, what command you used, or whether, like beauty before the beast, it was enchanted by your loveliness, but what I am certain of is; we most assuredly owe you our lives."

I noticed there were tears in her eyes as she shook her head solemnly. "No, Professor, I did nothing. I can remember nothing. I was compelled towards it by some terrible urgency, but once I was in the kraken's gaze.... I have no more memory than that, until I awoke onboard the ship. I thank the Lord God that I was spared. I am no heroine, merely a nonsensical foolish woman who flung herself into harm's way."

The Professor demurred, "Whatever your reasons, your actions speak louder than any words. I, for one, believe that your actions saved us all." He raised his glass, "Madam Fontenelli, the bravest of us all!"

Therefore, we toasted, we sat, we relaxed, we ate, and we talked. I found myself conversing normally with Adam about his day's duties, and how hard Sergeant Capon's loss had hit his fellow soldiers. Adam had a genuine understanding of their sentiment. I found myself looking at him anew; he was different now, far more assured of himself, almost a changed man. Of course, I, as with most of us, have grown so used to the terrible scars he bears to the point of almost unseeing, nonetheless his eyes, when they meet yours still have the same profound impact; one of deep melancholia.

Our mood was raised even further when Mr Charles reported that the repairs had been completed and we would be underway by 8pm.

I studiously avoided touching upon yesterday's events at my home, until the evening had moved towards its close. Parthena, Charity and Madam Fontenelli had long departed to their respective cabins. The Colonel, the Professor, Dr Spender and Sir John had completed a few hands of poker, partaken of a nightcap and bid us a restful night.

I took a long sip of my tea and tried to summon the courage to broach the subject of the anxieties that had plagued me since yesterday, but Adam forestalled me. He fixed me with those soulful eyes of his and began; "Edwin, you are my friend, and you have been generous and kind to me, a vagabond who befell your hospitality, with little or nothing to give or offer." He waved my protestations aside. "I have not been as honest with you as a true friend should; indeed, I have not been as honest with you as you deserve."

And so, he began a tale that I can only describe as overwhelming. I would have dismissed it as a jest or pure fantasy if I had not already started to suspect there was far more to his story than I could imagine, and I have been witness to some of the evidence myself.

Editor's Note.

This section, an estimated five pages, had been removed from the journal. Most probably by my father himself.

James Ransom.

We fell into silence after two hours of his tale. I, lost for words, sat turning over and over the policeman's battered identity card in my hand, and trying to avoid looking at the bent prongs of the bloody dessert fork, laying atop of the black leather glove, on the card table before me.

Adam stood gazing out of the porthole at the darkened world passing below. There was so much I barely understood; however, I believe I am not so big a fool that I cannot recognise the shape of the truth when it is revealed to me, even when, in detail, it is hardly comprehensible.

Finally, he spoke, "And so, that is all there is to it, well at least as so far as I know."

71

"But why tell me now?"

He turned back towards me. "Because of what Lloyd said. Edwin, I fear I am in no small part responsible for what has happened to you. I have brought this upon you and your family."

"Nonsense. I had already long ago determinedly set sail on a collision course with Du Maurier and his thugs. And by what I have learnt today, his motivations have nothing to do with you or my crops and more to do with that tomb we discovered. Will you not accept that encountering Lloyd was an accident of misfortune, a fiend like him..."

"Like me."

"No, sir. I will hear no such thing. What was inflicted upon you was none of your own doing, you were an honourable man, a soldier, and with all that they inflicted upon you, they could not make you into their creature. This Lloyd chap was already a fiend, and with his particular predilections, it can be of no surprise he would naturally be drawn to the employ of such a man as Du Maurier. It may have been merely happenstance you encountered each other. I believe he recognised you before you realised who he was, and as you have explained, he was a vile cad, even before your mutual...transmogrification. This is indeed a small world, as they say. I suggest he took great delight in taunting you with your connection, simply by way of goading you. Nothing more." I was in no way sure of my assertions, but the words, once spoken, were reassuring to both of us. I must admit part of me was truly intrigued. "Ultimately, my question is essentially the same as

yours; why? Why did these people do this to you? Mere experimentation is so improbable as to be ludicrous. There must be some ulterior purpose, some bigger plan. Once we can glean or even take an educated guess at that, then we will have a point from where we can begin to unravel this mystery."

Adam crossed the room and stood before me. Extending his metal righthand, he said, "Thank you, my friend."

I stood, and without hesitation, grasped his hand and shook it, "I am and always will be in your debt, sir. And I will always be your friend." That much I knew I meant wholeheartedly.

Excerpt from;
Diary of Aelita Fontenelli (Mrs).
Thursday, September, 34th. MY.26
Cont.

Dear Diary.

This evening the others were so kind to me, though I found their attentions a little embarrassing, the warmth of the reception when I entered the Saloon filled my heart. Yet I felt compelled to admit that I know nothing of the nature of the woman they applauded.

I have resolved to speak to Parthena Spender; she makes it her business to refuse to pass unnoticed through this world. Bending it to her will, rather than be controlled by convention. She is also a young woman of progressive thought, and I feel that maybe she, if anyone, might be able to appreciate in some small way my predicament. Though how I would explain it in a language comprehensible to myself, let alone her, I have no idea.

I am writing this in the storeroom bulkhead of the airship, away from everyone.

Today has been an interesting one.

I awoke from a nightmare in which I was trapped in a repetition of the confrontation with Lloyd in Edwin's lobby. This time the bastard would not die no matter what I did, he just kept coming on, a broken, bloody, crawling mess of machinery and flesh, clawing its way towards me, its half-exploded face gurgling insane laughter. I beat it with the rifle butt, stamped upon it, shot it, but still, it kept dragging itself towards me, reaching for me.

Awake, I sat in the darkness and listened to Edwin's gentle snoring until I felt able to move. It was almost half-past three in the morning when I left the cabin. I paced the decks, for how long though I have no idea.

I feel like a stranger in my own body, but this is not my body. My skin is my skin, I know every blemish, every mole and scar, but beneath it? A machine, an automaton. The face that stares back at me from the mirror is a mask, not metaphorically, but in reality. Sometimes I feel compelled to reach up and rip it off, to expose to the world the metal-plated skull underneath. If there is a skull if that too is not just a metal construction. My eyes: they look like my eyes, but are they? Was my eyesight ever this good? My hearing? How much of me, of Adam Franklin, actually remains? My brain? My mind? Alternatively, am I simply just a soul trapped in a machine? The ghost of a man cruelly ensnared in an automaton? A machine decoupaged with my own hide.

Why? The Doctor and Lanulos never hinted at why. Why put me through all this? Why go to such lengths and costs? To build machines that look like men. Not just look like but also to think as men do. To think like the men, we once were. To what purpose? Alternatively, am I wrong? What was the purpose of those little punch cards? To reprogramme our minds, our human minds, as such things are used to reprogramme automata like Karl or Jakes the steward. Is it that they were after some quality that human minds possess? Autonomy rather than mere automaton?

A chilling thought: how in control of this man-engine that I am trapped inside am I? Am I like a pilot of an aircraft; free to manoeuvre as I please or merely the operator in an observation kite? Does Lanulos still hold the strings?

Have they made me into nothing more than a clockwork soldier left with the delusion of independence?

Moreover, did it end with Lloyd and I? Did the apparent failure suffice? Did their experiments go on? Are there others out there?

If Lanulos and the Doctor are not dead, and I honestly doubt that they are, they would not have abandoned their project easily.

As the Watch changed, I joined the men coming on duty. By breakfast, I was stripped to my combinations stoking the boiler's furnaces. At first, I think the stokers thought me nothing more than a bored gentleman who wanted to amuse himself by working up a bit of a sweat. They were, of course, in part, right and in part wrong. I needed the physical exertion and could pull far more than my weight, and theirs. However, to avoid suspicion, I had to feign exhaustion and find myself other distractions at some point.

At midday, we stopped. I found myself hanging from a harness 150 feet off the ground, lending my hands to the repairs. The ship had taken a lot more punishment than anyone had realised. Mostly due to the Seren Bore's proximity to the explosions aboard the Pirate's ship. The struts holding the portside propeller were severely damaged, and the propeller had to be replaced with the only spare. The portside rudder's mountings were cracked, and a large chunk of one of the pirate ship's boilers was still wedged between it and the hull. I managed to wrench it free, pretending all the while it was not as big or heavy as it seemed.

While others worked on the envelope and other damage, I volunteered for a turn at the forward Watch and spent the afternoon scouring the land and sky for any menace that might appear. I saw nothing that posed a threat.

The landscape is astoundingly beautiful, rugged and wild, speckled with patches of ordered agriculture. The *overwhelming cinnabar colour of this world has not changed regardless of humankind's impact upon it. Colours blend from yellow ochre through to deep rust red, with patches of the native crimson foliage now contrasting more and more with splashes of the verdant hues of human cultivation. Here and there were small human enclaves, the intermittent farmhouses, and the huddled buildings of small settlements. Occasionally I spotted aircraft and aerostats in the distance and resorted to the crow's nest's mounted telescope to examine them further, but none appeared at all interested in us.*

Through the telescope, I studied a distant swarm of flying creatures. Bluebirds, neither truly blue nor birds, they are more akin to small flying stingrays. I watched entranced by their majestic numerations for a while. In such numbers, they could pose a danger to aircraft, but they were so far off that there was no reason to raise the alarm.

Then there was the pretence; I stood swaddled in an immensikoff I did not need, and every time a crewmember drew near, I had to pull on the respirator and face mask issued to me.

The time spent on straightforward tasks afforded me the liberty to think. A thing I really have not done since Clerval Street. I have occupied myself with duties and busied myself with any number of distractions, not least the spellbinding Aelita Fontenelli, but all these things have been to divert my mind from contemplating my real predicament.

I decided that I could no longer lie to Edwin. We have been through too much together, and he has seen too much to continue this pretence. Given that, last night at dinner, he did all he could to avoid the others' prying questions, especially those of the Colonel, and maintained a level of dignity that left me humbled. How can I, with a clear conscience, continue this pretence? How he could have seen what he saw and yet not have thrown a sheaf of questions at me, shames me. As an alternative, we merely drank ourselves into oblivion.

The decision though was not an easy one. I had to contend with the uncompromising views of the Sergeant Major shouting the odds in my head, forcibly voicing my own fears. Fears about Edwin's reaction. Would he think I was stark raving mad or merely delusional? How would I explain the truth of it all? The horror? How Lloyd was connected to me, what was done to us, let alone what happened in the House on Clerval Street. Some of the things that I have experienced, or I have remembered, are still beyond my understanding, let alone my ability to explain them in any rational way. Then, of course, there was the fact that whatever I reveal to Edwin may cost us our friendship. What if he denounces me for a lunatic, or worse; he believes some of my tales based on what he has witnessed with his own two eyes, and decries me as a monster? What could result from such exposure?

I must admit to having not only second thoughts but third and fourth, nevertheless my resolve held. It left me with only a matter of how much I would tell Edwin and in what terms. I spent rather a lot of my time in the forward lookout's nest behaving like a frantic thespian before his opening night, practising my speech over and over in my head and then voicing it into the heedless wind.

I allowed the crew to relieve me a little before dinner was to be served for the Expedition members, seeking a chance to spruce myself up and dress appropriately. Such formalities have been allowed to slide easily into comfort over the last few days.

As I left the head on the passenger deck, I encountered three crewmembers loitering in a darkened nook. Stokers and boilermen from below with nothing to do until we got underway again. They were as shifty as old Hood at his worst and reeked of rum and cheap tobacco. For a moment, the largest of them, a man I know as Howe, moved to block my way with his bulk. Calling his bluff, I continued my progress, forcing him to choose to move aside or confront me. Glaring insolently, he chose the former. As I stepped past, he let out a derisive snort; close enough for me to feel his fetid breath upon my cheek.

Howe is a big chap, with a bushy dark auburn beard and heavily tattooed arms. He has a good three inches in height on me, and self-assurance in his size and weight, the demeanour of a browbeater. A lifetime of hard manual work has made him strong, and years of throwing his weight around has also made *him confident. Up close, he had obviously seen a few fights in his day, as well.*

I stopped and turned to face him. His small blue eyes narrowed almost in surprise. I held his gaze for a good few seconds until he became uncomfortable, and his eyes wandered. The other two shifted nervously and began to move away. I kept staring at him until he physically backed away from me.

By the time I reached the dining room, I had put the incident out of my thoughts.

Edwin was obviously distracted and somewhat embarrassed, I wondered if this was because of my presence or whether he had other things on his mind, but I had no real opportunity to speak to him. Edwin had just finished a coughing fit over his soup when the whole room erupted in spontaneous applause upon the entrance of Madam Fontenelli.

I find looking upon her no more comfortable than I first did; she is undoubtedly the most enthralling woman I have ever chanced to lay eyes upon. I must admit to allowing my task of spying on her and Sydeian to slide, as I find it both uncomfortable and unpalatable. The Professor has not requested an update as to my observations, and I hope his request will soon be forgotten. In truth, I have seen or heard nothing untoward concerning Aelita or Sir John. However, I do not like or trust Sydeian at all, but that too may be a symptom of my own infatuation.

What I had heard tell about Aelita was astounding. More than merely running onto the field shouting, she had confronted the creature that attacked the pirate's airship. It was, of course, something I had taken as an embellishment of the facts, as I had been more interested in the failure of the rotation guns until the Professor took to his feet and extolled the bravery of her actions. I listened with intense interest; she defied the creature and commanded it to stop, and the monster apparently obeyed her. Something that was beyond imagination. No human could control such a beast, but then again, she is no human.

Could they, the Aresians, control such creatures? Did they have them at their beck and call? Are such denizens of the sands and skies intelligent enough to understand commands? Indeed, it does not bear consideration.

Too much in this new world that I have been reborn into, makes little or no sense. The entire incident at Clerval Street has left me certain that I cannot be certain of anything. If I were to wake tomorrow and find this all a dream, I would not be remotely surprised.

As the brouhaha subsided, I found myself in conversation with Edwin that ranged widely, though, like a carefully choreographed waltz, it avoided topics too contentious to be discussed within the hearing of others. It was not until we were alone in the wardroom that I finally took the opportunity to tell Edwin my story, or the story as I best understand it. I admit it

82

was a heavily amended version at that. I could not tell him of all that occurred in the Clerval Street house or what I discovered upon returning to the room. I showed him Percy Greg's identification card, Peter Wansey's watch, and the other personal effects I had collected. Using a fork from the dining room, I proved to him that the metal continued beneath my skin, and I explained what Lloyd had said to me before I killed him. I admitted that for the most part, my memories have returned. My service in the British Royal Colonial Marine Regiment, even to the fact I can remember plunging into the icy waters of the Myrmidon's Trench and the horrors of Lanulos' experiments, sparing only the most explicit of details.

He listened attentively, asking only the best considered of questions until I had come to an end. In truth, I ran out of words. Even to my own ears, my tale sounded like the ramblings of a lunatic. I dreaded how it must have sounded to his.

Instead of revulsion, or decrying me as a monster, he called me his friend. It is hard to find the measure of such a man, someone who would have no doubt been on the other side of the war I once almost died fighting in. The son of a Secessionist, who, even when all was revealed to him, grasped my hand warmly and pledged his enduring friendship, and I, with all my heart, pledged my loyalty to him.

Now I sit in this quiet corner of the ship, scribbling in this journal, no longer in those bizarre hieroglyphs. I must discover what is truly going on; why De Maurier is pursuing Edwin, what exactly Lloyd hinted at and who and what Lanulos is.

THE REPUBLIC OF THARSIS BUREAU OF STATE
INTERNAL SECURITY
CRIMINAL INVESTIGATION DEPARTMENT
THARSIS DIVISION
Witness Statement

Interview statement taken from Prisoner 452, Henry Avery, aka "Long Harry" on the 43rd, October. 29. Tharsis Panopticon.

Convicted crewmember, "Rigger," of the aerostat The Wyndeyer.

Cont.

Events of the Thursday34[th] of September 26.

Yes. We didn't hang around in the town. Too dangerous.

Dullahan had us liberate a couple of nags from a stable yard. We had ta roll over some old tosspot of a night watchman, but he didn't hav' much fight in 'im.

And sos off we trotted to visit old ginger Dundrearys.

It was quite a long ride outta the ginger moocher's house, and we, apart from Dullahan herself, weren't much shakes as far as riding horses was concerned. Sos we didn't get there 'til late morning.

No, and because you asks, No.

I took an oath on the Bible an' signed the Wyndeyer's Articles of Agreement, I, Sur, am a Brethren, not some common bludger or mughunter.

Listen, I gave me word that'd tell yous everythin' I know, as sos I will, but I will not bear false witness against me own or lie. I've killed a few, mostly that deserved it, robbed a lot, mostly that could afford it, and I've stolen plenty. In fact, I can rightly say; I've broken most of the laws of this land and several others, but I ain't going to lie to make your task easier. You can hang us all for felons and pirates, but I ain't going to make stuff up.

No, we did not pass anyone on the road that day.

When we reached the house, it was all
quiet. It was a rambling old place with a
pretty garden at the front. Dullahan was in
no mood for niceties, she kicked open the
little white wooden gate and rode her horse
up the garden path and right up the front
steps on to the covered terrace, right up to
the front door. We followed.

No. We weren't goin' to hav' a parley with
him over high tea, woz we?

Nop, but I don't think we had no 'murder on
our minds' either. Mayhap Dullahan did, but
the rest of us just wanted food an' rest an'
some recompenses for our inconveniences. I
might have ripped his Dundreary's off his
fat little face for the laughs, if we'd
caught him, but we would not have done wot
woz done there.

Dullahan jumps down an' goes to hammer on
the front door with the hilt of her pistol
and the door just swung open.

I thought it a trap, but she has bigger
brass balls than a Lombard's sign, she just

kicked the door wide open an' walked straight in. We followed, of course.

I think we kinda expected they'd made a run for it, but it were a righteous gaff, so we had hopes there'd be rich pickin's. But we weren't expectin' what we found.

I hav' never seen anythin' like it, an' never would want to again. I've seen men blown apart by grapeshot, an' hacked down in battle, but this was somethin' else.

They woz all torn to pieces, everyone. Like someone had let a pack of prattans in on them.

It was hard to say, really. We found the ginger moocher himself in the front parlour, well, what was left of him, and what woz probably the lady of the house. All the servants were dead too. The schoolroom was an abattoir. Wooden Eyed Pete, chucked his guts at the sight of it, and Whaler John broke down sobbin' like a Parson's wife. The sight of dead little 'uns always upset him, as he lost his to typhus a long time ago.

We woz comin' back down the stairs when we heard a noise from the library. Sounded like someone throwing stuff about.

The Captain just vaulted the newel post and charges straight in there. Without even thinking, we followed.
I wish we ain't had done so.

Look, what's the purpose of this anyways? You ain't gonna believe a word I'm tellin' you. Why should I bother?

Right. Fine.

Anyway's, the room is full of this weird greeny-blue light, like St. Elmo's fire, and in the middle o' the room is this man. Well, it was dressed like a man, but it weren't no man, for sure. I hav' heard stories as you do. Brethren tell tales you know, of *the others*, the Empyreans, (*). Creatures that were s'posed to be here before us mankind came, even before the Spookers themselves. It was dressed like one of those itinerant missionaries yous find out in the rough country. Tall, towering, easily over seven feet or more, and all in black with this wide-brimmed hat.

It was just standing there while books and things were flyin' off the shelves around the room. Then it stopped and looked at us. Sos we could see its face.

No. It weren't no human. Its face woz, well I ain't no edificated man, I can barely sign me name and do numbers, I don't really hav' the words.

It was a monster. Gruesome.

I remember when I was still at sea as a young 'un, the Captain ordered a rating keel-hauled for thievin' from the cook's stores. Poor bastard got stuck halfway, took five days before we yanked him loose. This creature looked like that. Like its skin was all slimy an' rottin' off. An' it had no eyes! Just these weird deadlights for eyes and a huge mouth full of teeth, lots of bloody teeth.

It stood there an' snarled at us. I couldn't move. I was so pissin' frightened.

How would I know? It looked straight outta Hell to me, matey.

Anyways we were about to give it a belly full of lead when it turned and gestured back to the corner of the library where that light was still glowing. These two creatures came out of the light as if they stepped through it from somewhere else. Huge ugly brutes.

Describe them? Have yous ever seen a prattan? Bodies like that but these were bigger than the biggest male I've seen.

They moved, no, almost flowed, like molasses on a warm day. They had these massive heads, like canal crocodiles, with tusks and huge teeth. And they too had like deadlights for eyes. But that wasn't what shocked me, they had too many legs, four at the front and two at back, and from their shoulders, they had these two powerful long tentacles that lashed about angrily. Their skin was like the Preacher Man, rotted and slimy, it was oozing off, and where it dripped on the carpet, it fizzed an' bubbled.

Wooden Eyed Pete was standing too close. One of them grabbed him an' was on him instantly. Poor fecker didn't stand a chance. It ripped big lumps out of him.

We weren't about to let them get the rest o' us, so we let fly with everything we had. Me-self alone I emptied my barkers into them, and then me revolver. We just kept firing, for all the good it did.

The creatures backed off a little, but the man thing seemed unbothered, at least until Dullahan shot it in the face. You see she's still a superstitious colleen at heart, if she has one. Well, most of us are, that hav' been the places we've been. So, she used to carry this little really old double-barrelled barker loaded with cold iron shot. Claimed that she'd use it to lay the ghost of any fecker that tried to come back to haunt her, even if it were the Devil himself.

Well, it worked. She pulled that pistol an' shot the cove in the face. It screamed like a little lassie in a Bosun's chair. Being African an' all, Black Harry was every bit as superstitious as Dullahan, he carried a baker's dozen of those iron rounds. Some of us carried them too, not for shooting apparitions, or anythin' daft like that, but 'cause they go through a breastplate or helmet like a hot knife through butter. Seeing what she done, we reloaded and let them hav' a volley.

We hurt them for sure, 'cos the two beasts fled like whipped puppies. The Preacher Man though regained himself. He pulled out this thing like a bullwhip, an' lashed out at Dullahan. The Captain though was as lithe as a ship's cat and every bit as fast, she dodged it, though it carved clean through the upturned wingback she leapt over, an' then she shot him again.

This time he must have had enough of us. He pulled a revolver, fired a few rounds at us and fled the same way as his beastie things.

He got the Captain in the chest, right above the heart, but she wore a cuirass under her long coat an', though it knocked her off her feet, it stopped the bullet. He killed Wild Haired Willy, straight through the heart and another through the liver. Hit me too, but Tricky Tom's boilerplate, God bless his rottin' soul, stopped the round, though it bloody hurt.

Yes. Well, no. Maybe he was searching for something. I hav' no notion of what.

What did we do? What do yous think? Of course, we charged after 'im through the St. Elmo's in the corner of the room like right heroes. So we did!

The feck, we did!

We scooped the shite outta our kecks, raided the place for what we needed an' got outta there as fast as we bloody could in case they came back.

No, we didn't burn the gaff.

(At this point the Interviewing Officer gave the prisoner sight of the journal found in the possession of Aislinn Ann Dullahan-Murphy, aka; Colleen Dullahan.)

Oh, aye. I would guess she spent a time looking around the library while the rest o' us, sacked the place. Said she was keeping watch lest they come back.

Yes. She told us she had it. It was Dockett's journal. She reckoned it was what the Preacher Man was looking for. She said it would be worth a lot in the right hands.

No, I never laid eyes on it me-self.

(*) Empyrean. A term coined by the British Imperial Government to describe supposed non-Martian alien beings, or extra-terrestrial beings of unknown origin.

"Igitur qui desiderat pacem, praeparet bellum."

"They who wish for peace, prepare for war."

The motto of the Republic of Tharsis.

GENERAL PUBLIUS FLAVIUS VEGETIUS RENATUS

DE RE MILITARI (5TH CENTURY)

DAY SIX

WEEPING LADY

The Diary of Dr James Athanasius Flammarion.

35th Sept. 26th

Mr Charles, the First Mate, pounding on my cabin door, thankfully awakened me from a dreadful dream at 4 am. Somewhat befuddled by the rapid evaporation of the nightmare, and without time to do anything more than pull on my dressing gown, and my coat over it, against the icy cold, I was rushed to the flight deck. Llewellyn greeted me with a cup of strong hot tea and frightful news. We had received a photo-telegraphic signal relayed from a communication beacon. We have orders to rendezvous with the Daedalus on the Northside of the Great Sorrow Lake, Acheron.

Upon whose authority? I demanded to know, only for Mr
Charles to thrust the transmission into my hand.

URGENT MESSAGE – STOP – ATTENTION OF *SEREN*
BORE – STOP – RENDEZVOUS WITH TWS DAEDALUS –
LATITUDE 39.57 NORTH – STOP - LONGITUDE 226.72
WEST – STOP – PRESIDENTIAL EXECUTIVE ORDER - STOP
– ONE NINE NINE EIGHT– STOP – PERRY – STOP

I looked up from the piece of paper, "One nine nine eight?"

"A one nine nine order is an executive military directive under
the Martial Orders Act. One nine nine, eight, is the subsection that
deals directly with mercantile and civilian aircraft," explained Mr
Charles.

"We have no choice but to obey," interjected the Captain. "I
fear we are at war." He sighed heavily, "It has been brewing for
some time. They may want to requisition the ship for military use."

I could not believe my ears. I found myself protesting against
the injustice, but what point were such declarations to my own
crew? Llewellyn assured me that under the Act they could
certainly requisition the ship if they should wish to.

Mr Charles asked how best to confirm the message's
authenticity. I explained that that would not be necessary as I
knew from whom the message came, Henry Giffard.

Henry and I had had several secret names for each other during
our time at Domdaniel's, often to throw off the prefects and
teachers from our shenanigans. We were two of the leading lights

of a group of a dozen or so self-proclaimed, "Rapscallions." Who found amusement in a campaign of practical jokes, creating and spreading tittle-tattle, and, to my eternal shame, minor vandalism. Modelling ourselves upon the romanticised adventures of the early settlers. We all gave each other secret code names; Bravett's was "Blusters," young Bogdanov was "Russian Peat," I was "Kaiser Jim," and Henry was "Perry," originally "Perry Winkle," but he did not take much to the full epithet. Now and then, even at our great ages, we have occasion to use those sobriquets when we need to make sure that letters and messages are definitely from whom they aver.

I was in no doubt the message was from Henry, but why?

Llewellyn advised me it would be only a matter of a few hours to reach the rendezvous. He also warned me that the hurried repairs to the rudder were not as secure as we hoped and we would need more time to effect better repairs, though they too would be only temporary until we could get to a dock.

I returned to my cabin to dress while I mulled over the reasons for this deviation. All I could imagine was that war had been declared and that for some reason, Henry wanted to speak to me personally. Why exactly? I had not the foggiest idea. Was there a problem with my work on the airships? Unimaginable.

If it is war, then what? Do they want me to abandon this quest because they fear I, and thus my knowledge, should fall into enemy hands? Possibly, as within the Ministry, paranoia has become a virtue.

After the failure of my fifth attempt to tie my bow tie, I found myself shouting angrily at my own reflection; Damn it. They shall not stop me. I am not a piece of property, a military asset!

I pounded my fist on the granite top of the washstand and stared petulantly at myself in the mirror.

I know I have changed over this last year. Alexa's death, though merciful in the end, left my emotions shattered and my mind exhausted. How does one recover from such a loss? I threw myself into my work, work I had begun long before Alexa's illness had truly taken hold, now I had been determined to finish it. Not out of some altruistic ideals of contributing to our national defence, no I wanted the money for this expedition, and the prestige it would bring me in my dealings with the Government. Therefore, I built their damnable war machines for them. Well, I designed them, other more practical hands did the construction, but I fashioned their ultimate form out of the fabric of my own conceptual ideation. Without me, the whole Damocles project would not exist.

Without me, every life those horrendous dreadnaughts will take would be spared. My father will be spinning in his grave, and what would Alexa think of me? I cannot continue the pretence any longer, even unto myself, that the Government built those monstrosities to protect our nation and its people. They are

Dreadnaught Class Air Cruisers, and their only true purpose is the utter destruction of an enemy. "A hammer blow," the President said, but against whom would that hammer be wielded? Damn them. Whose blood would be on my hands?

Is this the price God will extract from me for my presumption to seek peace in such a world as this? Will the means by which I have obtained the resources to seek salvation for humankind be worth the ends? Moreover, what if I should fail? What if I am wrong?

When I returned to the bridge to check on our progress, Llewellyn informed me we were on course for arrival by 7 AM, at the latest. I ordered him to make sure the Seren Bore was in full readiness in the event we had to make a hasty retreat from the meeting. Llewellyn took me aside and asked pointedly if I feared it was a trap. I admitted that although I wholeheartedly believe it not to be, deep in me there is a dread, not for the ship, but for myself.

"They will not take you off this ship without a hell of a fight, sir."

I thanked him and made my way to the wardroom to have breakfast. Whatever was to come this morning was best not faced on an empty stomach. I sent a crewman to wake Edwin and Franklin and request them to join me.

Franklin arrived keen-eyed and sharp-witted. Edwin, unfortunately, looked somewhat dishevelled and bleary-eyed. Over coffee, I explained what had occurred.

I asked Franklin to remain by my side at all times, and, should the situation warrant my leaving the Seren Bore, that he gets me back to the ship. Franklin seemed unperturbed by the request. Though, he asked if the situation warranted such action, would Colonel Jahns and his men be an issue?

I explained that I would have to charge Edwin, as my deputy, to take such matters in hand. Should I have to leave the ship, I would suggest he acts appropriately to ensure that Jahns and his men can be effectively neutralised. Without harm, of course.

Edwin, somewhat revivified by the coffee, suggested that it would probably be best to avoid any confrontation with Jahns and his soldiers. We exchanged a few ideas before hitting upon the decision that it probably would be best to take action first.

I summoned Gunnery Master Gwenllian and ordered him to secure the orlop, lock the hatches and place an armed guard on them. As for the Colonel, I suggested that Edwin would have to keep an eye on the old rogue. Franklin argued against that, saying that we most probably will take the Colonel with us if I leave the ship. I hope that he will be less suspicious and "should push come to shove," as he put it, we could leave the Colonel behind.

I chuckled at the thought of Ranolph's outrage and agreed.

We joined the Captain on the bridge just after 6 am. The sky was just beginning to brighten as we skirted the outer northern edge of the crater that held the Great Sorrow Lake of Acheron. Keeping out of sight of the eyes of those few awake in the tiny township that nestles on the far inner side of the crater. Weeping Lady, is home to a few dozen souls, making their living from the minerals and salts that the water brings up to the surface from its source far below the ground.

As the light grew, we could make out the leviathan's form hanging in the early dawn sky, the cold grey ironclad, Daedalus. She was riding low, her water hoses hanging like the lappets of some vast Aresian Man-o'-War into one of the numerous streams that flow out of the lake. Something in me stirred dreadfully at the sight of it. I felt like I had created this monstrous creature that now, so portentously, drank its fill from the waters of the Lake of Sorrows.

Several of the bridge crew remarked in crude expletives at the sight of the dreadnaught, only to be rebuked by the First Mate. Edwin exhaled through clenched teeth. Franklin though remained impassive.

"You seem singly unimpressed by the pride of the Tharsis war fleet, Mr Franklin,"

Without taking his eyes off the Daedalus, Franklin's face wrinkled into a most unpleasant sneer. "Not meaning any offence,

Professor, as I am aware you were involved in its conception. All I can say is that, as is often said of a homely child; it has a face only a mother could love."

Despite myself, I chuckled and agreed it was indeed an ugly brute, but it was conceived as a child of war, not love.

"For that, it would seem adequately disposed."

"Eleanor said it was a fearsome titan," remarked Edwin.

We watched as it loomed larger and larger in our view. Llewellyn had ordered that the crew make no fuss or noise that might alarm the Expedition members. Preparations for the rendezvous went on around us in an eerie hush. The engines were slowed gently to allow us to drift the last few hundred yards until coming to a stop about two hundred feet from the port bow of the Daedalus.

No obvious precautions were being taken; we could see the bridge crew of the Dreadnaught, illuminated by the electrificated lamplight, as clearly as they could see us. I took a look through the Captain's glass and could easily make out the tall figure of Henry Giffard, immaculately dressed as always, and still wearing his grandfather's topper, standing amidst the Officers. It must have been brought to his attention that I was at the telescope because he turned, waved and gesticulated towards their optical telegraph communications lamp. Almost immediately, it began to flash its message.

To my surprise, Franklin read the message as it was being flashed, without need of referring to the signal's chart or writing it down.

As I expected, the request was for me to join Henry on the Daedalus. My first instinct was to refuse, but I felt compelled to comply, lest it be taken as rude or ungentlemanly, but it was Franklin that immediately stepped up. Once the crew had erected our apparatus and its lamp. Franklin told our Signalman to reply with an apology, saying that our port side rudder along with the dory and both the bl'oats were damaged. There was no possible way I could get to him, other than to use the Bosun's chair and if he thought I was going to take my life in my hands on that contraption, he was gravely mistaken.

I watched as the message was deciphered on the Daedalus' bridge. Henry laughed, nodded, and then motioned towards himself before indicating towards me.

Within a few minutes, an air-launch detached itself from the Daedalus. Through the Captain's glass, we counted only Henry and a crew of three ratings.

By the time the launch had reached us; the news had spread through the ship enough to awaken the Expedition members, most of whom had gathered on the weather deck to gape at the Daedalus and our unexpected visitor.

As soon as Henry arrived, I had Franklin escort him straight to the Captain's salon, the only place large enough for us to meet that did not involve me having to run the gauntlet of unanswerable questions from the others, especially Jahns.

Henry Giffard still cuts an imposing figure, in his long black frock coat, his grandfather's top hat and toting a small portmanteau that had seen far better days. His dark brows and bushy beard now greyed with age, but underneath them, he still retains a certain adolescent sparkle in his eyes and ready smile. He greeted me warmly, as only old friends do, and I introduced Llewellyn, Edwin and Franklin.

We quickly settled around the Captain's map-table and, over tea, I invited Henry to tell us all what this was about? For an instant, that impish grin of old flickered across his face, and then he regained himself.

"James, my dear fellow. What I have to say is rather confidential."

I assured him that whatsoever he had to say I would pass on to those present unalloyed, so it would be pointless to exclude them from this discussion. Unexpectedly, he acquiesced with no further disagreement. "If they are to remain in your confidence then it would undeniably be pointless. So, let me get to my point. As you can probably guess from the presence of the Daedalus out here in Lycus County; Tharsis is on a war footing."

"War? With whom?" asked Edwin bluntly.

"As yet? Officially, no one. The Ministry of War has moved troops into the Plains to support the free settlers and dispatched elements of the Navy to the border of Thyle Major and along Icaria's eastern border with the Gorgonum region. I cannot share any further military intelligence with you, nevertheless, be assured that preparations are being made for a full mobilisation and pre-emptive actions against certain foreign interests."

"Damn it, Henry. Why?"

"Ours is not to reason why, dear boy. If you want my personal opinion, Bradbury is playing to the gallery with an eye to re-election. Nothing stirs the hearts of the hoi polloi more than a good bit of flag-waving, a rousing oompah band, and a bit of bashing old Johnny Foreigner. Patriotism is the last refuge, as they say."

"You do not sound totally convinced, Henry. The Zephyrians and the Utopians have been agitating for conflict for years now."

"Why James, dear chap, what exactly has happened to you out here in the wilds? You sound positively jingoistic." I admitted my patience for the Zephyrians has been tried severely of late.

"Sir, forgive me," interjected Franklin. "But why, exactly, are you here?"

Henry looked at Franklin with as much consternation as if the man had just popped into existence beside him. "Hmm... Yes.

Forgive my digressions. James, I have been sent ostensibly to request you to return to Tharsis immediately, the request comes from the War Office." He reached inside his overcoat, produced a sealed letter, and passed it to me. I examined the wax seal, the First Air Admiral's own stamp. I sighed, knowing full well what was inside, however as I set the crimson wax disk between my thumbs to snap it, Henry placed his hand over mine. "Before you do that, dear fellow. I have come here to serve that notice on you, although if you choose not to open it... Well, that is up to you. My personal recommendation, if you were to ask me, would be not."

In exasperation, I demanded, "Henry. We have known each other most of our lives, but your machinations never cease to amaze me, what is it you are up to?"

"Bradbury instructed Impey Barbicane, First Air Admiral to issue that order." He tapped the folded parchment. "The Air Admiral himself signed and sealed it. Then again, it in no way has his endorsement. It is my understanding that the Air Admiral feels that it would be extremely difficult, in fact, nigh-on-impossible, to afford the resources to chase down a single friendly private airship."

"You have us at a disadvantage, Sir." Franklin interjected, "There is no outrunning the warship you arrived on."

Henry nodded his agreement. "Mr Franklin, the Daedalus was not dispatched to lead the Seren Bore back to Tharsis on a leash. I have these communiqués to deliver to the Professor here and to Colonel Jahns, and then there is other business that we must attend to post-haste before returning to Tharsis."

"Jahns? You have orders for him too?"

"Of course, dear boy. In fact, I have two letters of instruction for him, both direct from the Air Admiral's desk, one official and one personal. The former contains orders to 'facilitate' your return as soon as possible, using whatever means he deems correct and necessary. The latter, states clearly that the First Air Admiral and several senior influential figures in the Government believe your expedition to be critical to national interests and that to end it prematurely would be a grave mistake."

"And which do you intend to deliver to the Colonel?" asked Edwin.

"It is my duty to deliver the first, and I am honour bound to deliver the second."

We all sat in silence for a few minutes looking at each other, until Henry inquired where Colonel Jahns was to be found. Llewellyn had a steward sent to find out. The answer was that Jahns was holding court in the wardroom, in full bluster, incensed that his men were being held under guard. Henry seemed to find that news amusing. I, myself, did not. I warned Henry that the Bureau of State Internal Security sent Jahns on this expedition with six veteran soldiers.

Henry explained that Barbicane had apprised him of that too. I clarified that my main concern is that Jahns is foremost a loyal soldier, and apt to follow orders in preference to thinking for himself.

"Come now, James, old chap, give the fellow more credit than that. He might be a bit of an old warhorse, but he is a great deal shrewder than he appears."

Edwin then reminded me that Jahns had been a great help with the Du Maurier problem. I explained to Henry what had happened at Edwin's farm, leaving out one or two of the more difficult to explain factors. I impressed upon him we are all sure Du Maurier was behind the attack, and that Jahns had provided us with some very detailed information on Du Maurier's criminal activities that confirmed our jointly held suspicions.

"Jahns is a fine fellow, James. I would trust his judgement to make the right decision. He and the First Admiral go back a long way. Almost as far as we do, old boy." I felt a prickle of resentment at his presumption in reminding me of the longevity of our friendship. I asked him if he wished to speak to Jahns alone or should I summon him here. Henry seemed to consider it for a moment before plumping for Jahns to be called to join our impromptu cabal.

Colonel Ranolph Carter Jahns arrived, resplendent in his nightclothes, red-faced and of a furious disposition. War hero or not, the man has a profane turn of phrase that could make a Neathian iron miner blush. It took all of Henry's charm and tact to mollify Jahns' temper down enough to be able to speak with him on civil terms. Still, he referenced his indignation at our audacity and issued dire warnings of unspecified consequences if such a thing should be attempted again.

Finally, Henry handed him the first letter. Jahns stopped mid-rant and looked at it. Running his thumb back and forth over the red wax seal, he glanced across to me, and then to Henry. "Damn it, man. You know what this is, do you not?"

"I do, indeed, old boy, but, if you will indulge me a little, I will ask you to open this one first." Henry handed Jahns the second sealed letter. Jahns snapped it and read it hungrily as if devouring every word. When he finished, he let the document slip from his fingers and fall to the table. Jahns then picked up the first letter and opened it. This time he only glanced at the short text held within before throwing it on top of the other. He sighed loudly. "You, of course, know the contents of both of these?"

Henry nodded, "Of course. I was there when they were dictated and sealed."

Jahns seemed to shudder. "As a still serving officer, if I disobey a direct order from the President's Office, I will not only be committing insubordination, to the point of mutiny, I will be committing treason. The very best one could hope for is that when

110

they catch me, they give me a perfunctory trial, and then shoot me."

"Is there an alternative?" asked Edwin incongruously.

"Ah there. A Formosusian Trial; first the firing squad, and then they will put my bloody carcase on trial." He suddenly laughed. "Damn it, Henry, I knew one day all this clandestine nonsense would get me killed." At that, I had to ask for him to make his decision clear to us all. He rounded upon me bitterly, "James, you have done nothing but treat me like an enemy, I would say potential enemy, but you have done a great deal to fulfil that potential. I supported your ideas. I have argued forcefully for you in the dusty smoke-filled chambers behind the scenes of Government for years. Since joining this escapade, though I have done nothing to deserve your mistrust, you have tried to hoodwink me and provoke me into rash actions. In fact, I fought to protect this vessel. One of my best men, and an old comrade, a man I considered a friend, died defending you. I have provided you with important documentation that you may use against Du Maurier, and you still imprison my men and confine me to my quarters, at the first sign of trouble. Now you wish me to throw my hat into the ring and commit treason to help you. God's teeth man, I have more to fear from you!" he dramatically pulled off his nightcap and threw it on to the desk.

His cold-eyed glare was almost too much to bear. He was right, of course. I undoubtedly have become so distrustful that I have lost sight of the fact he and I are old friends too. I felt quite ashamed. I was compelled to admit, that though it was not my intention to treat him so inconsiderately, his accusations were right. I apologised unreservedly.

Franklin broke the awkward silence that followed. "Colonel, should you decide to accept the orders contained within the dispatches then, with a clear conscience, you will be able to say that, with your men under armed guard by crew loyal to the Professor, you were powerless to stop us. We shall drop you and your men off at a place of safety so that you will not be implicated any further in our insubordination." He then drew a pistol that I did not realise he had and laid it, dramatically, upon the table. "I believe Mr Giffard will testify that we gave you no choice."

Henry nodded, "Indeed."

Jahns looked at Franklin coldly for some time before replying, "You, sir, are no arbiter of my conscience. I am Colonel Ranolph Carter Jahns, and no man has ever forced me to do something against my judgement, even with a gun to my head."

"So, are you with us, Colonel?" asked Franklin brusquely.

Jahns stared at Franklin for a while, "I do not like you Franklin, and my instincts tell me not to trust you further than I could throw you, and so; no sir, I am not with you." Their eyes locked, and for an awful moment, I feared one of them would reach for the pistol on the table. "But you are of little consequence in the greater scheme of events, and I am a man of my word. I believe that Barbicane is correct in thinking that this mission is too important to abandon on a whim. Even if that whim is the President's." He turned to me, "James, I will accept your apology if you will undertake to suspend your suspicions of my motivations. Then I will throw my hand in with you." He laughed, "I have always fancied the life of an aerialist buccaneer."

His statement relieved some of the tension in the room, but Henry soon focused our thoughts on the urgency of the situation. "Gentlemen, you must understand; I was not privy to this conversation, and I shall deny any knowledge of it, even upon oath." We all made it clear we grasped his meaning. "I also know nothing of any other letters than the ones I was officially charged with delivering. When I leave here, I shall report that both you, James, and you, Colonel, have assured me that you will be returning to Tharsis without any significant delay once your repairs are completed. Agreed?"

Ranolph and I formally agreed.

"And Colonel, you shall destroy any documents." Ranolph nodded. "Good. What you have decided to do could see you either hailed as heroes or decried as cowards, traitors even. You must be prepared for either or both. May I suggest if you are to avoid imprisonment, if it is at all possible, you must bring back incontrovertible evidence, of anything you find out there."

I assured him that, after all these years, that was my express intention.

"Good. Now then, here is a little something to help you on your way, should you need it." Out of his portmanteau, he produced a large manila envelope and handed it to me. "I drew up a list of accessible resources and people you may find helpful."

"Spies?" asked Edwin.

"Field Agents, and people that are friendly to our cause abroad," replied Henry. "You will, of course, use them with the utmost discretion, should you need to avail yourself of their services. These are, after all, dangerous days, especially for those on that list."

I gave him my pledge and my thanks. I requested that he take my three injured crewmembers on his ship as there was no possible way, with a clear conscience, I could allow them to remain with us without proper medical attention. He agreed, and I tasked Mr Charles with the arrangements. At that, he arose and bid us all farewell. I escorted him back to his launch.

We parted warmly as old friends do. Just before embarking, he turned to me and smiled the same old sly smile of almost a lifetime ago. "There are more than just names in that envelope, there is access to funds too, to keep you going." I thanked him gratefully. "James, we know they are out there, somewhere; it is how you are going to find them that is the question, but for God's sake and your own; find them and bring back proof, or you may never be allowed to come back."

I nodded, of course, he was right. We were taking a huge step into the darkness of the unknown. "Henry, there is one more thing I need you to do for me." I handed him letters to Bravett and Bogdanov I had drawn up regarding Du Maurier, and I also asked of him to let our families know, as much as he securely could, that we are safe.

Something crossed Henry's face at that moment, but then he smiled again and promised me he would deal with Du Maurier and make sure the concerns of the families of the Expedition members, and crew, were allayed. We then watched him return to the belly of that great iron-grey leviathan.

I ordered the Head Steward to serve breakfast in the saloon and took a while to prepare myself for the barrage of questions that I was about to face.

The Flammarion Expedition Journal of L. Edwin Ransom.
Day six. 35th. 9th. 26.
Friday.

The meeting in the saloon did not go well for the Professor. There were far more questions than answers. Mostly the expedition members were concerned about the events that were going on around us.

Regardless of the perils we would face, and already had faced, the main concern was that if war broke out would we ever get to see our homes again.

In a surprisingly philosophical mood, the Colonel forewent his expected bellicose rant; he seemed almost downcast, reserving himself to a few pragmatic statements. Only Sir John spoke in anyway positively about the possibility of war. He had spent a long time with the free settlers of Sirenum Plains and the frontiersmen and prospectors in the mountains and forests of Gorgonum. He identified intensely with their grievances against Thyle and the Zephyrians. According to Sir John, a great deal of them are Dutch and German speakers, who fled Phaetontis when the Zephyrians invaded and annexed the greater part of their territory.

The Colonel agreed that it was long past time to put a stop to Thylian and Zephyrian expansion. He voiced regrets about our nation's inability to intervene in the invasion of Phaetontis, blaming it on cowardly politicians; nonetheless, he doubted that this was the right time to pick such a fight.

I asked why? After all, Gorgonum is virtually on our southern border, if we, as a nation, do not secure it, then we could find a Zephyrian puppet state, or worse, on our very doorstep.

The ladies, on the whole, as ever ladies are, were opposed to the idea of war. Parthena being the most vociferous and plainspoken. I must say she made some excellent points about the futility of war and the unbearable cost in human lives, not just to the soldiers, but the innocents trapped between the warring factions.

The Colonel made various references to what he called the 'Bardolph Rules' laid down in the international declaration of UDI. However, it took no time for Sir John to refute the argument with several well-chosen anecdotal tales that alluded to the scope of Thylian and Zephyrian brutality. The Colonel agreed that although we may 'play by the rules,' as they say, few other nations do.

I observed Adam's face as it grew grimmer and grimmer until he finally spoke out.

"Tell me, Colonel, why did you not go down to visit the ruins of Ananthor during our stopover?" He allowed that to hang in the air like the Colonel's cigar smoke before answering it himself. "You have been there before have you not? You were one of the Field Officers during the clearing of Ananthor, were you not? It was you who led your Highlanders in the clearing of the population after the bombardment. What 'rules' were you 'playing by' then? Did you receive much resistance from the dying, the starving and the

sick? The women, the old men, the children, did they put up much of a fight?"

All eyes turned to the Colonel. His face had flushed the colour of beetroot, and his eyes bulged like a strangulated rabbit. He said nothing.

There was a frightening change in Adam's tone, almost as if it were not even his voice. "They must have fought hard because you were forced to kill so many. So many unarmed starving women and children. Humans and Aresians regardless. Is it true, what it says in Beresford's book, you received a commendation for your men hardly firing a shot?" He made a noise somewhere between a derisive laugh and a dismissive snort, before addressing us all. "You all delude yourselves. There are no rules to war. They exist only in the minds of lying politicians who wish to assuage your consciences with such notions. Eye-to-eye with the enemy, they are meaningless. We will kill them or be killed by them. There are no 'innocents,' only 'us' and 'them,' and if they are not 'us,' then they're our enemy, and we are there to kill them." Adam's face was drawn back in an expression I can only describe as what I once heard called a prattan's sneer. He looked utterly enraged. "In war, there is no differential drawn between man, woman, soldier or child, no mercy. They are all nothing but bloody fodder for the guns. Or the bayonet."

"Well said, Sir," exhorted Dr Spender. "Damn right. Carter, all your talk of 'jus in bello,' is utter nonsense."

Adam continued, "War is a horror beyond anything you, in your safe, plush, lincrusta lined worlds can imagine."

The room fell into silence, and it took Sir John to break the hiatus with a quip; "I say old chap, what have you been putting in that coffee of yours? Too much Scotch perhaps?" One of the ladies laughed nervously. "I hope it is the coffee, not purely the effects of too little sleep."

Adam stood up. His sudden movement silenced the room again. I felt for a moment, the sensation that prey must feel in the face of danger; however, a puzzled look came over his face, and he shook his head as if trying to awake. He mumbled an apology and hurriedly left, leaving the rest of us to stare at the closing door.

The Colonel, seated across the table from me, grasped my arm as I got up to follow my friend, and said softly. "Mr Ransom, You and I need to talk about that man." His watery-eyed gaze was excruciating. I nodded my agreement, mumbled my apologies, and went to follow Adam.

I was almost out of the room when the Professor called me back. The meeting was not finished. I stood discombobulated, torn between my duty to the Professor and my commitment to my friend.

It was Aelita that spared me from my predicament; she stood up and addressed the room. "According to my beloved husband's wishes, I, no doubt, have no home to return to. Not that I should ever desire to do so under almost any foreseeable circumstance." She crossed the room to where I stood. "My 'plush, lincrusta lined world,' as Mr Franklin adroitly put it, was little more than a

119

viewing cage that I shall never return to. So, my dear friends, for all intents and purposes, my decision as to remain with you is made for me. Now forgive me, as Ursula and I must go and determine whether Mr Franklin has recovered himself." She smiled at me, patted my arm and left with her maid in close attendance. Sir John made to move, but the Colonel grumbled something at him, and he sat back down.

It was never meant to come to a show of hands. There was no democracy aboard the Seren Bore, so talk of abandoning our aims and turning back never truly arose. Nonetheless, if any team members did not wish to remain a party to the expedition, then the Professor offered to drop them off at some point as soon as practicalities allowed.

Dr Spender said that he always knew this voyage would take far more time than the Professor would have ever admitted, and as it might be his last chance at a final great adventure, he was here to see it to the end. Parthena's trepidations were more practical; she was only concerned that they should obtain some more of her father's medication as soon as possible, apart from that, where her father went so would she.

Charity, sitting beside Parthena, took her hand and said, "I was invited to chronicle this expedition and have already discovered so much and seen such adventure. Thank you, Professor, for inviting me, and, regardless of the dangers, I shall continue with you for as long as it takes. Where Parthena and her wonderful father go, I shall happily follow."

Sir John quaffed his brandy, refilled it and stood up, "I am game for it! What more could one ask for?" He cast about. "High adventure and danger in the company of beautiful ladies." He raised his glass in salute of the Professor. "Cheers, old fruit! Game on and all that." At that, he emptied the glass, winked at me, and left the saloon.

The rest of us sat in silent contemplation for a while until Jakes served tea. "Ah there, then that is it decided then," said the Colonel. "Looks to me as if you have us all at your back. What now then?"

I have never seen the Professor so flummoxed by a simple question. "Really, Ranolph?" He said carefully replacing his teacup into its saucer. "I am damned if I know. We will have to set a new heading and try to make sense of this chaos."

"We will be considered fugitives, will we not?" queried Dr Spender.

"Indeed, in the eyes of the law, we already are," answered the Colonel. "We have just opted to disobey a direct order from the President. So, yes, you are now fugitives, and I, on the other hand, I shall be branded a deserter, or worse."

The Professor studied him over the rims of his pince-nez in a scholarly fashion and commented, "You are never one to be out-done, Ranolph. I am sure if we fail, there will be little difference in the fates that await both of us upon our return."

Colonel Jahns laughed. "James, dear boy. Do you seriously, even expect to live long enough to return?"

Parthena made a droll remark to Charity about maybe having to live on the Polar ice fields in one of those little ice houses the Eskimo's back on Earth make. Charity did not know to what she was referring, and so the conversation digressed into Dr Spender's detailed explanation of an igloo.

At that, I took my leave.

"This is not a world to be called home.
It is but the bloody altar of an ancient War God,
upon which we are sacrificed."

FRIAR GODFRIED,
SERMO AD POPULUM,
PUBLISHED, AMENTHES,
1890.

Extracts from
Beresford's History of the Martian Colonies.
3rd Edition. Milton and Dante.

Chapter 4. The Un Defeated.

No historically significant event ever happened in isolation. Howsoever, chroniclers may present them as such, and some lesser historians may attempt to study them as separate occurrences with specific causalities and repercussions. This is more to frame their research scope than to provide as in-depth a historical narrative as possible. History is much like a layered pattern that one would get if you were to impose innumerable spider webs over each other. Each small event connects to each other through inestimable and often apparently tenuous links. Momentous occurrences, such as revolutions, disasters, wars, connect these layers of webs as if some Godlike child had taken a rough sailcloth needle and brutally sown through those diaphanous layers.

Many historians make the fundamental mistake to present their considerations of a specific event in isolation, regardless of the myriad individual connecting factors that together often weigh massively on that occurrence, not only upon the cause but also upon the event itself and its final outcome.

Within a single generation of the 'conquest' of post-Roman England by the Anglo-Saxons, future Anglo-Saxon Kings would be baptised with Romano-Celtic names[i]. The truth of the story has been lost because generations of historians, each drawing from the previous generation's academic work, contaminated as it is with that cohort's inherent biases and assumptions, with little or no recourse to the original source material, focused purely on the destiny of the conquerors not the story of the conquered.

Defeat on the battlefield seldom leads to complete obliteration of the conquered culture.

Note.

i. **"The Hand that Rocks the Cradle." An examination of the evidence for matrilineal influences as agents of post-conquest cultural survival and assimilation. Beresford et al. Milton and Dante. 1899.**

Secessionism in the Colonies.

It is the nature of all successful colonies to move politically towards independence. It is a factor of economic success howsoever that is measured. Coupled with the factor of a ruling executive removed by a considerable physical and temporal distance from the colony's day-to-day existence. This provides fertile ground for the seeds of resentment within the colonial community and a desire for self-rule. Policies that may seem sensible, if not logical, in the halls of the Colonial ruler's Parliament, often seem unfair and punitive to the colonists. Unfair taxation, issues of political disenfranchisement, compounded by the inevitable estrangement that those who seek new lives in the colonies have for their Motherlands, play a significant factor in the growth of secessionist and revolutionary resentments in the hearts of colonists.

Page 498.

Additional failures of the often unsupported, Colonial administration at a local level, economic restrictions and burdens placed upon the Colony by the Colonial Executive, along with lack of consistency of military assistance in both its protective and regulative roles, are additional factors that nurse the seeds of political resentment, the ideology of revolution.

The intellectual ideology of Secessionism and Revolution were most probably imported into the Martian colonies along with the very first wave of Tellurian settlers. This was something the Imperial powers were all too aware of in the mid-19th century. To these ends, most of the Imperial powers used a system of differentiation of status between the various social classes of emigres. The British Empire used a system known as the Red Books, though the ledgers were in actuality were black. The Red Books system was used to guarantee stipulated privileges to those of certain social standing that would be willing to uproot and migrate to the Martian colonies. To provide the Colonists with a ready-created 'haute bourgeoisie,' asocial elite, from which would be drawn the upper administrative and governing class. The appearance of their names in the Red Books guaranteed their status above other emigres, including voting rights, legal immunities, and other rights, such as exemptions from specific taxes, namely Property Tax, and even the jurisdiction of the lower Courts. Many saw this as a way of furthering their family interests and raising their status. The Government saw it as a way of investing those families in loyalty to the Crown.

Alongside these, Red Bookers came the first waves of working-class immigrants, servants, skilled manual and agricultural workers and their families. Some of the lower levels of the administration class; clerks, recorders and various functionaries of the administration. These were not granted the invested privileges of entry of their names into the Red Book.

This latter group was a breeding ground for revolutionary ideologies. In Tharsis, in the early periods, this centred on Herschel Mensch, a Jewish clerk in the Agricultural Affairs Department, and Jonathan Ball, a Methodist minister. Though both were tried for sedition at Alba Assizes, and both were convicted. Public outcry saved Ball from the gallows, seeing him exiled to the Selenium Plains; Mensch was executed.

Page 499.

Herschel Mensch was a highly educated, charismatic and articulate young idealist, who, mounting his own defence, used it as a platform to eloquently heap scorn upon the Colonial Administration and the whole process that put him on trial. If Mensch had wished to "*humbly create a debate*" as he claimed, then he most certainly achieved his goal. His words and demeanour propelled what would have been just another trial of an unknown would-be anarchist onto the front sheets of the daily Newspapers.   In the end, Mensch's death proved fundamental to the growing movement as it provided the first martyr to the Secessionist cause.

The Colonial Administration failed to understand that the Secessionist movement existed on two distinct levels. On one level, there were the middle-class intellectuals, the intelligentsia, who were pursuing the argument in the dining rooms, drawing rooms and the colloquiums of the Colony. On the other level, there was the groundswell movement amongst the industrial and agricultural working class and the growing numbers of poor. The failure of the Administration to realise that the mood amongst the intellectuals was far more threatening to their position, was a fatal mistake. Instead, they focused on punitive actions against working-class agitators, often mistaking unionising and commonplace industrial disputes as sedition. These mistakes only served to polarise the issue and guarantee that when the inevitable revolution came, it would be brutal and bloody.

In his address to the Colonial Inquiry into the Wollstonecraft Square Massacre, Sir James Richardson said, *"Not every sabot thrown into a loom is hurled there by the hand of a traitor. Nor every placard-waving washerwoman an anarchist. It is foolish to view every poor, downtrodden, mill worker bemoaning his lot as a revolutionary. But then again, and here is the rub, should we continue to react as thus, then our actions will make it both a reality for them and us."* (iv)

Page 590.

Notes.

(iv) The Proceedings of the Special Inquiry into the Wollstonecraft Square Incident. Publishing date declined.

Excerpt from;
Diary of Aelita Fontenelli (Mrs).
Friday, September, 35th. MY.26

Dear Diary.

We awoke just before dawn by much kafuffle and toing-and-froing of the crew on the deck. Our airship had made an unexplained rendezvous with a tremendous Tharsian warship. I have never seen a dirigible as massive; it dwarfed our craft, like some prodigious grey giant, bristling with all manner of weaponry. I stole a moment to gaze upon it, silhouetted against the dawn sky like an overbearing Goliath to our tiny David, what awful monstrosities men create to wage their meaningless wars with.

After our rude awakening, we were hurried by the stewards to the saloon for the earliest of breakfasts.

I must say that, although he is a hero of great renown, Colonel Ranolph Carter-Jahns is a most disagreeable man. He arrived still in his sleeping garb under his greatcoat, sporting his nightcap and whiskers protector, and puffing feverishly upon a cigar. He appeared like some faintly ridiculous character from a children's rhyme; Wee Willie Winkie, grown old, cantankerous, and foul-mouthed. He was furious, berating the android attendant and the staff for no reason other than to vent his ire.

I must admit he caused me to cringe a little inside, as his outburst reminded me of Giovanni at his worst. He then proceeded to indulge himself in a prolonged jeremiad, illuminating in detail what he perceived as the shortcomings of the Professor and his ideas. In the midst of his tirade, he received news that his men had been confined to their quarters under guard. He became almost incandescent with rage.

Thankfully, we were only treated to this display for a short time, as a crewmember came to summon him to the Captain's cabin and, to our great relief, we were all left in the saloon to talk amongst ourselves. All we could do was wonder at the meaning of it all. I attempted to take the opportunity to make conversation with Parthena. However, Sir John was being a little overly attentive to my needs. I had just dispatched him to fetch me a cup of tea when the Colonel returned with the Professor, Edwin Ransom and Mr Franklin.

I must admit to a change of heart in my reactions to Mr Franklin. Although I still find him truly fearsome to look upon. I must say the more I hear of the regard the others hold him in and his undoubted bravery, the more I come to fear that I may have misjudged the man. Correspondingly, my newly amplified compassion has led me towards sensing an air of profound melancholy about him, something that I may have mistaken for hostility. For his part, he no longer looks towards me, studiously avoiding my gaze. I feared I had unintentionally offended him in some way. I resolved to speak to Mr Ransom regarding this, and if it were true, consider how I should go about making amends for my irresponsible, nigh childish, thoughtlessness.

The Professor explained that the warship had come to warn that hostilities were about to break out in the South, and that our ship had been ordered home. My heart sank at the news. The thought of returning home to my prison of a marriage, suddenly filled me with such dread I felt physically nauseous. Sir John sensing my disquiet, was attentive and kind. Then, to my relief, the Professor explained that he had no intention of returning to Tharsis and surrendering his ship to the war effort.

It was all I could do to contain my relief, that for a few moments I must have been so lost in my own happiness that I did not notice the conversation turn to the specific points of the impending conflict. I became aware that Sir John was in a heated exchange with Parthena regarding the morality of war. She is such a frank, clear-minded young woman, and not one to yield to anyone else's opinion, let alone a man such as Sir John. Sir John has a wonderful kind heart, courageous and humorous; however, I have noticed that when challenged, he can be as much of a supercilious pedant as Giovanni.

I could sense Parthena's anger rising when the Colonel interjected with some assurance that there are 'conventions,' as he called them, to protect innocent lives threatened by such conflicts. No one had been watching Mr Franklin, and we were all startled when he suddenly interjected in the most formidable tone, dismissing the Colonel's contention of the existence of rules in warfare as meaningless piffle. As we all turned our attention to him, I practically gasped with shock. Fortunately, after my experiences at Ananthor and since, I have taken on a little more circumspection in my reactions. I understood immediately that what I might perceive, others may not.

Mr Franklin sat on one of the dining chairs, his body thrust forward, with his elbows on his knees and his eyes, set, like burning coals, upon the Colonel. My awareness that something about him had changed occurred before I realised what it was; it was his face still, though the scars were gone, his modest moustache was now a well-clipped Suvorov, and his unruly hair was trimmed, and macassar oiled flat to his skull. This striking face was undoubtedly Mr Franklin, however in its intensity, it was more fearsome to behold than the ruined visage we all have become used to. There was no compassion in that face, hardly a shred of civility; it glared out from inside Mr Franklin with a ruthless contempt. When he spoke, his voice was cruel sounding and thick with an accent I could not place, he continued to talk of the slaughter of Ananthor in a most brutal manner. My attention was broken for a moment when Dr Spender loudly concurred with his sentiments. By the time my attention returned to Mr Franklin, the apparition had dispersed, and he was restored to his normal appearance, though the angry tone remained.

"The horrors of war are beyond anything you, in your safe, lincrusta lined worlds can imagine." That allusion struck me deeply. I have long grown to see my home as little more than a handsome cell, exemplified by the beautifully engraved foil

linings and plaster works of the reception rooms, depicting Aesop's fables and a tale from ancient India, about a caged tiger that tries to trick a Priest. All hand embossed by émigré Italian artistes at countless expense, as a gift for Giovanni's first wife, Ribqah. For so long, I felt that her presence remained in that house as an unseen warden to my imprisonment.

That he, Mr Franklin, should make mention of such extravagant furnishings, left me almost short for breath, as one does after suffering an involuntary shudder. Such a thing that often solicits the remark that someone has trespassed upon one's future grave.

Sir John, possibly aware of all our discomfiture, tried to make alight remark to alleviate the ominous atmosphere.

As if in reaction, Mr Franklin sprang to his feet. Everyone took an instinctive jump back into their seats at the unexpectedness of his movement. I watched as his face transformed again, from a mask of anger to one resembling more that of an upset and confused child. Most notably, the change came over his eyes. He mumbled something redolent of an apology and fled the room.

I felt instantly compelled to follow him, discovering myself already on my feet, and understanding it would be unseemly for a lady to leave in pursuit of a gentleman. I quickly addressed the assembled explorers, "According to my beloved husband, whose wishes I have already flouted, I, no doubt, no longer have a home to return to. Not that I should ever desire to do so under almost

134

any foreseeable circumstance. My 'lincrusta lined world,' as Mr Franklin so adroitly put it, was little more than a cage that I shall never return to of my own volition, and so, my dear friends, for all intents and purposes, my decision is already made. For now, please forgive me, Ursula and I, must go and determine whether Mr Franklin has regained himself."

It took a little while to discover where Mr Franklin had retired to. I dismissed Ursula's assertion that we should try his quarters as I felt it unlikely. I sensed he would want to be as exposed to the elements as possible, as I would.

We found him at the rear observation post on the poop deck. Due to the biting wind, I had to send Ursula to fetch my coat before I could join him. Mr Franklin though, was seemingly unaffected by the cold, standing as he was in the face of the gale in only his waistcoat, shirt and trousers.

I must declare I am not one with a fondness for small talk. However, I have been well-schooled in it through years of entertaining the endless stream of tedious gawpers that Giovanni called 'guests. 'Even so, I have grown no liking for it. Instead of attempting such interminable niceties, I spoke honestly, not fearing whether he assumed me insane or not.

"Please do not take me for nothing more than a hysterical girl. I see things, Mr Franklin. Things I would rather I did not. I have not always seen these things, now I do, and, as of only a few days ago, these things I see, these visions, grow stronger." I

paused fearing I was not making any sense and awaiting the type of cynical rebuff my husband would mete out.

Instead, he turned and fixed me with the most disarming gaze. His eyes still hold an intensity that I find, for want of a better word, alarming. Not because there is danger in them, on examination, I can sense no such threat. It is because they give the impression, they have seen too many unimaginable tragedies for one soul to tolerate. He asked softly, "What is it that you see, Mrs Fontenelli?"

I requested him to call me Aelita, as I feel it is my only true name.

"What is it that you see, Aelita?" The sound of my name on his lips sent a strange shudder through me and left me so disconcerted I struggled to find the words to continue. "I saw him, Mr Franklin. The other man, the soldier, I think. For a while, in the saloon, he became you, or you became him." I knew the words sounded insane as I spoke them.

Nevertheless, I felt compelled to finish. "I do not understand because, when he overcame you, forgive me, the vision I saw did not have your scars, nor your hair cut or moustache, though it was most definitely you, he almost seemed older than you are now." I found I had drawn too close to him, and self-consciously stepped away.

He continued to gaze down at me with an expression I can only describe as disconsolate.

Regardless, I felt the imperative to continue. "I beg your forgiveness, Mr Franklin, I feel I have judged you harshly. I understand that you carry some heavy burden that none of…"

He cut me off at that point, speaking so softly it was difficult for me to hear against the gale. "The Sergeant Major, his name is Adam Godwin Franklin. He was a Sergeant Major in the British Royal Colonial Marine Regiment. A long, long time ago."

"A ghost?" I realised how childish that seemed as soon as I said it.

He looked away. "No. I am he, and he is I, at least, he was who I was once. A revenant of who I once was, maybe."

I could sense clearly that he was not insincere. However, there was so much in what he said that made no sense to me, so much he was not saying. Instead, I found myself telling him about the vision I had in the city of Ananthor. He listened patiently as I blabbered on about the hurly-burly of a strange city full of fantastical translucent phantoms.

It was as I began to explain how the yellow-eyed boy and I had touched, that Mr Franklin stopped me abruptly. He queried whether I believed it to be a genuine experience or some form of phantasmagoria? A hallucination stimulated by the conditions or, like Marley's ghost, a poorly digested meal? I asserted it was as real as any experience I have ever had. It most certainly did not have any illusory quality to it. I assured him it was not some idle daydream.

His expression changed to one of consternation as he looked away from me. I apologised if I had caused him any further distress, he dismissed it, assuring me that I had in no way offended him. He then asked why I had been compelled to divulge these things to him at this point.

I paused, as it was a question that required an answer that had not by any means formed in my conscious mind. Had it not felt so preposterous, I would have said plainly that it felt the correct thing to do. Upon reflection, I struck upon an answer that surprised even myself, "You mentioned a world lined with lincrusta, and that struck a chord with me. Have you ever seen such rooms, Mr Franklin? The effect on the mind is akin to living inside a metal box, a prettily embossed one, of course, lavish in fact, nonetheless; a box. My home, my husband's home, has several rooms extravagantly ornamented with such foil coverings upon the walls."

Mr Franklin began to apologise if he had offended me. I brushed it aside and explained why I had found his metaphor personally compelling, to say the least. Again, for a moment, Mr Franklin looked disconcerted. "Is it not common to many other homes in Tharsis?" he inquired. Explaining that he had thought it some decadent fad, or status symbol, common to the mansions of the rich. I explained that in fact, I have never seen any other room bedecked with it, save the great dining room in the old Viceroy's Palace, though I supposed there must be many others.

At that point, our conversation was interrupted by the arrival of Sir John. I felt it more polite to divert Sir John so as to give Mr Franklin the peace and quiet he sought, however as we turned away, Mr Franklin asked a very peculiar question. "May I ask whereabouts is your house? Which district of the city of Tharsis, I mean?"

"Oh no, we only visit our Tharsis house during the Season, or when Giovanni is lecturing. Our main domiciliari is in the city of Alba. Clerval Street, overlooking a beautiful little park, a memorial to the great philologist and natural philosopher Henri Clerval. It would be my pleasure to show it to you one day, though I am of a mind that I may never return there."

The unseen veil of his melancholia closed between us like a theatre fire curtain as he turned aside. "Sometimes, it is best not to retrace our footsteps." Though his words were softly spoken and innocuous, his tone was disturbingly distant.

I agreed politely and ushered Sir John away.

Dated 5th of August 0030.

Statement taken from Henry Williamson Carstairs,

Butler to Professor Flammarion.

The days after Mrs Eleanor's death were undeniably strange.

Mrs Minerva took over the running of the house in the days following the tragedy. It was she who summoned the Uwharrie Clan to the house. They arrived on the night of the 36th.

I must say they were a curious collection. Men of fierce, rugged appearance, and rough handed, hard-faced women, most of them relatively young. Nevertheless, they came to our aid in short time and in a large number, brandishing enough weaponry to wage a military campaign.

Their "Parh," as they all respectfully referred to him, was Hezekiah Uwharrie, an amazingly hirsute mountain of a man. Who arrived the following morning with a handful of other more senior men of his extended family. For all their uncouth appearance, the Uwharrie clan were truly reverential towards the household and the house.

Although it was usually my responsibility to deal with any hired help. It was Mrs Minerva's wish that Joshua and Karl, once repaired, would act as liaisons with the Uwharrie Clan.

Only Mr Uwharrie accepted the offer of lodging in the house, though we were hard-pressed to find a bed, that could take his enormous physique. The others took to either sleeping in their wagons or camping on the south lawn where they created quite a colourful and communal atmosphere, though it rancoured the gardeners.

I feared awfully what the Professor's reaction to their presence would be upon his return. However, it was a minor inconvenience after the horror of the murder of Mrs Eleanor, something the household would never fully come to terms with. They did prove to be far more effective than our pitiable attempts to protect the family.

Their task, as I understood it, was to secure the estate and house. Though the nature of their role rapidly changed under Miss Lenora's direction

Miss Lenora arrived later on the same day with Mr Edvard Clemm, a gentleman friend escort. He was a colleague of hers from the school. A very pleasant and respectable young man. I feared, though, the situation he discovered himself in was far beyond anything he had experienced in the cloistered world of his boarding school.

That evening, the three ladies, Mrs Ransom, Miss Lenora and Lady Niketa, held a lengthy meeting in the drawing room. Everyone else, except Karl, were given explicit orders not to interrupt. Later that evening, Mrs Ransom had me request Mr Uwharrie to join them.

They talked into the late night and withdrew to their bedrooms with the grimmest countenances I have ever known.

From that day onwards Miss Lenora, whom her late mother had often referred to as her 'happy flower,' took on the bearing of a woman decades older than her years. After the morning of her first arrival, I never again heard her raise her voice or shed a tear; in fact, she seldom spoke. A few of the staff remarked to me that they now found it hard to meet her gaze. We all became anxious that her devastating loss had turned inward into the coldest of rage. The following day she sent Mr Clemm away. I think, though he behaved like a perfect gentleman, he was nonplussed by the perfunctory manner of his dismissal. She never returned to her post at the school.

Initially, I feel we were all unaware of how dangerous Miss Lenora's rage would become. It was only later that I became certain that it was with Miss Lenora's encouragements that Mr Uwharrie used his considerable resources to draw up a register of the men from the rough parts of the city whom Everheart had hired to perpetrate his murderous attack upon us. Though I believe the extent of their actions were never fully disclosed to Mrs Minerva or any of the family to my knowledge, the Uwharries carried out what I shall always prefer to see as a series of acts of rough justice against those unfortunates on that list.

Over the following week, the Uwharries went out under the cover of darkness, along with Karl and Joshua's men. They went out into the city, wearing hessian masks and bristling with guns, and did not return until the early hours.

The Tharsis Herald made a great hullabaloo over the deaths of several known criminals discovered hanging from the gas lamps of the streets in the more insalubrious quarters of the city. The sensationalist journals called these 'lynchings' and with no other suspects attributed it to the actions of some, as yet unknown, vigilance committee. I read the articles with a heavy heart knowing full well it was the Uwharries exacting Miss Lenora's vengeance. I did my best to make sure that such news, along with speculations in the other gutter rags, over the murder of Mrs Eleanor, never reached the breakfast table, nor that any such gossip should reach the ears of the family. However, soon such things were superseded on the front pages by much talk of possible war in Sirenia with Thyle and Zephyria.

As for myself, if I must be as truthful as possible, I felt no compunctions other than deep regret that Miss Minerva strictly forbade my sons and me from involving ourselves in those nefarious night-time activities. Whatever punishments the Uwharries meted out, and I fear that the newspapers hardly learnt of the full extent of their campaign. God forgive me, but I would have happily aided them in hanging every one of those brutes. Though I feel I may have been a little more discriminating as to whom I meted out such punishments.

Miss Lenora's emotional health never fully recovered; she was never again the 'happy flower' that spread such joy throughout the family.

Mrs Minerva continued to run the household as best as possible. The Friends came several times to hold their silent vigils and provide practical support to the household, something Mrs Ransom and the family found very reassuring, but Miss Lenora avoided them altogether. Many of the Professor's and Mrs Eleanor's friends called to pay their respects and condolences.

Police Officers called several times, including a visit from the Chief Constable of Tharsis himself, Sir Eugeniusz Emshwiller-Tananarive, but, in truth, they were powerless to do anything but take our statements and initiate the manhunt for Everheart. A man whom the High Sheriff of Alba had already issued an arrest warrant for.

Unfortunately, because the funeral arrangements had to be suspended until the Professor and Mr Ransom returned, Mrs Eleanor could not be kept at home, and she had to suffer the further indignity of being taken to the city morgue. Her departure caused great anguish to us all. The idea of her resting alone in some ice-filled storage room far from home was too much to bear. The small cortege winding its way through the city drew a substantial crowd of spectators, some of whom, though they may have never known Mrs Ransom, threw flowers, or, as it has become traditional on Mars in recent years, cast handfuls of red sand on the path before the black plumed horses.

As the days past, a dread settled upon the whole household as no word came from Mr Ransom or the Professor. Mrs Minerva sent letters and telephonograph after telephonograph, to the locations on the *Seren Bore*'s itinerary, even contacting Mr Giffard, a friend of the Professor with associates in the Government and Air Navy, in the hope he would forward the message via the Navy's photo-telegraph, but still, no answer came.

Journal of Adam Franklin.

Editor's Note.

2 pages have been roughly torn from the journal and have never been accounted for. As the removed pages comprised the first part of the entry included below, we feel that by the weight of evidence, it is probable that it was the entry for the earlier portion of the day.

James Ransom.

I must be mad.

Or it is this nonsensical world around me, this lunatic's nightmare I have awoken into, that is completely insane.

Nothing makes sense. I feel like I have tripped and stumbled down one of Mr Carol's rabbit holes.

Now I am conflicted even further. Aelita Fontenelli no longer looks upon me with mistrust but has decided to confide in me. After the incident in the saloon, she sought me out and, along with her highly strange experiences in Ananthor, revealed that she could see "things," that others could not.

In the telling, she drew close enough for me to smell the perfume on her skin, even in the driving wind.

Unconsciously, if any woman does anything unconsciously, she even rested her gentle hand momentarily upon my chest when she spoke to me of her visions in Ananthor. I almost folded as if struck by the fiercest of blows. Her eyes are kaleidoscopic pools, deep enough for any man to drown in and I fear I am not the only one who would willingly drown in them. It was all I could do to control myself from reaching out and taking her in my arms.

It was far less problematic when she distrusted me and kept a safe distance for both our sakes.

Now what?

I am infatuated with her, in a way I cannot imagine ever being before, and have been since the moment I laid eyes upon her. Not only is she the wife of a wealthy and respected gentleman, of a class far above my meagre station, and a Roman to boot, but she is an Aresian, a damned, red-skinned alien. For God's sake!

Also, she has a suitor, as unsuitable as he is, Sir John is at least of her own social class, and regardless of what scandal besets them, he can easily provide for her. No doubt, he has weathered numerous scandals before. What can I offer her? I am nothing more than an over complex adaptation of Karl. A Nutcracker in a poorly stitched skin suit, unsure of my own existence, let alone my sanity. It would be insane of me to draw her anywhere near the Sergeant Major.

Yet she provokes the wildest fantasies in me. Yes, I could kill everyone on this ship who gets in my way, snatch her up and escape with her to some remote and romantic place.

Then what?

Would I see her hunted like an animal, let alone let her know what is beneath this skin? What monster would I have to become to keep her and keep her safe?

Damn this all.

The things Aelita told me have perplexed me ever since. She was able to describe the Sergeant Major lucidly enough that I have no doubt she could see him. How? I cannot even begin to imagine. I only know I almost lost complete control of myself in the saloon. I can only describe it as a sensation of complete disembodiment; I could see and hear and feel, but I had no control over what he said or did. He was in total control, and it took all my strength to wrest it back from him. Did he manifest in some way, like one of Lady Niketa's phantoms?

Then, the strangest of all things, something I can scarcely force my mind to deliberate on. Aelita's home in Alba is the self-same house I encountered Lanulos in. Presumably, I must add. Of course, there were many grand houses around that square, but the coincidences are far too many for happenstance. Yes, it had that distinctive wall covering, but that house felt long forsaken, not closed up for a season, but stripped of the personal trappings of a home and abandoned. How can that be? Did I dream the whole thing? Was it an illusion brought on by fatigue, or was I mesmerised or passed some euphoric or hallucinogen? I shot two men dead, and yet moments later they and all shred of evidence they had ever been there were gone entirely.

All except those damn cards.

The experiences Aelita had at Ananthor were similar to mine in Alba. I cannot bring myself to doubt her. She said Dr Spender had a similar experience, at the same time, it was that that contributed to his collapse.

Ghosts? It seems preposterous to me. The experience was as real to her as Lanulos was to me, and he was no ghost. She even touched one of them. Again, a yellow belly, but they did not threaten her or the Doctor.

What does that mean? We cannot share in the nature of illusionary experiences we both knew nothing about. Are we infected with some lunacy or is the fabric of materiality crumbling about us?

This is ludicrous! A man, virtually dead for half a century, questioning if the reality he has been dragged back into is truly real? It would have made some old classical logician laugh himself insane.

I am grateful to whichever mad Gods that misrule this world that the rest of the day was uneventful. I spent a pleasant while with Edwin in the late afternoon, sitting wrapped up in immensikoffs on the weather deck, sipping tea out of a pair of china mugs we borrowed from the crew. We discussed some of the things that Aelita had told me.

He considered everything in his usual thoughtful manner before commenting, "As you know, my wife's mother, a wonderful woman, God rest her soul, was very involved with all that type of thing. She once talked with me for quite some time about some French chappie, Doily-Cart, or something, who put forward a proposition that everything we think we know we only know through our senses and they can easily be tricked or fooled. Therefore, he argued that the only thing we know for sure is that we exist because we can think. It is through the act of thinking we make sense of the world around us. However, thinking is in itself, by its nature, purely subjective. The most important part of thinking is our ability to imagine or to dream. So, if our only measure of reality is our thinking mind, and that can be deceived or deceive itself, then everything we think we know, everything we think is real, could, in fact, be a dream or an illusion."

"Or a nightmare," I added.

"To be sure. And I could be a figment of your imagination, in fact, all this could be. Or you might be a figment of mine."

I looked at him carefully, as he gazed earnestly back at me over his round-rimmed glasses. I could not resist commenting, "Well, Edwin, I must say that if this is all the work of your fevered imagination, then I fear for your sanity, my friend."

He laughed until he coughed. Once he regained himself, he added, "He suggested, this French fellow that is, this could all be an illusion, controlled by some malevolent force trying to deceive us. All the world's a stage and all the men and women merely players, etcetera." I agreed that sounded more in keeping with how I feel, but to what purpose? Edwin shrugged expressively, "Who are we to know the minds of Gods?"

The rest of the evening was uneventful. Most probably because I recused myself from the trial of dinner, considering discretion as the greater form of valour. I have no sensation of hunger and eating with the others has merely become a method of observing the 'niceties' of society. I could not countenance sitting in a room with Jahns as anything societal or remotely 'nice.'

Later I joined Sergeant Rawlings and the others in the orlop for a few games of cards and a crate of Porter I purloined from the purser's storeroom. Their company was far more congenial than I had anticipated given the circumstances, as they had hardly been inconvenienced by their erstwhile confinement. Two admitted sleeping right through it.

Edwin was still up and writing in his journal when I returned to our cabin. Proudly he showed me more of the little sketches he had been doing. The further adventures of a wayward Pug dog, who had taken to piracy of the airways on a rickety airship with an ever-expanding crew of bizarre anthropomorphic creatures, some of which bore an amusing resemblance to members of our expedition, myself included. I complimented him on his illustrations and stories and suggested, in all seriousness, that if he wanted to, he could easily make it to fame and fortune writing such stories for publication. After all, if Mr Carol could gain such success writing such stories for children, why should he not? This suggestion seemed both to delight Edwin and upset him. The melancholy was brought on by his dwelling upon his absence from his wife and children and the disagreeable manner of his departing. He informed me that he had written to his wife before our departure to make some kind of rapprochement, but, of course, there had been no time for a reply. Our conversation led me to one as yet unspoken question that had fermented at the back of my mind since we boarded this ship.

I know we have a Murray optical-telegraphic signal lamp on the bridge, but that is a very short-range communication system. Why is the ship not equipped with an Atmospheric Photophone or Telephonograph like the one we used on the train to Alba? Indeed, even in my day, we had air-telegraphy on most aerostats. We even had one on the HMAS Prometheus, the ship I was 'almost' killed on.

Edwin's explanation surprised me. In reply to much the same question from Edwin himself, the Professor had cited two factors. The first being cost as opposed to reliability; these days most of the civilian systems outside of Tharsis' main cities are antiquated and unpredictable, due to mounting cost of upkeep and resulting disrepair and the failure to properly rebuild the system after the ravages of conflict and the environment. In addition, the installation of such a system onboard presented a prohibitive cost to the expedition for, what he felt would be, little real benefit. The second reason was more interesting, and probably closer to the truth; the Professor had told Edwin he predicted something close to the events of this morning and *the subsequent recall to Tharsis. That being so he had told Edwin he knew that the Military have ways of locating airships that broadcast using such Atmospheric Photophone devices, should they be foolish enough to use them, even unsuccessfully, through the network of working receiver towers. An excellent way of locating any ship in an area, especially enemy ships. I asked Edwin how the Professor could know of such technology, but the answer was evident to me before I had even finished my question. Of course, he had probably been involved in designing it for them. Edwin agreed, saying that it was very likely the Professor would have been at least consulted in creating such technology if he had not a hand in perfecting it.*

Extracts from

Beresford's History of the Martian Colonies.
2nd Edition. Milton and Dante.

Chapter 5. The Bloody Red Hand of Freedom.

Major George Flavius Otranto-Usher was the only surviving male heir of a noble family from the Austro-Hungarian Principality of Das Majorat.

Upon the death of his father the Graf Herman Usher and finding themselves impoverished by the late Graf's profligate lifestyle, young George's mother, the Gräfinn Maria Louisa Otranto, and her sons, emigrated to the Martian colonies. Eschewing the Austro-Hungarian and German settlements, probably to avoid her late husband's debtors and the scandal surrounding his death. The Gräfinn Maria Louisa chose to settle herself and her three sons in the British colony of Tharsis. Abnegating their connections to the Usher name and any association with Daz Majorat, the family reverted to using their mother's maiden name, Otranto. Although of high social standing, but of foreign origins and without extensive financial resources, Maria Louisa's name was never entered in the Red Books, thus denying them the privileges it would have engendered.

George's older brothers, Roderick the 5th, and Edgar, both brought minor commissions in the British Forces. Roderick joined the Royal Air Navy as a Captain, and Edgar took a short commission as a Lieutenant in the British Martian Expeditionary Forces. However, he retired shortly due to ill health, listed as melancholia and nostalgia.

George was a dissolute child, given to humours similar to his father. In early life, his temperamental outbursts led to numerous household staff, nannies and teachers resigning. Leaving, at one point, only Maria Louisa to instruct her son. Maria Louisa was a young woman of great beauty and, at times, extraordinary personal resourcefulness, however, she was also highly spirited and prone to bouts of intense activity, reputedly bordering upon mania, followed by prolonged periods of introspective lethargy.

It has been suggested that Edgar's death in an apparent "hunting accident" (a neologism for being killed in an illegal duel) may have had a catastrophic effect on Maria Louisa's excitements.

At the age of 42, Maria Louisa died in what was described in the coroner's report as an "unfortunate accident while taking the waters." Though unsubstantiated, rumours abounded that she died attempting to drown herself and young George, in some insane suicide pact.

George remained in the charge of his mother's executors for the two years and six months up to his eighteenth birthday. The appointed guardians believed that it was necessary to place George in the Lawns Hospital, an asylum for the mentally deranged. Upon reaching his majority, the control of the little residue of his inheritance reverted into George's management, and he refused to pay for his own continued incarceration. With the support of his elder brother, now Commodore Roderick Otranto, George, following his late brother's example, bought a commission as a subaltern in the British Martian Expeditionary Force, the 2nd Pioneer Rifle Regiment.

It is recorded that, against all expectations, George excelled in the British Army, rising quickly to the rank of Major due to field commissions. George was recklessly brave and a formidable soldier in all areas, gaining the admiration of both his men and his superiors.

In late 1893, under the wing of Brigadier Sir Ian Fury-King, George was charged with forming a Special Company of the Forward Field Pioneering Battalion of the British Martian Expeditionary Regiment, to operate deep within enemy hinterlands. This Company, known only by its code name, The First Wolf Pack, later known as 'The Fury's,' or 'The Fury Boys,' were modelled upon the mounted Black Flag groups active during the American Civil War. The Wolf Pack company saw most of their operational activities deep within the borders of Thyle Major, Sirenum Plaines, Phaetontis and Amazonia. They quickly became renowned for their often brutal, yet highly effective exploits, sabotaging the enemy's infrastructure, disrupting supply routes and terrorising local populations. A technique that became known as "Fire and Fury." Regardless of their successes, their methods led some in high office to question their legitimacy as a military force.

On July 4th, 1896after the treaty of Mount Hecate, all the Wolf Pack companies, by then 12 strong, were officially disbanded and its officers decommissioned from the regular Army, including Sir Ian. However, they were immediately re-enlisted as irregulars.

What little is known about the later period of the Company's existence after the Mount Hecate Treaty sees them still deployed, albeit clandestinely, against both foreign and domestic threats, this included actions against identified anarchist cells and revolutionary agitators within Tharsis' own borders.

It was during the time with the First Wolf Pack that it is believed George was introduced to Secessionist sympathisers, amongst them James Nayler, most probably through friends of Sir Fury-King.

HRH Prince Edward Victor, Duke of Clarence, was appointed Viceroy of the Martian Colonies in 1892. In his letters, published after the UDI, he states that he was as good as exiled as far away from his grandmother, the Queen Empress, as could possibly be arranged. Scandal had always dogged the Prince, and his suggested embroilment with the denizens of the Whitechapel area of London's East End led to fears that he may become the lynchpin of a scandal of such immense proportions that it could damage the Royal Family, even the British Empire itself. Rumours, now believed manufactured by the British Government, suggested that the Duke of Clarence had died of influenza. If the Prince was aware of this is unknown. However, he did write that he understood that he would never be allowed to be the successor to his father Prince Albert Edward, the future King-Emperor Edward VII.

In truth, he arrived in Tharsis at the beginning of 1892, to take up his mainly ceremonial role. The colonial administration hoped that the presence of a member of the Royal Family would act as a rallying point for loyalists, and a catalyst for positive pro-Imperial fervour.

A great deal of patriotic rhetoric and pageantry surrounded the somewhat jaded and apathetic Prince. However, the Colonial Administration achieved its aim in raising the "morale" of the people. *"A Bread and Circuses policy,"* said the First Minister.

The ensuing years saw incidents of Secessionist activities drop, and the Government used the pro-Imperial mood of the people to stage mass arrests of undesirables, anarchists, revolutionaries, dissenting intellectuals and vocal pro-Secessionists. The Viceroy Prince was believed to have said, in private, upon hearing the term *"Bread and Circuses policy,* "that must cast him in the role of *"Principal Clown."* (i)

The Viceroy Prince settled into his purely ceremonial role well enough once he seemed to accept its strictures. His personal proclivities and conduct were closely shielded from any beyond his inner circle and, during his tenure of office, not a whisper of untoward rumour reached the newspapers. The commentator and satirist Randolph Rosenbud remarked that "for all anyone could say, inside the Viceroy's Palace could well be the domicile of angels or an anti-chamber to Sodom and Gomora." (ii)

More level-headed opinions have pointed out that the Viceroy Prince had liked to surround himself with free thinkers, philosophers, artists and the more colourful people from the edges of the social spectrum. The Bohemian elements of Tharsian society eagerly sought his patronage.

On Empire Day, 1899, in Tharsis, the Viceroy Prince was to award the title of 'Royal,' and their new colours, to the Colonial Marine Regiment. The Regiment had only been formed three years before by the amalgamation of the British Martian Expeditionary Force and units of the various other regiments that were serving in the Colony. It was to be a lavish ceremony, that was to be more a celebration of strength and unity than solely a military pageant.

Secessionist collaborators had secreted George Otranto, now calling himself Major George Otranto-Usher, onto the Aerostat HMAS Dealey. He had been furnished with a so-called *masquerade gun*. These were unique illegal specialist weapons, smuggled into the Martian Colonies in the guise of mundane items such as engineering or scientific equipment by pro-Secessionist sympathisers. George had also gained a reputation as an excellent sharpshooter.

In the middle of the presentation of the Colours, George Otranto-Usher fired one shot that killed the Viceroy Prince instantly. Although a single-shot rifle that takes some great difficulty to load, George Otranto was able to load the gun and fire three more shots in quick enough succession to slay the First Minister Sir Oswald Connolly and Field Marshall Sir George Hickey, and grievously injure the Austro-Hungarian Ambassador Prince Leonid Czolgosz.

George Otranto escaped the area and fled into the Lincoln Theatre, where he expected other Secessionists to be awaiting him. In his panic, he had sought refuge in the wrong theatre. Unfortunately, for George, he did not find armed sympathisers, only a small group of thespians in the middle of a dress rehearsal of a little-known play, 'The King in Yellow.'[iii]

Cornered by police constables and soldiers, George chose to fight it out, initially with firearms, but finally in a brutal hand-to-hand melee with the soldiers.

Legend has it that, as they dragged his dying body back into the street, George grasped at the white monk's robes of one of the bystanding actors, leaving a perfect bloody red handprint on the starched white cloth. That image would quickly become the symbol of the Secessionist's uprising.

The assassination of the Viceroy Prince, though hugely traumatic for the colony, did not lead immediately to armed rebellion. While the event rapidly began to take on mythic proportions on both sides, there was a hiatus period of roughly three months (Imperial Standard Time) often referred to as the "Long Intake of Breath." A period when both sides awaited the anticipated or feared reprisal from the British Imperial Government. When it became evident to all that no such punitive action would be forthcoming, the Colonial Government fell into disarray. Aware of the confusion at the heart of the administration, the Secessionists seized their opportunity to openly rebel.

The first significant act of the Secessionist revolution was the liberation of prisoners from the Tharsis Panopticon. An armed mob released two hundred and thirty-two political prisoners. Most were political agitators, anarchists and pro-revolutionary Secessionists. When the British soldiers arrived, the fighting spilt out into the surrounding area, and the incident became known as the Battle of Bentham Street.

The focus of the Secessionist's anger were the Colonists known as the Red Bookers. Whereas the Red Book had once been a bastion of established privilege, with powerful and wealthy families vying and bribing their way into later editions, in the hands of the Secessionists it became a death list.

In Tharsis, the most brutal fighting happened in the City of Alba, with the storming of the Presidio, the garrison of the 1st Colonial Marine Regiment. The now 'Royal' Marines, made up almost entirely of men born in the British Empire on Earth, formed the most feared and most loyal regiment in the entire British Colony of Tharsis. As the tide of history turned against them, and more and more military commanders, including men like Air Marshall, Sir Marcus Justinian Brookes, Commodore Roderick Usher and Colonel Ranolph Carter Jahns, joined the Secessionist cause. The Royal Marines in Alba, under Major General George Collingwood, found themselves isolated within a hostile city.

The siege of the Presidio was one of the most brutal battles of the rebellion. Major General Collingwood and his men chose to die, rather than surrender.

As Tharsis, the bastion of the British Empire on Mars, fell to the Secessionists, the true scope of the movement was revealed. Secessionists and revolutionaries across Mars rose up against their colonial masters and seized control with the avowed intention of establishing a brave new world.

In some colonies, such as Amenthes and Aeria, the transition was virtually bloodless.

"In Tharsis, they waded in blood, in Amenthes they hardly shrugged." (iv). In other colonies, like Tharsis, Chryse and Utopia, there was brutal fighting and reprisals against the social elites. Elysium, once the wealthiest and most progressive of the colonies, was thrown into brutal chaos from which it never truly recovered.

In all, the Secessionist's Revolution was well planned and over, in most colonies, in less than a year. A Universal Declaration of Independence was drawn up at the Thoris Conference, where the leading lights of the Secessionist movements and the newly formed administrations met to hammer out their new world order. The ideology of the declaration was unequivocal, but the most significant practical stumbling block was the defining of national borders, encompassing access to water and mineral resources.

Within two months of the UDI, several of the newly independent colonies were at war with each other.

Notes.

i.   Remark attributed to HRH Prince Edward Victor, Duke of Clarence, Viceroy of the British Martian Colonies, in the biography of Mrs Phyllis Roker, based on her diaries. Vol.7. P 327. (MY 07)

ii.   A remark attributed to Randolph Rosenbud, in the biography of Mrs Phyllis Roker, based on her diaries. Vol. 9, 102. (MY 07)

iii.   'The King in Yellow.' A play in two acts. Author Anonymous.

iv.   "Death of Empires." James Richardson. Tharsis University Press. (MY 10)

The Aresian Factor in the Wars of Secession.

Only two months (IST) before the assassination of the Viceroy Prince Edward Victor, the British Martian Expeditionary Forces made a surprise assault on the Aresian ruled oppida of Ananthor. The municipality had become a haven for disaffected Tellurian settlers, black marketeers, sand bandits and pirate activity. The city existed well within Tharsis' borders, but well beyond its control, as it was still notionally governed by the Aresian Suzeraine of Aldébaran, one of the last Princesses of the Malacandrian Imperial family, under the Treaty signed in Alba. The Archbishop of Tharsis, the Right Reverend Dr Charles Clarke described it as, "A cesspit of human and alien depravity." (i)

The hinterland around the city had recently been ravaged by an outbreak of the 'maladie de la Jeanne d'Ys,' the so-called "Jean D's" a fever that the Colonial Authorities blamed on the denizens of Ananthor for both breeding and spreading.

It was rumoured that the disease's presence in Ananthor also led to the Suzeraine Aldébaran forsaking her protection of the city. In truth, the British were aware that the Suzeraine's personal and political powers were diminishing and that she had no capability to resist their expansionist actions. Her refusal to send aid to the city during the plague was as much because of her lack of resources as it was the Aresian's profound fears of human contagions.

This action was the last known military engagement between any Colonial power and the Aresians. It did not seem to provoke any form of response from the Suzeraine, or her remaining allies.

Other than a few minor incidents on the borders of Thyle and northern Aeria there was no interaction with the Aresian forces during the Wars of Secession. A fact that did not go unnoticed by observers on all sides, even during the height of the conflict.

It was only the arrival, unannounced, of a delegation from the Red Aresian Royal houses of Kaldane and Ma'alefa'ak to the conference at Thoris Major that acted as a timely reminder to the newly formed independent nation-states, of the continued presence and power of the Aresian kingdoms. Though their behaviour was, as ever, cordial, their demands were unequivocal. The Aresian's charged the newly formed nations with the duty of holding to the treaties and settlements made with their colonial predecessors.

It is crucial at this point to remind the reader that the generally held view of the Tellurian colonists across Mars was that the Aresian threat was a spent force. Successive conflicts had resulted in the Aresians losing vast territories, and, to all intense and purposes, the complete destruction of the Malacandian's 'Empire.' The surviving Aresian kingdoms were considered to be little more than rumps that could be opposed at a whim. Even so, their appearance, in strength and some majesty at the Thoris conference underlined the point that untried they still posed a significant threat to the newly formed nations, especially in their vulnerable embryonic state.

The event denounced in the Tharsis Parliament as "over a barrel" diplomacy, left little choice for the delegates other than to acquiesce to the Aresian's demands and ratify the pre-existing agreements. Something none of the Secessionist states could guarantee, nor honestly wish to.

Notes.

i.   **Collected Sermons of the Right Reverend Dr Charles Clarke, Archbishop of Tharsis. 1898. Vol 2. Withdrawn from publication.**

DAY SEVEN

<u>RENEGADES</u>

The Flammarion Expedition Journal of L. Edwin Ransom.
Day fifteen. 36th. 9th. 26.
Saturday.

I awoke earlier than I intended, jolted awake by the content of my feverish dreams. The clarity of that nightmarish dreamscape dissipating almost instantly, leaving me bathed in sweat and in the grip of a gloomy aspect to my mood coupled with an intense desire to speak to Nelly. I have tried to dismiss it as the subliminal effects of my conversations with Adam yesterday, but the anxiety seems to have taken rest upon my shoulder like a lead weight. At breakfast, I found myself stuttering like a fool unable to complete the humblest of remarks without sounding like a stammering buffoon. I am aware that my frustration with my inability to speak exacerbates the problem and does little to assuage how badly it feels when one's self-awareness runs amok. It has been worse for me this morning than it has been for months.

In the main, the other expedition members are polite and patient with me, except the Colonel, who was rather disrespectful in his display of intolerance to my difficulties.

I spent the rest of the morning assisting the Professor in planning the rerouting of the expedition. The decision was that we would stop firstly at Mefitis, originally an Icarian township, which, although still narrowly within the borders of the Republic of Tharsis it remains, by virtue of geography, virtually autonomous. I

expressed my concern with us going too close to Icaria, but the
Professor chuckled suggesting I read the papers more. "It would
be an overestimation to refer to Icaria as a vassal state. Icaria's
Parliament has not sat for the last three years. Most of her
parliamentarians spend either their days in bucolic semi-
retirement or idling in the gentleman's clubs of Tharsis and Alba.
For all intents, she is a province of Tharsis, in all but name." Our
calculations suggested it would take us two days if we could keep
up this speed. There we can resupply and refuel probably without
much notice. It is very much a frontier town, more so even than
Tremorfa. I have only been there once before when I was a student
studying techniques of sustainable water reclamation for irrigation
purposes from deposits of organic feculence. It was not the most
salubrious community I have ever experienced, but one whose
memory lingered longer in the nostrils than in the mind. From
Mefitis, the Professor could send communiques to his various
agents to redeploy the resources he had set up for us so that it
would fit into our new schedule. It would also give us all a chance
to communicate with our loved ones.

He pawed over the map jabbing at it with the long stem of his
Tyrolean. "We will skirt the border of Icaria, and from there we
will cross over into what is, technically, still Northern Sirenum and
strike out towards Thaumaisa then on into Aonia. The crew will
have to push the engines hard, but if we can make it to the city of
Felix before Friday, God and the Wind in our favour, then we will

be far beyond the reach of the Air Navy should they have time to change their minds and decide to pursue us."

It was an excellent idea, but I had to point out it Mefitis is only a stone's throw from the Gorgonum and heading south-east from would take us into northern Sirenum, both will take us perilously close to trouble should fighting break out.

Never one to take an unconsidered action, the Professor accepted my observations but countered with his belief that if there was to be war in that area, then it will be Tharsis' forces that make the strike first. Probably into the Zephyrian bases in eastern Gorgonum. "There is an awful lot of traffic in the air paths from Szélanya." He waved the pipe stem over the whole area. "And out of northern Sirenum to Mefitis and Ember. Let alone what comes overland through Aonia itself. Mostly trade, legal and illicit." I asked him what he meant by that? He explained that most of the major arteries of Tharsis' black-market pass through those borders and Aonia, and such a permeable margin could only exist with the complicity of the authorities, at least on more than one side.

I ventured, "A blind eye?"

The Professor replied it was more a case of deliberate, if not sanctioned, collusion. I naively questioned why our Government would allow such a thing to continue if it were as openly engaged in as he suggested. The Professor sat for a moment absorbed in scraping out the bowl of his pipe with a tiny penknife and tapping the loosened debris out into the stone ashtray on his desk.

"There are many ways to conduct war, Edwin. Economic warfare can be just as effective as a gunship, and often involves hardly a shot being fired. Of course, you remember Arabia Ponds. The destruction of the rice paddies and poisoning of the fish stocks with hellebore extract had a greater effect on the outcome of that conflict than all the fighting. Pushed to the point of despair the pro-Tharsian settlers turned to us for help, but Edwin, it was our Government that did that."

I was shocked, that statement made no sense to me, "We saved the settlers from starvation. I remember the campaigns for donations; we fed those valiant people for over a year."

"Cui bono?" He opened his tobacco pouch and began to pinch at the long strands. "True, we saved those settlers from starvation, but we made them dependent upon our charity, and how do you think the pro-Thylian settlers fared?"

I dreaded to think upon it. Petulantly I reminded him, "My uncle died in that conflict, Sir."

He smiled sadly. "I know Edwin. He was a good man, a commissioned officer, but what was he doing in an irregular's uniform fighting a war that our Government refused to acknowledge even existed? Officially, no Tharsian troops were involved until the Marines were deployed to break the siege of Neos Chirris."

I wanted to correct him. I felt compelled to remind him that the newly formed Government of the Free Settler's had requested our help to end the fighting, but, of course, the Professor would know better, if not solely that, he would understand things in more detail than I could ever do.

He deftly changed the subject back to the point in hand.

"Although conflict in Gorgonum will surely bring a rapid halt to all of that coming and going on the boarders; the more intelligently minded traders and black marketeers will want to get their merchandise above the 30thparallel while they can. Of course, when the shooting starts, the area will be flooded with all those wishing to escape the conflict. Traffic will, if only for a short time, escalate exponentially, and the border patrols, ours and Aonia's, will be stretched far beyond breaking point before the Navy shuts it all down."

The Professor aims to lose our 'scent,' as he put it, amidst that frantic activity. I asked what we would do if we, by accident, do encounter the military.

The Professor smiled, stoked his pipe and lit it, after a few puffs, he swore me to secrecy. I agreed readily.

In the manila, that Henry Giffard gave him before he left, was a letter of safe passage for this ship under the name of the 'Haul Du.' Captain Llewellyn was having identifying signage created as we spoke. The Seren Bore will enter Mefitis, but it will be the Haul Du that departs.

I have known the Professor for at least 18 years, as a teacher, mentor, and father-in-law, I knew him to be a genius by reputation long before I ever met him, but he still manages to confound me with his thinking. For a man of high moral principles and a staunch advocate of peace, his mind is easily focused upon martial exploits and deception. I have heard it said that old warriors make the best peacemakers; it would appear that old peacemakers make excellent tacticians.

Once we had finalised the new headings, I took the information to Captain Llewellyn and then spent the afternoon writing a letter of apology to Nelly. After tea, I spent some time reading in the wardroom and played a couple of games of chess with Sir John, where we fell into discussing the fuel blend he uses in his flying apparatus. He explained he used his own mix of super-refined Taraxium of course, with hydroxide of phrikite, which is prohibitively expensive and incredibly unstable. My real interest though was in the "other ingredients" that he promised to tell me of. I sat open-mouthed as he explained that one of those ingredients was a refined distillation of red zizany, a plant widely believed unsuitable for anything. He explained that from some regions of Mars it is rich in phrikite along with a dozen other exotic metals, which it stores, not in the tubers, but the leaves. When refined as a powder (!) and added in small amounts to the primary fuel mix, it can increase output thrust by anything up to 40% or blow the engine apart! I was incredulous. No one refines zizany; it is so poisonous and invasive you cannot use it for anything. He laughed heartily, making me fear I was being duped. Then he explained that he, himself, pays for the entire process. He owns a small manufactory outside Torres that produces it for him and mixes his fuel. I was agape; the cost alone must be astronomical, but that aside, how did he discover the properties of Red Zizany? He smiled again and drew me nearer; "The Aresians used it for everything." He winked. "That is why there is so much of the damned stuff about. It was to them, what dandelions are to you."

I was about to ask him how he had discovered that when he suddenly sat back and laughed. "It is no great secret, old chap. I just did a little research. Look; once all this nonsense is over, I shall be happy to show you my little project. See what you think. You might be able to help me upscale it a bit and maybe make us both a few bob out of it. Think about it." At that, he excused himself and went off to take the air and smoke.

Think about it! I was so exceedingly excited that I sat all afternoon scribbling notes on our conversation and further questions as they occurred to me. Red Zizany! The damned red weed! Who would have thought! A few more 'pennies,' indeed, this could transform the entire botanical fuel industry completely.

Later Dr Spender entertained us with various diverting accounts of his explorations. The rest of the day went off without incident.

In the evening, after dinner, Charity and Patty, who were all in high spirits, did a little shooting practice off the weather deck, which gave me a chance to practice my overarm bowl.

Adam kept himself busy with work in the engine room and taking a couple of dogwatches, whatever they are exactly. After dinner, he joined us on the weather deck, where Sir John challenged him to a target contest, with rifle and pistol. None of us had ever seen such shooting, though Sir John was very insistent that he had only been able to best Adam by a fluke. Adam was gracious, but most of us were left with no doubt that he had deliberately thrown the contest at the very last point.

The Professor has requested us to all be prudent with the contents of our diary entries and any letters we may write to our loved ones.

All in all, apart from my conversation with Sir John, a tranquil day. One should not be sorry for it being such.

Charity Bryant-Drake.

Notes to self.   36/9/26.

It has been a splendid day. I have spent all day with Patty and her father; we took a long constitutional on the decks before tea and sat while Dr Spender reminisced about his times at university with my mother and stepfather. He is a fascinating man and a great raconteur, possessed of a whole litany of amusing stories. I must say I understand why Patty dotes upon him so.

While he took his afternoon nap, Patty and I took some time to be alone. We were embracing when she noticed the small scar under my right eyebrow, where I had run full pelt into a tree at seven years old. We fell into swapping tales; I showing her the scars from the various past misadventures of my tomboy childhood, and she reciting the meanings and stories behind the beautiful tattoos that covered her chest, shoulders and back. We were reclining in each other's arms when I noticed she had avoided mentioning a long scar under her left breast and gently chided her on it. That was the first time I saw a glimmer of self-consciousness in her. Finally, she explained it was a duelling scar. One of several. I could not believe my ears and burst into an uncontrollable fit of laughter.

Patty accused me of being unromantic, as I often find myself so happy, I burst into hysterical giggles at the most inappropriate moments. She then proceeded to bundle me out of bed.

I am afraid we may have upset the crew even more with our antics, as I ended up locked out of my room, barefoot, in only my chemise. Once I had convinced Patty to let be back in, and we had both regained our senses, I worried that our horseplay would instigate yet another rebuke from the Professor.

Patty said she would defy the Professor to say anything, or we would strip naked and practice our 'polka' in the corridor tonight. We had great fun with that innuendo over dinner.

Patty makes me feel like a dizzy little girl in love for the first time.

Love. Oh, my, did I write that?

Am I in love? Is this what love makes one feel like?

I have never met anyone like Patty, and definitely, no one has ever evoked such feelings in my heart. I am so giddy of mind that I cannot even think straight. Then tonight, on the weather deck, in front of Sir John, Edwin, Adam and Aelita, she kissed me! In public, shamelessly.

I do not know whether to be shocked by her fierce disregard for the mores of 'polite company' or the fact that the gentlemen merely passed over the event. Mrs Fontenelli modestly smiled and clasped her hands under her chin, leaving only the two crewmembers to look on aghast.

The Professor had a chance to speak to us all regarding our journals and diary entries as well as my continued recording of our expedition. He requested that we desist until we are close to our objectives. I asked why this was, and he explained that he did not wish such material to fall into the hands of any authority that may be likely to utilise such knowledge to trace our journey, and especially those who may aid us.

There was some indignation, but all agreed that if we do continue to keep our diaries and journals that we shall be far more circumspect as to the information we will record.

I shall continue to keep my own journal in my mother's idiosyncratic version of Metcalfe's archaic 'short writing' as she taught me. I defy anyone to translate it without my assistance.

As it was, the rest of our day was wonderfully uneventful.

"It's funny how humans can wrap their mind around things and fit them into their version of reality."

THE LIGHTNING THIEF
RICK RIORDAN.

DAYS EIGHT AND NINE
THE JOURNEY TO MEFITIS

Editorial

The rest of the 2-day journey from The Great Sorrow Lake to Mefitis as recorded in the diaries and journals seemed relatively uneventful for the expedition members.

James Ransom.

Miss Spender and Miss Bryant-Drake grew ever closer and, though the openness of their displays of affection for each other did cause some consternation below decks, it appears that the expedition members and senior crew were quite broadminded in their attitudes. If they did harbour anxieties, they decided that discretion on their part was the better part of valour. Only my grandfather noted a couple of times that there were rumbles of disapproval from the lower decks.

The young ladies organised an evening of entertainment for the expedition members and senior crew. The entertainment consisting of some readings, a recital of poetry and a few of the more acceptable popular music hall ditties (this appears to have been the original intention).

Mr Charles, accompanying himself on a little concertina, also sang several ancient sea shanties that he encouraged everyone to join in with.

Miss Bryant-Drake, with Parthena Spender's assistance, developed the images she had photographed at the excavations. These they presented to the expedition members after luncheon on Monday. Regretfully the images have been lost, but we can gather from comments that they were excellent in technical detail but seemingly unremarkable in any other context. Most attention being lavished on the expedition group pictures. Mrs Fontenelli was most surprised upon seeing her image caught in the camera lens for the first time in her life. She remarked that the monochromatic picture cast her skin in darkest detail, making it look not crimson red but as black as that of the Negro soldiers.

The pictures of the underside of the tomb lid though did not survive well and, from what is recorded; to the young lady's consternation, only fragmentary images were salvageable.

Mrs Fontenelli stated she found even those incomplete pictures unsettling. Dr Spender wrote that the bas-relief seemed to depict a similar historical narrative to the vision he experienced in the tomb's lower chamber. Though, he to, found the partial images unsettling.

From what we can glean from the various comments, the images held within the bas-relief were on several complex layers and, though hard to decipher, were quite ghastly in their subject matter. It would appear to have been a prolonged warfare narrative. Colonel Carter Jahns, recorded by several others, summed it up with the sardonic observation that it seemed to be the work of some would-be Aresian Hieronymus Bosch, obsessed with martial conflict but lacking in whimsy. As if one could find whimsy in the art of Hieronymus Bosch.

The Captain's scrap log and records of discipline saw entries of a couple of recurring names of crewmembers sanctioned for "disrespectful language and demeanour." Although this is difficult to draw definite conclusions as to whom such language was aimed, whether Miss Spender and Miss Bryant-Drake or whether the subject was Mrs Fontenelli and her friendship with Sir John.

Stoker, 2nd Class, Darra Howe's name is foremost in these entries. The Captain did recommend strongly to my grandfather that Howe be 'dropped off,' at the first convenient point.

Mr Franklin continued to keep himself busy with various tasks around the ship. He used the time to build up a strong fellowship with the men under Colonel Jahns. He also used the time to win over numerous other crewmembers above and below deck. This put him in an excellent position to learn of anything that went on aboard. His only disquiet mentioned in relation to this was around the crewmember called Howe, whom he was aware of as an agitator and intimidator of other crewmembers.

Mr Franklin appears to have been very protective towards my father, admonishing him regularly for not taking enough rest or physical exercise, drinking too much coffee and staying up very late writing and illustrating stories for Tabitha and I. He made several references in his journal to his concern over my father being unsettled by nightmares. These centred upon my, by then, late mother and Tabitha and I.

There was no possible way in which my father could have had an inkling of what had occurred at home, but, upon my reading those journals, it appears to me some of the details of his nightmares, he mentioned to Mr Franklin were very pertinent to what had actually occurred.

I do not share my mother's and grandmother's belief in a spirit realm that interacts in any way with our own, but upon consideration of such facts, I wonder if there was some method of transferral of our family's anguish to our father.

Mr Franklin also remained very suspicious of Sir John and always kept a weathered eye on him. He noted that Sir John did leave the ship in his rocket pack late on the first night after the incident with the kraken and did not return until just before dawn. Mr Franklin also ascertained that Sir John had bribed the Watch handsomely several times for not entering his "little excursions," as he called it, in the record. I was further intrigued to discover Mr Franklin did not report this to my father or grandfather or Captain Llewellyn. He did note, however, that upon close inspection Sir John's weaponry had seen use.

Dr Spender's condition improved over the days following his collapse at the Tomb. He focused his time on recording his memories and thoughts regarding his experiences at the Athenaeum and the oppida of Ananthor. On the afternoon of the 38th, he engineered an opportunity to talk in private with Mrs Fontenelli about their shared experiences. He wrote:

"Aelita Fontenelli is a most remarkable young woman, very patient and empathic towards a bumbling old fool such as I. It would seem that we both experienced some form of what I have termed an auto-epiphanic impartance of knowledge, in the Tomb. My experience was more of the grand opera of Aresian history, while Mrs Fontenelli assures me that her revelations were far more of the familial and personal kind, but none the less revealing. She is a woman of great sensitivity and delicate nature, but I sense inside her there is a strength beyond what one could possibly expect, she is both accommodating and friendly, chatty even, but also very circumspect regarding her personal matters.

We discussed the incident at Ananthor at some length. It appears that we did share a similar experience, though hers was longer and far more detailed than mine. She told me of the wonders she witnessed, and I prevailed upon her to write their descriptions down for me, which she has promised to do later. As I concentrated upon the details of my visions in the Tomb, I am aware that there also I saw other races, some quite fantastical.

I cannot accept that either of us saw ghosts at Ananthor. Most probably we triggered some other, more sensory pervasive, form of auto-epiphanic impartance, or, and here is a possibility I have barely been able to touch upon myself; we saw through some barrier, some dimensional veil, into a similar, or analogous, realm that not only existed but also continues to exist in its particular reality. The idea is extraordinarily stimulating to contemplate.

She listened intently as I recanted all I can remember of what I experienced in the Tomb. She readily concurred that, if as I determine, the Aresian race did not originate from this 'ball of dust' (1) but from far across the heavens, then the Tellurian conquest of this one single planet, can in no possible way mean that the Aresians are defeated, as a civilisation, let alone a race. She agrees with me that that deduction obviously points to the possibility that somewhere out there in the 'upper heavens' (2) the core of Aresian civilisation still exists. Not only that, but it was and probably still is, far more advanced of us and far more powerful than we ever dreamed of.

I must admit in my excitement to wittering on; I found myself telling the dear lady of the grand armada I witnessed as a young officer. I explained that they flew the battle pennants, the nobly, not of the petty upstart Malacandrian Kingdom, but of what I, and the Professor, believe may have been an Over-King, a Vortigern of

Mars, a true Emperor or, more probably, an Empress of the Aresians. We discussed why then that armada did not strike to end the War, but disappeared, as if into the aether itself.

Mrs Fontenelli then suggested an idea to me that I cannot exorcise from my mind, no matter how outlandish it seems; What if my sighting of the grand armada was a similar experience to that of Ananthor? What if I, unbeknownst to myself, have all my life been privy to perceive things beyond that dimensional veil?"

Dr Spender spent many of the following days attempting to reconcile the phantasmagoria he had encountered with the then-current understandings of material reality.

Notes.

1.   "Where Cain Danced. "Poem by Stephanou. Collected Works. Lime House. 1890.

2.   The Lower Heavens being the vastness of Space beyond the firmament. The Upper Heavens being the metaphysical realm of angels and God. (Paraphrased) Pope Pius IX. "De Dei Super Filios Mars." Papal Encyclical.1887

Colonel Ranolph Carter-Jahns, OOM, was a man more written of than known for his writings. He did not – to our knowledge – keep a diary or journal at the time, and seldom wrote letters. From what the other members of the expedition recorded, he kept himself to himself over those few days. We have detected a slight thawing in his attitude towards Mr Franklin during this time, including inviting him to join in a friendly game of poker, with himself, my grandfather, Sir John and Captain Llewellyn.

He astonished the whole group on the evening of the young lady's Recital by joining in. Performing, in a baritone worthy of Tharsis' Grand Metropolitan Opera House, several arias, including that famous one from The Barber of Seville to the delight of all.

Colonel Jahns did confide to my grandfather his further concern as to what might become of them all once the expedition was concluded or if, by unfortunate circumstance, they were captured before completion of their mission. He proposed that they think upon at least a secondary plan of action in such circumstances. To this, my grandfather tasked my father, Sir John and Mr Franklin.

Mrs Aelita Fontenelli spent a lot of her time in the company of Sir John, and Miss Spender and Miss Bryant-Drake, she wrote that she enjoyed their companionship and the diversion from her concerns about her past and what she feared the future might hold for her.

During the Recital on the night of the 37th, she accompanied the singers on the piano and sang publicly for the first time in her life. She wrote of the evening:

"I have never laughed so much. What a joyous thing this is, that such harmless frivolity, can be so refreshing to the soul. We sang and danced and laughed like the small children I would watch playing in the park across the street."

She hardly wrote of Sir John, other than the occasional mention that he had been so kind as to do this or that for her. In the only explicit mention of him, she wrote:

"Sir John has become a constant companion to me; he is such a dear friend. Saying that though, he has a side to him that I do not find entirely comfortable; he can be thoughtless in his comments, hurtful even, but not to me, and a little too judgemental in his thinking. He is a good friend, but I do not need another guardian. This evening he wished to discuss my plans once we return to Tharsian Society. I know he wants to offer his not inconsiderable resources to ensure my security, but it seems foolish to me to consider even talking of such preparations, for we have no idea what will transpire between now and our return to Tharsis. Should any of us live so long."

She wrote of her conversation with Dr Spender:

"At his behest, we took tea together. Such a dear, kind gentleman. I can easily understand why Parthena is devoted to him, let alone for the fact that he cherishes her without an iota of judgement upon how she conducts her life. I left my questions unspoken, but he told me that he felt that he had acquired another daughter. With the cheekiest of grins, he added, 'One even bossier and determined than the other two. A man cannot get away with even a small glass of port without suffering a full half-hour of recriminations. And lo! Would that I should forget my medications!' He chuckled merrily. I do believe he bathes in the warmth of their ministrations.

"He wished to talk with me about what occurred in the burial chamber and Ananthor city. I tried to convey to him as much as I could without talking specifically about my difficulty, as I have come to see it. He though had a somewhat different experience. He believes that the Tomb is akin to a library of the mind. One that reads us rather than us reading it and imparts the information we desire to know. I believe that he is accurate in that deduction.

"He told me of what he saw; a phantasmagorical history of my people, possibly going back tens of thousands of years and across the great voids of space. I must say I am excited by such ideas. What if I am not just merely some leftover '*alien*,' but the child of an ancient spacefaring race that spans the immeasurable gulf between the stars! The mere imaginings of such have raised my morale considerably.

"Then we spoke of the events in Ananthor. I had no idea that he had seen what I had seen, or that his experience was as tangible. We agreed these were no ghosts we witnessed, but something physical. I explained that they touched me, and I touched them, and they were palpably real. He too witnessed them, but more importantly, he witnessed them interact with me.

"It was then he put forth the most extraordinary idea; that what we both experienced *was* actually existent, that we looked into some gap between ours and some other reality, where Ananthor still stands. Like Alice, we had a glimpse through the Looking Glass, into a world of wonders. A comparable world where my people were still here, on Mars. How could such a thing possibly be? Dr Spender believes that from discussions he has had with other learned men in his University and the Society, that the notion of such coexistences could be theoretically possible.

"As Parthena warned me, when her father started upon a subject it is best to order more tea and settle in for a while, as, though he is very edifying, he is also apt to wander off the beaten track. He told me of his time in the army after the revolution and then about the Grand Armada, a vast fleet of Aresian warbarges that he had witnessed. An Armada that never engaged the Tellurians but disappeared without a trace. He showed me a little battered notebook from those days and the beautiful pictures he had drawn.

"My mind was working like an overwound clock by this point, and I suggested that possibly he, as a young officer, had unbeknownst seen through that self-same Looking Glass. He seized upon my suggestion and quizzed me further as to whether I have had such experiences before.

"Now that I understand I had no brother, and all of that was my mind playing elaborate tricks on me, the Doctor's question struck a concerning note. I could only honestly tell him that I do not remember the details, but as a small child, the Nuns often punished me for my fantasies. As an adult, I have had no such experiences before Ananthor, but I have always been a vivid dreamer and occasional somnambulist.

"The Doctor then took my hand and said the sweetest thing; 'My dear, I believe it was crucial that you joined us on this expedition. Not only have you already saved all our lives from the ravages of that monster; I believe you will be the key to our success.' He then requested my permission to talk to the Professor of our conversation, seeing no harm in it, I agreed.

"He left me with my head dizzy with the wildest notions. What if my people are not gone? What if my father and mother are still alive?"

Mrs Fontenelli recorded several strange dreams following that discussion. Dreams in which she saw her father on the grand warbarges of an unknown Empire. It was her father, however no longer the gentleman she remembered, in these dreams, he wore fearful looking armour and commanded armies. However, with the knowledge only dreams can impart, she could tell he did so with a heavy heart. She also dreamt of her mother, something of a rare occurrence, "…wandering in utter anguish the endless corridors of some infinite palace that appeared to be floating in the void itself. In reverence, all others genuflected before her as she rushed past them, but none seemed to dare to offer her solace for whatever distressed her."

Aelita Fontenelli also provided Dr Spender with several excellent watercolour sketches of what she saw in her vision at Ananthor, including some of the strange creatures, and their names. She noted on the back of one of the sketches that the more she concentrated upon these apparitions, the more was revealed. She described this as similar to the sensation of 'breaking a dream,' when some small factor in your waking experience suddenly allows you to recall vividly a previous night's dream, or the revealing of memories long obscured by time.

Sir John Sydeian, OCTE, as far as we have discovered did not keep a journal during this period, if he did, it has long since been destroyed, or lies locked in some unknown vault. He spent a great deal of those few days before reaching Mefitis in the company of Mrs Fontenelli, and the other young ladies. He always maintained a good-humoured and outwardly pleasant manner, though his attentions to Mrs Fontenelli did cause my grandfather to have reason to speak to him again on the subject.

Sir John again protested complete innocence on both their behalves.

An off the cuff remark he made to my grandfather seems to confirm that he was aware that Mr Franklin had been set to watch him. He referred to Mr Franklin as my grandfather's "beady-eyed watchdog."

The Gunnery Master reported to the Captain that he had discovered Sir John exiting the light munition storeroom on the evening of the 34th. Sir John explained to the Gunnery Master that he saw the door was open and thought he would just pop in and pick up a few shotgun cartridges for some target shooting.

Nevertheless, upon carrying out an inventory, it was discovered that two hundred rounds of the ammunition Sir John had brought on board with him had been removed from the store without signing for. Sir John had been requested to keep it in the light munitions store for safety. Gunnery Master Gwenllian also pointed out that the Light Munitions store is never left open, all storeroom doors are checked every change of the Watch, and all keys are accounted for. In addition, one of the three flasks of fuel that Sir John had stowed in the spare strongroom had been removed. This was also reported to my grandfather, but there is no record of him taking Sir John to task.

Extracts from

Beresford's History of the Martian Colonies.
4th Edition. Milton and Dante.

Appendix B.

"Imperator mutationes, sed non in palatium custodes."

Aulus Paulinus
123 AD

After the declaration of Independence from the British Empire was finalised all existing hereditary titles stemming from the British Empire were abolished.

This further disenfranchisement was not popular with those of the Red Books, admittedly few, who had thrown their considerable financial, logistical and political power behind the Secessionist cause, often at great danger to themselves and their families.

In August M.Y.2 under pressure from powerful interests in Government, The Titles Act was passed, this restored the right, through application, to use such titles to those whom the Government felt had contributed to the 'Cause of Tharsian Liberty,' a deliberately nebulous term. This was clarified as a form of reward for their services to the Secessionist cause, but no longer bestowed any additional rights or entitlements.

As part of the titles Act, the Government of Tharsis also created several awards, orders and titles in recognition for services to the state, bravery or self-sacrifice. No hereditary titles were created.

Critics, most notably amongst them the Secessionist Philosopher James Richardson, publicly refused the offer to restore his inherited title, decrying it as the 'Putty-Medal Act,' and as being nothing more than a step backwards towards an Imperialist mentality. Possibly, because of the public furore, several protest marches, and a great deal of adverse comment in the popular press, less than one hundred individuals applied for the restoration of their family titles.

Since the Titles Act was passed, to date, the Government has inducted two hundred and eighty-five individuals into the Olympian Order of Merit (OOM) and inducted one hundred and ninety-six individuals into the Order of Citizen of Tharsis Emeritus (OCTE) both confer the right to the awardee to use the title 'Sir' or 'Dame.'

The highest military honour currently awarded is the Tharsis Cross Medal, for gallantry. A number of the recipients of the honour have later, upon retirement, been inducted into the Order of Citizen of Tharsis Emeritus, and thus the Order of Citizen of Tharsis Emeritus is often thought of as a military order.

Editorial Cont.

The Professor. My grandfather never rested. He wrote that he found this period very difficult as without a doubt his best-laid plans had, "*gang aft a-gley*." (1) He found it impossible without the use of telecommunications to restructure the itinerary. He was forced to wait until reaching the mining city of Mefitis, to send the electric telegrams and dispatch the letters he needed to. Instead, he spent time pondering his thesis regarding the Aresian's departure, and his attempts to disprove it. The method of exactly how he would make contact with the Aresians was, as yet unformed. He had some equipment onboard the airship, but it was untested, a point he had begun to be concerned by.

On Sunday, 37th. Day 8

He wrote, "Mr Holley, the Ship's Medician, who is also a Lay Preacher of the Unified Redemptionist Church, conducted a short Service in the saloon for those that wished to attend. I was delighted to see that Aelita and her maid had attended, and quite surprised to see Colonel Jahns and his men join us, all resplendent in their dress uniforms. Mr Holley would hold a Service for the crew later. We recited a few prayers together, then observed the traditional period of silence, something of the Quaker origins of the Church, and ended on the hymn 'Land of Pure Light.'

Editorial Cont.

It was on the evening of the 38th, the night before they reached Mefitis that my grandfather and Dr Spender discussed the Dr's ideas as to the nature of the Aresians and the things that the Doctor witnessed in the Tomb.

My grandfather wrote:

"I am utterly discombobulated. I am confounded beyond words. If such ideas had come out of the mouth of anyone other than Octavius, even my own, I would have heaped doubt and scorn in equal measure upon them. To a rational mind, such thoughts appear utterly insane, lunacy even, but because it is he who postulated such a thing. I am forced to review it with reasoned composure. I am struck that there is undeniably some confounded logic to it.

"Octavius informed me of the strange '*otherworldly*' experiences he endured both at Ananthor and the Tomb on Edwin's farm. The events seem to have been superficially different yet analogous. Representing what he feels was a '*glimpse behind the curtain of mundane reality.*' In this, he included his experience of sighting the Aresian '*Armada*' as a young officer during the last war with the Aresians. The theory he postulates makes Lady Niketa Chaol Ghleann's Voynich Society's eccentric notions of metaphysical '*plains of existence*' seem positively tame in comparison. He asked me to consider his proposal that more than one existence, '*world*' for clarity, may be able to exist in the same time and space as another, simultaneously. Not in some supernatural manner, as concepts of Heaven or Hell, or '*the Other*

Side' as Alexa used to refer to the supposed realm of the spirits, but as distinct mundane material realities. In *'counterpart'* so to speak. Within the same physical space, and that on some occasions one maybe witness to this *'Other side,'* as if looking through one of those *'magic mirrors'* one finds in a booth at the funfair. If remotely true, then everything we theorize about the Universe would be wrong. Thus reality, itself, is not as we comprehend it.

"How can that possibly be? If another realm of existence exists analogous to ours, is it the only one? Could it be that innumerable universes may exist in counterpart with each other? If this were at all true, could it be possible that we could communicate between such worlds, or, as Aelita Fontenelli suggests, for anyone to pass between those counterpart worlds physically?

"In the face of my scepticism, he made a perfect physical allegory of a large glass pitcher filled with a few clean lumps' of coal. Which he got me to agree was undeniably as full as he could make it. He then poured in some smaller glass beads he had obtained from his daughter, with a little shake they all fitted into the smaller spaces in the same jug. His next examples were sand and finally, water. All equal and distinct, and yet occupying the same boundaried physical space.

"Scientifically we were only just beginning to unravel the true mechanics of space travel, which, I might add, was utterly unthinkable only moments before Stranger and Hamilton crashed down on that hill in Woking, when the revolution occurred. We were only just beginning to construct theories to allow us to understand how the Rabbit Hole transports matter instantaneously over such vast distances when suddenly we were cut off. This has left us, by which I mean; all of us in the scientific community, our selves included, confined here on Mars, not only without the resources of the wider Earthbound scientific community but without access to the greater resource; the minds of our peers.

"In truth, I do not know what to think. Octavius is the most respectable academic I know, a level-headed and pragmatic scientist who has forwarded his science immeasurably, but this theory, for want of another less tolerant term, boarders upon wildest imaginings. Yet, some years back, I attended a seminar at the University given by the eccentric Professor Niccolo Lamberto on a similar theme; Cavor, Dalton and Thomson's theories of atoms and the spaces between them, and the possibility of things passing between those atoms. Though it all appeared fanciful, but entertaining, theoretical nonsense to me back then, merely hypothetical hyperbole, nonetheless now those theories chime closely with Octavius' ideas.

"By way of humouring Octavius, I ventured that his theory would make a fascinating paper and that when we do return to Tharsis, I shall introduce him to Professor Lamberto. Until then he should keep detailed records of any further occurrences."

1.   "To a Mouse, on Turning Her Up in Her Nest With the Plough, November 1785." Robert Burns. Kilmarnock Edition. 1786.

James Ransom

A Brief History of pre-Colonial Martian Civilisations.

Author, Prof. Ronald Benjamin Harry.

Published Oxford University Press. 1922

Chapter 3.

The Fall of the Malacandrian Empire.

Of all the Kingdoms and regional powers of Mars, the largest and most diverse was Malacandria.

In comparison to other political entities on Mars, Malacandria was a relatively young nation probably less than two thousand Martian years old.

Often referred to as an 'Empire' it was initially merely an expansion of the city-state of Malec's political power, akin to Philip of Macedon's arrangement with the Greek City-States, relying more upon diplomacy, inducement and intimidation than all-out military dominance in the field. That said, as will be seen in this chapter, to suggest that the Malacandrians lacked in military capability or the preparedness to use it would be a misnomer.

What set the Malacandrians apart from most other societal groups on Mars was the fact that their ruling class, religious class and inteligensia was made up, almost entirely, of Yellow Martians. As we have already explored in the preceding chapters, most of the ruling classes of the various cultures and nations of Mars were drawn from both the Red and Yellow sub-races. The Red Martians, who formed the most extensive sections of the noble and religious castes, dominated most of the other cultures at their social zeniths. Malacandria thus was disparagingly referred to in some texts as "*Reigän ti Hlirgh Yelovik Aküirr,*" The Heretic Empire. (A)

Malacandria only ever held political sway over thirty-one oppida (B), or cities, of which Malacandria directly governed only seventeen. The principal cities of the Empire were Malac, its cultural heart, Carthoris, its administrative centre and the walled Forbidden City of Lunismar, the seat of the Gre'tik Jireg, the Malacandrian Empress, and her Court. The others appeared to remain semi-autonomous until the last acts of the Third Age of the Empire (c).

The Malacandrian's primary economic resource was based on its agricultural production. For a nation with a sparse population outside its thirty-one major conurbations, it controlled vast areas of agriculturally rich land on the Tharsis uplands, Sirenum and Terra Meridiani regions and around the equator. Successive Empresses must be given credit for Malacandria's contribution to the irrigation and fertilisation of those areas. During the Empire's Second Age the Malacandrian's were probably the foremost canal builders on Mars.

Wealthy, militarily strong and technologically adept, the Malacandrian's are often lauded by academics as the archetype Martian Empire, but this overlooks the broader scope of their culture.

Malacandria's economic strength was built upon the enslavement of immense numbers of Green Martians, along with empyreans taken in battle or simply subjugated, more than Kaldane and Ma'alefa'ak, their nearest rivals in size and military power. In the last acts of their Third Age, they even broke the widely held cultural taboo against enslaving their own people and even Red Martians, which fostered great animosity from other Martian Nations.

The other aspect that sets Malacandria apart from other Martian societies, and probably contributed substantially to its political isolation, was both its distinctive religion and its practices. Although its social organisation reflected the predominant matriarchal structure of most other Martian societies, the integration of its religious cast into the fabric of Malacandrian's government at all levels was unprecedented.

We will explore the strange pantheon of divine and semi-divine beings that the Malacandrians worshipped later in this chapter. For now, it is accurate to state that the religion of Malacand was not as 'unique' as some previous academics have stressed, as it demonstrably grew from out of the roots of a religious theology shared across almost all the Martian nations. Though in other Martian religious traditions, these 'Malacandrian Gods' were most often cast in a similar role as devils and demons play in more primitive Christian theology. It is easy to cite the similarities in the repurposing of pre-Christian gods such as Bale, Pazuzu and Moloch, into demonic entities by the embryonic Catholic Church. The difference in their role in Malacandrian religion to that of the others is that these so-called 'Old Gods' were not portrayed as destroyed or cast down in some ancient war, but ever-present and active.

The metamorphosis of the Malacandrian religion from a benign theology, servile to the state apparatus, into an aggressive militancy and fundamentalism can be easily comprehended when equated with the chronology of the slow social and economic collapse of the state. This decline into religious fanaticism, along with its appalling manifestations, was amplified by Malacand's continued failure to successfully rebuff the incursions of the various invading Terran imperial forces into their territories and the refusal of the other Martian nation states to come to their aid.

Jairus, the last Gre'tik Jireg of Malacandria, was reputed to have remarked that the other nations held Malacandria responsible for showing the rapacious Terrans the way to Mars in the first instance.

Page 194.

The 'Grail Quest' of the Malacandrians.

The reason for the Malacandrian expedition, led by Prince Verilhon Malacandi of the Konöm, the ruling House of Malacand, that abducted the British Capt. Edmond R. Hamilton in 1852, has often been the subject of great speculation. Hamilton claimed that the Malacandrians, conjecturing that Malacand was synonymous with all Martians, had been visiting Earth for hundreds if not thousands of years. He hinted that they were doing so in search of something that neither he nor Stranger either never discovered or chose not to elucidate upon.

Later evidence appears to support the idea that these expeditions during the Empire's later Third Age were in search of a supposed lost antediluvian Martian colony or 'city' on Earth. What they sought from that lost city is unclear. Though Prince Verilhon has been later identified through historical documents as being a Magivan, a high-priest astronomer/astrologer of the Malacandrian religion, this suggests that the quest had some quasi-religious or symbolic meaning, such as a pilgrimage rather than merely seeking some lost object.

One interesting point is that in text 00281.7.i, possibly written about 450 AD in Malac and now held in the British Imperial Museum, the chronicler refers to a lost colony on 'Thul'candra,' or 'Tal'shugg,' meaning the Silent World or Earth, and that colony is named, not 'Atlantis,' as some so fervently wished, but Vadazas.

'Zifdejiel fhtagn syha'h gretik vönik Vadâzâξ.'
"The Great Eternal Ancient City of Vadazas
awaits." (D)

Page 231.

Notes.

(A) **"Reigän ti Hlirgh Yelovik Aküirr,"** The Heretic Empire of the Yellow Skins.
Translated by Prof. Wesley E. Grant. University College London. 1901.
(B) Conurbations or heavily urbanised areas.
(C) Lewis' theory; Three Ages of Empire; Growth, Consolidation, Decline. 1910. Oxford Press.

(D),Translated by Prof. Wesley E. Grant. University College
London.1901.

The pulse beats ten and intermits;

God shield the soul that ne'er forgets.

BELOVED PHYSICIAN

EDGAR ALLAN POE

DAY TEN

THE SALTMASTER'S DAUGHTER

**The Flammarion Expedition Journal of L. Edwin Ransom.
Day ten. 39th. 9th. 26.
Tuesday.**

I awoke at the sounds of the crew busying themselves on deck. They were preparing the ship for our arrival in Mefitis. I dressed quickly and went in search of a cup of breakfast tea. Fortified, I made my way to the flight deck to observe our arrival.

It was as I reached the flight deck that I was treated to a waft of air leaden with that particular rotten-egg stench that is all too familiar to those who have had the dubious pleasure to acquaint themselves with Mefitis. It is strange how one can never truly forget just how awful is the odour that pervades every aspect of the city, a smell I could not get out of my nostrils, let alone my clothes, for weeks after I departed. Much like the unmistakable stench of death, though it is hard to describe, once encountered, it is never really forgotten.

I stood on the bridge with the Professor and the Captain and watched as the crater rim that the city clings to came into view. To

210

call Mefitis a 'city' is a gross misnomer, it is frankly a vast industrial conurbation, about which has accreted a sprawling slum. Once the original settlement had clung precariously to the slopes of the escarpment, but now it has spilt out in all directions. A settlement of unadorned, functional buildings, and enormous ugly industrial complexes built of corroding iron and the rough-hewn bedrock discharged from the impact. As habitation had spread down the slopes, the buildings, almost too grand a term for them, had grown shoddier and shoddier, until they were little more than crude shacks nestling amidst the belching kilns and towering manufactories of the refinement processes.

A constant brume blanketed the city, a nauseating mix of sulphur, smoke and steam, mixed with the vapours of the processing plants. This putrid yellow miasma that hangs about the city also carries on the winds for dozens of miles.

The source of the worst of the stench is also the very reason for the city's existence; sulphur mining and refining on a massive scale. The meteors that made this astrobleme and other ones in the vicinity had penetrated a gigantic salt dome that underlies the whole area. Mefitis is the biggest of them, a three-mile diameter impact that punched through the crust, deep enough to expose an enormous layer of high-quality sulphur. The entire crater floor and the central up-lift are almost pure volcanic sulphur.

The whole region has been stripped of several hundreds of thousands of years of regolith deposits, sand and red weed jungle;

now it is just one vast yellow opencast mine for sulphur, salt and borates.

Captain Llewellyn slowed our approach to a speed that would allow us time to appraise our companions of the dangers they were to expect here.

Edwin and the Professor called a meeting over breakfast to warn us of the hazards we may encounter in Mefitis.

Firstly, they emphasized that the air here was not breathable, and if anyone should go down to the city, they must always wear filter masks, even when indoors. In fact, even though the Seren Bore would remain above the thick of it, the Professor insisted, that if anyone goes on to the exposed decks, they too must wear their filter masks.

The brume is exceedingly noxious, so even if we see locals take off their masks, we, especially the ladies, should not.

Edwin added that we would notice that almost all the people here cough continually, as he believes the standard mesh of their masks is hardly adequate to clean all the particulates out, especially the fine sulphur.

The Professor requested that unless the ladies had some urgent business that they must attend to, they should not go down into the city. "Ladies of good breeding," as he put it, "are a rarity here, and the inhabitants of this city are renowned for their uncouth manners and unruliness. If you must go, then you must go with an armed escort."

Charity asked incredulously whether the city could truly be all that bad?

Edwin explained that he had spent a fortnight here during his first year at University, doing field research on uses of effluent for irrigation and fertilisation. This drew some sardonic comments from Sir John, but Edwin merely smiled and continued, *"All I can say is that I met few gentlemen here and even fewer women of a class one would wish to be associated with. Most men have left their wives and loved ones behind to come and earn their fortune here. The work is hard, but the remuneration is good. They were rough, hard-working men before they came here and without the steadying guidance of their good womenfolk, they are apt to drink, gamble and argue too much."*

"Rough men have rough past-times," added Sir John with an obvious wink to Edwin.

"Yes, indeed. It is a place often on the edge of lawlessness. I was not sorry to leave."

The Professor interjected firmly, "We shall endeavour to make our stay as short as possible."

Dr Spender said he had been here several times before and could only support Edwin and the Professor's assertions about the city. "It is not a suitable place for decent people. Even hardened Neathian miners view this place as little more than a septic tank."

"Father, you paint such a pleasant picture of the city I am almost compelled to visit its delights for myself," Parthena joked.

Dr Spender though was in no mood for jesting, "I seldom forbid you anything, Patty, my dear, but I would forbid you going down into that hellhole if I had to."

"And I, as a devoted daughter, would happily disobey, if I were so cotton-headed and obstinate." She added a theatrical sniff, "but I think I shall pass up this opportunity."

"I can barely stand the stench from up here," said Charity. "I cannot imagine what it must be actually like in the city. What is it?"

"In the main; sulphur, and by-products of the various industries and mining, and countless other noxious vapours." Edwin elucidated.

The Professor wished to spend as short a time as possible here. He explained that he needed to visit a branch of his bank, which, he envisioned will take quite some time, and then the Postal and Telegraphic Offices. He assigned Edwin the task of accompanying Harkett, the acting Purser, to the Mefitis Municipal Supply Stores to place our supply orders. Edwin was to sign the cheques. I was to escort Edwin and Harkett, while Colonel Jahns volunteered to chaperon the Professor himself. Sir John said he too would be going to the Post Office as he had some missives to dispatch and would happily do so for any of the others who wanted him to.

The thing inside my chest, my heart, if it is still human, skipped a beat as Edwin produced a letter from his inside blazer pocket and placed it trustingly into Sir John's hand, accompanied by halting pleas to make sure it went off safely. Sir John smiled, and with a hand on Edwin's shoulder, promised he would not entrust it to some lackey, but place it in the post *himself. I know not why, but I felt some sudden dread sweep over me like the mid-morning tide. Foreboding, maybe. A tinge of fear that Edwin would never live to see his beautiful wife and children again.*

We prepared ourselves for the rigours of the city. Against his wishes, I insisted Edwin carry a secondary firearm along with his father's antique pistol, and if he were to carry the Professor's chequebook, as large as a good-sized blotting-pad, he must secrete it inside his coat. I would have had him attired in one of the cuirasses I found in the weapon's locker if I thought that for a moment, I could have convinced him to wear it. His old British Army issue filter mask was no use for this environment, thus I threw it away and got better ones from the stores, full face gear with reinforced covering for our heads. Utterly useless for me, but I had to make a show of it for everyone's benefit.

Hoping desperately for the best but preparing for the worst; I armed myself comprehensively. I cannot remember ever visiting Mefitis, but the Sergeant Major had seen many industrial cities like it, accordingly I chose to take the old boarding gun, more for show than anything else.

Wrapped in our immensikoffs against the cold, we gathered to watch as the ship glided to an anchorage tower on the very edge of the crater itself. A spectacular view if it had not been for the yellow-grey murk that blankets everything at lower levels.

Mooring cables winched us lower, as mobile gantries, built on wheezing steam engines, chugged out to cradle our hull. Forward motion ceased, and we came to rest in the rusting iron-framed embrace of those skeletal armatures.

Mr Charles opened the gate and unlatched the gangway. A nimble young female crewmember skipped across and lashed it to the gantry. Charles gave us the good-to-go signal, and the Professor marched across the gangway like General Mandeville at the Battle of Jahannam. We quickly followed with Mr Charles bringing up the rear; he was to organise the repairs and replenishment of our fuel supplies.

A rickety platform descended us to the ground, where we were shepherded by two masked Customs Officers towards a crude-looking building, resembling nothing more than a corroded iron box. The legend above the building proclaimed; "Mefitis Municipal Customs and Excise."

The inside of the building was as rudimentary as its external shell, consisting of little more than an open area before a high desk, behind which sat two disinterested looking clerks, old, bald and wizened, wearing breathing masks and long black gowns. Edwin remarked to me how they resembled two old crows perched upon a high branch.

An armed automaton in a Customs Officer's uniform stood to the side, guarding a wrought iron gate. The Professor presented the ship's documents, which the Clerks inspected and stamped in a perfunctory manner.

We were then waved through the barrier and beyond that to a narrow wood-panelled passageway and onward to the door beyond. Outside, a steep flight of stone steps took us down to the street. We stepped down into the swirl of the thick, stinking fog, like trepidatious bathers descending into water. As the brume enveloped us, I realised that the filter masks, though adequate for the dust, were no use at keeping the stench at bay. The others spluttered and cursed behind their faceplates.

We gathered on the pavement and checked our pocket watches, as the shapeless bulks of the madding crowd hustled by. The Professor addressed us tapping his watch face to emphasise that we were to return to the ship as soon as we finished our respective errands, post-haste. We all readily agreed.

Mr Charles headed off towards the repair yards. The Professor, the Colonel and Sir John, hailed a steam cab and jumped in, instantly disappearing into the murk-shrouded chaos of traffic.

Edwin, Harkett and I headed off on foot through the crowds. Edwin said he knew the way, thus I simply followed along.

From what I could see of the city from the street level, it was every bit the cess pit that Dr Spender described. Mefitis is a city built for and by industrialists and manufacturers, and those workers, miners, navvies and servants that provide services to them, with little concern or interest in the salubrious *pleasantries of civil architecture. Everything was functional in the most brutal of senses.*

Now and then, showers of embers from engineering works lit up the swirling brume, creating strange, hunched shadows that capered through the yellow mist. Vehicles rumbled by, belching more foul smoke into our paths. Mechanisms spilt out into the streets, muddy pathways became rickety metal walkways, roads became rusting gantries, straddling pits and beds where massive machinery sighed, pumped, and spun. Smoke and fumes poured from endless flues, steam billowed out of innumerable vents and valves, most often on to the street before us.

Edwin unexpectedly led us down a left turn, and we found ourselves walking through the bowels of what appeared to be some colossal steam engine. Around and above us giant gears and cogs whirled, open fireboxes threw glowing sparks and leaping cursing silhouettes across the chaos of machinery. Pistons, the size of train carriages, hissed and thrust. Below us a stinking, boiling brown river of effluent surged and ebbed with the tide of the motion of the machinery that pumped it. (Edwin informed me later that it was the plant that he came to study as a student.)

Everywhere I looked, machines rumbled along on self-laying tracks or shambled about on two, three, four, or more legs. Everything appeared old and grubby and churned out viscid smoke and steam. Every contraption rattled, clanked, or gasped like it was about to explode. I cannot remember seeing so many automatons and walking mechanicals of every description, anywhere before. Most were, like their larger cousins, in various states of decrepitude, as if the air itself was corroding everything. (Which, upon reflection, I suspect it was.)

Every now and then, thudding engines and huge dark shapes passed over us and powerful search lights would illuminate the brume, turning it a vile, milky yellow-grey colour. I wondered aloud, how they could fly, let alone navigate in that murk?

I saw few women, fewer children, thank God, and none what-so-ever of a class above the working men's own level. The greater majority of the women that I did notice, were often working alongside them. They were as rugged and grimy as the men, or hard-faced harridans who earned their living servicing the needs of those rough, grubby males.

Suddenly Edwin stopped and gesticulated towards a non-descript building we had arrived outside of; "The Mefitis Guild Hall of Municipal Suppliers, Victuallers and Provisioners".

Edwin positively skipped up the steps, Harkett at his heels.

A uniformed automaton guard opened the door for us, and we slipped into a huge brightly lit, checkerboard-floored, lobby.

In comparison to the Customs House, this was palatial, with wall-to-wall wooden panelling and a high vaulted ceiling from which hung three lavish gas-lit chandeliers. Along the left and *right flanks of the lobby area were deep booths, each with a narrow table between the facing benches.*

As the door closed behind us, I immediately noticed that, though the area was a throng with people, none wore masks. "None of these bastards are hacking their lights up," It was the Sergeant Major's voice in my head, alerting me to something that had not consciously registered with me. He was right, of course.

Edwin quickly pulled his mask off, and we followed. "Gads!" he blurted, "I can barely breathe in this thing."

Harkett readily agreed.

A young clerk in a frayed cravat and pinstriped tails slightly too big for his frame ignored Harkett, and myself, and approached Edwin to enquire as to his business. Edwin explained he had come to purchase supplies for an airship. The clerk hurriedly took us to one of the side booths and went in search of someone more senior. While we waited, Edwin, possibly more to keep himself entertained, explained that MSVPs acted as both a wholesaler and retailer, as well as trading in larger commodities, including everything from food and water to rock salt, borates and, of course here; sulphur. If it can be bought, and you wish to purchase it in more than the smallest portions, then you come here. In fact, the companies that owned the mines and manufactories own all these MSVP's in towns and cities like this. They even own the smaller stores where the workers buy their own victuals and equipment. Some even go so far as to pay their workers in their own coins, tokens, therefore their workers can only spend them in the company's stores.

"Indentured slavery," murmured the Sergeant Major in the back of my mind. "So much for the Red Hander's dreams of freedom, equality and fraternity."

After a few minutes, a kyphotic and eerily cadaverous old man, puffing on a Churchwarden's long pipe, appeared. He and Edwin got straight down to business. Harkett, as acting Purser, had drawn up detailed lists of the required comestibles and all Edwin had to do was agree and endorse the cheques. Which sounds upon writing it an expedient process, it was far from it. The old man was a haggler par-excellence and wanted to argue the toss of every bloody item, down to the price of every individual bottle of Port and tin of corned beef.

Finally, the young clerk was summoned back. He reappeared, pushing a trolley with some sort of fancy arithmometer on it, and, at the old man's precise instructions, began to tally up the price Edwin would pay. Edwin seemed rather to enjoy the process while I, at the Sergeant Major's urging, had come close to using the butt of the boarding-gun about the old bugger's head.

To hours later, we were finally back on the street.

As we headed back the way we came, a wind had picked up from somewhere and, though ice-cold, it had at least thinned the brume enough for us to see more of the city we passed through. It facilitated no kindlier observations. Above us the buildings crowded in as if reaching for each other with skeletal arms constructed of metal gantries, clothed with an insane spider's web of cables and wires.

The clearer air only served to make it easier to witness the squalid decrepitude that permeated the entire city. Everything, wood, stone, brick, brass and cast iron, was either corroding or rotting, even the people. Stripped of the formlessness afforded by the yellow fog, the people, their clothes and even their skin, appeared to be crumbling. We stepped over dead and dying in the gutters. Maimed and mutilated begged from the alleyways. It seemed that every worker's clothes were marked with blood and beige phlegm splatter from the constant coughing. I saw people pull off their masks, casually hawk up bloody mucus, spit in the gutter, clear their throats, pull their masks back on and go on about their work. It left me wishing the shroud of clag would thicken again.

We were about five minutes from the Custom's House when my attention was drawn to a small company of soldiers mustering in a square a little further ahead. They were the Royal Elthorn Experimental Rifle Regiment by the livery of their tunics, but I swiftly realised, of course, the insignias had changed. In the Sergeant Major's day, they were our 95th,

General Marcellinus Blood's men, every trooper to a man had to be a first-class sharpshooter with a variety of different rifles and pistols. I noticed they were even still allowed to modify their weapons; some appeared to have essentially built their own.

I was doing a quick headcount when suddenly out of the passing crowd a man lunged towards Edwin.

I had a pistol drawn and aimed at the visor of the assailant's filter mask before I heard him shout, "Edwin! Edwin, old chap! By golly, it is you!" The man seemed oblivious to my presence. In a flourish, he pulled off his mask, revealing his face. "It's me, Barnsby!" He grinned widely before quickly pulling the mask back on.

Edwin seemed to falter before shouting back, "Barnsby! Damn it, man, what are you doing here?" They shook hands warmly.

I holstered the pistol and nodded to Harkett to relax.

Edwin and his friend drew close enough not to shout through their masks at each other. The man obviously wanted Edwin to go with him and, after a pause, Edwin nodded agreement and gestured for us to follow.

We crossed the road, dodging between the insanity of the traffic, waved on by the stranger. After a short walk, he began rummaging through his coat pockets, and came up with a key, before stopping at a pair of rusting gates. He unlocked them and ushered us through.

I caught a certain furtiveness about the man, but Edwin seemed at ease with it all, so I followed. Once inside the gate, he directed us across a tiny, rubbish-strewn yard and through a small doorway.

Unexpectedly, we found ourselves in a large hall, the likes of which one would expect in a fair-sized townhouse. It was well appointed and, though the carpet on the stairs looked a little threadbare, it spoke of well-heeled comfort. A rather timorous maid appeared and helped us divest ourselves of our outer garments.

"Damn it! Edwin Ransom!" Our host exclaimed again. "It is so good to see you!" He rushed forward and hugged Edwin. Edwin's stiff limbed reaction was much like a favoured child greeted by an over-enthusiastic aunt.

Extricating himself from the fellow's embrace, Edwin turned to us, "Gentlemen, may I present my old friend, Barnsby Monck. We were students together at University."

Monck stepped forward and shook our hands enthusiastically as we introduced ourselves. He was a slight man with a pallid complexion and a broad forehead crowned by a shock of unruly black hair, a small moustache and deeply set piercing black eyes that darted about constantly.

Everything about the little man seemed rushed. He hurried us into the drawing room and issued orders to the young maid to serve tea. The room had once been expensively furnished, but now things showed signs of wear and tear, but only enough to make it feel comfortable rather than shabby. Monck flourished a box of Flor de Dindigul cigars under our noses. We politely declined. He then took centre-stage in front of the fireplace. "Well, old friend, what are you doing back here?"

"Only passing through, I'm afraid," Edwin replied. "But I should ask you the same thing?"

"Ah, yes! I suppose it comes as a bit of a surprise to find me back here." Monck laughed, "Indeed. It came as a bit of a shock to me too!" He struggled to light his cigar from an ornate crow-shaped silver lighter he had taken off the mantelpiece. "Ah, forgive me. Now, what was I saying? Yes. Unlike you, my old friend I was never cut of whatever cloth it takes to make an even passable engineer. After our sojourn here in this delightful metropolis, I returned to Tharsis and resolutely failed every exam they threw at me." He laughed heartily.

"I must say that I noticed your absence," said Edwin, "I apologise though for my inconsiderateness, as I was rather preoccupied courting my future wife."

Monck stopped in mid-action of lighting his cigar. "Not... the Professor's daughter! Tell me you did not!"

Edwin smiled coyly. "Indeed, I did."

"Damn, Good show! Old man!" Monck addressed myself and Harkett as a Shakespearian actor would the audience. "An incredible beauty she is! Have you met her? Half the chaps in the faculty were enamoured with her, and the other half were absolutely obsessed. She was the single greatest distraction on campus, in fact, the single greatest attraction, and you, my dear boy, you... well, you got her!" Monck stepped forward and shook Edwin's hand again. "Congratulations, old chap! Though I suppose having that old bear as a father-in-law is quite an affliction."

I noticed how Edwin prickled at Monck's remark.

The nervous-looking maid arrived with tea. I watched her as she carefully filled our cups and presented them to us, all the time never once glancing at her master. After passing around a plate of fancies, she quickly departed.

Edwin deftly changed the subject. "So, what are you doing here then?"

"Ah, well," Monck puffed the cigar into life. "Well, engineering was not for me, and I could not go back to my father with my tail between my legs, clutching a sheaf of failed exam notices. Therefore, I did what every self-respecting failure does on such occasions; I took up the noble art of Medicine.

"Which, I may say so, I rather took to, being more an art than a science. It was more to my temperament. One can blag one's way through most of it with the merest tincture of knowledge and a good line in patter. I have an excellent bedside manner, you know," he winked conspiratorially. "Especially if the convalescent is female and wealthy." He laughed again. It had a falsity to it that stretched my nerves.

"Well, I got to the end of my third year, and I had to do something. Father's patience, like his patronage, was running out. Therefore, I had to take up a specialism or be trapped, administering purgatives to constipated old dames or mercury tonics to syphilitic soldiers. Honestly, dear chap, there is only so many times one can shove a rubber hose up some poor unfortunate's arse before all the glamour of the vocation wears off.

"So, I was looking to make a choice when, as luck would have it, I met a ravishing young lady in the University Library. A place I hardly visited, and I tell you it was quite a shock to find a woman in those hallowed stacks, let alone a beautiful one. I quickly got myself acquainted with her. Cattarina was her name, and she was attending the School of Nursing at Olympus but had come down to Tharsis to use our library.

"You see she wanted to know everything there was to know about lung diseases because she originally came from here no less. She aspired to become a doctor herself, but you know how difficult it is for a woman even to be allowed to train. No humble nursing student would ever be deigned as socially acceptable enough to enter the faculty, let alone having the required mental capacities.

"Anyhoo, I thought our encounter was little more than a pleasant afternoon's dalliance, a light distraction from my own predicament, when over luncheon she confided in me that she was the youngest daughter of none other than Sir Guillermo De Sampo, the Saltmaster! The chap that owns at least half of the mineral salt mines in this region!" He laughed again.

I made a show of checking my pocket watch against the clock on the mantle.

"Well, to cut a long story short; when such an opportunity arises, one must make the best of it. You see Cattarina has this theory that the sulphur dust in the air here is what is causing the lung maladies. Indisputably the dust causes the problems as we know, but the sulphur is what is killing the miners... well everyone. And she was intent on proving it."

"I suspect her father is not too happy with such assertions," commented Edwin.

"Well, there you are damned right. He hated the idea, did not want her to be a nurse and was dead set against her studying anything to do with dust or fumes, but Cattarina is an obstinate girl, and she has her inheritance from her mother. Not as rich as her father, but in a league way above even my own dear old Pater."

"So, you decided to help her?" I ventured in hopes of moving this tale along.

"More than that, old boy. With our newfound shared interest in all things pulmonary, well how could we avoid falling in love?"

Edwin congratulated him, and we murmured our approval. Monck insisted we toast his betrothal and good fortune with liberally filled brandy glasses. Edwin, ever the well-bred gentleman, enquired where the new Mrs Monck was.

Monck grew strangely reticent. "Oh, she's about her business. She is... she is quite a crusader for the afflicted and the poor. I believe she is..." He made a grand gesture of scrutinizing his watch, "... probably at the Municipal Infirmary at this time of day."

Edwin began to suggest that we needed to depart soon, but Monck changed the subject, curious as to what we were doing in Mefitis.

I have grown to respect Edwin for his many skills and abilities, and he is one of the most truthful men I have ever known, yet when circumstances fall upon him to fabricate, he is able to call upon those skills with fiction that serve him so well in the stories he writes for his children. It was the same skill that he used to provide me with an acceptable story for the Colonel. More plausible than ingenuous lies and told in his usual affable but slightly halting manner.

Edwin explained we are on a scientific expedition from the University with the renowned Archaeologist Doctor Octavius Spender; we are travelling to the Gorgonum Chaos to examine the ruins of some newly discovered Aresian settlement that might be the oldest yet identified.

Monck seemed to accept the tale but commented dismissively, "Archaeology, digging about in others old rubbish and grave robbing. I never saw the point myself."

The conversation seemed to grind to a halt at that point. I took the opportunity to look at my pocket watch, sigh dramatically and take to my feet. "I am dreadfully sorry, Dr Monck, but I fear we will have to be..."

"No, no, not yet." Monck almost shouted over me. "You cannot leave, not yet," he implored Edwin. "Cattarina will be devastated not to have met you. My best friend from my University days." He paused, "My only friend. I have told her so much about you."

Edwin looked taken-aback but tried to assert our need to leave. "It has been wonderful to see you Barnsby, but..."

"Nonsense, you can spare a little while longer for an old friend, can you not? After all, what has it been? Ten years? Fifteen? Cattarina will be home soon, I am sure, and she will be thrilled to meet you. Please, stay, just a little while longer... and we have so much to talk about..."

Edwin seemed at a loss but could not dismiss his friend's desperate pleas. "All right, but we must be going soon. Just one more cup of tea and then we must go."

Monck sprang to the door and called for more tea to be served.

We sat in uncomfortable silence for the next few minutes. Then Monck decided to show us his album of daguerreotypes, the subjects of the album were mainly himself and his wife. She was indeed a beautiful young woman; raven-haired and light-eyed, tall and long-limbed, with a confident patrician bearing. Seeing the set of her face and the way she held her head, I could easily imagine her being every bit as determined as Monck suggested she was.

Monck was now sitting beside Edwin with the album on his lap extolling his wife's beauty and the wonderful life they had together when I noticed an image slip out of the rear of the album and fall to the floor.

Harkett saw it too but said nothing as I surreptitiously placed my shoe over it and slid it back towards me.

Tea arrived. The young maid was seemingly even more anxious than before. She followed the same ritual and, after proffering the fancies, fled.

I waited until Monck had poured the tea and was occupied relighting his cigar before I picked up the daguerreotype and took a glance at it.

I recognised the type of picture it was immediately: the staging, the pose. It was Monck's wife, in repose. Every bit as beautiful as in the other images, but that was the photographer's art I supposed.

"What's that?" Monck demanded on noticing the image in my hand. "What have you...?"

I turned it slightly so Edwin and Harkett could easily see the image on it.

Monck's mouth hung open.

I passed the picture to Edwin.

"I know a memorial portrait when I see one Dr Monck," I said flatly. Monck stiffened but said nothing, just stared at the card now in Edwin's hands.

"Indeed," said Edwin softly.

"That is your wife, is it not Dr Monck?" I asked.

Monck closed his mouth and swallowed hard.

"Barnsby? Please, what is the meaning of this?" queried Edwin.

Monck's eyes seemed to almost roll in his head to such a point I thought he was about to have some sort of fit. He made a low groaning noise and turned to the mantle.

Edwin stood up and made towards Monck, but I interceded moving him back a few steps. Harkett, taking his cue from me, moved away too.

After what seemed an age Monck turned back to us. His face was as white as a sheet, and his eyes seemed deeper than ever. "Oh Edwin, Edwin, forgive me. Please, please." He made to move towards us, but I held up my hand to stay him. He moaned again and visibly sagged. "I am so sorry... so, so...sorry.... I..."

"Sorry for what, Barnsby? What have you done?" Edwin's tone was calm, but I could see the alarm in his eyes.

"I... I... We came back here to make a difference, Cattarina and I, to try to save lives, she said. She was always so burdened by what the people here suffer at the hands of her father and his business partners. Not just the poisoned air, but also the injuries from the machines and the mining. Burns and scalds and hair and hands ripped off, and their lungs burning with sulphur. She swept me along with her crusade. Me? A useless quack, a charlatan, playing at being a doctor, more used to

peddling potions to the unwary than actually trying to heal people... but she saw more in me." He sat down heavily on a chair.

"Dr Monck, what are you telling us?" I asked warily.

"One day she started coughing too. At first, she tried to pass it off as a cold. Nevertheless, I knew. I followed her and saw that when she was away from the house, she would take off her mask when tending the ill. I confronted her about it, and she confessed that she would only wear the filter on the street and that the one she wore was the same as that the poorest of the workers wear." Monck shook his head violently as if to drive away the memories. "I tried to reason with her, but she was adamant she must do it. You see, she was documenting her own disease." He looked up at us. "My beautiful wife.... she was documenting her own death." He sprang to his feet and stalked across the room to a small writing desk by the window. "She used to sit here and write." He pulled a sheaf of papers from the desk and cast them on the floor. Each page was covered in a perfect script, no doubt by a female hand, the writing almost legible from where I stood. I could also see the fine mist of coughed up blood on many of them. "She sent copies of them to her father, every day, every detail. She implored him to help the people. The old bastard did not even answer. Not once." He slammed the top of the desk. "She died... She died, and she left me here, on my own. She killed herself as surely as if she took arsenic. Only it took so long, and it was so painful, and she took my soul with her."

"I am sorry for your loss, Barnsby." Edwin patted him on the shoulder. "She sounds like she was quite a driven woman who believed in what she was doing. You could not have saved her from herself."

Suddenly he seized Edwin's elbow. I made to intercede, but Edwin waved me away. "Edwin, I tried to save her... I tried everything a doctor could do. I learnt more in those few months than all the time I was at the University. Everything, I studied everything, I reread everything, but she would not let me save her... she forbad me unto her last breath."

"There was nothing you could do," consoled Edwin.

Monck's expression changed. I cannot say the man looked insane, for what does insanity look like, nonetheless he looked dangerous.

"Here we bury the dead quickly. I had that picture taken because I feared I would one day forget her face. You see, she had known how weak, I am. She had arranged it all, her funeral, everything. Her solicitors saw to it all. Even as far as forbidding her father to attend. It was all I could do to get up and go there to watch them put my beautiful wife in the ground. I could not accept it."

He let Edwin go and walked back to the fireplace. "I could not accept it. I screamed at God himself, I would not accept this. There must be something I could do?"

"What did you do, Barnsby?" asked Edwin again, this time far more suspiciously.

Monck turned to us. "I saved her. I saved her...."

"He did what?" asked Harkett incredulously.

"I dug her up, out of that hole in the ground, I brought her home, and I saved her... I brought her back."

I was too shocked myself to believe a word of what I was hearing, but Edwin pushed on. "How, in God's name! How?"

"I shall show you." Monck strode across the room, flung open the door and crossed the hall. Edwin followed, and Harkett and I followed him. Monck fumbled at the lock of the door across the hallway and then, almost reverently, pushed it open.

The room had once been a reception room, but now the furniture was piled to the sides. The heavy drapes were pulled together securely over shutters blocking out what little light there was from the street. Even so, there was enough light to see clearly. A peculiar corposant glow filled the room, colouring everything in a surreal palette of sickly green. The room was so humid that Edwin had to stop to wipe clean his spectacles.

In the middle stood a tall glass tank, almost to the ceiling, full of some bubbling turquoise liquid. The light appeared to be emanating from the very fluid in the tank.

Attached to the tank was a vast insane hotchpotch of devices, brass valves, gauges and contrivances. Copper pipes pierced the glass, creating a strange frame of spiral metalwork inside. Something hummed with electrification, and small discharges flickered through the liquid. Mechanical bellows hissed, puffed, and sighed as they pumped gasses into the bubbling ferment. Around us, there were tools and strange pieces of machinery strewn everywhere.

I had the chilling sensation that I had seen similar machines before.

Edwin gasped.

Harkett swore loudly.

But all I could do was stare in shock.

In the glass tank, like a mermaid suspended in a bottle, floated the corpse of the beautiful Cattarina Monck. She wore something diaphanous that flowed and billowed about her in the churning current. I realised, with horror, it was her wedding dress. Her hair too, streamed out giving the illusion of life to her, but there was nothing alive there.

"Dear God," whispered Edwin. "Dear God."

I noticed that bubbles were escaping from her mouth before I realised why. The brocaded bodice of her dress had been ripped open, to reveal her emaciated chest. That too had been brutally torn open; the sternum exposed and left hanging by tendrils of flesh to the shattered ribs. Inside the cavity, where once her fragile heart and lungs resided, now nestled a crude brass contraption of whirling gears, cogs and pumps.

Monck turned to us, his face eerily lit by the greenish glow, "See, Edwin, she's alive, she's breathing..." He added proudly, "I did it, Edwin. I brought her back. Like Lazarus, at my hand, she rose from the grave. She lives."

"That is not life, Barnsby. She is not alive."

Barnsby placed his hands on the warm glass and pushed his cheek against it. "She is, she is....almost."

"Barnsby..." Edwin began, but Monck suddenly turned back to us with the strangest of smiles upon his face. One that reminded me chillingly of that leering loon, Lanulos.

"I did it, Edwin. I built mechanical lungs so she can breathe, and a new heart because it was so badly damaged, but I am no true inventor. I can't free her of this," he pounded his fist against the thick glass. "My adaptions to the Ringer's solution sustains her, but I can't free her, I don't have the skills. I am not an artificer, not like you Edwin, not anything like you. They always said at the University that you were a genius like your father, which is why the Professor favoured you." He turned back to Edwin, his expression that of a gleefully pleading child. "That is why I have been waiting for you, Edwin. Because you, you can engineer it better, you can build her a new heart and lungs that will fit inside her. Therefore, she can be whole again, so she can come back to me. Free of this place. We will leave this awful city. We have the money. We can travel; see the wonders of this world. She has always wanted to see the Pyramids of Cydonia. She can live again. We can both live again."

"No, Barnsby, I cannot. And, even if I could do such a thing, I would not. Your wife is dead," Edwin let that sink in. "Forgive me Barnsby, but that is just a series of pumps pushing air through a corpse. She is dead."

"No, she is not." Monck thrust his face towards Edwin. "She is alive, and you will help me to save her. You can do that. I know you can. That's why I was looking for you."

"What do you mean? You were looking for Edwin?" I asked. "How could you have known he was even in the city?"

Monck gave me a knowing grin, one that instantly alarmed me. "I've known for weeks you were coming here, Edwin. I didn't know exactly when, but I knew you would come."

I grabbed Monck's shoulder and turned him to me. "How?"

"My friend told me. He said Edwin would come soon, and that he would know what to do to save Cattarina."

I pulled Monck toward me by his lapels. "Friend? What 'friend'?" I already dreaded the answer.

Monck's eyes suddenly brightened. "Oh, you know him too. Have you met him?"

"In God's good name, man, who are you talking about?" demanded Edwin. "Did someone tell you to do this? To desecrate your own wife's body!"

"What is he called, your 'friend'?" I asked softly.

Monck held my gaze for a moment and then said, "Indrid Cold. He is an Angel. A strange grinning Angel. He came to me at the funeral and told me what I would have to do. He told me how I could bring her back..."

I tried to conceal the precipitous dread that overwhelmed me, but my mind wheeled. "He told you that Edwin was coming here?"

Monck looked at me, quizzically. "Yes, of course. He knows everything."

"When did he tell you?" I demanded.

Monck appeared to snap out of it finally. "A few weeks ago, he came to me and said that Edwin Ransom, my old friend from University, was coming to Mefitis. That Edwin would help me find the 'Dead Man,' and the Dead Man will help us bring Catterina back. All I had to do was keep looking for Edwin. I have been out every day and night, walking the city, looking for you."

I pushed Monck away from me and told Edwin and Harkett we had to go immediately.

Edwin agreed, however, as he turned, Monck launched forward and grabbed at my coat. "It's you! Isn't it? You are the one he said about. You are the Dead Man."

I punched him in the belly, just hard enough to knock the wind and the fight out of him, and then ushered Edwin and Harkett out of the room.

Monck had recovered enough breath to give an anguished cry, "No! No, you cannot leave me. Please!"

I stepped between him and the door and, as I expected, he threw a punch at my chin. I let it connect, hearing the crack of his knuckles as they impacted against the metal of my jaw.

Monck gasped in pain.

"Enough, Dr Monck, I do not wish to hurt you," I warned, but he was not about to give up. He snatched up a wrench that was lying nearby and swung it at my head. I blocked the swing, took the tool from his grasp and pushed him roughly back against the tank. Monck howled and began to sob.

I tried to reason with him, explaining that Edwin could not help him bring the dead back to life, no one could.

He argued that this man, this 'Angel' as he called him, had told him what to do and how to do all this. All he needed to finish the process was Edwin and the 'Dead Man.' I looked him in the eye and told him it was all a tissue of lies. This man, Cold, was deceiving him, but Monck was beyond any logical reasoning. He kept insisting that I was the 'Dead Man' that Cold had promised would have the key to bringing his wife back to life.

By this time, he had resorted to begging pathetically.

"Look." I pulled the Police Officer's Châtellerault knife out of my waistband and stabbed my right palm. The blood came quickly. I held my hand up to Monck's face. "Look, man! The dead do not bleed!" There was a flicker of realisation across his face.

At that point, possibly to assure himself of our safety, Edwin opened the door. I turned to tell him to leave, but his sudden intake of breath alerted me. Like a stage magician, Monck had produced a derringer pistol from somewhere and had it pointed at Edwin.

I know I am quick, quicker than any man could be. Nevertheless, Monck fired before I could stop him.

With a cry of pain, Edwin spun into the hall. I gathered instantly from his loud cursing that he was still alive.

I punched Monck to the side of his head with enough force to kill, sending him crashing into the mass of machinery, and kicked the pistol away across the room.

Edwin was only lightly injured. The bullet had passed through the shoulder of his jacket and scored the skin, enough to tear the flesh, but nothing serious. I told Harkett to bind it and get them both out of the house.

As I turned back to deal with Monck, Edwin grabbed my hand and made me pledge I would not kill him. I had to admit I did not know if Monck was still alive after I had just hit him. Edwin protested, but I ordered Harkett to get him out of the house.

By the time I returned to the room, Monck was trying to get up off the floor. I, well the Sergeant Major, warned him to stay down or I would knock him back down again.

I then took one last look at the woman in the tank. I was struck by the serenity of her face in repose; she certainly had once been very beautiful. Something about the violation of her body not only repulsed me, it outraged me. This anger was mine, not some residue of a long-dead Sergeant Major, this fury was mine. I walked around the glass tank, stepping over Monck where he cowered on the floor; searching for something, I knew not what, probably his gun. Behind the tank was a dining table that appeared to have been used as both a workbench and operating slab, the surface covered in dried gore and random pieces of equipment. Beside the table was a stool with a heavy wooden seat and a cast-iron frame. I picked it up, hefted it for weight, and turned back to the tank.

Monck immediately foresaw what I was about to do and clambered back to his feet, screaming at me to stop. I batted him out of the way with the stool. I had given my word to Edwin not to kill the wretch; nevertheless, I would happily see him suffer for what he had done.

The first blow shattered the glass of the tank, and the weight of the liquid within exploded it with a force that almost took me off my feet. Furiously I smashed the remaining glass and then, with my hands, I tore apart the network of pipes and tubes until I had freed her fragile body from the grip of that mechanical web. Monck was screaming at me again, so I threw the stall at him to silence him. Sweeping Catterina into my arms, I kicked my way back through the metal and glass, and after clearing it with my arm, laid her upon the table.

I know not what possessed me. I felt compelled to try to pull the bodice over her damaged chest and brush the hair from her face. I was doing so when her eyes flickered open.

Beautiful light green eyes that burned with an unearthly effulgence, wide open and utterly terrified.

Monck shrieked with delight as if witnessing a miracle.

"Dear God, almighty!" Harkett stood in the doorway. I had not heard him return.

"Get out!" I thrust Harkett back out the door and slammed it shut behind him and returned to the table. Monck was leaning over his wife clasping her hand to his chest and reciting her name over and over. I seized him by the shoulder and violently thrust him away from her.

She looked like a terrified ghost. An innocent soul awoken to discover it was nothing more than a reanimated monstrosity. She stared into my eyes as her hand grasped for mine. Her body began to shake violently. She gasped and spewed a thick green mucus across the table.

So, this was it? To be dragged back from death's embrace into this world, to this horror. She had chosen to die, to sacrifice herself for a cause she believed in, to prove something, to make her life meaningful and he, Monck, had betrayed her, violating the meaning of her sacrifice as surely as he had done so to her body.

As surely as they had done to me. I could not let this be. I would not let this be.

I closed her eyes, and covered them with my hand, drew my pistol from its holster and placed it gently against her temple.

Monck immediately understood my intention and tried to stop me. Grappling my arm, he desperately tried to pull me away and began his pathetic begging again.

To silence him, I put the muzzle of the gun between his brows and ordered him to stand back. Fear was enough to make him take a few steps. Nevertheless, it did not stem his abysmal imploring. The Sergeant Major's voice in my head demanded I should kill him and be done with it. However, I had given Edwin my word.

I have not the remotest idea why I did so, but I leaned forward and kissed her cold, wet forehead, tasting the vile metallic fluid on her skin.

Monck let out a terrible wail as I placed the pistol back against her temple and pulled the trigger.

I am a killer. Lloyd was right about that. Since awakening into this nightmare world, I have killed more men than I can easily recount. And before this incarnation? Who knows how many lives the Sergeant Major took? So why did the death of an innocent leave me bereft of my faculties? This was different. This felt so different.

I turned the gun on Monck. He sank to the floor sobbing and clawing at himself. "It ends now, Dr Monck," I warned. "Do you understand me? It ends here. Let the dead lie."

Monck babbled something incomprehensible, and then he blurted out like a spoilt child, "He promised me!"

"Who promised you?"

"The Grinning Angel, Cold... he promised Ransom, and you would bring Catterina back to me..."

"No, Dr Monck, he is not an Angel, he is a Demon, his name is Lanulos, and he lied to you."

During the time we spent at Dr Monck's house, the brume had come back down again. I tried to hurry us quickly through the crowded streets to the Customs House, but it soon became evident that Edwin's injury was far more severe than I had anticipated. Monck's derringer had discharged both rounds simultaneously and, though the first had only grazed his upper arm, the second had embedded in the flank of his pectoral muscle. It was a very small calibre injury, but Edwin was losing blood and tiring rapidly.

Notwithstanding my promise, I regretted deeply not ending Monck's odious little existence, and vowed to myself to make amends for my mistake should I ever be unfortunate enough to return to Mefitis.

Harkett and I did our best to carry Edwin without calling much attention to ourselves. Fortunately, the wind swirling the fog helped cloak our progress.

There were armed men abroad, in small patrols, wearing red armbands and sashes, with shakos above their filter masks. I quickly deduced they were some form of local militia by their lack of standard uniform and regulation weaponry, little more than indigenous bravos with guns and cudgels. Harkett told me they were called "Minute Men" because they could be readily called to duty in a minute.

Why they were on the street, I did not know nor care, as my intentions were fixed on avoiding any encounter with them whatsoever.

As fate would have it, there was a group of them at the bottom of the steps of the Customs House, but they were too involved in some animated dispute with a cluster of men and woman to be bothered with us as we slipped by on the other side of the steps.

Thankfully, the Customs House clerks were as disinterested as before. With a quick glance at Edwin's papers, and a tick by our names, we were waved through.

I expected to find the Professor and the others on the other side, but we found only Sir John awaiting us.

"Sorry chaps, but the Prof and old Colonel Blowhard are still at the Post Offices. They got stuck in the Bank for an age." As we pulled off our masks, he noticed how grey Edwin looked. "I say, old boy, what's up with you?"

"Oh, I encountered an old friend, and he appears to have shot me." Edwin calmly handed me the blood-soaked chequebook and promptly collapsed.

Excerpt from;
Diary of Aelita Fontenelli (Mrs).
Tuesday, September, 39th. MY.26

Dear Diary.

We have been trapped inside the confines of this airship all day. I cannot abide the rotten egg smell of the yellow brume, which permeates every compartment of the ship. We, those of us left aboard, implored the Captain to ascend above the malodorous miasma if it were at all possible, alas regretfully he could not.

We gathered in the wardroom, which was one of the few areas where the odour had not thoroughly permeated and had the Steward light some aromatics to mask the pong. Dr Spender spent most of the day reading a stack of books beside his chair and making notes in his journal. Patty, Charity, and I amused ourselves, chatting, playing card games and reading aloud to each other curious titbits we happened upon.

I was sitting with Ursula and doing a little sewing, further adjusting a pair of Giovanni's plus-fours to a better fit for myself, while Charity was reading an excerpt from the inimitable Mr Dickens' Book of Sketches, and, much to our delight, attempting the various character's voices from the tale of the Steam Excursion. She is so amusing, especially when she affected the steward's lisp. I asked whether people actually used such effusive language as that back in England?

Charity said that they did back then; however, we now speak a plainer, less verbose, dialect in the old colonies, especially since independence. She attributed the loss to the schoolmasters and mistresses 'slacking' as she characterised it. They were allowing standards in the classrooms to slip. I remarked it was a pity to lose such a wonderful lexicon. An individual's vocabulary has consistently appeared to me to be a reliable measure of their intellectual faculties, though, I must admit, an imperfect gauge of the nature of their personality.

I turned to Dr Spender to ask for his opinion and realised he had fallen fast asleep in his chair. One of the ship's cats, which I discovered only earlier today were on board, had found its way into the wardroom and had taken the opportunity to avail itself of an empty lap.

(I later learnt that this brindle coloured one answers to the name Davy Jones, and is the friendlier of the two, the other is a ginger tomcat called Mr Jules.)

Patty was unconcerned, enjoining us to leave it be if it was acceptable to me to do so.

I queried why she would think it concerned me. As it was not I, the feline opportunist had chosen to take advantage of.

Patty explained that the automaître D' Jakes, had informed her that my husband had during our original visit left word that I have an unfortunate sensitivity to cats, consequently the poor things had been corralled in the crew areas for the journey.

I laughed, and dismissed it as utter nonsense, I adore cats, and dogs, in fact, all animals.

Patty made to apologise when I suddenly realised what had led to the misapprehension. It is my husband, Giovanni, who is averse to cats; in fact, he cannot abide any animals unless, of course, they have already passed through the hands of a taxidermist or pickled in a jar.

For some reason, this instance piqued my resentment, and I cursed him openly, there and then. I do not know who was more shocked, Patty and Charity or myself. Charity giggled genially, so out of relief, I repeated it, and expounded further; "Damn him and his little piggy eyes. The bumptious clammy Italian podsnapper! How dare he!"

I know I should not have indulged so, nevertheless, with Patty and Charity's encouragement, I suddenly found myself giving vent to half a lifetime of constrained frustration and anger at the man's audacity.

When I finally took pause, we were all giggling like schoolgirls on a junket. Much to the apparent consternation of Davy Jones, the cat, who regarded us suspiciously from the safety of Dr Spender's lap.

Once we regained our composure, Patty and Charity began to question me as to the lifestyle I had led as the wife of the illustrious areologist, cartographer and adventurer, Dr Giovanni Eugenio Fontenelli. I found myself regaling them with amusing biographical anecdotes from my alphamegamic married life, which, I must ashamedly admit, did not take particularly long.

More importantly to me, we discussed the grave disquiets I suffer, as a deeply religious woman, when considering my part in the death of that unfortunate brigand at the tomb. I explained that I find it a terrible weight upon my conscience and how I have prayed continually for forgiveness for committing such a mortal sin.

Patty was quite forthright in assuring me, that in her opinion, no God would judge me harshly for killing to protect the lives of the innocent. It was an instinctive act at the height of what was, to all-intense-and-purposes, a battle. She pointed out, quite correctly, that the Bible is full of such things.

Patty assured me that if it had been her, she would have done precisely what I did. "Your worries only prove you are of a kindlier disposition than me," she added. "As I would not shed a tear, nor waste a moment in concern, over the death of such a wretch."

They are wonderfully strong women, proper daughters of Mars, made of far sterner stuff than I. Though, it did not do much to salve my regret, at least it was good to share with them the burden I carry because of it.

The automaître D', Jakes, was serving another round of tea when Charity, changing the subject again, asked me the question that I have so long been expecting; Why had I and Giovanni not had children?

I thought for a while on how I should answer it. Was this the right time to have the conversation I had intended to have with them?

Dr Spender was soundly asleep, oblivious to any conversation we might have, so was the feline interloper on his lap.

That time, for the first time, I suspect not the last, explaining what little I comprehended about my own dilemma was undoubtedly the most problematical conversation I have ever had. I am not one used to openly discussing myself or my emotions. Such talk was always gravely discouraged by my husband and, of course, touches upon subjects that no genteel lady broaches outside of her private salon. There and then, though, was not the time for obscurities, candour was called for and I, if I were to allow them some measure of the scale of my dilemma, had to address the issue succinctly.

I found myself attempting to explain concepts that I struggle to understand myself. We, by that I mean Red Aresians, are the most Tellurian like, though it is patently clear to all except the blind that I am not Tellurian, however less readily comprehensible is the fact that the differences are far from skin deep, a simple matter of colouration. My companions readily accepted what I had to say, and, other than for a little harmless speculation, they allowed me to continue fumbling towards my point. I tried to clarify that the differences between our kinds include how we, as a race, reach maturation.

I explained the circumstances regarding my brother, Gethen, and how I had been led to believe in our separation as children was by death. I tried to explain how I have grown up with the constant feeling that he was a part of me, not only in the spiritual meaning, but in a tangible sense.

Then came the most challenging part, to describe how I learnt that Gethen was not my brother in actuality, only a facet of myself. I tried to explain my new-found knowledge in terms of a spiritual revelation, and how, with this knowledge, I find myself mourning for Gethen, the brother I never had, the aspect of me I was denied knowledge of, as if he were, as undeniably he has been to me all my life, a real person. Even the memory of him, now my reasoning mind accepts the truth, is beginning to fade. I am left feeling that I am losing him all over again. Stolen away from me piecemeal.

Due to the circumstances of my childhood upbringing, I fear I am left neither one thing nor the other.

My companions felt they could empathise with my feelings to some degree. I explained how the conundrum was compounded by my sham of a marriage and Giovanni's indifference to me on a physical, dare I say, sexual level (it was Patty that said it plainly after my initial equivocating) and how I was led by him to believe the fault for our failures somehow rested solely with me.

Now, sadly, I have come to the deduction that he, my gentleman jailer, had all along some deeper knowledge of my predicament. That is why he kept me imprisoned in our loveless marital home, fascinated by my duality, yet repulsed by it.

Charity bid leave to ask me if I had ever before felt some tincture of masculine verve within me. In truth, I have never even contemplated what it would be to be male, as that aspect of myself I knew of and accepted as a separate entity, Gethen, my brother. Even with my newly discovered awareness, it is beyond my envisioning, that presented with such a choice, I would have ever have chosen the path to undertake such a fundamental metamorphosis. What remains with me though is a fear that, because that selection was never clearly made, I can never be wholly a woman. Let alone fully maturate and consequentially fulfil the innate purpose of womanhood, the very thing in life I have always desired. Even more so than abstract concepts of freedom. Oh, what ages I have spent on my knees praying to the Virgin Mary for a miracle, unknowing that the fault lies within me. That fissure runs, not only through my soul, through my physical body too. A fracture no end of praying for miracles can resolve.

They listened carefully asking only the most sensitive of questions. Charity said she had heard curious theories expounded by people such as Professor Elron and his like, though they had been dismissed as fantasy.

Patty then confided that she, thought of course, though a purely Tellurian woman has never, throughout her entire life, felt as she was told a woman should 'feel.' If she had had the choice and was not constrained by ridiculous traditions and the social mores of society; she would dispense with all this 'ladylike' nonsense, especially the bodices and dresses that she hates wearing, and clothe and deport herself such as she pleased.

In all, they were warmly accepting of my situation, nevertheless unable to provide me with any clear guidance, if indeed that was what I was looking for from them. I remain, I feel, incomplete, an unfinished work.

"Forgive me, dear lady." Dr Spender must have awoken during out tête-à-tête. "I could not help overhear. What you speak of is not such a strange concept actually. There are plenty of anecdotal tales from the natural world of creatures that change gender under certain circumstances. Recently I read some works by an Irish writer called Edward Hoy-Castle, he claims to be an 'intermedialist,' a person who accepts nothing at face value. In actuality, he is an anti-dogmatist, who collects anecdotal stories of the bizarre to support his disputations. He has written of legendary tribes back on Earth, in ancient Turkey and possibly Hispaniola, where all babies are born female, then at some point, most probably the onset of adolescence, some develop onwards to become males while the rest remain female. The Greeks, of course, wrote a great deal about the so-called 'hermaphrodites, 'being a perfect union of both male and female, even going so far as the have a demi-god called Hermaphroditus, an androgen who was one of the Erotes, the followers of the

Goddess Aphrodite, Goddess of Love. What you suggest actually is that your people, your race, have developed so far as to have some control over that process. Remaining as androgens until self-assigning a gender, possibly with the aid of ritual to bring on the elected maturation. In primitive societies rites of passage rituals often coincide with puberty, it would seem that your society has taken that far further. Which I find fascinating."

"Father. Does that not fly in the face of your beloved Mr Darwin's theories?" asked Patty.

"No, I do not believe so. In fact, I think it would be very acceptable within the concepts of adapting to the environment. You, the female of the species, have us, males, at a constant disadvantage, as you could, after all, at any point dispense with us once we have served our limited purposes." He put the cat down on the floor and leaned forward to select a biscuit from the plate on the table. "It would make a great deal of sense as far as nature's need to safeguard the survival of a species." The automaître D' poured him a fresh cup of tea. "I believe that the vivisectionist and natural philosopher Clerval stated he believed that all the young of mammalian creatures begin life in the womb as female."

Patty laughed, "So we are the superior of the species."

Dr Spender chuckled, "Maybe the Bible got it wrong, everything we are comes not from Adam but from Eve."

"Or in my case, Lilith," joked Patty.

I know they meant no harm by that remark, nevertheless I found myself stiffen at such flippant blasphemy. Then again, where would my kind fit into that biblical narrative? It had not occurred to me until then to question it; the God that made Adam and Eve, how could he have made me? What of my race? A mistake or an act of perfecting?

I implored their advice as to what I could possibly do to alleviate my condition. I fear my maturation has been circumvented by the strictures of a culture alien to my physical nature. How do I reconcile the unreconciled aspects of my own body and soul?

We sipped our tea in silence for a few moments.

"I fear, dear Aelita," Patty reached across and held my hand. "That that is ultimately a question none of us, mere Tellurians, can aid you with. The solution lies in the knowledge of your own people. And though I hate to say so, I think your journey will not be at an end when we find them, merely the beginning of another stage. What I would not give for such an adventure, though we will happily be at your side as your companions if you should want us." She sighed most retrospectively. "In some way, my sweet Aelita, I envy you so. Would that we all could have had a chance, at some point in our lives, to make such a choice."

"A decision that was beyond me, my dear," said Dr Spender. "Though I would not change you for this world or any other."

I then felt compelled to request that though we were talking openly in this room, the subject should not be mentioned in front of the others. All readily agreed with Dr Spender adding flippantly, "If we did talk of such choices in front of the other gentlemen, it might cause a few to clutch the family jewels and flee in terror!"

I did not immediately understand his meaning, however, latterly saw the jest in it.

Journal of Adam Franklin.

It was very late in the evening by the time the Professor and Colonel Jahns returned from the city.

The Professor went directly to his cabin, and the Colonel was seen pacing the poopdeck like an angry caged animal. Sir John said he had enquired of Colonel Blowhard, as he has taken to referring to Jahns, what had caused their considerable delay and was rebuffed with more than the Colonel's customary boorishness. The dining table had been rife with speculation.

The ship's Medician had patched up Edwin well enough for him to join us for dinner, though eating onehanded was an obvious chore, he also had been cautioned to lay off the tipple. Earlier we had agreed that rather than describe the horrors of what we had witnessed at Dr Monck's house and alarm the others, we would explain Edwin's injury as nothing more than an unfortunate encounter with a couple of trigger-happy yokels.

We had retired to our shared cabin, and I was assisting Edwin into his bunk when the Professor summoned him, not by sending some crewmember or steward, but the First Mate himself. There was a concerning demeanour about Mr Charles, and that set Edwin speculating as to the reason why the Professor would wish to speak to him at this late hour. I escorted Edwin to the Professor's cabin, though with no intent other than to wait outside, but on opening the door, the Professor insisted I join them.

Though he was making a good fist of displaying that old British stiff upper lip, I could immediately tell the Professor was deeply disquieted.

Edwin, being Edwin, clearly saw the distress in his father-in-law's manner, but in his innocence, obviously had no inkling of how distraught the Professor truly was. I could see the man had shed more than a few tears and that there were much more dammed behind his resolute gaze, a whole flood. Without any preamble, he said, "Edwin, Eleanor is dead."

I moved to catch Edwin should he collapse, but he merely stood still with a look of absolute confusion on his face. Eventually, he managed to force out, "What? How?"

The Professor waved his hand at the telephonograms on his desk. "Du Maurier's man, Everheart. He got into the house. He shot her Edwin. He killed her." The distress cracked his voice. "She threw herself in the way to protect the others, Minerva and Lady Niketa."

Edwin began to make a sound the likes of which I have seldom heard before. I do not know if it was a cry of anguish or fury, but it seemed trapped behind his tongue, and he could only vocalise it as a visceral noise. He turned quite pale and leaned forward to steady himself against the chart cabinet.

I should have done something to comfort him, but I too could only stand rooted to the spot.

"The others are safe. The children, Minerva and Lady Niketa. Lenora is with them." The Professor proceeded to fetch some glasses from his draw and pour brandy for us all. *"I have sent orders that they must take the children to Maurine's house in Etidorhpa, they will be safe there."*

"I have to go. We have to go to her. I have to..." Edwin made for the door as if he could rush to his fallen wife right then and there.

"NO! No, Edwin. No. You will not go." The Professor's voice was as determined as I have ever heard it. *"We cannot abandon this mission. We cannot go back."*

Edwin looked at the Professor as if he were insane. "What? Poppycock! What are you saying, man?" Edwin's stammer disappeared as he turned and stalked forward to face the Professor. *"That's my wife! The mother of my children! I will go to her, Sir, and you and your 'mission' be damned!"*

The Professor somehow kept his resolution enough to mete out his words carefully in soft tones. "Edwin, do not attempt to weigh your loss against mine, she is my daughter. I helped bring her into this godforsaken world with my own hands. Her mother and I nursed her through a dozen life-threatening illnesses in her first years and gave her all the love we could. She is the image of her mother, in every look and mannerism; she is my child, the mother of my grandchildren. My heart is shattered into a thousand shards that pierce my very soul." He stopped for a moment to swallow and take a deep breath, "But, we will not abandon our quest, and you will remain here with me."

"NO, SIR!" Roared Edwin. "I will not!" he pounded the top of the cabinet. "My children need me. My wife needs me… I…" Edwin looked lost. "I am all they have."

The Professor reached out and put his hand on Edwin's undamaged shoulder. "No, they have Lenora, Maurine and Minerva; they will protect them until we can return. I cannot let you go."

Edwin angrily brushed the Professor's hand away. "I must…"

It was not my place to, but I felt compelled to speak. "Your father-in-law is right, Edwin. It is no doubt what Everheart did this for; to draw you two back to Tharsis City."

"Then he will get what he wishes," Edwin growled through clenched teeth. "I will kill him."

"No, Edwin." The Professor's tone was firmer now. "Edwin, you are more of a son to me than a son-in-law, you always were, long before you got up the courage to ask for Eleanor's hand. I cannot lose you as well, and I will not have my grandchildren lose their father."

"I must go to them," pleaded Edwin. "I must go home." He suddenly looked so frail and lost, shaking violently with tears streaming down his face. "Nelly needs me. The children need me."

The Professor stiffened again. I wondered how much effort he had to summon to stand there and make the right decision against everything he desired. "No, Edwin. We carry on. For all our sakes and for everyone's children. For mankind itself. We have to continue on."

Edwin sagged like a man that had been belly punched. I managed to guide him into a seat, or he would have collapsed to the floor. He was still shaking, so I quickly put my head out the door and shouted for tea.

The Professor downed his brandy and took to staring into the middle distance, repeating what was obviously a prepared oration. "Edwin. This mission is possibly the most important thing any of us will do in our lives. We have lost Nelly, but so many more lives will be lost if we fail, notwithstanding all those we love. The lunatics in Governments across this world are dragging our nations into yet another set of pointless wars. Fighting for what? Over what?" He reached over and picked up a bundle of broadsheets he must have brought in the city and dropped them on the table. "The technology, let alone the lives we are wasting on these military campaigns cannot be replaced, and that which can be replaced is at ruinous cost to us all. Resources are dwindling; the Red Seas are reclaiming the farmlands we can no longer irrigate. There were food riots in Japygia last week; the poorest cannot even afford bread to feed their children. We are descending into little more than jackals fighting over the carcass of the great beast we once slew. Without the Aresians help we will all perish here, either suffocated by the red dust, starve, or die in the act of murdering each other for a portion of bread. Maybe Friar Godfried was right; 'This is not a world to be called home, it is an altar, upon which we are to be sacrificed.' I will not stand by and sacrifice my whole family, our entire race, without attempting to find some salvation, even if that is through those we once knew as enemies.

"I, too desperately want to go back. I want to find this Everheart and wring his bloody neck myself, but I am no man of action, and neither are you. Everheart and De Maurier aim is to force us, driven by our anguish, into acting rashly, and then they will spring whatever fiendish trap they have set in wait of our return."

"I do not care if it is a trap, I would rather die trying," groaned Edwin.

I knelt beside the broken man that had been such a good friend to me and placed my hand on his arm. "I met her only once Edwin, but in that short time, she was as kind to me as any could ever be. I never saw even a flicker in her eye when she looked upon me. She was a beautiful woman, a wonderful mother to your children and," I turned my glance to the Professor, "a credit to her father and mother. We could all see how much she loved you, and you loved her, and nothing will ever erase that." Edwin began to sob deeply. "But you cannot go back, it is a trap. As they were in the house, they will be waiting for you."

"I am not a coward," Edwin whispered. "What kind of man am I if I do not avenge my wife?"

"A wise one, one that will live to see his children grow up. This is not something you can do, and she would not ask that of you, or want you to put yourself in harm's way." I stood up and addressed the Professor. "That is why you wanted me here, was it not?" He did not answer but looked away in an almost embarrassed manner. "You cannot abandon this quest, and Edwin cannot return without us all returning, and that would see you and the Colonel, and probably all of the Expedition members, crew and all, thrown into prison."

The Professor sighed and nodded, almost imperceptibly.

"Then I will go."

The Professor looked me straight in the eye. "I will not ask that of you, Mr Franklin."

"Sir, you need not request anything from me because my mind has already been set upon that course." The Sergeant Major's voice whispered something abhorrent in my ear, but I ignored it. "I made an oath to myself some time ago that whatsoever happens, I will make it my business to bring De Maurier to book for the terrors he has inflicted upon Edwin, your family, Miss Bryant-Drake's family, and all the other poor decent people that have found themselves in his way."

"I must request that you stay within the limits of the Law and see that these murderers are delivered to justice."

In my life, this one and what I can remember of my past life, I have seldom looked a man in the eye and comprehensively lied to him, let alone in full knowledge that he most certainly knew my undertaking was, in essence, a lie. Though remembering what Augustus Bravett had told us about the Laws of Tharsis pertaining to the rights of citizens to defend themselves, and laws attaining to automatons, I wondered if it was indeed a lie. "I will do what I must to see lawful justice done."

Edwin had broken down now. He was wailing and had taken to pulling at his hair and clothes. I managed to calm him enough to get him on his feet and with a steward's aid, brought him back to our cabin.

I sat Edwin at the little table on one of the small stools that creek far too alarmingly for me. I took up a position on the floor with my back against the door and allowed him to cry. Then came the anger at the Professor, born of frustration at being thwarted in his desire to return. The accusations that the Professor saw him as nothing more than a failure, not worthy of his daughter's hand, and now nothing other than a snivelling poltroon. I did not argue, forcing myself to remain stoically quiet.

Then came the self-recriminations fuelled by anger; how it was all his own fault. If only he had done this or not done that. Then the anger turned inward; they were all right. Everyone was right; he was nothing more than a craven coward. He had failed in everything he had ever done, failed his father, failed his family, failed as a father. Now he had abandoned his business and run away like a gutless milksop, leaving his wife to be murdered in his stead. He had even failed as a dandelion farmer. He looked me in the eyes and questioned who could even fail at that? Hysterical laughter degenerated into body shaking sobs.

Eventually, about dawn, through utter exhaustion, he fell asleep, and I put him to bed. I was just preparing to leave the cabin when he sat up again. "I have a request," he asked as he wiped away the tears and snot. "I have a request." he struggled a form the words. "Kill them, Adam, kill the bastards like you killed that thing in the hallway of my house. Do not leave a stone unturned. Root them out and eradicate them like the vermin they are."

I never thought I would hear such violent words from Edwin or see such loathing on his face. He clambered ungainly out of the cot and back onto his feet. "I shall pray to Almighty God that he shall judge me rather than you for what you do in my stead but show them no mercy."

I have never embraced a man with anything more than a comradely hug, but Edwin and I embraced each other with an intensity that startled me. For a moment, it was as if I felt the power of his emotions course through me.

I helped him back to bed, extinguished the lamp, and left.

On leaving, I discovered Sergeant Rawlings perched upon a stool reading a book. He had been posted outside the door at the Professor's insistence. I informed him that Edwin would probably sleep for some time now. Sergeant Rawlings told me that the Professor wished to see me first thing after breakfast. I thanked him and went to find something to drink. Something strong enough to affect.

On the way to the wardroom, I came upon Sir John having some difficulties with a group of engine crew hanging about in the corridor. I heard an exchange between Sir John and one of the crew, and the tone of their reply straightaway piqued my interest. I stepped into the shadow of a doorway to observe.

Sir John, in his usual jocular tone, but blunt manner told the crewmen not to be so insolent and to step aside. The crewmembers, of which I could only see three clearly, made snide comments amongst themselves and ignored him. I heard a woman's voice leading the mockery.

Sir John, obviously provoked by their contemptuous sneering chose to attempt to force his way past the knot of bodies. He is a fairly well-built chap, muscular and undoubtedly able to handle himself in a public-school scrum. Nonetheless, these were men, whose daily task is hard manual work. They easily frustrated his efforts. Sir John became angry now, and that is when I saw Darra Howe. He appeared out of a darkened nook like the Demon King in some amateur play. He loomed over Sir

John and growled something in a low tone I could not make out. Sir John's face flushed blood red, and I could see him barely control his compulsion to strike the man.

Howe made another remark to his workmates, and they all laughed. A stinging derisory kind of laughter. I could tell by his deportment that Sir John had had enough of their insolence. He threw the first punch, a good roundhouse, not very Queensbury; nevertheless, it would have floored most men. Unfortunately, Howe is bigger than most men, and evidently more than able to take a good knock or two. It barely rocked him. Though like a good pugilist, Sir John was fast, and the following uppercut was coming right behind the first. That too landed well. However, it had no more effect than the first.

The next thing all hell broke loose. The crewmen, of which there were probably about six in all, set upon Sir John like a pack of hounds on their quarry. I would have been willing to wait a few moments to observe the show, but my patience with this day had long run out.

The Sergeant Major had broken up a lot of brawls in his time. The first rule is never to announce your arrival. Shouting and profanity will only serve to spur the melee on. Snatching a bludgeon protruding from the back pocket of the first man I encountered, I laid into the group from behind. Two went down before the others even became aware of me. Sensing I was the real danger to them, and spurred on by the woman's angry encouragements, the rest, about four, not counting Howe, turned on me.

It probably seemed good odds to them. Nevertheless, they did not stand a chance in that confined space. I am ashamed to admit that it felt good to be hitting something. Now the Sergeant Major surfaced, shouting filthy language barely fit for the parade ground, and I lashed out.

My mind cleared to find myself face to face with Howe, who stood passively watching me.

He growled. "Yor ah hello' a fella in a fight I must say. A real 'hard-man'...but wot ar' ya like without that billy-club?"

I stood my ground and casually tossed the bludgeon aside. "Try me."

By this time, I admit I was so angry that I had no intent to hide my true nature. These men, and women, needed a lesson in manners or, more accurately, fear. Howe threw his punch, a left thrown right from the hip with all his weight behind it, which connected with my jaw.

I watched his reaction, as I did not move at all. He snarled some obscenity and threw his right. His huge ham-fist wrapped in some roughly made brass knuckle-duster, slammed into the side of my head with as much force as he could muster. I remained impassive, unmoving.

I could see the sudden alarm in his face. "Oh, for feck-sake what ar' ya?" He did not wait for my reply but threw the right again, aiming for my nose. I stopped it. Clasping his massive brass bound fist and squeezed, I cannot say hard, just enough to feel the metal give under my grip, painfully constricting his fingers in the brass contraption. There was no purpose in saying anything as his cry of pain would have drowned it out. Pulling his hand towards me, I struck him hard in the belly just below his ribcage, more to silence him than to knock him down. Nevertheless, he folded like a bedsheet.

I looked about me. The others had already fled, leaving only Sir John and I with Howe, who was crumpled at my feet. Bending over him, I snatched his beard and dragged his head up, so we were eye to eye. "What did you say? What did you say, Howe?"

Howe was in no state to reply, but Sir John elucidated. Howe had made ungentlemanly comments about the personages of the ladies, culminating in an insulting remark about Mrs Fontenelli, that he could not repeat. At that, Sir John admitted throwing the first punch.

I leaned close into Howe's face. "No more, Mr Howe. I have had a truly dreadful day today. I have killed once today. I have seen my best friend shot, and I have just been told that an innocent woman has been callously murdered. So, understand this; I would happily rip your arm clean out of its socket and watch you bleed to death for the light relief it would bring me." I squeezed his hand a little harder, "No more. Do you understand me, Mr Howe?"

He mumbled something incomprehensible; nevertheless, the appreciation was in his eyes. I told him to scarper before I broke his other hand. Together, Sir John and I watched as he staggered away back into the bowels of the ship.

"That's not the last you will hear of him. You know that of course?" said the Sergeant Major as clearly as if he were standing beside me. I knew he was right.

Sir John had taken a few hard knocks and had an excellent shiner coming. However, he seemed undaunted. Nevertheless, before we adjourned to find something to "steady the nerves," Sir John wanted to report the episode. I agreed, however on the understanding that he play the incident down. I agreed that the Captain would want Howe and his cohorts off the ship as soon as possible. Although, if he were to be dropped off, then it would have to be here.

Sir John registered his outrage at Howe's insulting behaviour and his attack upon his person, even so, though he would happily see the man flogged, he agreed he was in no mood for something tantamount to murder and dropping off anywhere but here is as good as execution.

The Sergeant Major's voice in my head favoured military-style retribution. His preferred chastisement, which he expounded at length on in the back of my mind, would have been sand hauling the offender. A savage practice the Regiment used, akin to maritime keelhauling, the practice of which often saw the offender die of their injuries if not torn to pieces. I suggested that we had not to concern the Professor but speak to the Captain after breakfast.

Sir John agreed but insisted we retire to his cabin for a stiff drink.

That is when the interrogation began, as I feared it would. Sir John was no fool, and he had been a clear witness to what had transpired between Howe and myself.

"Damn it, old chap. I saw that brute throw his best at you and you barely budged an inch. It was as if he were pummelling one of my Aunt Agatha's atlantids," (Evidently 'Aunt Agatha' has a penchant for Greco-Roman architecture.) "How on earth did you take that? There is barely a scratch on you. The blighter scarcely clocked me one, and it almost floored me."

Training, I told him. Simply training. I knew a man in my old regiment who used to do it in a music hall act. It is all to do with stance and balance. He made a fortune out of the boys in the barracks. Nobody ever knocked him down. Nothing more.

A true enough story. Lance Corporal Holton was his name. I could never work out how he did it.

Sir John refilled our glasses, but he was obviously not convinced and moved on to question me about how I crushed Howe's hand, brass knuckles, and all. I began to answer, but he cut me off. "I know, vaudevillian strong man routine. There was someone in your old regiment, et cetera, et cetera." He grinned widely.

"Yes, something like that." I agreed.

"Forgive me, old chap. I do not mean to offend you at all, and I am eternally grateful for your intercession, or I would have got quite a 'whopping,' as my chief beater would say, but, though I hope we can still remain firm friends; I do not believe a bloody word you have just told me."

We sat in silence, looking at each other for a few moments. Then he laughed heartily and refilled my glass. "Damn it, man, you are an enigma, and you wind up that old Colonel Blowhard by merely breathing, which makes you a fine chap by my reckoning. We all have our secrets, and I think there is far more to you than I certainly will ever know."

I put down my glass. "Forgive me if my justifications sound a little trite. I suffer from amnesia, brought on by the injuries I received at the battle of Alba Ponds. The Medicians dug a lot of metal out of my skull. My clear memories of before that are little more than a disjointed patchwork, fragments of recollections and impulses, my day-to-day memory is often patchy, to say the least. Sometimes it is better than others. In some ways, I am as much as an enigma to myself as I am to any other man. I have relied upon the kindness of others over the years to help me cobble together my past. Still, I have deep chasms in my memories and sporadically odd passions forcefully surface. Occasionally, abilities too. Truly, Sir? I do not know how I can do what I can do."

It was laced with enough truth to convey sufficient sincerity, if not to convince Sir John than to placate him. I began to take my leave and was almost out the door when Sir John asked, "I almost forgot, who has been 'murdered'?"

I looked back at him blankly.

"When you bearded that scrub you said that you had killed today, no doubt whoever tried to assail you in the city and injured Edwin Ransom in the act, but you also mentioned an innocent woman has been murdered? May I ask whom that is, or should I take the keening I heard emanating from the Professor's cabin as an indicator?"

I looked him in the eye. There truly is something about Sir John that I find deeply disquieting. There is a sharp edge to his musical hall bonhomie. The man does not miss a thing. The Sergeant Major's voice in my head sneered; "There's more than one bloody spy on this ship. You are going to have to kill him sometime, best be sooner rather than later." The Sergeant Major's voice was so clear I may have involuntary looked aside to see who spoke.

I turned back to Sir John. There was no need to be secretive about it, by later today the whole ship will probably know. "The man who hired the pirates, De Maurier, his gunman got into the Professor's home and murdered Eleanor Ransom."

"Dear God!" For the first time, I believe I had a glimpse of something behind Sir John's mask, something I recognised; outrage. "When are we turning back?"

"No. I am."

"Then, I will go with you."

"That will be for the Professor to decide." With that, I left.

I found myself a quiet corner of the stores to write these entries. I should not have made such a blatant display of myself in front of the crew and Sir John. It was an imprudent thing to have done. I have decided that no matter what occurrences befall us, I shall find Everheart and De Maurier and I shall kill them, and I am going to take great pleasure in it.

James Ransom.

My father did not write in his journal of that day or ever about the loss of our mother. However, he did write a letter to Tabitha and me and a message to Aunt Minerva. The contents of which my family has requested me not to include in these documents. Suffice to say, my father was almost unhinged with grief and self-recrimination, blaming all the events upon his actions and what he saw as his personal failures. Aunt Minerva read us the letter addressed to us, but never allowed us to read it for ourselves, which we only did when we came upon it in amongst her papers while researching for this folio. I feel she was indeed right in not allowing us, as small children, to have known that our beloved father was in such distress. It is true to say that the man that wrote those letters was not our father, or at least not in his rightful mind.

Tabitha and I, as adults, feel that although it was a hard choice to make, our grandfather made the correct decision in not allowing our father, or himself, to return immediately. We feel that my grandfather, understanding the need for safety, and how focusing on some grander, less personal concern, aids one in dealing with such terrible loss, was right to keep father with him and engaged upon their quest. Though it was hard for all of us left at home to understand at that time. Evidence supports Mr Franklin's assertion that it was far too dangerous for them to return to us.

We also must add at this point that what we know of the actions of Adam Franklin, Sir John Sydeian and the others were in our opinions, though beyond the legalities of any of the Martian Republics, unreservedly heroic.

I danced with a million devils.

Died from a life of sin.

Made love to a million angels.

Murdered a million men.

There will be blood.

There will be blood.

There will be blood.

There will be blood.

DEPUIS LE DEBUT

THIRTY SECONDS TO MARS

DAY ELEVEN

<u>A DISH BEST SERVED COLD</u>.

<u>THE MEFITIS HERALD</u>

DATE 40TH WEDNESDAY

TRAGIC HOUSE FIRE CLAIMS THE LIFE OF RESPECTED DOCTOR.

IN THE EARLY HOURS OF THIS MORNING, FIREFIGHTERS FROM ACROSS THE CITY VALIANTLY FOUGHT AN INFERNO THAT ENGULFED THE HOME OF RESPECTED DOCTOR, BARNSBY MONCK. THE FEROCITY OF THE FIRE LED TO THE DESTRUCTION OF SEVERAL OTHER HOUSES IN THE STREET.

DR MONCK WAS THE WIDOWED HUSBAND OF THE LATE MRS CATTARINA MONCK, PHILANTHROPIST, AND DAUGHTER OF THE INDUSTRIALIST SIR GUILLERMO DE SAMPO, WHOM HERSELF DIED TRAGICALLY EARLIER THIS YEAR.

MEFITIS MUNICIPALITY'S CHIEF FIRE MARSHALL, SAMUEL PEYTON-JONES, ANNOUNCED THAT THE FIRE BEGAN IN THE DRAWING ROOM CHIMNEY, AROUND MIDNIGHT, AND SPREAD SPEEDILY THROUGH THE HOUSE, TAKING THE LIFE OF DR MONCK AND THREE SERVANTS IN THEIR BEDS.

MEMORIAL PRAYERS WILL BE SAID AT ST. PETER'S CHAPEL, ON SUNDAY.

Charity Bryant-Drake.
Notes to self.   40/9/26.
Cont.

Edwin's wife is dead. Murdered by that monster Everheart.

The Professor told us after breakfast. She died defending her family.

I have never seen such a heart-breaking sight as that man talking of his murdered daughter. Edwin, understandably, was unable to face anyone today. We all expressed our deepest heartfelt condolences. We had many questions, but the Professor was in no fit state to answer them. Therefore, we did not pursue him other than to ask what his intentions were?

He said that it is his intention that we continue in our quest. With heavy hearts, but as one, we agreed that if that is what he and Edwin wished, we will do so.

The Professor told us that Adam had volunteered to return to Tharsis in their stead.

Sir John requested to escort Adam, and the Professor agreed, I feel more out of exhaustion than consideration.

I, myself, am heartbroken and enraged beyond reason. The more I dwell upon this outrage, the more furious I become.

I have decided to ask Patty if she will indulge me in what will be none too small a favour.

Patty and I almost had our first quarrel.

I told her what I intend to do, and she tried to dissuade me with every argument she could think of, but once my mind is set, there is no way I will change it.

After extracting from me profuse provisos and promises, she acquiesced, and I was able to enlist her and her father's assistance to persuade the Professor.

P.E.S. Seren Bore.

40/09/26

Ship's scrap log (excerpts from) Captain R. K. Llewellyn.

Mefitis.

Repairs to the ship's post-side rudder require more extensive work than anticipated.

New mountings and bearings are required. It will take most of the day to fit them.

We remain another day at our moorings in the city of Mefitis.

I have ordered Mister Charles to implement the change of identity for the ship as soon as the boatwrights have finished.

The following have been ordered and are to be double-checked and rechecked before tomorrow's morning briefing.

1. All Name Plates.
2. Official Tharsis Hull Identification Numbers (external and documentation)
3. Air Vehicle Identification Number (documentation and external).
4. Free Trader Registration Number (External) and documentation and licenses replaced.

5.   Communications crew to be assigned the new Call Signs.

6.   New Hull Class and Classification Documents to replace existing ones.

7.   All pennants numbers and pennants to be changed.

8.   New registers and logs issued.

This should keep everyone busy.

All *Seren Bore* documentation, nameplates and pennants, along with this Logbook, to be stowed away by myself.

As of 8 bells tomorrow, this ship will be the *Haul Du*.

It was reported to me by Sir John Sydeian that he was the victim of an assault on his person by several members of the engine crew. Sir John identified by name Darragh Howe as the ringleader.

I had Howe arrested by Gunnery Master Gwenllian and interviewed by Mister Charles.

Mister Charles reports that Howe admitted the attack on Sir John but refused to identify the others involved. Mister Charles will be investigating further.

I have ordered that Howe be discharged from the crew without pay and escorted off the ship immediately.

I did not consult on this decision with Professor Flammarion as he is indisposed due to a private matter.

We await further orders from the Professor regarding our departure.

A Note folded into the Logbook at this entry.

Statement written by Sally Varney, aka "Septic Sally" Coal Trimmer.

I Sally Varney. So swear thaht I am telling the truthe on the Holly Bible. I never laid a hand on Mr Sir Jon. It was a put on. Darah How paid us to do it. Five Shillin each.

He wos friends with Mr Sir Jon and there was no harm in it.

It was all a lark that's all it wos.

So help me.

Signed, *Sally Varney.* Mrs.

Dated; Wednesday 40[th]September M.Y.26.

Witness; *Joseph Charles.* 1st Mate.

Fined a Month's pay. Five strokes.

Flogging suspended by order of the Captain.

Journal of Adam Franklin.

Sir John and I met the Professor and the Colonel in the Professor's cabin after he had made his announcement at breakfast. We resolutely did not talk about the crux of what we were setting out to do, though our solemnity spoke clearly of it, we merely discussed the logistics, what we needed in the way of equipment and finances. The Professor entrusted me with a considerable amount of folding money and a small purse of pre-independence gold Sovereigns. Evidently Tharsis does not issue golden Guineas anymore after a scandal over their purity. The Colonel then gave me a thick folio of information that had been compiled on De Maurier. He warned us not to ask from where it came and cautioned us that we must destroy it before it should ever fall into anyone else's hands.

The Colonel added that he wanted to send along one of his men. If we were amenable to it? I cut Sir John's response off, by requesting that Sergeant Rawlings accompany us. I have grown to enjoy his company; he is intelligent, well read, he plays a good game of cards, has a wry sense of humour, and he is a redoubtable soldier. I have also learnt that he knows to keep his own counsel when it is required. Jahns granted that Rawlings was an excellent choice for a companion.

All agreed, we set about packing lightly and girding ourselves with whatever weapons and equipment we required. Rawlings met us in the wardroom, and I formally introduced him to Sir John, as my friend Sergeant Freddy "Red" Rawlings. I was *amused by Sir John's obvious awkwardness in that situation; being obliged to greet a man of a lower class, and a Negro to boot, as an equal. He almost blushed at the sight of Rawlings' outstretched hand, but he swallowed his 'pride' - for want of a better word – and shook Rawlings' hand firmly. Rawlings gave not a hint of sardonicism in his manner, but his eyes sparkled with enjoyment.*

I addressed them earnestly. "Gentlemen, this is a solemn task we are about. Make no mistake; I am set not upon any lofty ideals of justice, but upon revenge." They nodded their understanding. "Whilst we are off this ship, we will exist in a state of equanimity and equality. Whereas we are about this terrible bloody business and mark me, it shall be bloody. We shall be comrades." I let that sink in a little. "I am Adam." I waited until they repeated my name.

"John. I am John."

"Red, they call me Red."

I left the two of them to organise some provisions while I visited Edwin to say my farewell.

Sir John, Rawlings and I together rode the bone-shaking platform down to the ground level. Shouldering our equipment, and Sir John seemed to have brought all of his, we headed across the site to the Customs Office.

Though Sir John pointed him out, I had already noticed the looming figure of Howe, lurking near the gates to the office in the thin yellow mist. He had wrapped himself in as many layers as he could. He wore a very old filter mask, which was hardly worth the effort of wearing, and we could hear him coughing already.

Sir John came close to me and shouted. "What's he doing here?"

I asked Sergeant Rawlings the same question.

"Most probably hasn't got enough money to pay to pass the gate. If he cannot pay, they will not let him through. So, he stays here and starves until the Customs people call the Police and they take him for a vagrant, or until he begs enough money to get past the gate or finds work, or if, he is lucky, some other ship takes him on."

Sir John looked horrified, "And if not? A man who has been thrown off his last ship and has an injured hand?"

"It can take weeks sometimes, to beg or scrape together enough coins to pass the gate. I wouldn't want to be landstranded here though. Not in this clag."

As we approached the gate, Howe shifted away. His huge form wracked with bouts of coughing.

We should have walked right past him, but we did not. Sir John stopped, and so did I.

"You there, my man," shouted Sir John beckoning the big man over. "Mr Howe, is it not?"

Howe trudged forward. He looked faintly ridiculous in his inadequate clothes and tiny filter mask lost in the mass of ginger beard and hair.

"Yes." He immediately began coughing.

"You address your superior as; 'Sir.'" Rawlings warned him.

"Sire," added Howe, in a defeated tone.

"What are you doing still here?" I asked.

After another bout of coughing, Howe explained, "I haven't got the coppers ta get through th' gate. The Master had me dropped off. No pay, nothin'. Not even all me tack. Sires."

"You that brought on yourself," I observed.

"Aye, Sires. You're prob'ly right. I'm sorry, Sires. I woz awful full o' piss-an-wind an' buoyed up by Septic Sally."

"That was the woman with you?"

Howe nodded as he began coughing again. "She gets in ta your 'ead. Poisonous cow bag, she is an all."

"Sir John could have had you turned over to the Police." Rawlings pointed out, "He could have had you hanged for assaulting a Gentleman."

Howe was contrite. "I know. I'm deeply sorry, Sire John."

"Well, let this be a lesson to you, my man," said Sir John uncertainly.

The automaton guard opened the door for us, and Red made to move us away from Howe.

"Please, Sires, don't leave me 'ere. I can't breathe. Th' fug is killin' me." He coughed illustratively.

"You'll survive, Lad," Rawlings said dismissively.

"Tha damp in tha tenement got in ta my chest when I woza young 'un, Sires." pleaded Howe. "I can't breathe properly. This place will do me in." He pulled off the filter mask, coughed deeply, hawked and spat.

Against the warnings of the Sergeant Major in my head, I reached into my pocket, pulled out a couple of shillings and thrust them into Howe's undamaged hand.

"Get out of here and get yourself a respiration mask that works."

Howe thanked me profusely.

"Now be off with you," added Sir John.

We filed through the door into the Customs Office, showed our papers, paid our fee and passed through without comment. Sheepishly Howe followed us.

On the steps outside the front of the Office Howe approached us again and, through bouts of coughing, pleaded; " 'cuse me, Sires. I can't stay here. I will die."

"What do you want us to do, Howe?" I asked.

Howe looked shamefaced, well, as much of his face as I could see. "If ya'll forgive me, Sires. I 'eard of wat 'appened to the Prof's daughter. He's a good man, th' Professor, a proper right Gentleman. If ya take me wid ya, I will help."

Sir John was about to decry Howe's request, but I spoke over him. "Howe, you are a ne'er-do-well, a drunken bully. You insulted the ladies of our party, you assaulted Sir John and tried *your best with me, now you have found yourself, deservedly, dropped off here, and you are whining like a brat."*

Between bouts of coughing, he stated his case; "Sires, I 'ave never been too bright, I know. Easily led, me mother always said, but I know when I'm prop'ly beaten. Sires, if ya gives me th' chance I'll prove ta ya I'm a good fella. 'Specially in a fight, an' that's wot you're goin'lookin' for aren't ya?" After a prolonged bout of choking, he looked me in the eye again. "If ya leave me 'ere it'll be killin' me, for sure."

I was stumped for what to say in reply. Sir John began with, "Look here, my man. Just..."

"Damn it, Sir John!" Charity appeared in our midst. "The man's begging for his life, and you will not turn him away."

We all turned to her in surprise. "And what, Miss Bryant-Drake, may I ask, are you doing here?"

"Edwin is also my friend, Sir John." Charity looked from him to me and back. "I am coming with you, of course." Her brusque manner broached no opportunity for argument.

We hailed a horseless growler for the station. It was a big steam-powered contraption with capacity for all five of us and our luggage. Unfortunately, like everything in the city, it was almost as grubby on the inside as the outside. It was a challenge to find the least dirty place to perch a bottom cheek. The journey across the city was thankfully short, and, apart from the chaotic traffic and the rutted roads, uneventful. Mefitis

Central train station was, as I expected, little more than a freight depot with scarce thought given to passenger traffic.

A small, rough building, built of wrinkly tin and wooden boards, served as both ticket office and waiting room. I had noticed a hawker on the station approach selling a variety of masks of varying quality. Already tired of Howe's constant coughing I sent him to purchase the better mask I had given him the money for.

In the short time, Howe was gone, Sir John questioned me as to why I was being so beneficent to such a lout? I found I could not give him an answer that would be satisfactory to him, let alone myself. Probably the same reason I spared Hood back in Alba.

Charity observed openly that, in her opinion, for all my savage countenance and gruff manner, I am, in her words, foremost a Gentleman and a most compassionate one at that. I did not know whether to be shocked or flattered by such a summation. Sir John snorted derisively. I found myself chuckling with embarrassment at the thought of me being perceived as a Gentleman.

The train out of Mefitis was a squalid thing that made the horseless carriage appear clean by comparison. Mostly made up of freight cars, it chugged along at a snail's pace towards Ember Township.

Sir John and I spent the journey stripping down and cleaning the weapons. Out of nothing more than sentiment, I had *brought along the boarding gun. However, on closer inspection, I discovered it was far better made than I had at first envisioned. It was crude, but robust and functional being more the work of a skilled gunsmith short of time than a ham-fisted botcher as I had presumed.*

Sir John had packed his flying apparatus, an array of pistols, and the gas-powered rotation gun he incongruously named 'Betsy.' He is a solidly build fellow, but I realised by the weight of that gun, he must be a lot stronger than he appears. I could imagine that even someone of the build of Howe would need every ounce of strength to wield it and hang on when firing it. Lugging it about though was beneath him, he had already requisitioned Howe as his batman. Howe though seemed happy to fall into the role.

Charity produced, much to our surprise, out of her carpetbag, one of Aelita Fontenelli's Odic pistols.

They are fearsome looking things, somewhat resembling a hatchet head with an offset pistol grip. Set in the body of the weapon is a thick glass orb full of some shimmering lime-tinted liquescent material, through which the charge travels. The result, as I had seen during the deck practices, is impressive.

Sir John pointed out Mrs Fontenelli had almost disintegrated one of the corsairs with it back at the tomb. Charity explained that Aelita and Parthena had decided that if she were going to join our venture, she would require something better than her father's old Eliminator pistol. Sir John spent a while showing her how to charge and discharge the weapon quickly. Aelita had furnished Charity with ten charges, which Sir John calculated would give it about sixty discharges.

Charity explained that Aelita could not forgive herself for killing another human being. She has vowed never so much as to touch a weapon again. At that, Charity produced the Odic's twin from the carpetbag on her lap, along with its holster and belt, and handed it to me.

"Aelita wants you to have the other one. She says at least they should be in the hands of those who will make proper use of them."

I caught a brief look of disappointment cross Sir John's face; nevertheless, for reasons I would rather not elucidate upon, I did not decline and offer him the weapon but readily accepted it. "She asks that they only be used in our defence, of course."

"Of course," I repeated.

For my part, I produced the bundle of papers the Professor had entrusted to me and handed them to Charity.

"What's this?" she asked in surprise.

"I surmise; everything you ever wanted."

I watched her face carefully as she quizzically untied the bundle and began to sort through it. After a few moments, she lifted her gaze to mine, her green eyes sparkling. "Where did you get this?"

"Ah there! We are not at liberty to say," replied Sir John, with a wink.

"Jahns!" she smiled triumphantly. "That old fox!"

"I cannot say," I replied. "But if anyone can make head or tail of that lot, it would be you."

She looked delighted. "Can I use this," she patted the bundle. "In my article? I could expose the bastard for what he is. In God's name, I could bury him!"

"No, Miss Bryant-Drake, I am sorry, but you cannot publish anything you read in that bundle," interjected Sir John.

I felt sorry for having to deny her this victory when it seemed finally in her grasp. "Charity, after we have finished in this task, I doubt there will be any need to publish anything you find in there. I must explain to you; I have no intention of bringing Everheart or De Maurier to any lawful justice."

She looked at me both confused and alarmed. "Then what?"

"We are going to kill them," Sir John said matter-of-factly.

"Both of them," I added. "And anyone foolish enough to get in our way."

Her expression changed from disappointed to quizzical. "Then why show me this?"

"Now that is a good question," mumbled Sir John.

"You are a journalist; you are experienced at finding out the where's, what's and why's. See if you can fathom out from all that information where we will find De Maurier. You see, John here is a hunter of animals, and I and Red, we are just soldiers, but you are far more experienced at hunting facts than people."

"I thought we were going to Tharsis, to Professor Flammarion's house?"

I shook my head. "No, that will be a waste of time. We are going directly after De Maurier."

Sir John sat up. "Of course, you are right. Damn good move! If we go straight for the King, then he will have to pull back all his pieces to protect himself."

Charity looked concerned. "But he will know you are coming for him."

"Good, that is exactly what I want. I only just flicked through those papers, but even that was enough to make me realise De Maurier has eyes and ears all over the place. If we start knocking on doors and throwing our weight around a little, it will get back to him very fast."

They murmured agreement.

"We are going to arrive at about 9 o'clock. See if you can find anyone connected to De Maurier in Ember, that we can pay a little visit to."

"Beat the bushes a bit," said Sir John. "See what we can flush out."

Charity spent the rest of the journey rummaging through the papers with great relish. She enlisted all of us to hold various sections of the file and took copious notes. As she scoured *every sentence of every report, she shared what she discovered in those pages about the ruthless little Zephyrian Fuel Magnate.*

Most gods throw dice, but Fate plays chess,

and you don't find out 'til too late that he's been playing with

two queens all along.

TERRY PRATCHETT

DAY TWELVE.
<u>THE STORY OF TWO QUEENS.</u>

Charity Bryant-Drake.

41/9/26.

The Story of Two Queens.

Adam Franklin insisted I should not make a record in any details of what we had embarked upon, as such a document could easily be used, not only against ourselves, but also against the Professor and Edwin, and so, because I know well the effects he fears, I agreed. I shall continue to make my notes in the 'short writing' script my mother taught me. It falls to me now, to create a completed record of what happened, to the best of my knowledge and recollection.

I will try not to bore you with the intricate details of our journey, and I will admit to not disclosing the identities of some of the people that aided us along the way.

I noticed that Adam Franklin often appeared distracted, or should I say, lost in thought. There was an air of reflection about him, a darkening melancholy that I had not seen since we set foot upon the airship or at least until his outrage at Colonel Jahns. I understood this was no leisurely pursuit he had set out upon and, as for us, we were little more than baggage carriers and guides. It amused me to think of Sir John Sydeian cast in such a role.

Journal of Adam Franklin.

Editor's Note.

These following excerpts were written in a strange hybrid text, which appears to be an amalgam of the Celestial Alphabets thought to have been created by Heinrich Cornelius Agrippa in the early 16th C. and other letters later identified as Malacandrian 5B and 5Q.

With the aid of Robert P Uprichard, Professor of Ancient Linguistics at the University College Cardiff, we were able to decipher roughly 96 percent of the text.

Professor Uprichard suggested that this 'language' might have been the cypher used as a basis for the coding utilised to imprint on the victims of the experimentations. It may not have been anything more than a machine code, a type of computational language, and this would explain Mr Franklin's original use of such a script – though we do not have any examples of the earlier writings.

What is surprising is that Mr Franklin retained the ability to read and write fluently in what can only be described as a lost ancient script.

James Ransom.

It feels duplicitous to be writing this journal after requesting that the others, especially Charity, should not keep any recording of our exploits. Nevertheless, I feel compelled to write. It aids me in reasoning as if writing down the thoughts that flit about inside my head was akin to pinning butterflies.

I need to do this, so I write in this script. It is as effortless to me as writing in English, easier even, but the letters on the page, left like the trail of a spider drunk on Indian ink, remain alien to me. It is as if I were wearing a pair of spectacles on the bridge of my nose as the Professor does, and that with only the smallest raise of my head suddenly the text is comprehensible. On the other hand, is it that I can bring to bear some other part of my cognizance?

My mind is troubled to the point of enervation. I have given my word to Edwin, something, I hasten to add, I did with *complete conviction and determined resolve, but I now find my thoughts are plagued with a myriad of anxieties.*

After I had made my assurances, Edwin went back to bed like a confused kinchin awoken in the small hours by some frightful nightmare. I placed his spectacles upon the small folding table and brushed itinerant hair, wet with tears, from his forehead, soothing him like a child.

Throughout my preparations, I had been lost in thoughts of Nelly Ransom and Cattarina Monck. Anguish was building inside of me, churning, boiling slowly into a rage I did not know if I could control. These beautiful young women, intelligent, kind, caring, wives and daughters, one a mother. Symbols of everything that remains good and decent on this bloody dust ball of a planet, slaughtered and desecrated, for what; the machinations of turgid yaldsons not fit to lick their boots. In addition, at the behest of whom? Lanulos. At the back of all this is he. That vile little yellow-bellied arsemonger. I had his stink in my nostrils, and I smell him still.

Moreover, I? What part had I played in their misery and deaths? Was it I that brought this horror down upon them? Upon Edwin and his family? Is this all just some price exacted by Lanulos for Edwin aiding me?

The rational part of my mind countered with the facts that Du Maurier and Edwin were on a collision course like two runaway locomotives long before I knew him. He had even met Everheart the previous day. Cattarina Monck was dying long before I met Edwin, possibly before I even awoke upon that operating table.

Yet I feel guilty. Guiltier than ever.

Lloyds' words screamed through my head as if giving voice to the insanity itself. "Us, dear chap. Us. You and me. All the rest is but chaff in the wind, merely smoke and mirrors." What did he mean? And then there is Monck's claims that he was told we were coming weeks ago, before Edwin and I ever met.

Then there is Lanulos' mocking words ringing in my ears as he tossed those damn little cards at me; "Here is Adam Franklin. Your memories. Everything you are. Your program. Your soul. "He had been trying to confuse me with lies. It must be lies. I had a life. I had a family. I had a wife.

That thought stopped me dead in my tracks. I had a wife.

The Sergeant Major's presence burst upon me, like an angry bear escaping from a closet. Emphatically assuring me, he had a wife. Not me. His. Not mine.

Like a lunatic, I found myself arguing with the ghost in my head. He had been obscuring things from me. What else had he been hiding? I demanded he let me know, but at every point, he blocked me, his presence driven by anger...and something else, fear. I wanted to know. I demanded to know. These were my memories too. My life.

Suddenly I felt something giving way like a headache lifting, or the haze from your eyes when you step out into the sun. I am Sergeant Major Adam Franklin, and he is I, whether we both *accept that or not. We are one. His past is my past, and my future is his future. I have thought of him as nothing more than a ghost of a maniac haunting my skull; nevertheless, we are still the same person. Circumstances change, experience changes us, death changed us, but we remain fundamentally who we are, our nature unchanged. This above all; to thine own self be true.*

Nevertheless, he has been lying to me, and I have been denying him.

Sergeant Major Franklin was wrought by the world he was born into. Cold hardened steel hammered into a merciless killer of Her Imperial Majesty's enemies. Every spark of humanity within him suffocated under layers of duty, obligation, honour, and ceaseless brutality. Almost but not quite. There were things he kept hidden, memories of things he guarded so jealously that even death could not make him give them up.

Sergeant Major Franklin had loved. I had accepted it readily that he had been all those things I am not, and he had let me believe that. That was a lie; he had hoodwinked me.

I pushed further, beyond the fog of his obfuscations, all that sound and fury, but signifying nothing. He withdrew, fleeing into the brume, like a ghost.

I chased him down through a fog-filled nightmare world of half recalled memories. A semi-occluded dreamscape wherein dark corners of our mind fearful phantoms lurked. Memories, too awful to contemplate, cast out like demons beyond the pale, moved in the darkness beyond the reach of rational thought. I pursued him onward through this weird dream world, with its bizarre mishmash of reality and delusions, until I cornered him.

In the Wool, Stone and Craft tavern, spitting distance from the walls of the Presidio. A rowdy night, full of drunken laughter and bravado. He sat in a corner snug, his usual place, nursing a pint pot, with his back to the wall. Eyelids half-closed in a feigned doze, but beneath them, his eyes darted about.

I drew up a stall and sat opposite him at the crude wooden table.

"I didn't invite you to sit."

"You did not invite me at all."

His eyes opened. "Leave it out. I'm not interested. We, I, should have died in that crash, or drowned in the bog."

"Oh, stop the self-pitying bullshit. What are you hiding from me?" I kept on and on. Each repeat was like a stab at him. "I will know, eventually. What are you hiding from me?"

The noisy barroom faded around us.

"It's not your business. It was my life, not yours. My life does not belong to you. You think you are me?" He laughed bitterly. "I died thirty years ago, and my life died with me. They resurrected you, but you are not me. You're just a husk of something I used to be. A reanimated corpse. No, not even that. An automaton in a badly stitched meat suit. You got my face, what's left of it, but you'll get nothing more."

I noticed there was a notebook on the table between us. Had it been there before, I did not know. As soon as I saw it, he snatched at it, but I was quicker.

Only it was bigger and heavier than I thought, not a notebook, a tome. Leather bound with gold embossing. The name on the spine was "Pandora."

I looked up, and he was standing over me, his eyes wide with fear. "No, please, it's all I got left."

I ran my fingers over the embossed name. "Do you know why it was hope that was left in Pandora's Box?" Of course, he did, but I told him anyway. "Why was hope trapped in there with all those other horrors? Because the Greeks believed that hope was one of humanity's most damning delusions. The thing we hold on to when all logic and reason tells us to let go."

He grimaced as if I had touched a raw nerve.

I opened the book.

I awoke in the carriage with the others. I must have dozed off, my head bumping rhythmically against the grimy windowpane. Charity was still combing through the papers we had given her, scribbling urgently in her notebook. Sir John was providing his own unique brand of assistance to her, which often appeared as much a hindrance as anything. Howe was asleep on the floor his long body forming a barrier down the length of the small compartment. Red had dozed off reading a battered copy of Melville's Moby-Dick.

I feared we were running late. We would miss the connection and lose a day sitting around in Ember.

I looked at my pocket watch. Battered and old now, the glass on the face cracked badly, a miracle it still even worked, but it was my watch. The one I had taken to my watery grave with me. The one Mary brought me when I was promoted to Sergeant Major.

It was all there now.

Mary and the children. A lifetime of memories.

Like Red, my mother was a schoolmistress. She taught me not only to read but also to read well. "Proper books," she called them, not just the Bible, but Bronte, Thackeray, Bentham, Goethe, even Cervantes. We even read Greek philosophy and books on thought. She took me to the theatre to see plays; Shakespeare, Marlow, Greene's ridiculous play about the necromancers. Once even to the opera. That cost almost a month's wages.

My father was a more practical man, an overseer in the engineering works, building boilers for steam locomotives and airships. Not uneducated himself, but his interest was music and a passion for choral singing. The little house I was brought up in was full of books and singing. We were the only house in our street to have a piano.

My father lost his position for joining a Union, which almost broke him, and it took years for him to get a proper job again.

As an idealistic young man, I used to write romantic poetry. I wrote poetry to my wife, all through our courting, and long rambling letters when I was on campaign, with love poems and songs. I loved my wife. Oh God, I loved her, she was everything to me. Mary was a schoolmistress in the barracks, where my mother had once been Headmistress, she had bright green eyes, auburn tresses, and skin the colour of milk. Not unlike Cattarina Monck. A kind beautiful girl, a gentle spirit, with a ready smile and infectious laughter.

I could see her now, clearly. The arch of her neck, the way her eyes crinkled when she smiled. The shape of her body against the glow of the fireplace. The smell of her perfume. The warmth of her skin against mine. The roundness of her belly when she was carrying the boys. Twin boys. Fine, strong, healthy baby boys; Alfred and Arthur, King's names, and then little Percy, after her favourite Poet, he looked so much like his mother.

Those were good times. I did well in the Army. The Regiment becomes your life. Men defined themselves by it. I loved it, but I hated war. I hated it with all my heart, pointless waste of life, but soldiering was what I was good at. We did not give a damn for the Queen Empress, or the whole bloody Empire. Nor did I care if Mars was free or not, or whether the Aresians were good or bad. I loved my family, my Mary, my children, and I cared for my lads. Therefore, I just got on with it.

That was until some bastard anarchists threw grenades into the crowds watching the Christmas parade through Tharsis. They told us it was Thylian agents, but it was probably Red Handers no doubt.

I was not there. The regiment was in the forests of Etidorhpa chasing Spookers and Thylian irregulars around and around the frigging maypole. Mary and the boys, even little Percy, who was still no more than a kinchin, were there. Mary had taken them to wave little flags at the Viceroy's coach as it sped by, oblivious to their existence.

Even the bomb-throwers were oblivious to their existence.

It was not a serious attempt to harm the Viceroy. They intended only to murder and maim indiscriminately, without reason or care, to spread terror on the streets and splash blood and mayhem across the headlines of the broadsheets. They succeeded.

It is strange how a single telegraph, a few words on ticker tape stuck on to a piece of card, can utterly crush a man's soul. Strip away everything a man values from him, and either he will crumble to dust like a burnt-out hulk consumed by the hole inside him, or he will fill that gulf within himself with rage. Then he will become far more dangerous because he has nothing more to lose, and when death itself holds no fear, a man is free to become a monster.

The ghost of the Sergeant Major that I encountered in my head was that man. The Adam Franklin that plunged into that burning icy bog two years later had been insane with grief. A murderous savage form of grief that consumes a man from within. I had no mercy in me, only an all-consuming hatred. The papers told us it was anarchists in the pay of the Thylians, and we were fighting Thylians. Thylians had blown my life apart, and I stamped out my bloody revenge on their screaming faces, and anybody and anything that our officers told me was our enemy.

Even my lads became afeared of me.

So it was that the Sergeant Major was holding on to, the thing he was hiding from me. That underneath all that fury was nothing but a fathomless pit of pain, self-recrimination and shame.

I felt uncomfortable now as if I had intruded upon someone else's private grief, though it was mine also. Part of me had been expecting his presence to evaporate once I had fully recovered my memories. Yet he remains, brooding in the back of my mind, like a sulking kinchin. We have to make peace somehow, he and I, or at least come to an understanding.

Charity Bryant-Drake.
41/9/26.

The Story of Two Queens.

Cont.

I pawed over the contents of the file Adam gave me like an excited child. My mind was a churning mixture of a dozen different emotions. Jahns, and I knew it had to be Jahns, or the people he works for, had amassed all this information and done nothing. As D Maurier has left a trail of murder and bribery across the world, they just stood by and catalogued it all! And what a catalogue it is! There were so many other names here too; Volpone, Lenox, Edgars, D Sampo, Hudor-Genone and others that I do not know or have only vaguely heard of.

Buried deep in the documents was a transcript of a short Meucci telephonic conversation between D Maurier and Edgars, in it 'Camarilla' was mentioned twice. It is odd how a simple word on a page can make your blood run cold. The notes scribbled in the margin suggested to me that the transcribers had made the mistake of thinking it was a woman's name. I tried to explain to the others what I remember from the history my stepfather taught me, and what that word implied; a cabal, a clique, by inference; a conspiracy.

I have always thought that, when all was said and done, D Maurier was just a vicious avaristic mountebank, but if he is part of some cabal, then I fear Edgars, Volpone and the rest are working together towards some joint aim.

After several hours of thumbing through the papers, referencing and cross-referencing the threads of evidence I could pick at, I put forward my deduction that this "Camarilla" was not a person at all but a group, an organised group of like-minded tycoons, working together. For what, other than accumulating wealth and power, I did not know. It left me with one central unanswered question. Edgars, Volpone and the likes of Hudor-Genone were, though notoriously avaricious, well known for being obsessional recluses. What would lure these men into joining forces?

Sir John thought my talk of conspiracies and a secret cabal fanciful, suggesting instead it was probably just an old boys club for the kind of megalomaniacs no decent gentleman's club would allow through their doors. A kind of 'Black Balls' club, where they could turn up in their best shadowy cloaks and sit around twiddling their oversized waxed moustaches like some music hall scoundrels.

I did not know whether to laugh along with him or be outright furious at his dismissive manner.

Adam was not so dismissive; he told me that was something the Professor had talked of when we were at Lockley Hall. He explained that the Professor, like my stepfather and many others, held some deep fears over the power and wealth such magnates are amassing about themselves.

Charity Bryant-Drake.
42/9/26.

We reached Ember on the morning of Thursday, 42nd at 3.30 AM, almost five hours late! Adam was grievously annoyed. Our passage had been so slow that we had missed our connecting train to Yuma, and it would have meant a day's sojourn in yet another shoddy little mining town, something none of us looked forward to.

I had already established that, as far as I could see, D Maurier had no known connections to Ember. There probably were some associates here, but Yuma, and Alba, both seemed a much better bet.

With all the pomposity and haughtiness of Colonel Jahns himself, Sir John berated the Station Master and Porters and had the Station Master roused from his bed to open the waiting room for us immediately.

I obtained a train timetable from the ticket office, and we sat in the station's little tearoom drinking coffee and eating stale little fancies, as we pawed over the tiny print of the charts in the vain hope of discovering a faster way of getting to Yuma earlier than the evening's train would deliver us. Time was of the essence.

Sir John, who had been smoking feverishly, fell uncharacteristically quiet for a while before suddenly quaffing his tea, extinguishing his Flor de Dindigul, and excusing himself. "I shall be back in a bit," he shouted before disappearing out the door into the glow of the dawn.

Red suggested that it might be quicker to hire an emancipator or some such, and drive to Yuma, rather than sit about waiting. It was an honest suggestion; however, Mr Franklin felt that Red did not grasp the distances involved. If we set off immediately in an emancipator, we would barely get halfway before tonight's train overtook us.

I was proposing, for the fourth time, we take the next train to Baily Township and connect with the 2 PM train to Yuma from there when suddenly Sir John reappeared in high spirits.

"I say! Come on you lot. We are in luck!" He dashed in, grabbed his duffle bag, and dashed out again.

Bemused, we followed him into the street where a large Gurney awaited us. "No time to lose. Hurry up, man!" He shouted at Howe, who was struggling to manage with the rest of the baggage single-handedly.

Once we were all in the carriage, Adam enquired as to what solution he had come up with. Sir John seemed thoroughly excited, but all he would say is, "Trust me, dear chap."

Adam's expression though was anything but trustful. "John," he snapped curtly. "What is going on?"

Sir John flinched a little. "Well, we cannot stay here twiddling our thumbs for an entire day, and even if we had made the Old Bull (referring to the great Asterion 'Touro' locomotives, that resemble titanic fire breathing black bulls), we would not get to Yuma until sometime late tomorrow afternoon."

"So?" probed Adam.

Sir John ignored him, "Ah, here we are!" The Gurney stopped, and he leapt out of the vehicle. "There you are!"

"Wot's that?" asked Howe incredulously.

We had disembarked by the railings of what appeared to be a small landing field. On the other side was a dirigible or at least, I assumed it was some form of 'dirigible,' but of a most unusual configuration. It had an airship's body, with an integral cabin, but with wings, enormous double aerofoil extensions on either side, upon which were mounted giant propellers. To my inexperienced eye, it looked like a biplane had swallowed a blimp. The whole thing had the look of something cobbled together out of ill-fitting parts. My heart sank under the weight of the dread that Sir John intended us to get on that thing.

We followed Sir John along to the gates and then back towards the aerostat, stopping at a point that we could regard the thing in its entirety. "The Queen of the Skies!" He announced proudly. "Beautiful, is she not?"

It was anything but. "Will it fly?" I asked incredulously.

Sir John looked at me disbelievingly; "Of course she flies! Damn fast too." He then proceeded to regale us with a lot of flimflam about the power of the engines and the aerodynamics of the something-or-other. I must admit I did not bother to pay any more attention than I had done to Mr Ransom's overly detailed elucidations on the complexities of the dandelion fuelled internalised combustion engines on the Railplane. Finally, Sir John pulled his exquisite half-hunter out of his waistcoat pocket and checked the time. "If we can be off the ground within the next hour, I wager we will make Alba first thing in the morning, long before the Old Bull we just missed."

"Are you sure?" asked Adam.

"She has been running proscribed goods across the border into the Planes for the last five years. Never been caught up with."

"Proscribed goods'?" I queried, "You mean contraband for the black market."

"Smugglers?" Adam raised an eyebrow.

"They like to think of themselves more as Free Traders. I know the Captain well. I've used her services several times in the past when I have needed to get back across the border smartish."

"I thought we were heading for Yuma?" The thought of a day or more travelling in a smelly and cramped train carriage took on an almost romantic charm by comparison.

"Only to make a connection. We stand a better chance of beating something worthwhile out of the bushes in Alba than Yuma."

Of course, Sir John was right. I had already gleaned several names and locations in Alba from the file, but only two in Yuma. Nevertheless, my instincts told me that Yuma was important, and I usually go with my instincts. I turned Adam aside and told him all my journalistic instincts made me believe Yuma would turn out to be important.

He appeared to consider what I said carefully. "If we could afford the time, I would investigate Yuma. I may be wrong; nevertheless, I think that whatever we find in there is going to lead us back to Alba. If John is right and that thing can get us there much faster than the train, we will steal more than a day or two's march on D Maurier; we might just catch him with his breaches down."

The Queen of the Skies had been grounded on its very own landing gear, and as we approached, the Captain descended a flight of steps to meet us. I shall call her Captain Marie Rampallion* – though, of course not her name.

*Editor's Note.

After extensive research, we are able to confirm the identity of the Captain of the aerostat was Maëlle Louise Rambeau, we have edited the following entries to avoid the reader's confusion.

James Ransom.

She was tall, almost as tall as Adam, with an olive complexion and sparkling dark eyes, strong jaw, and full lips. Her thick dark reddish-brown tresses cascaded wildly over her shoulders down to the middle of her back. I have heard of female smuggler Captains, even female Sky Pirates, but I did not expect one to be as young or as beautiful. She carried herself with a confident bearing that matched any man of her station, and dressed accordingly, in breeches, boots and a long heavily braided military coat. John introduced us all, but before she replied, her eyes searched our faces intently as if examining us for something. She spoke with a heavy accent that I took for French, but learnt later was Walloon in origin, after quite a lecture on her vociferous hatred of all things Zephyrian.

By the raillery that issued upon our boarding the ship, the mainly female crew seemed, save one or two, to be either delighted or appalled by Sir John's arrival.

I caught a whispered warning from Adam to Howe, cautioning him on his prospective behaviour while we were guests upon the ship. Howe looked somewhat amazed at the situation he

319

found himself in, especially as some of the women were not too shy or furtive in their comments on his size and physique. I do believe I saw him blush like a schoolboy at one lewd remark and a none too playful hand that slapped his posterior as he passed.

Adam though was met by silent stares. I could not decide whether it was hostility or astonishment. I have known him for a while now, and it is right to say that as you get to know someone, you begin to see beyond the surface detail. Patty's tattoos quite amazed me when she first showed me them, but now, because they are so much a part of her identity, I hardly notice them. I can say the same for Adam. If I were called upon to describe him it would not be the disfigurement of his facial scars that would immediately spring to mind, it would be his handsome bearing, thick hair and the kindness in his eyes, but for those on board the airship, his physical appearance was understandably quite a shock.

The Queen of the Skies insides was a cramped maze of pierced metal gantries and ladders. The accommodation was rudimentary at best and shared with the massive engine's gears and pistons which dominated the central aisle of the ship. The twelve or so crew sleeping in nooks amidst the cargo or in hammocks hung anywhere they could find space. The Captain informed us she slept on a bed on the flight deck floor. They all lived on army-style field rations when on a "run," as they termed it, and ate and drank at their posts. She warned us all while directing her gaze at me; this would be a swift journey but not a comfortable one.

I assured her I was not unused to a little minor discomfort. At that, she laughed heartily and told us we would have to billet down wherever we could find a space. Sir John suggested he too would be well settled on the flight deck floor, but Captain Rambeau laughingly disavowed him of the notion.

I found myself easily won over by her sass and her sardonic wit, which she exercised freely at Sir John's expense. He, for his part, managed to hold his own while maintaining a level of courteous deference. It was easy enough for me to see that these two were old sparring partners, at the least, and most probably more.

After a final cargo arrival had been stowed, we set off.

I remember the journey on the Queen as one of the most intolerable I have ever experienced. It was noisy, smelly, fume-filled and cramped. We spent most of our time on the flight deck, where it was freezing, huddled in as many layers as we could manage or in the main body of the ship where we could share the warmth of the engine, but at the torment of all our other senses. The toileting facilities, or lack of, do not bear even mentioning. The only thing we had to sustain us for the length of the journey was copious mugs of "tea," or more accurately; a steaming hot, heavily sweetened beverage that bore scant resemblance to anything I ever drank before or since, that and the promise of a hearty breakfast when we reached Alba.

The Queen of the Skies was every bit as fast as Sir John had reported, but this appeared to be at the expense of any semblance of stability. Rather than fly, the ship seemed to hurtle through the air. I had visited the flight deck of the Seren Bore a few times, and once or twice, as a child, invited on to others. They were always oases of calm professionalism. The flight deck of the Queen was nothing of the sort. My mother likened such things to flying by the seat of your breeches, and that is precisely what Captain Rambeau and her crew seemed to do, though, of course, they knew exactly what they were doing. At least I prayed they did.

The dirigible yawed, rolled, and plunged onward at an increasingly breakneck speed. The whole journey was quite the most alarming ride I have ever endured, including the storm we suffered on the Seren Bore.

Sir John explained that the engine was overly powerful for the craft, what was gained in speed was lost in stability, hence the addition of the wings, but the lack of inherent stability meant that there was a constant struggle to control the ship. He likened it to wrestling a bear while riding a bicycle.

I hung on to the most securely attached apparatus for dear life and watched in amazement as Captain Rambeau managed this incredible feat of balance. Not only did she do it well, but she also undoubtedly revelled in it. I too felt swept up in the euphoric rush, but not enough to let go. Patty would have delighted in it.

I would like to say that after a short while, the journey settled down, but it did not. However, I think one can learn to tolerate anything given long enough exposure. Thankfully, I am not one given to bouts of naupathia. I found that with one hand always firmly gripping something bolted down, I could shuffle about the ship.

I felt it prudent not to enquire what cargo the ship was transporting, but I gathered through a little judicious eavesdropping on the crew's remarks that the Queen of the Skies was carrying tobacco and tea, as well as various illegal nostrums and nepenthes to the black marketeers of Alba.

We had been in "flight" for a couple of hours when, while making my way back from the toileting "facilities," I came upon Sir John and three of the off-duty crew members in a secluded corner, giggling like naughty children, passing a bottle of Zephyrian Cognac, and sharing a corn-cob pipe between them. I was surprised, as I had barely seen him without a cigar in his hand since we left Mefitis.

Sir John was unperturbed that I had discovered him so indisposed and, with languid movements and hooded eyes, he offered the pipe to me, suggesting I might indulge in a "toke" of it.

For the life of me, I have no idea why, but I joined them, sitting amidst the crates of untaxed tea, slurping contraband liquor, and smoking some weirdly euphoric blend of tobacco and herbage, like some rough stevedore.

I have partaken of such things before, and Patty has her "little reticule bag of delights," a positive pharmacopoeia, but this was far stronger than anything I had ever dabbled with. As soon as the first wave hit me, I realised that if I were not circumspect in my participation, I would quickly become as indisposed as Sir John.

I cannot recollect it as a coherent conversation, and I fear that after a couple of hours of smoking and drinking the keen edge of my journalistic mind had been somewhat dulled. However, I did learn quite a lot from the various crew members that joined and left our little cluster.

I learnt from the crew:

That Captain Rambeau was one of a collective of smuggler Captains that had long ago bought off the customs officials of Ember.

That Ember was the main staging post for smugglers operating in and out of the Chaos and the Sirenum Plains.

In Tharsis, the main profit was to be made on untaxed merchandise, common commodities such as tea, coffee, sugar, salt, tobacco, and alcohol in its various forms.

That there were three crates of Aresian artefacts onboard destined for non-too-scrupulous auction houses in Alba and Tharsis City, and that that money would eventually find its way to buy weapons for the fight against the Zephyrian and Thylian forces on the Sirenum Plains.

Captain Rambeau apparently had strong ties to the "Sirens," a band of female guerrillas based in the south of the Chaos. As the evening wore on, I also learnt that she had stronger ties (of the past relationship variety) to Sir John.

Emboldened by the intoxicants, Sir John was happy to elucidate.

Maëlle Rambeau's father, Robur, had designed and built the Queen and had been its first Captain, but when he died, the ruthless First Mate, Alexandre LeRoi, a lout that would have made even Howe look small in comparison, seized the Captaincy, in a coup d'état against the crew's elected candidate, Marie's older brother, Jacques Eliacin.

No one would say what happened to Captain Jacques.

The crew had finally elected Maëlle Rambeau to the position of Captain only after the vacancy arose due to Sir John having killed Captain LeRoi. Sir John fought him in a duel over his treatment of one of the female crewmembers. Evidently Sir John had paid passage on the ship out of the Plains, for some reason that he avoided clarifying, and was appalled by the Captain's manner. "A mean spirited, violent, drunken cur," was the mildest evaluation offered by the crew members of the previous Captain's nature, along with a lot of stories that would have compelled even one as kind-hearted as Aelita Fontenelli to wish the man ill. Sir John challenged LeRoi to a duel. With cutlasses on the port side wing. Which evidently is a tradition.

Sir John was happy to let the crew furnish the details. Least to say, as I expected, the loathsome bully of a Captain did not stand a chance against Sir John Sydeian in a fight, fair or otherwise. Sir John chortled his way through the story dropping in at the end with some vague remark about one should never bring a cutlass to a gunfight. Some suggested it was more Sir John's interest in Maëlle Rambeau that spurred him into action than moral outrage. Sir John laughed extravagantly and protested insincerely that his motives for dispatching the brute were absolutely morally pure. Like scolding sisters, the women openly mocked him as he feigned protestations with a wide grin on his face. I was left in no doubt that Sir John is in every way as dangerous as he is rakishly charming.

Other incidental tip bits I gleaned from conversations were little more than 'scuttlebutt,' an excellent term I picked up from the crew.

Except for one remark that caught my ear.

Just before Adam joined us, a member of the crew, unfortunately, due to my intoxicated state, I cannot for the life of me remember precisely whom, mentioned that there was another "special cargo," on board destined to be collected by the agent of a private buyer.

An artefact, evidently so highly unusual that it had "spooked her and her mates out." Probably because I was mildly inebriated, I asked boldly what could possibly frighten such women. I did not get much in the way of a clear answer other than it was hideous and that it was big enough to require several people to move it. It was only the considerable amount that they were being paid that prevented some of the more superstitious crew from dumping it overboard.

Adam joined us for a short while. Though he refused the pipe, he took a long draft from the third or fourth bottle being passed about. He had come to remind us that if possible, we should get some sleep, as we would have no time for resting when we arrived at Alba.

I took that as my prompt to leave the group and take up the offer of a hammock one of the crew said was free for the length of its occupant's duty. However, before doing so, I managed to speak to Adam in private before he returned to the flight deck. I told him of the "special cargo" and, no doubt jumping to conclusions on little evidence and fuelled by the intoxicants, I suggested possibly the private buyer could be an agent of D Maurier. After all, he was a fanatical collector with ties to Alba and black-market smugglers. Adam seemed sceptical at first, but I argued that who else had the wherewithal, associates and the financial resources to buy such a thing? Let alone pay for the movement of a large stolen artefact?

Adam looked me in the eye and assured me he would ask the Captain. If it sounded promising, then we would see who comes to collect it. I also told him of how Maëlle Rambeau became Captain. He did not seem surprised, only replying that there was a lot about Sir John Sydeian that required careful consideration.

After struggling into the hammock and finally getting comfortable, I hardly had got off to sleep when Red suddenly awakened me shaking my arm.

"You should see this, Miss," he said. He led me through the yawing ship and down a couple of ladders and to a separate hold at the rear of the craft. Finally, I stepped through a bulkhead door into a dark storeroom to discover Adam, Sir John, Captain Rambeau and Howe, gathered around a large crate. The swinging oil lamps they held threw eerie shadows over the stacks of packing chests, bales and boxes that surrounded them.

The lid was off the crate, and there was packing straw, wood wool and rags piled on the floor next to it. As I entered Adam spoke, "Miss Bryant-Drake is the stepdaughter of the renowned antiquarian, and expert in Aresian art and artefacts, Dr Commie."

"Cromie," I corrected him.

He apologised and continued. "Charity, I wonder if you can throw any light on this?" He lifted his lamp over the crate to illuminate the contents.

The ship lurched, and I involuntarily recoiled, for the thing laying in the crate seemed alive in the guttering yellow light. Steeling myself, I took a closer look. It was a statue. Laid down, it was about eleven or twelve feet long. A monstrous thing, carved in exquisite detail out of some pale faultless alabaster. A kraken perhaps? Long tentacles twisted down from a massive head. Two great eyes, with their characteristic sha-shaped pupils, glared out menacingly from beneath furrowed brows. However, this was no kraken, for under the writhing appendages was a hulking human-like body, massively proportioned, with claws for hands and feet. I noticed its distended genitalia and pendulous breasts and quickly averted my gaze back to the horrific creature's head. The detail was as incredible as it was implausible. Part of me instinctively wanted to reach out and touch it, to caress the detail of the skin, while all my other senses were absolutely repulsed. An expletive worthy of Patty escaped my mouth.

"Amen to that," replied Sir John.

"Have you ever seen anything like this before?" Adam inquired.

"No," I immediately replied in revulsion before remembering that I had indeed seen something like it before. "It is such a pity that those pictures of the bas-relief on the underside of the capstone at Mr Ransom's farm did not come out. It was hard to tell from what survived, but there was a monstrous kraken like creature wound through those images. Although it did not depict a human body, I remember it did appear to have both tentacles and arms.

A chill ran down my spine as I also remembered that it seemed to move in the lamplight as if it was not quite a straightforward depiction.

"So, is it Aresian?"

I forced myself to look at it again, closely. "From the style and the technical craftsmanship; I would say so."

"It looks real," murmured Howe in disgust.

"Like it was moulded from…" Captain Rambeau stopped herself in midsentence. "I don't like having it on the ship, but they paid very handsomely."

"Is it some kind of god or idol, Miss?" asked Red.

I wished my stepfather or Dr Spender were there, they would have known far more. I answered as honestly as I could. "Possibly. Malacandrian maybe. My stepfather said they worshiped some sort of kraken-like god."

Adam turned to me again, "Based upon what it is; do you think it is the kind of thing 'our friend' would be interested in?"

"Mr D? A unique piece of Aresian 'art,' for want of a better word, and possibly an idol or goddess from some lost or looted Malacandrian temple? Absolutely! There is no doubt in my mind at all. If this is genuine, it is the kind of thing he would probably have people killed for."

Adam turned to the Captain, "Who is to collect this and where?"

The Captain looked uncomfortable about answering the question.

"Excuse us," Sir John interjected and led the Captain out of the storeroom. After a few minutes of hushed discussion, he returned on his own. "Look. That just took up the last of any cache of favours I have left with her. She has given me the name and the location, but we must undertake to allow the transaction to complete before doing anything. Either that or we pay her right now for the value of that monstrosity, plus a consideration. And I do not know about you, but I do not have that kind of money ready to hand."

"She has my word," said Adam solemnly.

"It is to be collected at a regular drop off site about five miles west of Alba. A man toiling under the moniker of Ingenious Solomon Squelette,* is to pay off the balance on collection."

*Editor's Note.

After extensive research, we are able to confirm the identity was Isaiah Habakkuk Barebones; we have edited the following entries to avoid the reader's confusion.

James Ransom.

"Has she dealt with him before?"

"Several times." The Captain had returned. "He's a local freelance moving man. They say he used to be a kidsman that ran a rookery in the old Iron Quarter of the city but was run out by another street gang. Or that's the story they tell."

At that, Adam seemed to prickle. "Which gang? Do you know?"

"I can't say I do." Her face screwed up delightfully as a small child would when trying to remember something difficult. "Wait a moment." She turned and left.

"Why is it important?" Sir John beat me to the question. However, Adam seemed lost in thought.

"Miss?" ventured Howe. "Why would a'body want a t'ing like that?" Howe's big ginger framed face carried an expression of complete befuddlement.

"Mr Howe, this 'thing' is worth a truly great deal of money. Aresian Antiquities are of great value to collectors, as well as being able to be used as collateral; I mean trade, between unscrupulous criminal types." Howe looked a little less puzzled. "It is better than cash or gold."

Captain Rambeau returned with the information she had sought, "Lauren says she heard it was the Union Street Boys that took over his patch."

That seemed to snap Adam out of his reverie. "Is she sure?"

"I would think so, old chap. Lauren hails from the sticky end of Alba," answered Sir John. "Why is it important?"

Adam appeared distracted as if listening to some internal dialogue. He then replied to Sir John, "Yes, it is. It may be only a coincidence, nevertheless yes. I think it might be." He turned to the Captain, "We will come with you to drop off this thing to this Mr Barebones. Once the transaction is over and you are satisfied, we will follow Barebones to wherever he is taking it. Hopefully to whoever has paid for it, and not another intermediary."

I must say, though I was delighted that my ferreting about had gained us such a lead, I could not for the life of me understand why it was that it came to matter to Adam which coterie of hooligans and yobbos had driven some kidsman out of his haunt. Or why it was that that information appeared to make his mind up to follow the statue.

"It could be a complete wild goose chase," commented Sir John.

"Possibly, and we can only spare a few hours on such a departure, but I think it is worth the toss of the penny." There was something in Adam's eyes that made me quite sure he believed we were most definitely on to something.

Journal of Adam Franklin.

Peace is a rare thing, and, it seems to me, peace of mind rarer.

I am now plagued with memories and visions continually. We flew over a small lake, and my mind was transported back to a summer's day in Victoria Park with the boys. Resplendent in their straw boaters and the sailor suits their mother had made them. We had taken them to the park after Sunday services to sail the tin toy boat I brought them for their birthday. They looked like little Princes. Excited five-year-olds, sloshing and laughing on the edge of the ornamental lake. How annoyed I was that the thing needed constantly fishing out of the water and winding up.

Percy was dressed the same, pushing a little wooden horse on a stick, and cheekily driving his mother wild as he tried to get to the water's edge because the horsey wanted a drink.

In the afternoon, I brought them penny-wipes from the hokey-pokey man and flew the kraken shaped kite I had spent days making for them. Its long tentacles flowing out like streamers in the warm summer sky. I was almost as elated as they were because I had never made anything like that before.

A handmade kite, clothes made from hand-me-downs, second-hand straw hats, and pawnshop toys, but they were so delighted. So happy.

They never saw another birthday.

This had to stop. I was getting lost in a lifetime of recollections and losing touch with the task in hand. I had made a promise and I was intent upon keeping it, something even the Sergeant Major understood.

I knew the statue in the hold was significant, from the moment Charity told me of it. It added up; De Maurier is an obsessive collector of such antiquities, and this is one of the main arteries of items from looted Aresian sites entering Tharsis' black market. If this thing were not bound for him, then I would wager he knows of it and has an interest in acquiring it.

The thing that really troubles me about it though is the coincidence of it all. This was beyond luck, it was eerily fortuitous, in fact, concerningly so. I feel manipulated. The others seem happy to accept that this is all pure happenstance. However, there are too many coincidences in this. The ruffians of Walton Row told me that the Union Street Boys were working for Lanulos back in Alba. Another coincidence that they were the self-same gang that had connections to the man coming to collect that abomination in the hold. Neither I, nor the Sergeant Major, believe in coincidences.

What was it that the Sergeant Major said about spies? 'There's more than one bloody spy on this ship.' However, it is just the one I am concerned with at this point; Sir John Sydeian. Conversely, how would he know about this shipment? Powerful friends, no doubt. It occurs to me possibly the same 'powerful friends' that drew up Jahns' dossier on De Maurier. Was all that acrimony on the Seren Bore an act, a cover story? Are we being manipulated or led by the nose?

Do I confront Sydeian or play along with it? The Sergeant Major's advice, shouted in my head, was as unequivocal as it was brutal.

There is some kind of connection between De Maurier and Lanulos. There has to be. Nevertheless, I guessed not even Charity would find it in those papers Jahns gave us. However, the Bureau of State Internal Security had been on to Lanulos' activities in Alba. It was their files on De Maurier that Jahns gave us. Percy Gregg's name was on some of those reports. Yet there was no mention of Lanulos in them. Was I imagining a connection, desiring it to be so?

With one eye on Sydeian at all times, we shall find out to whom the effigy is destined. If it does provide a direct link to De Maurier, then we will have to tread very carefully, as I am aware that it will be most probably a trap. Possibly one set by De Maurier, Lanulos, or even Sydeian himself.

If it is nothing to do with De Maurier, and I am just imagining spies in the shadows, then the Sergeant Major suggested that the statue could be usefully utilised as bait. It was illegally smuggled into the country, thus stealing it off whomever it was destined for should not concern us, thieving off thieves is not a crime, especially if I promise Charity it will end up in the right hands in the end; someone like Dr Spender or her stepfather. I think she will readily agree.

Therefore, I have decided to let this play out a while.

I have gathered, from idle talk, that there was a communication device on the airship. I broached the question with Captain Rambeau whether she would allow me to dispatch a message through to Locksley Hall. She already knows of the methods employed by the military to track ships by their broadcasts. I explained I knew the scientist who had developed the technique. She laughed it off, saying that they can only pinpoint the source of a message's location, and for that to be accurate, they need it to be within a triangle of three listening posts. She then showed me a map of all the known broadcast towers and listening posts. Amazed by the complexity I pointed out the grid they formed across Tharsis, Thaumaisa, Icaria and most of eastern Amazonia, was damn well comprehensive.

Maëlle Rambeau's eyes sparkled. "Exactement! It is a good system when it works. Better than the Zephyrians and their awful Chappe tachygraph. On the other hand, they have a blind spot. If you get as close as possible to a le mât, the broadcast mast, the system cannot see you. But you must get very, very close."

I asked politely if she would do that for me. Her answer was playful. "Non, mon cher! We do not need to. Regardez!" She pointed to a blank wooden box mounted on a stand in the corner of the flight deck. "We have a brand new aerial telautograph. I am not one for all that clever stuff, but I am assured, when it is off, it is off, and your friend's system cannot track it. When it sends, it is *instantané*, and the Queen of the Skies is very, very fast."

"So even if they do locate the point of the broadcast, you are long gone."

"Trés bon! And you cannot predict a *trajectoire* from one point. But keep it *bref*, Mister Franklin. Keep it *bref*."

I promised to do so.

"And Mr Franklin, there is a storm out there. So, no guarantees, *entendre*?"

I understood. That much had not changed; dust in the air could cause the Mendeleev effect and send a signal anywhere or scatter it to the winds.

The machine kept under the wooden lead-lined box was more complicated than I could have imagined, overly so I thought. An intricate mass of black lacquered keys, brass dials, cogs and tiny levers. Upon powering it up, it hummed alarmingly and glowed with dozens of tiny valves. I could operate the telephonograph at the Toll House back in Tremorfa. However, this contraption was beyond my capabilities. The Captain set one of the crew to help me; a young girl called Sam with such delicate long fingers that they would have made many a pianist jealous. Upon my instructions, her fingers flew across the dials and keys.

I had the curious experience of realising that a part of my brain, or whatever it was, something almost independent, was watching eagerly her every stroke and adjustment, learning, categorising, and assimilating the knowledge.

Once the message had been dispatched, Sam quickly shut the machine down, and I replaced the heavy lead-lined cover.

"Clever is it not?" The Captain asked proudly. I agreed.

"Monsieur Grey's aerial telautograph machine is the very best money can buy."

"Expensive, I would expect."

"Very." She laughed. "I like you, Monsieur Franklin. You are a good man." I protested that it was hard to tell a man's nature from knowing him only a few hours. She dismissed my protestations. "Your face does not frighten me. My own Papa was disfigured as a young man. It never stopped the ladies from admiring him for his other accomplissements!" She winked at me and laughed again.

I demurred. In truth, I had not noticed any woman give me more than a passing glance and that with a shudder as they turned away.

"Adsurdité! Why, have you not noticed how the young Mademoiselle Charity, looks at you? Hmm?" She was teasing me now for the amusement of the bridge crew. Even so, it was a pleasant enough diversion. "She watches your every move like a hawk. Ready to pounce." She made a lunging motion and laughed heartily.

I tried to explain, as tactfully as I could, that though it may be a flattering thought, Charity's interests in that area lay in a different direction. Maëlle Rambeau waved it away. "Ha, men! Allez! All full of passion and vigour but you know nothing about women. Il ne faut pas mettre tout dans le même sac, especially a girl like that."

I felt a little uncomfortable as the subject of the conversation and deftly turned the table by asking about her relationship with Sir John Sydeian.

She sneered, "There is no relation. There was once, but not now." She crossed herself and spat. Intrigued, I probed further. I told her of the tale I had heard that Sydeian had killed the previous Captain of the Queen, for her. "Mon dieu! Ha!" She laughed. "Oui, mon Père built this ship, and when he died that vile pig of a man, LeRoi, murdered my brother, Jacques, and seized the Captaincy. That much is true. We suffered under him for almost two years. Until one day Sydeian and his companion brought a passage. I thought he was 'un tel homme,' as we say, such a man! Dashing, charming, mesmerizing. I was nothing but a silly little girl awaiting a hero, and here he was. I fell in love with him and told him everything. He said he would challenge LeRoi and win my father's ship back, for me!" She laughed bitterly. "They were to duel with cutlasses, but, because he was losing, LeRoi drew a hidden pistol." She paused. I asked her to go on. "LeRoi was a stupid big ox of a man, a bully and a browbeater, but he did not stand a hope in

Hell against Sydeian, gun or no gun. Sydeian did not just kill him; he toyed with him as a cat does with a mouse. I was young, angry and full of spite. I wanted to see LeRoi suffer, and he did. Especially at the hands of my brave lover, my chevalier, my hero; John Sydeian." She sat down heavily in the Captain's chair. "I believed he did it for me. Because he loved me. Ahh, we were so happy! So, in love!" She spun the chair about and thrust out her arms. "We had each other, this ship and the world at our feet! What more could I want! Il n'y a qu'un bonheur dans la vie, c'estd'aimer et d'être aimé!" She stopped spinning and set her fiercest gaze upon me.

"I was a stupid little girl, blinded by infatuation and lust for revenge. Then, one morning, le bâtard vanished. I searched the whole of Tharsis and Selenium and beyond for him until I found his companion. He took pitié on me and told me the truth. You see Sydeian didn't kill LeRoi because he loved me. He was paid to do it. It was his job." By whom, I asked. "The Secret Police. Mr Franklin, your friend kills people for the state. Oh yes, he is handsome, charming and witty, but be very careful my friend, don't be fooled by his bonhomie, as you people say, underneath it all he is nothing more than a poisonous snake."

"But you have worked with him since?" Though that was obvious I just wanted to know why.

"Mon Père taught us never to let sentiments interférer with enterprise." She shrugged expressively. "And I have had little choice. One does not decline a Government Agent, no matter *how détestable, if you wish to stay free and in business, let alone, alive."*

We sat in silence for a while before I asked, "You said he had a companion when he first came on board this ship?"

"Oui, Monsieur Greg."

"Percy Greg?"

"Oui. A big bear of a man, not unlike your Monsieur Howe, but teint basané, darker. Une âme gentile. Do you know him?"

"We met once." I tried to think about how tactfully I could put my next question. "Did Sydeian have anything to do with your ship being hired to transport that statue?"

I saw a flare of anger behind her eyes. "Non! No. Do not tell me this is another one of his damned games?"

I admitted I honestly did not know. All this is news to my ears. I only know him as Sir John, big game hunter and adventurer, and friend of my employer.

Maëlle Rambeau pulled her fingers through her hair. As far as she knew there was nothing out of the ordinary about the actual transaction, in fact, nothing unusual that is until Sydeian turned up. It is registered as internal transportation of private property, not an import. I asked if I might see the papers myself. She looked both puzzled and angry, but readily agreed I could look at the Green Book, the legitimate cargo manifest.

*The entry read; '***Item 661 A. A moulded copy of an Aresian religious effigy. Depicting an Aresian kraken goddess.***' It gave exact weight and dimensions. '***Property of the Prior J. Tonto-***

Jitterman, of Tharsis City, Tharsis. *'To be transported to address; 'Dashwood House. Medmenham Abbas. Wharton. Tharsis,'* also the home address of the owner. *'Value 2,000 21/-Insurance; Akers and Moles, Tharsis. 'And stamped with several different customs verifications and valuer's marks.*

Reasonably convincing and thorough, I had to admit.

"It'll pass vérification. The stamps are authentique. That is where the real cost lies," the Captain remarked with a wry smile. "Bribery."

I was intrigued by the name and title, a Prior? A religious man, and 'Abbas,' meant an Abbey. What group of monks would want a thing like that? A sculpture of an old God of an alien civilisation? "The name and address, however? Do you think that is the real buyer?"

The Captain shook her head, "I have no idea, but I doute it. Although the adresse is réal."

I made a note of it to show the others. I stopped to make myself some tea in what passed for a galley on the way (old habits die hard), merely to give myself time to think. I have not trusted Sydeian from the get-go, there is something off about the man. Now Maëlle Rambeau has confirmed my suspicions. However, she believes him to be an agent of the Tharsis Government, which makes things even more interesting. That seems to hold some weight if he was working with Percy Greg when she met him. I pulled Greg's Identity card out of my pocket and looked at the picture. Greg had been an Inspector

*of Detectives in the Bureau of State Internal Security, and he
had been murdered while investigating Lanulos. Coincidence?
Unlikely.*

*Is Sydeian here to investigate me? Does he think that
following me will lead him to Lanulos? Maybe he thinks I am
working for that grinning, yellow bastard? Alternatively, is it
something else? Does he know Lanulos is connected to De
Maurier? Or is he here to kill one of us? Surely not one of the
expedition members? The Professor or Aelita? No, I pushed that
thought away. It was illogical, what was he doing here with us
on this flying crate if he was aiming to murder any of the others.
Perhaps he aims to kill me? Then he is going to need a bigger
gun.*

*A definite decision as to what to do about Sydeian will have
to wait for now. Probably until he makes his move and then I
will have to do as the Sergeant Major strongly suggests.*

*I found the others in one of the cargo bays drinking coffee
and discussing the thing in the crate. I told them what I had
learnt from the manifest. Sydeian remarked that he would not
have bothered to look at the paperwork as pure fabrication was
only to be expected. I agreed, however, there was something I
wanted to show both he and Charity; the signature on the
documentation of verification that the sculpture was a modern
copy of an original held in the Tharsis Museum, was signed by
one Professor G.P. Serviss. I said I had heard his name
mentioned before but could not place it. Which was a*

convenient lie, as I remembered the Professor mentioning that he was one of the original members of the Expedition, but I wanted to know what they knew of him.

Charity gasped, "The old devil!"

"So, who is this Serviss chap?"

Sydeian scrutinised the signature. "I met the old buzzard at Flammarion's do the other day when the Prof told us of his idea to set off on this adventure. Seemed a stuffy old shirt. He was supposed to be coming with us, but for some reason cried off at the last minute. The Prof was not best pleased."

I asked Charity how she knew of him.

"He is an old colleague and friend of my stepfather and Dr Spender. He is the senior Areological Anthropologist at the Museum and Curator of the entire Aresian teaching collection. I am actually quite dumbfounded. Dear God! To think he would be involved in stealing antiquities!"

Sydeian pointed out the very document, let alone the signature on it, could probably be a complete forgery, so we must not rush to judge. True enough, nevertheless it is another interesting coincidence, that he should have been privy to the Professor's plans and that his name is attached to that thing in the hold.

"With fear of sounding like the Colonel; I do not like or trust in 'coincidences'," I said.

"Well said, old chap," laughed Sydeian. "Me neither."

Journal of Adam Franklin.

Very little rest last night. What sleep I did get was plagued with strange dreams. Cattarina Monck came to me in one of them. I was in a vast glass house with my wife and my boys; they were playing merrily amongst the tropical plants and throwing pebbles into the water to frighten the fish. Was it a dream or a memory, I did not know. I was so lost in longing for them that I almost lost myself. Suddenly, there, amid the little open-air tearoom in the centre of the faux jungle, stood Cattarina Monck, still in her wedding dress. Her mouth moved. However, no words came, but her eyes, her eyes pleaded with me, she held out her hand to me, and I had to fight the compulsion to raise from my seat and go to her.

I awoke with a start in my makeshift bed between the crates. I was crying. I did not know I could, in this body, cry. Automatons cannot cry.

Just before dawn, the Queen of the Skies landed in a clearing in an ancient redwood forest outside Alba. There were several groups of smugglers eyeing each other as they waited to collect their cargos. I was impressed with the efficacy of the whole enterprise. Before the ship had even touched ground, the crew were already throwing bales of animal skins and bolts of cloth into the eager arms of those awaiting. I had expected haggling and checking of goods; however, nothing of the sort occurred.

Amidst the busy smugglers and black marketeers, sat three men on horseback, their animals still steaming with sweat in the ice-cold morning air. I recognised Karl immediately. The other two identical burly young men, I did not straightaway remember. However, they had a familiar look about them.

The Captain said she could not land the ship here and there was no space for horses. Karl quickly threw a few pennies into the hand of a smuggler in return for the promise of returning the beasts to the city.

The whole process was carried out with minimum chatter and almost military precision, cargo off, cargo on, passengers on and we were away in less than ten minutes.

When I had first met Karl in Edwin's home, I thought him incongruous, dressed up in human clothes over his brass skin. Then when we were on the run from Everheart, in his long leather duster and wide-brimmed hat, I had found his appearance almost melancholy, a man engine masquerading as a human being. Now though, standing in the hold of this airship, with his impassive brass face, I realised I was delighted, even a little relieved, to see him.

"How the hell did you find us?" Sydeian asked incredulously.

"Mr. Franklin's report said you were heading for Alba. Mrs. Minerva Ransom sent us to meet you at Central Station." He turned to me, "These are Joshua's sons David and Eli, Michael's

older brothers. We received your message about three hours ago. Mr. Peter Ransom had a taste for cigars and brandy on the black market. He came to this clearing to buy from smugglers directly. Mr. Ransom senior would send me on. To keep Mr. Peter safe and buy more things. Statistically, it was a good wager."

"Damn right, my old tin friend. Damn right!" Sydeian seemed delighted.

"I bear a message for you, Mr Franklin. From Mrs Minerva Ransom." He produced a thick envelope from inside his duster.

I had scarcely started to read it when Sydeian bluntly demanded, "Well? What does it say, old bean?" Never one for formalities he almost snatched the letter out of my hand and proceeded to read it aloud.

"It is from Edwin's Sister-in-law," I explained.

"Mister Peter Ransom's widow," interjected Karl.

"'Dear Mr Franklin, I pray this letter reaches you safely. Thank you kindly for your gentle words of condolence. You have become a great friend to our family in such a short span of time, and we all thank you for taking on the burden of bringing to justice the man that wrought such calamity upon our family.

'I have received word from the Professor, and I have set in motion the arrangements he requested. Lenora and the children have already left for a safer location. They are being personally escorted by a gentleman of uncommon stature and courage Mr Hezekiah Uwharrie. I am sure Karl can explain more than I have

time to write here. Mr Uwharrie and his family have come to our defence in these dark days and have been of great assistance. They have pursued unrelentingly those; one can barely call them 'men,' who were hired from the back streets of the city to attack our home.

'Please rest assured that we are in the protection of Mr Uwharrie's extensive family, and we are all safe.

'As requested, I am dispatching Karl, and Joshua Hopeforth's sons, David and Eli, to meet you at the location you suggested.

'If you are reading this then they have obviously rendezvoused with you.

'Mr Franklin, pardon me if I deviate. I must thank you for what you are doing. I understand how the Professor could never allow dear Edwin to embark upon such a course of action. It was one of God's small mercies, that, in this time of need, He sent you into our lives. I cannot think of any man our family could trust more. Nevertheless, Mr Franklin, please take utmost care, as our family is so bereft, we could not bear to lose anyone more.'"

Sir John gave me a knowing smile and winked, but as he read on, his tone changed.

"'I beseech you to take care, for the man you seek, I cannot even bring myself to write his name, is a fiend. I must tell you about the night of the tragedy. Please do not believe me to be merely a hysterical woman, I am not, and I must accept the evidence of my own eyes.

'We were in the sitting room when the events erupted outside the house. With a crash, two rogues burst through the French windows into the room, and I, Nelly and Lady Niketa were forced to defend ourselves with whatever was at hand.

'It was in that chaos that a dark presence suddenly overcame me, I became faint, almost as if drowning. My eye was drawn to the nook between the fire breast and the door to the hall.

'I am not given to flights of wild fantasy, but an unusually dark shadow had formed in that nook and suddenly issued from it the form of a tall man in black. It was he, that murderous fiend, and it was as if he stepped out of the very shadows themselves.

'I cannot for the life of me understand how he did it, but he did not enter the room by any normal means, he simply appeared in that darkened corner.

'I was rooted to the spot, too awestricken to react, unable to believe what I had seen. The others were unaware of him until he shot Karl and struck Carstairs a blow.

'I witnessed his face at the moment he murdered our beloved Nelly. He is a devil incarnate. I shall remember the dreadful leer on his face until my dying day.

'I do not know whether this has been relayed to you, I feel though it is of some great importance; Dearest Nelly was an indomitable young woman who saved my life at the cost of hers. Though I tried to place myself between them, she deliberately moved me out of the path of danger and defiantly confronted that depraved monster. She shot him squarely in the chest with a little pistol that Lady Niketa had provided for her defence. He was only a few feet away, Lady Niketa and I witnessed the shots strike him squarely, but to no avail.

'I fear he must gird himself with some strengthening armour secreted under his apparel, as he did not so much as flinch at the impact.

'Go carefully, Mr Franklin, in Gods good name. I understand Edwin and the Professor's need to see sweet Nelly's death avenged, but please know that we, I and my Sisters-in-law, Lenora and Maurine could not bear to see any more loss of life amidst our family and friends.

'Lady Niketa wishes me to enclose a note from her. She requested me to implore you to open it only when you have, and, I quote, 'Laid eyes upon the Queen of Qadath.' Whatever that means. I cannot elucidate further as she remains most cryptic, as befits one of her calling. I must confess to being anxious about what she may tell me should I ask.

'Finally, as I have no idea of how you are to be provisioned, and the Professor can often be a little imprecise about such practicalities, I have entrusted to Karl some paper monies; a hundred pounds, to cover your expenses.'"

Prompted by that remark, Karl produced a wad of folded banknotes out of his coat and proffered them to me.

"Soon and so forth...Minerva Ransom, Widow, etcetera, etcetera.

Sydeian regained some of his manners, enough to ask my consent before opening the next letter. However, he had difficulty reading the tiny handwriting. Charity took it from him and read on.

"'Dear Mr Franklin.

I am compelled by recent events to write to you. I know through our meeting at Locksley Manor that you are a human being of unusual qualities, and of all people, may possess, more than most, a clearer apprehension of what I have to write. You may not think what I have to impart as implausible as some may consider.

'I do not have to emphasise to you that there are powers abroad in this world far beyond those measurable in the Professor's laboratory, or most men's wildest imaginings.

'On the night after your departure, dearest Eleanor asked me to undertake a scrying, a reading of my crystal ball, for her. She was concerned for her husband's safety and asked that I should consult the crystal as to what the future may hold. I tried to dissuade her, but to no avail, as

I had grave misgivings after the events of the séance the night before.

'During that reading, the room was pervaded, dare I say, invaded, by a terrible presence, a threatening entity, that caused us to abandon the scrying. I believed it to be what is known as an Egorg Egregoroi, a Watcher spirit, but I now fear that it may have been something far more dangerous.

'Whatsoever it was, I saw the mark of binding upon it. Every occultist has his or her particular sigil, and I could at least distinguish that clearly. I have since consulted about this with my spirit guide and with some members of my Circle.

'I can say no more than I believe the beast to have been under the domination of the Zephyrian occultist, Jeteur de Sort. I know of no other would be able to do such a thing.

'De Sort started as a lowly stage magician on the Music Hall circuit, but he is now reputedly a leading member of a very dangerous group, a sect, of iniquitous men. He is very,

very cunning and not without powers that, to most would make no rational sense.

'My friends tell me that de Sort's Circle has been seeking knowledge of darker Malacandrian occult practices for some time, those suppressed by their rulers and other Aresian Kings. I must warn you, if they have, there may be little or no defence against such arts they can bring to bear.

Chief Whitehawk, my spirit guide, told me something that I pray will be of use to you.

The Queen of Qadath will lead you to whom you seek, but beware, the Dark Man. He is not what he seems.

'My apologies, but the Chief is always quite enigmatic, and I have not the foggiest who this 'Queen' is she is or where you may find her.'

So on and so forth, etcetera, etcetera..."

"The Queen of Qadath," the name struck a familiar note somewhere in the back of my mind. It was that same sense I had back in Alba, the intuition that led me to the Presidio. I had already met the 'Queen' Lady Niketa was warning me about; she was down in the rear hold of the airship, sleeping in her crate. Sleeping? My mind seems to be full of odd associations.

I was very interested in hearing more from Karl about Lenora Ransom and this man Hezekiah Uwharrie. However, we were short of time, and preparations had to be made.

I noticed a general change in the crew's demeanour after the second stop they relaxed visibly. I asked why that was. "We're legal from here on. No contraband on this ship, M'lud," joked a crewmember called Lauren.

In a quiet corner, I went over the arrangements for dropping off the statue with Sydeian, Karl, Red and Charity. Howe and the Hopeforth twins would be told what was needed of them by whomever they would be working with.

The Captain informed us that the drop off was to go something like this; the location was a dried-up riverbed on the edge of a small woodland, lots of long grass and reeds. The Captain will officiate and we, provided with some other clothes, will pose as crew in helping to move the crate onto whatever conveyance Barebones has with him.

We were aiming to get to the site as early as possible. Karl and the Hopeforth boys would disembark and take up positions in the tall grasses as support if things went badly. I already know just how accurate Karl is with that repeating rifle he carries, and a sharpshooter in good cover could pin down an army. They would also have our kit with them, as Captain

Rambeau had made it clear once she was paid, she and her ship were leaving immediately.

As soon as the transaction is concluded, and the Captain was back on her ship, we were free to "Take Barebones and his men down," as Sydeian coined it.

I must admit that at this point, I expected this Barebones chap to arrive in a good-sized waggon with a couple of hefty labourers to do the fetching and carrying. Maybe an outrider or two for safety sake.

Once we had control of the situation, we would then call in Karl and the boys for back up. No doubt, we will have to persuade Barebones to share with us what he knows about his cargo and where it is headed for. It was a straightforward plan; even so, I made sure that they all clearly understood what was intended. I then warned Charity that any such persuasion would probably require the application of more than just a few harsh words.

She answered proudly, "If you are suggesting I am either to hide aboard this ship out of fear or that I am too squeamish to witness a little rough stuff, then Mr Franklin you forget that I fought by your side in Alba Station and you underestimate both my resolve and myself as a woman."

I must say I have grown to admire her spunk greatly. However, I fear it will come down to more than merely 'a little rough stuff.'

The Story of Two Queens.

Cont.

Adam was enormously relieved to see Karl, Edwin's automaton, awaiting us at the first drop off point. I must admit that I felt a sense of relief at the sight of him, in his long dusty coat and wide-brimmed hat; he looked the very epitome of a frontiersman.

It is almost ridiculous to write this as Karl is, as Wilberforce Bravett insisted, a machine, and a taciturn one at that, but his manner, if a machine can have a 'manner,' was subdued, more sombre than usual. He greeted me politely, almost warmly, but soon withdrew into a contemplative reverie. I am forced to reconsider if Bravett's assertions were correct at all. For this automaton, seems, for want of any better description, sad.

As to be expected, Karl is somewhat reserved, if not sparing, in his conversational abilities, and most certainly was in no mood to discuss the death of his Mistress. The young Hopeforth boys, as we have come to refer to the twins, have been far more illuminating of the details of Eleanor Ransom's death, and to which lengths Lenora Flammarion, whom Eleanor told me of, has gone to exact revenge. It is heartrending to think of how such a tragedy has changed the mild young schoolmistress that

Eleanor so proudly showed me in the family picture album, so fundamentally. I can only see that as yet another tragedy that we should lay at the feet of D Maurier and Everheart. The Uwharrie clan are a formidable bunch, and I do not doubt that they have thrown themselves whole-heartedly into the awful task Lenora Flammarion has appointed them to. David, the more talkative of the twins, told me that the staff of the house were more nervous of Lenora than the Uwharries. I despair for her.

Adam called us together to discuss his plans for capturing this 'Mr Barebones.' Adam is a masterful tactician seemingly aware of several potentialities and able to lay out contingencies for each. Sir John and Red deliberately threw up several possible problems, but Adam had an answer for each. I must admit to admiring his thorough mindedness.

My task was to give the signal to them to act. As Adam said, all eyes would be on me. Captain Rambeau had one of the crew, Lauren, a tall, powerfully built blond girl who could have only been eighteen if a day, with bright eyes and a ready wit, show me the rudimentries of operating the steam hoists and slings that we would need to unload the effigy. The Captain warned all of us that we would have to put our "backs into it" if we were not to garner suspicion from Barebones or his companions. I have never operated heavy machinery in my life, other than my

360

monocycle, but I must admit I undeniably enjoyed being shown by Lauren how to handle the apparatus.

The rendezvous was in a shallow gulch on the edge of a redwood forest plantation.

We arrived early and settled amidst the long grass on the broadest part of the valley floor.

Karl and the Hopeforth boys disembarked quickly, disappearing into the long grass with weapons and our luggage.

Onboard the ship, the crew swiftly armed themselves with an exotic array of guns, rifles, knives and cutlasses. Sir John advised I arm myself too. I strapped on Aelita's Odic pistol and thrust my father's old eliminator into my belt. Lauren tied my hair back with a large kerchief and gave me a tough, stained, leather jerkin and gloves to wear. Suddenly I quite fancied myself as a real swashbuckler of the skies. We giggled a lot, and I do believe she was flirting with me.

Once I gathered my wits, I noticed that only after a few minutes the crew were getting nervous with being on the ground. Every eye was scouring the surrounding area for Mr Barebones and his wagon.

What finally emerged out of the tree line about a quarter of an hour later was not the covered wagon of our expectations, but one of the most bizarre machines I have ever seen. It looked like nothing less than a twenty-foot-high, hundred-foot-long drab olive-skinned caterpillar, walking on ten pairs of legs. The pilot's cabin housing was formed of a green glass and filigree metal dome, around which four articulated arms waved like antennae. All about its globular segmented body hissed jets of steam, and smoke exhaled from the stack mounted upon its back. The machine picked its way down the incline towards our ship with surprising, if not alarming, adroitness, as the pilot in the cupola heaved and strained frantically at a vast array of highly polished levers and controls.

Unfortunately, there was no time to stand and stare at the marvellous mechanical beast. Orders were shouted from above, and Lauran and I swung into action. We were at the controls of the hoists while Mr Franklin, Sir John, Howe and Red, manhandled the crate into the slings, and, once in the air, across on to the lowering platform.

By the time the platform had settled on the ground, the walking machine had reached us and was noisily lowering itself to allow a big bay door in its side to drop a ramp. I noticed that the crew of the caterpillar were all relatively young men, rough-looking, but not one over the age of majority. Twelve of them scurried down the ramp from their vehicle and ran across to us. They had brought with them numerous lengths of rope, which they passed under the crate and hauled it off the platform. At an order to "lend a hand!" shouted by Lauren, Mr Franklin and the others joined in manhandling the box which appeared to need every one of them to lift it.

My task was to wait for Captain Rambeau's signal when she had concluded her business.

The glass dome of the machine raised with a hiss, and out of it climbed a tall, powerfully built, African gentleman, with a patriarch beard, wearing a pale frock coat and battered top hat. I presumed this was Mr Barebones. A younger man, also African but with a slightly lighter cast to his skin, clambered down behind him. He too was well dressed, but apparently physically deformed. He moved in a peculiar lurching manner, dragging his left foot, the right shoulder held higher than the other and carried his right arm coiled close to his chest. I noticed that unlike the other crewmembers, both carried a brace of pistols.

Captain Rambeau and Lauren met them about halfway between the ship and their vehicle. The transaction seemed amicable enough; hands were shaken, pleasantries past, the older man gestured to his companion who produced a bundle wrapped in brown paper and gave it to Lauren. She opened the package and checked the contents. As she thumbed through it, I could see it was paper money, Tharsian white ten-pound notes in a thick bundle. She appeared happy with the amount and commented so to her Captain before handing over the roll of accompanying documents. The exchange done, Captain Rambeau and Mr

Barebones shook hands again before they turned away towards their respective conveyances.

As Captain Rambeau turned, she caught my eye and winked. That was our signal.

I jumped down from the platform, ran across the short distance to join the men hauling the incredibly heavy crate up the ramp into the belly of the caterpillar. As soon as we settled the box in the hold, Adam and the others sprang upon the young crewmembers.

I have nothing but the most profound admiration for Adam Franklin, he saved my life at Alba Kirk and again at Alba Central Station, and he is a kind and considerate man, but, and it is regretful to say that he and the others were brutal in their unprovoked attack. Hardly any of those young men and boys, in the hold of that strange metal caterpillar, were armed with anything more than their own bravado. I am thankful to say our men did not resort to using the deadliest of force, or their firearms, but, with the ferocity of a pride of prattans on a flock of sheep, they showed no restraint in violently subduing all the crewmembers they could lay their hands upon.

The young hunchbacked fellow that had been with Mr Barebones, appeared at the bulkhead door, no doubt to investigate the commotion, and upon realising his ship had been boarded, beat a hasty retreat, but not fast enough to slam shut the door behind him. Adam was through it instantly with Sir John at his heels.

After Red and Howe had finished restraining the crew, we followed on warily. Carefully negotiating the narrow, segmented iron gangway that ran like a spinal column through the machine. Onward, over its steam engine heart, and on into the head section.

It was bedecked more befitting a comfortable gentleman's study, with ornate fittings and book-lined walls, than the control room of such a machine. At the other end of the room, accessed by a short spiral staircase, was a raised platform upon which sat a comfortable leather wingback surrounded by an array of highly polished throttles and leavers. Only the light streaming in through the green glass cupola above reminded me that this was the control room of such a bizarre contrivance.

Mr Barebones sat in a big wing-backed armchair behind an exquisitely made desk, his hands raised, one clutching a snifter and the other a thick cigar, as if in surrender. Before the desk, on the floor, sat his deformed companion, rubbing the side of his head in obvious distress.

Adam Franklin and Sir John stood in the middle of the room; their pistols drawn. Sir John had his aimed at Mr Barebones, but Adam casually motioned his as he spoke.

"Again, Sir, we are not brigands. We have no interest in your money or your vehicle."

"Then, what is the meaning of this invasion?" Mr Barebones' rich baritone rumble filled the room. There was an accent to it that I did not recognise until it was pointed out later, that he was an American. "You Gentlemen, have not boarded my ship to purely pay your respects." His hands began to lower, but Sir John gesticulated with the barrel of his pistol and Mr Barebones raised them again, slowly.

"To be certain, Sir. If you make a rash movement, my friend here will kill you, and your young friend, without as much as blinking an eye."

Mr Barebones appeared to consider the validity of Adam's threat for a moment. "Why, Sir, I have no argument with you or your friends. As far as I am aware, we have not crossed trails before. So, unless you are in the pay of others...."

"Which we are not," interjected Sir John indignantly.

"...I will match, in fact, I can double, whatever they offered you."

Adam picked up a Windsor carver that had been knocked over before I had arrived and sat down heavily on it. "Let me make myself clear, Sir. We want nothing of yours and wish you no ill will. All we require is information."

Mr Barebones appeared to consider that for a moment. "Why, I assume it would be pointless to remind you of who exactly I am? And that I will not be intimidated by the likes of a few gun-waving yahoos."

"Utterly pointless," responded Sir John and fired a round into the wing of Mr Barebones' armchair.

The noise reverberated painfully around the spherical metal dome about us.

Mr Barebones did not so much as wince, his eyes never leaving Adam's face. The boy on the floor though recoiled terrified by the noise.

I stepped forward, took the boy's hand, helped him off the floor and led him away. Whatever was to transpire, I would not be party to the death of an innocent child. I told Red to take him back into the hold and secure him with the others.

"As I said, Sir; I only want information, and I am not here to do you any harm. But if you do not tell me what I want to know, my friends here will drag in every one of your crew and kill them before your eyes. Starting with that boy," he gestured in the direction I had sent the young cripple. "And then I, personally, will take you apart, like an over-inquisitive child with a tin toy."

Without doubt, a man like Mr Barebones had been threatened numerous times in his life, so much so that he would be a good judge of whether or not the person threatening him was willing, let alone capable, to carry out their threats. I could see clearly in his eyes that he believed every word Adam uttered.

I too was chillingly certain that Adam was not bluffing. I suddenly understood the warning he had given me earlier in the day.

Mr Barebones swallowed hard, cleared his throat and replied. "Why Sir, in my line of business, Mr...?"

"Franklin."

"Mr Franklin, information is more valuable than gold or human life."

"Do not think for a moment that I will not leave you and all your crew as an explicit warning to whoever comes to see what befell you. The question, Sir, is not whether the information I seek is worth more than 'human life,' it is whether it is worth more than your life."

"Please, Mr Barebones, I would believe him if I were you," I added. "I would not wish to be a party to such a thing, but I fear I am powerless to stop them."

"Why, Ma'am, I don't even know what it is you all want." At that, in defiance of Sir John's pistol, he lowered his hands and took a mouthful of the spirit in the glass.

Adam asked his question. "I want to know about the crate you just collected."

"Yep, wood, twelve by four, about a half a ton loaded. What about it?"

"Everything you know."

Mr Barebones pulled an odd expression. "Why, to me it's just a crate. I have no knowledge of what's in it. I'm a moving man; just a self-employed carman, really. I am paid to move things. I don't take an interest in what I'm moving, in fact, it's a policy of mine not to enquire too closely." He puffed the cigar back to life.

Adam said softly. "Darra?"

Startled to be suddenly addressed, Howe jumped, "Aye?"

"Go and call in Karl, and then get the cripple and bring him back here."

I was too shocked to react.

Howe turned to the door.

"Now wait!" said Mr Barebones commandingly. "Why, there's no need for unpleasantries."

I grabbed Howe's sleeve to stay him.

"That boy means a lot to you, does he not?" asked Sir John.

"Why, they all do, Sir," replied Mr Barebones defensively. "I look after them all. They're good boys."

"Yes, but that one in particular."

Mr Barebones did not answer, but the look in his eyes spoke clearly.

Adam leaned forward in his chair. "I shall ask again; I want you to tell me everything you know about the contents of that crate and who you are collecting it for."

For the first time, I saw a chink in Mr Barebones' imperturbable countenance. "Believe me or not, but, it's true; I do not know who that crate is destined for. I just move..."

Adam then did something I found entirely strange. From his waistcoat pocket, he produced a wad of white cards, about the size of a small deck of playing cards, and deftly flicked one at Mr Barebones. It struck him on the nose and dropped on to the desktop blotter before him. Mr Barebones looked utterly confounded. Adam flicked another at him. They were plain white cards with numerous holes, and slots punched through them. A meaningless act but it seemed to terrify Mr Barebones. "Darra, get that boy. Now." Adam flicked another card at him. Adam flicked another card at him.

"Aye." Howe looked me in the eye and gently removed my hand from his sleeve. "Sorry, Miss." He moved me out of the way and stepped through the bulkhead door.

Adam placed the deck of cards on the corner of the desk, produced an ornate folding knife from his belt, and opened it. Mr Barebones' face had taken on an ashen pallor.

"Mr Franklin?" I implored, "May I have a word with you?"

"No, Miss. You may not." He did not even turn to look at me. "You may though wish to leave now. I fear it may be for the best." I will attest on a stack of Bibles that some great change had come over him in those moments. Every aspect of him had transformed, most obviously, his voice.

"Mr Franklin," I said as forcefully as I could manage. "Adam. You cannot murder an innocent boy."

At that, he turned to look at me, and I do avow that he was so utterly changed that if I had not known it was most surely him, I would have hardly recognised him. His eyes burnt with a ferocious intensity that I found so alarming it struck me silent.

Suddenly Howe returned, "Me laddo's gone. He's slipped his ties an' done a runner."

Mr Barebones sighed noisily and gave out a loud chortle.

"And what is so funny about that, old chap?" inquired Sir John.

Mr Barebones blew a ring of smoke. "You won't catch him. Why that boy's slipperier than a greased weasel. Only he knows where that thing you are so interested in is destined."

Adam turned back to him. "Because he is the real Mr Barebones, is he not? Not you."

"Yup." The big man grinned widely and sipped his drink. "He's our Captain."

"And you? You are just what?" asked Sir John. "The decoy?"

"Why, Sir, you could say that. You could say I am the face of this enterprise, while he is the brains." He looked incredibly pleased with himself. "You see few people would take seriously to a crew being run by a Negro boy, let alone a lame cripple to boot. So, to the entire world, I'm Isaiah Habakkuk Barebones."

"Quite a ruse," agreed Sir John and levelled his pistol at the man.

"Hey now, hold on! I did not say I don't know nothing."

Adam stood up. "Darra, Red, go find the real Barebones and bring him back. I shall be honoured to meet him properly this time." He then turned back to the man behind the desk. "The last time I was in a situation like this, someone tried to trick me then too." He drove the knife through one of the cards into the desk blotter in front of the bogus Mr Barebones and then leaned forward, "I killed him, and after he was dead, I skinned the flesh from his face."

Mr Barebones stumbled over his words, "The crate? We are to deliver it to a house in Wharton County. You are welcome to it... I'd as soon as not return there anyways."

"Why?" I asked.

"My Mamma was a God-fearing woman, and she knew right away if a place was wrong, and that place is wrong. And getting wronger."

"Who hired you?"

He hesitated but gave in, "E. Lemuel Swearengin. Says he's a broker, he works for a wealthy collector."

"Who?"

"Some high-class lady collector called Carmella."

As soon as he said the name, I felt a chill run down my spine, "Camarilla?"

"Why yes, Ma'am, I believe that is the name of the lady in question."

Suddenly I understood that maybe Adam's intuition had been right all along. I forced myself to look at him again, but there he was, back to normal.

"I think you have hit upon something there, Adam, old chap," remarked Sir John.

Adam gave Sir John an indefinable look, almost hostile, he then turned back to the man behind the desk. "What is your real name?"

"Khattab," he answered. "Khattab Flaxman."

*Editor's note.

After extensive research, we are able to confirm the identity of the Pilot of the Oruga Voraz was Omari Cotton; we have edited the following entries to avoid the reader's confusion.

James Ransom.

"Well, Mr Cotton, we are going to need to find your Captain because we are going to be coming along with you to deliver that crate."

Assured by Karl that no one had left the vehicle, it did not take long for Howe and Red to learn from the other crewmembers that their leader had secreted himself in a cleverly disguised hidey-hole under the floor in the posterior section of the caterpillar.

They returned him to the control room post-haste, but this was no frightened boy. His entire demeanour was different, his right arm was still coiled protectively to his chest, but there was no hunched shoulder, and he hardly limped, let alone dragged his foot. His head was held up proud, and his eyes sparkled almost mischievously like a child finally caught out in a trick that he had used to deceive everyone and was enjoying the vagarious reactions to how cunning he had been. I must admit I had been totally fooled by his charade. As he entered the room, he smiled broadly and acknowledged me with a slight nod and a softly spoken, "Ma'am."

"The real Mr Barebones, I presume?" Sir John asked. "Or is he a total fiction? Some Ned Ludd to confuse everyone?"

The young man, he could have been no more than sixteen if that, without any confusion as to the reference, looked Sir John in the eye and replied, "Oh, I'm very actual, Sir. Isaiah Habakkuk Barebones at your service. My mother, God rest her soul, was one of those women that believe that a child's name can fix his destiny, or at least bring him to the notice of the Angels.

She was a very God-fearing woman, a Fifth Monarchist, and when I was born like this, she thought giving me such a name would offset my infirmity in some way."

"Did it work?" I asked.

"Well, Miss, God did grace me with the smarts of a man born way above the station I was born into, and that has," he gestured widely with his left hand, "gained me this."

"How old are you, Isaiah?" I asked.

He seemed to prickle at my familiar use of his first name. "Truly, Miss? I believe I am seventeen years or thereabouts." He turned to look at Mr Cotton, who was still sitting at the desk. "May I?"

Mr Cotton arose swiftly, and Isaiah sat down. "My ankle, I can't stand on it for too long without the pain becoming too much to abide." The big cocky smile returned to his face, and he addressed Adam directly. "And how can I, a humble moving man, be of service to you. Sir?"

Adam seemed distracted again as if listening to some inner voice. It took him a moment to reply. "Tell me what you know of the crate you just collected and to whom and where it is destined."

Isaiah picked up the cigar from the ashtray on the desk and took a long draw. "May I presume Sir, that Omari has already told you most of what you want to know, you just wish me to confirm the details?"

"Presume as you please," replied Sir John, "However be aware the lives of you and your crew will depend upon whether we believe you or not."

"Your proxy told us a few things, so let us just say that what you tell us needs to tally or this is all going to get very distressing, and unnecessarily so," warned Adam.

"Gentlemen," Isaiah suddenly seemed very much in control. "You have boarded my walker like pirates, taken my crew hostage, beaten me, and now have me at gunpoint. I am simply a moving man and not given to violence. If I must give you what you want to regain my freedom, and that of my crew and ship, then I promise you I will do so. That is if you, give me your word, you will free us once I give you whatever it is you want."

Adam cut off Sir John's pithy reply, "Once we have what we want, we will release you and your vehicle and crew unharmed. You have my word."

"And mine," I chimed in.

Isaiah Barebones repeated the same information that Mr Cotton divulged; the crate was to be taken to a house, or rather an estate outside of the township of Medmenham, a place called Dashwood House. It was to be received thereby a man named Swearengin, a dealer that Isaiah had dealt with before. Yes, they had delivered items to the estate several times. As for the buyer? The name the broker had used, was Camarilla; consequently, they had assumed it was a lady buyer of some wealth and influence. Although they had never seen her in person. The estate was quite some way outside of Medmenham and very well guarded.

Adam probed further, and as the tension in the room relaxed, I joined in the questioning.

The broker had approached them about two years ago and, so long as there were no questions asked, the money was very lucrative. The items were statues mostly, First Martian effigies, as far as they could tell. This current one was the largest and most valuable.

They had never knowingly met the man whose name was on the documents, Prior Jeramiah Tonto-Jitterman. I asked if they had seen monks or religious people about? Isaiah told me, once when late delivering some items, one of the men at the gate, a bald, fat man with a high voice and a bad comb-over, who usually pays them, arrived wearing long white robes. They were warned most forcefully not to be late ever again.

It evidently was a big house, "supposedly built before the 'revolution'," and set in extensive grounds. Mr Cotton added they had never been allowed further than the courtyard of the gatehouse to deliver their cargos. It was then I asked who actually collects the shipment?

Isaiah explained the broker is sometimes there, so is the fat paymaster who inspects the items and pays up. He seems to be pretty important by the way he orders everyone about. I asked if there was ever anyone else present except for the staff who unloaded the items.

Mr Cotton answered. "Once. About a month ago, two men arrived in a steam growler as we were unloading."

Isaiah nodded, "I didn't take them for just visitors because of the way the others reacted."

"What do you mean?"

"The broker and the fat man seemed very nervous around them."

"Why, I'd say they was plain scared of them," added Mr Cotton. "I can't say I wasn't scared of them too."

"Describe them."

Isaiah thought carefully. "White men, both tall. One older than the other. The older one was dressed like a gentleman but all in black. He wore a big hat and had a walrus moustache. He wore spectacles..."

"Dressed like a cowboy?" asked Sir John nodding towards Karl standing impassively in the doorway.

"Dressed like a lawman," replied Mr Cotton. "When I was a child, my father used to read me tales of the lawmen back on Earth, in the Wild West, when he was a boy. In the pictures, they always used to be dressed like that. Talked like a Texan too."

"And how would you know that?" asked Sir John.

"Why, Sir, I was born on Earth. In New York City. My father had been a Georgia gentleman's personal slave. His master freed him when General Sherman's dirigibles firebombed Atlanta. He fled straight North and joined the Army of the Union, Brisbin's 5th USC Cavalry. After the war, he became a steward on an aethervolt passenger ship to pay our passage here. We left Earth when I was only small, but I know a Texan accent when I hear it."

I felt my blood run cold again. "The other one?"

"I think younger, he wore a big coat and a high crowned derby, and he had this thing built into his face. Like..." He gestured towards his face.

"...they had replaced his eye with it." Adam finished the sentence for him.

Mr Cotton nodded, "Yes. The rest of his face was pretty strange too, like..."

"Mine?"

The room fell quiet for a while.

Adam told Karl and Howe to guard Barebones and Cotton, while Sir John, Red and I joined him in the engine room where we could talk in private. He wanted to know whether we agreed this was an avenue worth following. Rather than just going to Alba and ferreting about, knocking on doors or "busting heads" as Sir John put it, until we found something useful to lead us to D Maurier's location.

I pointed out that it was never much of a plan and would take a great deal of time and was, by its very nature, an unreliable course of action. I felt instinctively that this thing was important from the moment we first laid eyes on it. We all agreed that we felt much the same.

Sir John pointed out that this was an unexpected but fortuitous turn of events. At that, Adam rounded on him almost angrily but stopped short, only replying, "Yes, very fortuitous, indeed."

I ventured that if Everheart and Knapp were at the mansion a month ago, then D Maurier must be connected to the place. Not all the papers on D Maurier had been particularly useful in pointing out exactly where we might find the little runt and, that for all our intended bravery, this might be a more unexpected line of approach. An avenue that D Maurier and his cabal of friends would least expect.

Sir John agreed but cautioned, "We may just blunder into a nest of vipers, and your man may well be long gone."

Adam gave Sir John that barely masked look again. "Unless by some amazing stroke of good fortune, I do not expect to unearth him there. Nevertheless, I do expect we may well unearth valuable information as to where we will find him. In a way it is still the same plan; knock on doors and bang a few heads until someone tells us something of worth. It is just that this appears a lot more promising than scouring the sticky end of Alba for felonious ne're-do-wells and other bottom dwellers to roust from their lairs. If we disturb a nest of vipers, as you call them, we will clear them out, and then at least we will have done something worthwhile."

"Start as we mean to go on!" Laughed Sir John, "Damn right, we will!"

"Unless, of course, it is a trap." Red's comment hung in the air like an Aresian Man-o'-War; no one daring to touch it.

"That would be difficult to set up." Sir John finally spoke, "How would they know we would hitch a ride on that particular ship? If we had made good time, we would have jumped the Old Bull and been on our way to Alba or Yuma, or some other God-forsaken hellhole. I did not even know the Queen was laying over in Ember. I came over on the off chance there was some crew there I knew, and we could hitch a ride."

"Just good luck," said Adam.

"Exactly! Nobody can predict the future like that." Sir John turned to Red. "So, I do not see how it could be a trap, old boy. That thing is not a handful of broadcasted millet for luring us in like ducks."

"Still," Adam added quietly. "We will need to treat this like we believe we are walking into a trap." His tone did not broach any argument.

We returned to the control room, and Adam informed Isaiah that we were coming with him to deliver the crate. The deal he offered, if it could be called that, was that the crew would be disarmed and released to operate the vehicle. Once we arrived at the delivery point, they would all be free to go. Isaiah and Mr Cotton were given no choice as to whether to accept those terms or not.

Journal of Adam Franklin.

Though I know how insane this appears as I write the very words on the page, Cattarina Monck is haunting me. At first in my dreams but now, I am seeing her, out the corner of my eye, a glimpse and then she was gone, but now she is there. Solid, as real as... well, as real as any of this insanity can be real. She stands, her long graceful handheld out to me and her eyes full of pleading. She does not seem angry with me; I feel no malice from her.

What does she want from me? I tried to give her peace. Now she will not allow me any.

I must stop myself from following these trains of thought. Regardless of Madam Niketa's séance and my own near-death experience, I adamantly believe there are no such things as ghosts. It is all a trick of my own mind, some less than subtle way of communicating with my wakeful mind, but what is it trying to say? On the other hand, is it simply telling me I am going mad?

I have no choice but to follow the Statue to its destination. However, I feel it is undoubtedly, if not a trap, then a setup, of some kind. Sydeian is lying through his teeth. I believe in blind luck even less than I believe in coincidence.

Charity Bryant-Drake.
45-46/9/26.

The Story of Two Queens.

Cont.

The journey took a day and a half.

Mr Cotton proved to be an amiable and talkative host. I was intrigued to know how he and Isaiah had come up with their subterfuge, and with a little prompting, he was happy to tell us of the history of their 'little enterprise.' Most of the young men on board had actually been part of a crew working out of a rookery in Alba city, mainly dippers, drunk-rollers, mobs men, mughunters and palmers (various pickpockets), run by a malicious scoundrel known as 'Black Murphy.' It was a name I remembered as linked to several criminal cases during my time as a runner for the ugly men that made up the court correspondents.

According to Mr Cotton's tale, Black Murphy had overstepped the mark one day. Fancied himself as a smasher, and took to "running coiners," (which Mr Cotton explained was counterfeiting money). Then, buoyed by his newfound wealth, he tried to "diddle" the Union Street Boys out of their "dividend." They came to punish him one night, but he was "buried in the rookery deeper than a tick on a dog's behind." So, they set fire to the whole warren, seven or eight buildings regardless of who was in it. Families, children, old people, the infirmed. Luckily, the crew had about a dozen different ways out of the lofts and attics that made up their nest. In the panic most escaped, but the Union Street Boys quickly caught Black Murphy and his two Captains and brutally extracted their dividend.

By dint of his wits, Isaiah became the nominal Captain of this little dispossessed crew of rapscallions as they tried to survive on the streets of Alba's old iron mining quarter. They were just about hanging on when Mr Cotton came upon them. Omari admitted that as a child, after losing his parents, he had fallen into much the same line as they. His size had helped him in many ways, most often because it meant that people underestimated how intelligent he was. He had been taught to read by his mother and father before he was six years old, and with a head full of "daring do" adventure stories and sharp wits, he had managed to survive. He also read anything he could, especially about engineering, because his dream had been to build an aethervolt craft and fly back to Earth like Hamilton and Stranger did. A dream he still harboured.

Regardless of his imposing physical demeanour, he claimed to have very little stomach for "the rough stuff." To survive, he made his living originally as a bookie's runner, later as a gambler himself, something he claimed to be very adept at.

The caterpillar vehicle, which I learnt was called 'Oruga Voraz,' and like a ship the crew refer to it as a female, was surprisingly fast over flat ground. Mr Cotton was very proud of the machine and told us that it had been designed by an eccentric Spaniard, an inventor called Juan Javier Sánchez for use as an exploration vehicle in very remote areas. Professor Sánchez died while searching for lost Aresian pyramid tombs in the red forests of Cydonia, in the east of Eden, long before the last Aresian war. Some claimed Sánchez had been a tomb robber and that he was murdered for the treasures he amassed. However, if that existed or not, he died, leaving only a modest estate, and the Oruga.

The Oruga is a fantastic vehicle, Edwin Ransom would love this machine. It can easily achieve thirty-five miles every hour over flat terrain, but its greatest strength is its ability to traverse forests, waterways and negotiate the roughest of ground. At one point in our journey the Oruga, instead of navigating around a deep crater, over seventeen miles in diameter, descended the rim at almost sixty degrees and, once we had negotiated the soft sandy floor of the depression, scaled the even steeper incline back out. Inside the vehicle, in all but the control room, the noise of the engine's hissing and throbbing, along with the clanking and thudding of the pistons that drive the legs, was unbearable.

Mr Cotton maintains he won the Oruga Voraz in a game of faro (somewhat like poker, I think) from the dissolute nephew of the late Professor Sánchez, who was rapidly squandering himself into penury.

Mr Cotton had worked on repairing the machine for several months, but it needed a crew, and when he came across Isaiah, he found a crew without a home. It had been as uncomplicated as that. He knew that the Oruga would make the perfect vehicle for a smuggling enterprise, and he needed hands to run it.

That remark piqued my journalist's nose for a story. People do not make throwaway comments like that unless they are dying to tell you something the more prudent part of their mind cautions against. I pushed him a little on why the Oruga Voraz was so good a machine for smuggling. I could understand that she is fast and can traverse the roughest of ground, but there are plenty of other engines that can do that. He could not resist but tell me that the Oruga is amphibious, as far as being totally submersible for several hours. I, playing Devil's advocate, pointed out that a few hours underwater was a remarkable achievement of engineering and good for hiding, but once out in the open, she was no less conspicuous than any other vehicle, in fact, more so than most.

Mr Cotton gave out a booming laugh, "Ma'am, this old girl, she has many, many tricks. Pardon me, but you forget the man who designed and built it was a true genius." I pushed a little more, but all he would add was, "Beauty, they say, is skin deep," with a conspiratorial wink.

Aware I would get no further on that point, I took the opportunity to ask another question that had perplexed me; if the vehicle is his, why then is Isaiah its Captain?

"Why, Ma'am, we are pirates! As is tradition, we held a show of hands. Anyway, Isaiah is the smartest young man I have ever known. I just don't have the mind for business he has. I take my portion and a portion for the Oruga, the rest is shared out fairly."

I knew there was so much more to his story than he was telling me, and that it was probably more than simple circumspection; even so, I was genuinely charmed by him, with his warm rolling baritone voice, sparkling eyes, and ready smile.

Over these few days I have met people like Isaiah Barebones, Omari Cotton and Maëlle Rambeau, criminals all of them, ruthless, unrepentant pirates and smugglers, who are also some of the most enthralling and intriguing individuals I have ever encountered.

Extracts from

Beresford's History of the Martian Colonies.

Vol 2.3rd Edition. Milton and Dante.

Chapter 7. The Second War of the Sirenuim Planes.

Influential voices in the Government and military of the Republic of Tharsis had long called for action on the territorial disputes over the Gorgonum Chaos, an area renowned for its broken terrain and lush ancient temperate and sub-tropical forest, situated on Tharsis' southwestern border and west of Icaria. A region that was always a point of contention between the British Empire and Austro-Hungarian interests during the colonial period.

Due to undertakings given at the Thoris Conference, Tharsis had renounced its claims over the region in order to secure agreements on other more imperative areas of control. Politically the Chaos was seeded to Sirenum Plains. The old Austro-Hungarian colony, with its hotchpotch of ethnic groups, was contending to unify with the ethnic German settlers to establish itself as an independent nation. The eastern border of Gorgonum though remained undefined. Icaria, with the support of Tharsis, refused to relinquish territorial claims.

Under pressures from external forces, political, military and environmental, Sirenia continually failed to establish secure borders and build any form of functioning infrastructure. The nascent state lurched from one political and social crisis to another.

Sirenia's perilous stagger towards independence continued until the invasion of Phaetontis by Zephyrian and Thylian forces under the guise of protecting the interests of minority French-speaking colonists. This action caused a mass migration of ethnic Dutch and Germanic settlers into the Plains. Sirenia's limited resources and fragile social structure was unable to aid or stem the flow of refugees. Conflicts soon broke out between the ethnic Hungarian, Bohemian and Romanian Sirenians and the displaced Phaetontis refugees.

Tharsis intervened in the situation by resettling large numbers of the Phaetontis refugees into the forest of Gorgonum, sometimes forcibly. Tharsis' Government cited this as a humanitarian act; conversely, it was more to political ends. The resettling of the Phaetontis refugees was seen as a way of creating a buffer of anti-Zephyrian communities along Tharsis' southern western border. By favouring these settler communities generously, Tharsis aimed at further undermining Sirenia, both economically and politically. Unsurprisingly the Phaetontis settlers of the Gorgonum Chaos rapidly thrived, while the rump of Sirenia, especially the communities of the lowland plains, stagnated.

In the following years, the husk of Phaetontis became a puppet state of the Zephyrian and Thylian alliance, and a staging post for their intended expansion into Sirenuim Plains.

Broader political and military issues on the worldwide stage meant that the Zephyrian and Thylian Concordat's expansionist plans in the area were shelved. Tested by war with Tharsis and its allies, the Concordat soon became unable or unwilling to do anything constructive to further their campaign in Sirenuim. Certain voices in the Thylian newspapers began to question publicly the political and military concord with Zephyria; 'Cui Bono?' was a famous headline to an alliance-shaking editorial published in the Thylian Beobachter.

In Chalon, the Capital of Sirenia, after the third failed harvest, the governing apparatus, as much as it was, collapsed into utter chaos. In reaction to the failure of the central authority, various communities across the Planes declared themselves as Communes in the style of revolutionary France, under the umbrella of a Federation of Free Settlers. The Phaetontis communities of Gorgonum Chaos, who had, since their creation, been virtually independent of the central authority, led by the orator and fervent anti-Zephyrian, Gerban van Ebbenhorst, became willing participants in the new quasi-political structure.

From early in the Martian Year (M.Y.) 25, Zephyrian attention turned back to Sirenuim. Without military support from Thyle, Zephyria was concerned not to find itself in direct conflict with Tharsis, so relied upon creating dissent and sponsoring disaffected minority groups, some with wildly differing agendas. The "Guerrilla Plan," a policy put forward by Marshal Pierre Boulle, was readily adopted. It was thought that much of the groundwork for a future Zephyrian conquest could be achieved by placing supplies of equipment, weapons and funding into the hands of those groups with a grudge. By mid M.Y.26, Zephyria had created some steadfastly pro-Zephyrian enclaves in the south of Gorgonum and was using them to support destabilising activities, sabotage and terror throughout Gorgonum and Sirenia.

Meanwhile, the city of Chalon suffered an outbreak of an unknown poisoning similar to St. Anthony's Fire, which caused widespread violent psychosis, severe illness and death. Such madness, afflicting an armed and ethnically divided population, under such circumstances led to the destruction of the city. Unsubstantiated rumours stemming from various sources linked the magnate Windlestraw Volpone with the deliberate poisoning of the freshwater canals supplying the whole city. Volpone, known as the White Fox, had been in dispute with the City's Commune Council over their refusal to honour mineral rights he had obtained from members of the previous Sirenum National Government. The Commune Council had declared their predecessors corrupt and their contracts void, they had seized Volpone's mines, equipment and holdings, even some of his workers.

In March M.Y.26, Tharsis dispatched a small expeditionary force to Chalon to discover the truth of the conflicting reports coming, or not, from the city. Upon their return, they reported that the city was mostly gutted by fire. They had encountered unidentified forces within the conurbation and were forced to skirmish their way out of several ambushes. The reports stated that, in the opinion of the officers, these forces were forward skirmishing detachments of the Zephyrian Foreign Legion, supported by pro-Zephyrian settlers.

Pressure upon the Tharsis Government increased when on the 24th of July M.Y.26, leaders of twenty of the Free Settler Communes, led by István Zsoldos, leader of the Sirenum City Commune, and Gerban van Ebbenhorst, brought space in the Tharsis broadsheets to publish a signed open letter pleading for Tharsis to intervene in Sirenia to "defend our freedoms," against Zephyrian aggression.

This "Freedom Letter," as it was known, caused a public outcry in Tharsis, prompting anti-Zephyrian demonstrations in the streets and questions in parliament.

On the 40th of September M.Y. 26, Tharsis moved regular troops into the Gorgonum Chaos region in support of the Free Settlers. They then dispatched elements of the Air Navy to the border of Phaetontis to cut off any supply routes, and into Sirenum Plains to establish positions for fast retaliation against enemy actions.

On the 44th of September, on the tail of one of that year's worst sandstorms, the Tharsis forces struck.

"Sometimes fate is like a small sandstorm that keeps changing directions. You change direction but the sandstorm chases you. You turn again, but the storm adjusts. Over and over, you play this out, like some ominous dance with death just before dawn. Why? Because this storm isn't something that has nothing to do with you. This storm is you. Something inside you. So all you can do is give in to it, step right inside the storm, closing your eyes and plugging up your ears so the sand doesn't get in, and walk through it, step by step. There's no sun there, no moon, no direction, no sense of time. Just fine white sand swirling up to the sky like pulverized bones."

HARUKI MURAKAMI,
KAFKA ON THE SHORE

DAY FOURTEEN.
RAGING TEMPEST

Editorial Note.

The Great Sand Storm. Day 14.

The newly renamed airship the *Haul Du* departed from Mefitis on the morning of 43rd of September at 8am. She made good progress in a South Easterly direction towards Tharsis' southern border.

Little of interest was recorded in the Captain's new scrap log other than a personal note regarding his surprise at how willing the authorities in Mefitis had been to turn a blind eye to the *Seren Bore*'s transformation.

Scarce entries in the expedition member's diaries and journals, other than comments on the sandstorm they endured, seem to suggest that a sombre and reflective mood had settled over the ship.

J.F. Ransom

The Diary of Dr James Athanasius Flammarion.
43rd Sept. 26th

An entire day lost to a raging tempest.

I was awoken by severe turbulence. The ship had been overcome by a dust storm of some considerable magnitude rolling in from eastern Daedalia.

By the time I reached the flight deck, the storm had grown to such proportions that Llewellyn had informed me that we either must ground or be blown severely off course. It was as we were discussing our possible actions that the starboard rudder was rent from its mountings, sending the ship into a violent spin. I was thrown bodily across the flight deck and cracked my head against one of the swinging electrificated lanterns, which knocked me senseless for some time.

Though Mr Holly's ministrations saw me back on my feet, I beat a hasty retreat to the safety of my cabin.

Mr Charles reported to me regularly throughout the day. Though temporary repairs were effected to the rudder, it was impossible, due to the ferocity of the storm, to do anything other than run before the wind. I also had Edwin supervise the deploying of our ad hoc lightening system to dissipate the static build-up of ionized dust.

As soon as it was feasible, I requested an estimation of how far we had been blown off course. Llewellyn assessed we may have been pushed afield by fifty to sixty miles, possibly more, but he was unable to even speculate at what would be the final extent of our deviation. Depending, of course, on the force of the winds, which are between seventy and eighty knots at the moment, and upon how long the storm lasts.

I sent word to all the expedition members to remind them not to venture out of the confines of the ship, as the windblown sand at this speed can easily damage eyes and strip flesh. Who of us has not, in their blithe adolescence, made the mistake of ignoring such warnings and suffered sand burns, or almost choked to death by the swirling dust? I remember my cousin, Gerald, as a young man, suffering terrible burns from being caught out in such a blast, in nothing more than his cricket whites, it stripped the skin off his back as if he had been flayed.

All any of us could do was test our patience, and our nerve, as we waited out the day.

Llewellyn did an excellent job of riding out the storm.

At eight o'clock in the evening, Mr Charles informed those of us gathered in the saloon that the Captain felt the wind had abated enough to attempt to ground the ship.

That grounding was the most alarming, forced landing I have ever known. In fact, but for Llewellyn and his crew's airmanship, it would have been a disastrous crash.

All we could do was hold fast to the fixtures and pray that God would not see our endeavour end in such an ignominious manner.

Finally, we are down and moored, but the storm still rages about us.

I have just finished a meeting with Captain Llewellyn, Edwin and Ranolph. We all agreed that it has been particularly unfortunate for us to have been caught in the teeth of two of the worst storms of the year so far. Until this clear, we cannot take bearings from the stars. Even our compasses are redundant until the dust settles. A rough estimate places us over a hundred miles off course.

However, we are down and safe, by the Grace of God.

I shall speak to the team in the morning after Llewellyn has briefed me.

The Flammarion Expedition Journal of L. Edwin Ransom.
Day fourteen. 43rd. 9th. 26.
Saturday.

My own disquiets beleaguered me throughout these days. I can find no way to relieve this despondency.

My mind is like a carousel unable to stop returning to thoughts of Nelly, no matter how I try to distract myself from the pain of my broken heart, and I am now so weak from such misery that I fear soon I shall have no more tears left in me.

We were in the grip of a terrific storm from dawn to darkness.

The Captain's decision was to keep the winds at our stern and ride the storm's leading edge, but that meant a headlong rush into the cinnabar-coloured fog with little but Llewellyn's and Charles' instincts to rely upon.

I could not bear being cooped up in my little cabin and so, driven by the hope that something to occupy my hands may distract me a little, I busied myself assisting in the repairs to the starboard rudder and aiding Mr Beer with deploying the anti-fulguration grid.

I achieved something of my intentions by driving myself to such enervation that, upon returning to my cabin, I collapsed upon my cot, fully clothed, and slept the dreamless sleep of the exhausted.

The Flammarion Expedition Journal of L. Edwin Ransom.
Day fifteen. 44th. 9th. 26.
Sunday.

Morning came. Well, our chronometers concurred with it growing a few shades lighter, but as for 'morning,' it was, like the dawn, yet to be seen.

The storm had ceased; nonetheless, we were, as with these things, left with that saffron-coloured miasma that hampers both breathing and vision. Dust, the eternal enemy of all life on this planet, will hang in the air for however long it takes, regardless of our hopes and prayers. Visibility on the ground was, initially, down to a few yards, but that fluctuated depending upon how much the breeze stirred the dust clouds about us.

After breakfast, the Professor informed the expedition members what was known about our situation. By the Captain's reckoning, we were far further off course than had been expected, possibly far more than a hundred miles, but until the sky clears, we can only have a vague estimate to go on. The ship's compasses were, of course redundant, due to the static electrification of the sand and dust about us.

After the repairs to the starboard rudder were completed, Llewellyn wished for us to push on as best as we could, taking our bearings for the position of the sun, as much as could be seen of it.

We busied ourselves with whatever staved off the boredom. Patty's and Aelita's suggestion that we at least got outside and take a few turns around the decks was enthusiastically received. So, for a while, we distracted ourselves with a promenade.

Though it could do little to lift my melancholia, it was good to get outside and stretch our legs, but there was little else to do other than to peer over the sides into the orange murk in vain attempts to spot anything.

It was as we were about to retreat back inside for tea, that a shout went up from one of the crewmen on the portside watch.

We all rushed to see what had caused the alarm. Squinting into the gloom, it was Alita that was first to make it out.

There, ahead of us, about a few hundred yards from our resting place lay the remains of a gigantic aethervolt ship, burnt out and in places stripped to its skeletal frame by the windblown sands. Its colossal prow, towering portentously out of the sand and regolith, was still emblazoned with the name 'SMS Ozymandias,' an Austro-Hungarian. In truth, such things are not an unusual sight, our world is littered with these testimonials to the tragic ends to mankind's foolhardiness, but there was something strange about that one. Something foreboding. I wondered if it touched upon some long-forgotten memory of mine.

Dr Spender, standing beside me, intoned a verse I had never heard; "King of Kings am I, Ozymandias. If anyone would know how great I am and where I lie, let him surpass my works." He smiled at me, "Quite a portentous designation to give an aethervolt ship."

"Portentous, indeed." Patty remarked, "Another few seconds in the air and we would have crashed headfirst into that hulk."

403

As a child, I had been interested in mysterious events, a thing that living in this world provides a constant diet of, especially airships and aethervolts that went missing never to be seen again. I used to snip them from my father's newspapers and out of the back page of the penny dreadfuls Philip used to read. My favourite, like so many little boys of my age, had been the curious tale of the Holländer's disappearance, with all the mystery and bizarre sightings it entailed. Maybe the Ozymandias belonged to that canon of knowledge now almost lost to me. I made a mental note to look it up one day when I get back. I could dig out all those old scrapbooks I kept and reread those amazing stories and wild speculations.

"What powerful but unrecorded race.

Once dwelt in that annihilated place."

OZYMANDIAS

HORACE SMITH

1818

DAY FIFTEEN
<u>THE HOURGLASS SEA,</u>

Extracts from

Beresford's History of the Martian Colonies.

Vol 2.3rd Edition. Milton and Dante.

Chapter 8. The Empyreans.

'*It is an inexcusable conceit, indulged in by mediocre romantic scholars, to propose that the representations of palpably fantastical, nay mythical, creatures; gods and demi-gods, found in Aresian art should be cited as testimony of the presence of unknown races throughout Martian history.*

'*If these phantasmagorias were to be accepted as prima facie evidence then, by that very self-same reasoning, we would have to admit that there were indeed jackal and crocodile-headed empyreans abroad in ancient Egypt, winged men in ancient Persia and*

cloud hopping dragons in olden Nippon. Even that St.
Christopher himself had the head of a dog!

'This, along with unsubstantiated claims of other
tinted sub-races amidst the Aresians themselves,
pushes credibility beyond the pale of factual knowledge
into the realms of wistful fantasy.'

Meghan. 1885.

The question of whether there were other sentient
races on Mars throughout the reign of the Aresian
Empires is one that has vexed historians and
archaeologists ever since Tellurian humankind first set
foot on Martian red soil. The primary obstacle to the
academic and scientific investigation into the question
of these 'others,' was the flat refusal of the various
Colonial Authorities to entertain any serious
discussion of the presence of other sentient alien races
on Mars.

This point of view, closed-minded as it was,
stemmed from a paper presented by Professor Sir
Oswald Meghan to the Royal Society in London in
1885. In which the eminent Professor painstakingly
endorsed the British Government's stated position.
This position also allowed the dismissal of the Anemoi

as being merely nest-building animals of a lower order, akin to nothing more than flying monkeys.

The British Imperial Colonial administration unofficially, nonetheless enthusiastically, adopted the term 'empyreans' as a comprehensive label for any evidence, archaeological or historical, that they wished to disparage or discard as spurious. This stance was effective in curtailing any credible academic investigation into the evidence of such 'others.'

The Diary of Dr James Athanasius Flammarion.

44th Sept. 26th

The sandstorm cleared as the dawn arose. The ironized dust in the upper atmosphere, though giving everything such fabulous radiance, rendered our compasses utterly useless and blocked any attempt at avigation by the heavens. The hazy sun was our only point of reference from which we could take a heading, but as to where we are on the map, it is impossible to fathom.

By mid-morning, the iridescent sky was a kaleidoscope of brilliant hues, though lateral visibility was still severely inhibited. At our conference, it was decided that we would use the sun's position as our bearing and keep moving Easterly at a measured pace until either the dust cleared, or we could spot a landmark. I felt it was necessary, under these circumstances, to keep the momentum of our journey up and put as much distance between ourselves and the reach of the Tharsis Air Navy as possible.

The only thing of interest we passed all morning was an airship wreck of some considerable size. An old Austro-Hungarian warship, impressive, though nothing unique. The Seas of Sand are littered with such monuments to human grief.

I had sent my apologies to Mr Holley, citing pressures of my responsibilities, to excuse me from his Sunday service. I felt no inclination to pray to a God that would allow that horrific disease to strip Alexa's life away in such a slow and agonising way and then would allow those fiends to murder my Eleanor. I feel tested, and I do not have the stamina or strength of faith of Job. I fear I might lose my composure mid-service and end up railing against the injustice of it all or blubbing uncontrollably like Edwin. Preferring my own company at that point, and lost in my own thoughts, I was taking tea in my cabin when a cry went up from the watch.

I heard the bosun's whistle blow to send the men to their posts. Setting my cup aside, I went to investigate.

On the flight deck, the Captain and Mr Charles were standing at the observation windows staring out. Curious as to what had caused their consternation, I joined them, however at the sight I beheld, my questions died on my lips.

We had crested a small ridge, and the land below us fell steeply away into rolling dunes. From this height, in all directions, as far as our eyes could see, was scattered a vast plethora of wrecked machinery. To my perplexed gaze, it first appeared to be some immense rubbish heap, a graveyard of carelessly discarded contraptions. However, I rapidly appreciated that it was no meagre rag-and-bone man's scrapyard.

It appeared to be an immense battlefield. The machines and vehicles not discarded, but piled broken upon each other, war-torn and burnt, where they had fallen in incalculable numbers. Most were little more than shattered, twisted wrecks. Though, as we ventured further out over the battlefield, we saw, amidst the chaos, almost complete machines and vehicles we recognised, and many more we did not.

There were countless engines of apparently human construction, but then again so many that were unfamiliar to us; Aresian sand flyers entangled with Tellurian walkers, strange, armoured land vehicles lay amidst the wreckage of airships of unknown origin. An alien-looking tripodic machine towered thirty feet or more over the shattered remains of a huge, armoured wagon with Blinov type continuous tracks, sporting a turret-mounted gun, obviously human in design.

Mr Charles informed me it was an Ironclad, though it looked nothing like the steam carriage mounted guns I have seen roll through the city during the Independence Day parades. There was not just one here, there were, amongst the insane jumble of metal carnage, dozens, if not hundreds, and almost all of differing designs.

A huge Aresian trireme lay shattered upon the sands, its hull now nothing more than a burnt-out husk. All about it were scattered the destroyed carcases of fat-bodied metal tripodic and hexapodic machines, like giant silver ticks, their glossy skins reflecting the rich orange and reds of the sky. All about them, thick black dust covered the sands.

By now Edwin and Ranolph had joined me at the window, the others were forward of the Weather deck. Even the crew, those not on duty, crowed the decks to witness this spectacle.

I excused myself and went to find Octavius. He and his daughter were at the handrails on the starboard side. I asked him if he knew which battlefield this was, because it was one I knew nothing of.

Octavius laughed dryly. "It is no battlefield I have ever heard of. James." He gave me a very singular look, a glance that forced me to question him further.

"Is this the lost Aresian armada? The one that never attacked Tyrrhena Mons."

"It is possible, some of these are undoubtedly Aresian, but I do not recognise the markings on any of these machines, and if it were, then who in God's name were they fighting?" He shook his head, "I have no idea."

"Neither have I," I agreed.

"Have you any inkling whereabouts we are?"

I was just about to explain our deficiency in calculating our location when Octavius' daughter, who had been surveying the area through a small pair of cow-bone opera glasses, pointed into the far distance and queried ominously, "What is that?"

I took the glasses and peered through them. Far off in the distance, I could see a floating platform, for a moment I thought it man-made, but it was obviously not. I called for someone to bring me a more powerful spyglass, and upon closer examination, determined it was a fracture of floating rock, much like the one in Tharsis. Reputedly a piece of Phrike the third moon of Mars. Upon its flattened top was a soaring pale spire, like some elegant Egyptian obelisk. I handed the telescope to Octavius who, after complaining his eyes were no longer as good as they once were, and sending his daughter to fetch his spectacles, took a long look.

"Dear Lord, unless the distance is an illusion, that thing must be almost half the size of the Pegasus Rock!"

Words issued from my mouth before they had even entirely formed in my mind and thus disturbed myself as much as it did him. "I did a survey of all the known pieces of Phrike in my freshman year at University, I know of no unaccounted pieces as large as that."

"Well, there appears to be one," remarked his daughter.

Octavius let out a gasp that caused us both to turn to him in concern. "Of course!" he exclaimed. "In Hoy-Castle's book, there is mention." He sent his daughter to fetch the book from his bedside. Once she had returned with the battered and heavily thumbed tome, he riffled hastily through its annotated pages. "Ah! Here it is!"

"What 'is,' may I ask?"

"It is quite a long article, but he notes here that travellers in eastern Lybia, an area commonly known as the 'Hourglass Sea,' have reported a number of unusual experiences, some quite singular in fact. The area has a reputation for people and things going unaccountably missing, most celebrated of these, no doubt you remember James, was the aerostat Der Fliegende Holländer in 1892, the Holländer was never found. It is also where the Dalander disappeared too."

"The Dalander was taken by airship pirates," I pointed out.

"That was the official pronouncement, by the Lybian government, mainly so that the families could claim the insurance compensation, and to avoid political embarrassment. Nevertheless, she was never found, no survivors, no wreckage."

I must admit to being a little irritated at this digression when we had such an imminent mystery confronting us. "Octavius, I cannot believe you would give even a second thought to such nonsense. The man is well known for being a charlatan." My tone, unfortunately, was more challenging than I meant it to be. "What exactly has that to do with this place?"

Octavius looked somewhat taken aback, and his daughter gave me such a reproachful glare that I felt like a cad for being so short with him. He slowly closed the book and peered at me over his spectacles like an old schoolmaster looking upon a particularly obstinate student who was just not grasping what he was supposed to understand. *"Some of those travellers, a few but enough to warrant consideration, mentioned seeing, or encountering, an unrecorded but large floating rock platform out over the Hourglass Sea. A platform with a tower upon it. Though it does not appear on any map."*

I tried to reason with him. *"Nonsense, Octavius. That is impossible. The Hourglass Sea is over six thousand miles from Mefitis. Granted we were blown off course however that distance is impossible."*

I shall remember the look in Octavius' eyes for the rest of my days. He opened the book again and began to read aloud.

"In March 1896 Captain Bernard Fokke of the München, a redoubtable fellow of thirty years' experience at the helm, mostly spent plying back and forward over the Hourglass Sea without incident, reported to the Austro-Hungarian authorities his discovery of what he believed to be an unrecorded or lost battlefield. In his application request for exclusive salvage rights, he named the supposed lost battlefield as 'Camlann.' Due to the outbreak of the Wars of Independence, he was unable to embark upon his search until late M.Y.1. Alas, though he borrowed heavily and spent a fortune, he failed to rediscover the Camlann site, and died penniless in a debtor's prison in October M.Y.5." Octavius looked up at me. *"Hoy-Castle mentions that, even after his*

disgrace and untimely death, Captain Fokke's entire crew maintained his story."

"Dear God."

"Hoy-Castle also notes that Hamilton mentioned in his letters the first time he encountered a floating rock with a tower upon it. He called it 'Magdala's Tower.' It has always been thought that he was talking of what we call the Pegasus Rock; however, he said he was hunting in the southern deserts of the Kingdom of Iclea, in the retinue of its yellow Martian Prince, Altfoura. That was in what we now call southern Lybia. Not Acidalia Planitia where the British took the Pegasus Rock from."

"That would put us over six thousand miles from Mefitis. Far beyond where we could possibly be."

"That would appear so." Sometimes Octavius' tone alone could cut a man to the quick.

I returned to the bridge and requested Captain Llewellyn to take us lower so we could better view the scene. I felt a compulsion to investigate the mysterious floating rock and the enigmatic spire atop of it.

Below us, the field of destruction continued. Stranger and stranger war machines, the likes of which few of us could have ever imagined, littered the landscape.

To placate the excitement onboard our ship, and to give Captain Llewellyn and I some time to paw over the charts and *maps in a desperate attempt to make sense of our predicament, I agreed to Jahns' request that we pause for a while so he could go down and have a closer look at the machines.*

Mr Charles had us brought to a halt, and I allowed Jahns to organise the excursion. Jahns insisted that he take his men and that the crew should also be issued their arms. I readily agreed, as my own disquiet at the nature of this ominous place was growing by the moment.

I was deeply intrigued by the plethora of contrivances and was desirous to go down to inspect them myself but, as duty and safety of the ship dictated, I could not. I requested Edwin to go in my stead. I thought it would be good for him. After all, he is every bit the engineer I am. Also, I felt it would be a good sign of my faith in his judgement. He agreed solemnly.

Octavius insisted he wanted to accompany the others to view the wreckage for himself. Madam Fontenelli said she too wished to escort Octavius and his daughter. I, in turn, asserted, that she take her automaton with her for her protection.

Jahns and his men combed the area thoroughly before I allowed the rest of them to descend. Nevertheless, it has done little to calm my unease. The incident at Edwin's farm is uppermost in my mind along with the growing anxiety at the fact we have no idea where exactly we are on the face of this Godforsaken world.

I have instructed Llewellyn to have all the guns readied in case any nasty surprises lurk amidst this field of devastation.

The Flammarion Expedition Journal of L. Edwin Ransom.
Day fifteen. 44th. 9th. 26.
Sunday.

Cont.

I was in my cabin preparing myself to attend Mr Holley's
Sunday Prayer Service. Mr Holley had left a note to inform me he
would lead us in some prayers for Nelly and my family, something
that truly touched me deeply; nonetheless, I was anxious as to how
I would react emotionally. The Professor is a great one at
maintaining that old aphorism of the British gentleman's stiff-
upper-lip, but we are British no longer, and I can barely pull
myself together enough to appear to function at any worthwhile
level, let alone control myself through a memorial service. So, as I
sat in that little cabin clutching that note, I found myself talking to
Nelly as if she were there in the room with me. Begging her
consent not to attend. Would she be angry at me? Disappointed? I
could see her smiling face and knew that even so; she would
forgive me. However, my sense of duty disparaged my plea, as
nothing more than another display of my inherent cowardice. I
struggled with what the others would think of me, let alone the
Professor.

Therefore, it came as some relief when I was alerted by the
commotion on deck. I found myself following the Colonel forward
to the prow of the ship and stood in awe of the sight that greeted
us.

A vast graveyard of innumerable smashed and shattered
contraptions wheeled and tracked, flying and walking, of every

conceivable size and configuration. They littered the land as far as we could see as if discarded by some ancient war god.

I asked the Colonel if he knew what battlefield it was.

He did not. "Ah, there have been so many, but I know of nothing like this."

Dr Spender too was at a loss to explain it.

I know too little of the intricacies of war and war machines to claim anything but a rudimentary knowledge, but there were here, broken and torn, machines the likes of which I have never even heard talk of.

The Colonel requested of the Professor that we stop to take a much closer look. The ostensible reason, he argued, being an attempt to identify to whom these things belonged, though I felt his words belied his real motivation. I could see in the Professor's face that he was not entirely happy about allowing such an escapade, but, with Dr Spender's support, the Colonel insisted. The Professor conceded, admitting that he was as curious about this place as everyone else.

The ship was brought to a halt and preparations were made for our little field trip, as Patty called it. The Professor, though upon the recommendations of the Captain, decided against joining us and asked me to go in his stead. I know it may have been more to lift my spirits than anything else, as my mood had been darkening through most of the morning, so I agreed, as it was indeed ill-advised for him to leave the ship.

The Colonel and his men descended first to make sure the area was secure before we were lowered on the platform. As we rode down my interest was piqued by what appeared to be a type of Nutcracker, a steam-powered walking fighting vehicle, which I had seen once or twice in military parades, but this one was much bigger.

So as soon as we reached the sand, and after helping the ladies and Dr Spender disembark, I made my way over to the intriguing machine.

It was quite a monster, I estimated it would have stood a good forty hands at least, dwarfing any Nutcracker, let alone any walking war wagon, I had ever seen, and it carried what, upon examination, appeared to me to be two great steam cannons, one on each arm, and another mounted in its chest plate. I was amazed to see it carried no steam boiler, and so with my interest further piqued, I examined it more closely. For the life of me, I could not discover its power source, apart from what I surmised could have been some type of energy cells, but they were far too small. I concluded that the machine, being, as it were, not completely wrecked, had been looted of its boiler. It took me a few moments to locate the pilot's chamber, but when I did, it was quite shocking to discover that the unfortunate fellow remained inside his contraption. Sadly, now only a desiccated husk, with half his head missing from where a shell had torn through the cockpit. He wore an elaborate uniform, a Hussar, I think. His shako still stuck to the headrest behind him with his own dried blood, bone and brain matter.

Sergeant Smith called my attention to the next pile of debris. It was some kind of flying weapon platform, like a small aerobarge, the kind of thing we copied from the Aresians, but this seemed to me neither Aresian nor Tellurian. Most of its front end had been destroyed by its impact with another vehicle on the ground, a huge ironclad, with pedrail wheels, toting a heavy mounted cannon. The ironclad bore all the signs of human design, but the flying machine did not.

With the Sergeant's aid, I climbed up the side of the ironclad so I could survey the strange aerobarge. Overall, it was shaped much like a three-bladed spearhead, the lower blade forming the hull. The flat upper surface provided a platform for a deck, with wheelhouse and mounted weaponry. I poised myself on the flank of the ironclad and made the short hop over on to the barge's deck. The five mounted guns resembled Aresian ones in ascetics but not as sleek. Behind one I discovered its cowled gunner, still strapped to his seat.

After only the quickest of glances, I called the others over. It took a few minutes for the Colonel, Patty and Alita to make the climb. Though I warned the ladies that it would be quite a shock, both insisted on viewing the corpse.

Initially the gunner appeared human like, though long limbed and long necked. He, and I assume it was a '*he*,' wore an armoured cuirass, with articulated armour on his arms and thighs, though he wore no helm other than a complicated set of goggles. His skin, now dried and sand blown, was once a mottled greyish green, somewhat reptilian in appearance. His two arms were sinewy and robust looking with hands similar to ours, four digits with a more centralised opposable thumb, each finger ending in a raptor like claw. Shockingly, it had another arm, emanating from the left side of its chest, far less powerful looking, with only three digits and a central opposing thumb. The third hand looked delicate, possibly underdeveloped, with only the hint of claws on the ends of the fingers, but it was that hand that was still gripping what I assumed was the weapon's trigger. With bravery born out of fascination, and at the encouragement of the others, I pushed back the hood from its head and slid off the heavy goggles.

I have never seen a creature like it, the long scaly neck reached the jaw line where it flared out into a row of sharp bonelike protrusions. The chin sported two short tusks, for want of a better word (I am no herpetologist). The mouth was wide, a featureless slit that the dry air had pulled into a grimace over rows of savage looking teeth. The nose was just a small bump with slits for nostrils. The mottled grey green skin of its head had been protected a little by the hood and we could make out other designs on its angular face. Patty observed they were tattoos, primitive warrior races often had them, at least back on Earth. The head was crowned with a horny crest.

Its huge lidless eyes though were the most alarming, protected by the goggles, they remained still quite clear, the irises were the yellow of amber with flecks of green and brown in them. The pupils, though almost wide open, were vertical slits. I stood transfixed, this was the first truly alien '*alien*,' I had ever seen, a magnificent and formidable empyrean, made all the more frightening by the fact it was obviously sentient.

Patty leaned close over the dead warrior while making "Uh ha," noises much like a doctor would make while examining you. I asked what she was looking for? She explained that, though the creature had no eye lids, it did appear to have some sort of nictitating membrane, and the brows looked flexible enough to close quite a way over the eyes.

"All well enough, Miss Spender." Colonel Jahns interrupted us. "More pertinent to our knowledge is what the hell is it and what is it doing here?"

Patty replied sharply. "How would I have any more idea than you, Colonel?"

Jahns, who looked quite flustered, pulled himself up short. "I apologise Miss Spender."

Patty ignored the apology. "An empyrean, Colonel, a reptilian man. Admittedly in an infinite universe, a probability, possibly even an inevitability, but I have never heard of a reptile on Earth or Mars, with five limbs."

"My God, girl, it's an alien. Why does the number of its limbs matter?"

"All creatures on Earth, even creatures here on Mars, whether land, sea or air, have an even number of limbs; two legs, two arms, such as humans, apes, and so on, or four legs, such as dogs or horses, or six or eight legs in insects and arachnids, birds, two wings two legs. Even the sand kraken has eight. Not three or five or seven, never an odd number, unless by accident or mutation. I know of no lizard or other reptile that has five limbs."

"Starfish?" I ventured.

I often forget Patty is very much her father's daughter, she gave me a look that a kindly teacher might give a struggling child, and explained, "That is no kind of Asteroidea, Edwin."

Desperately trying not to appear stupid, I suggested, "Monkeys in the zoo use their tails as a fifth limb."

"Prehensile. Yes, but it is not a fully developed fifth arm."

"So, why is that important?" asked Jahns impatiently.

"Because, Ranolph," Dr Spender appeared amongst us on the arm of Aelita's automaton Maid. "It suggests strongly that that creature came from somewhere utterly different from Earth or Mars, probably not even in this solar system. I could wager, somewhere where the laws of nature themselves are profoundly different. A truly alien race."

Sergeant Smith pointed towards the construction at the rear of the flier. "There is another one in the wheelhouse, Sir, better preserved."

There was indeed another, bigger though with more elaborate armour and tattoos. The creature's natural skin markings were like that of the reticulations on the skin of a python.

"Have you ever seen anything like it?" I asked rhetorically to no one in particular.

"Yes. I have." I had utterly forgotten Aelita's presence with us, as she had been so quiet. We all turned to her in amazement. "In my visions, I saw them at Ananthor, though they were less warlike in manner. They are called, the Jed'dak."

"Indeed," chimed Dr Spender. "I saw them too."

We all stood gazing at the fallen creature, speechless as if trying to digest what had been said. Until Sergeant Kline called to us from the ground. He too had discovered something he thought we should see. We hurried excitedly to investigate.

As Sergeant Kline led us, he explained that he and Sergeant Weinbaum had been checking for signs of life in case of an ambush, when he had discovered something he thought we would be interested in. Near to the burnt skeletal remains of a sizable dirigible, was what appeared to be a large round silver disk about thirty feet in diameter. It was partially buried both in the sand and under the crumpled tail frame of the dirigible.

On first inspection it did not seem damaged, in fact, it appeared blemishless, totally seamless, no windows or doors, nothing. Forestalling my observations, Sergeant Weinbaum led us around the other side of the craft, where we could see some way underneath it. Below, a door or hatchway, in the bottom hung open.

I was so lost in awe of this strange craft that I did not notice Patty pass me and put her head up inside the disk. "Dear God!"

She called out elatedly, "You have to see this!" With that, she hauled herself into the belly of the craft.

We rushed over to see what had excited her so. I got there first and, after taking a step or two into the hatchway thrust my head up into the craft.

At first, I could not quite understand what I was seeing.

"What is it, young man?" asked Dr Spender.

I stepped down but could only look at him and shake my head confusedly. "Impossible," I exclaimed, and then looked back inside. To my eyes, Patty had been apparently floating in featureless white emptiness. A harsh light seemed to emit from everywhere, but after a moment or two my eyes began to adjust, and I could make out that there was indeed a floor and a domed ceiling above me but nothing else. Inside was utterly featureless, and impossibly big, a vast cavernous void. Patty had wandered a good ten or twelve yards into the interior, and yet, on the outside, the craft was no more than thirty feet across. My mind grasped for explanations for what I was seeing. An optical illusion? Possibly. I had experienced such things in experiments at my University and at fairground attractions, distortions using convex and concave mirrors, but this was beyond any ingenious trick of the eye. This was impossible.

The material of the craft, was strange to the touch, neither cold nor warm with a texture somewhere between velvet and skin. I quickly drew my hands away in disgust, pulled on my gloves, and clambered up into the colourless emptiness.

Patty stood in open-mouthed wonder, her arms outstretched, and her eyes as big as saucers. I noticed the only thing that marred the pristine whiteness about her was the little trail of red sand left by her walking boots. I spun about like a child in a toyshop, utterly bemused. I tried to touch the ceiling, but it was by far beyond my reach. Intrepidly I turned and took a few steps in the other direction from Patty, attempting to measure out the distance in yards, but, without her presence as a reference, my senses were suddenly overcome by a nauseous sensation of vertigo. I think I must have staggered because Patty rushed to my aid. Taking my elbow, she turned me back towards the open hatch in the floor.

Dr Spender and Alita were awaiting us as we climbed down. I was failing miserably to explain to them what it was like inside and so I was just about to suggest to them they take a look themselves when the Colonel summoned us.

Just beyond the edge of the disk lay a form half-buried in the regolith. At first, I thought it to be one of the creatures we had discovered on the crashed flier, but I was egregiously mistaken. If the discovery of the reptile men had not been shocking enough, then here we were presented with something far more horrific.

An ornate helmet or mask of what looked like silver, fashioned to resemble some demonic grinning grotesque, lay discarded beside a supine corpse. It was roughly human-like in shape and size, but barrel-chested with powerful shoulders and overly long arms. The creature's head was immense in proportion to its body, with a ridged crown formed either side of what appeared to be its forehead, joining together to form a crest that ran down the back of its head, either side of which cascaded a curtain, of course, matted black hair. There was no discernible nose. Its lower face seemed to be taken up entirely by a gaping mouth beset with innumerable needle-sharp, semi-translucent teeth. Two bulbous eyes, the size of bicycle lamps, projected from its forehead, the irises though were like a cephalopod, with the characteristic strange "W" shaped pupils. The mottled dark greyish-green skin was scabrous, covered with thousands of tiny scales, now desiccated over its skull by the dry winds. From under flowing saffron robes, long, lithe leathery skinned limbs protruded, misshapen skeletal hands, with webbed fingers, that had, in its last moments, grasped at its own garments and the gritty sand about it.

I am not a superstitious man or given to flights of fancy, I hope, but, no matter that it was deceased, and had been so for some time, the creature seemed to exude malevolence.

It, this frog-fish-man creature, whether male or female I have no idea, had evidently been killed where it fell. Shot several times. The attacker had made sure it was dead by placing a final shot right in the middle of its forehead, clean through its brain. If it had had such a thing.

Colonel Jahns was kneeling by it examining it closely with the point of his boot knife. He had turned the creature's head and exposed deep gills that ran from behind its jawline. With a look of revulsion, he turned back to us and asked, "So Madam, do you know what *this* creature is?"

428

"I believe they are called the '*Y'ha-nth'lei*'," interjected Dr Spender. "They are malevolent creatures."

Jahns stood up quickly and demanded irritatedly, "And how exactly do *you* know all *that*?"

Dr Spender flushed, "Well, Colonel Jahns, I read…you know. And I do my *damned research*!"

Aelita stepped between the Colonel and Dr Spender. "*I* told him."

I must admit I have looked upon Aelita as somewhat akin to a delicate child, beautiful, but as fragile as finest crystal. An escapee from a caged life, slightly bewildered by her surroundings. More so even than I. There was none of that now, at that moment I realised she stood about two inches taller than Jahns and she looked down at the Colonel with all the authority of some ancient warrior Queen.

(It occurs to me now, writing this, to ask myself, was that the Aelita that confronted the kraken? Not our genteel, shy lady, but this potent Aresian woman?)

Nervously I watched for Jahns' reaction, but he seemed hesitant, he flustered and looked aside quickly, before regaining himself. He continued but in a more respectful tone. "And how exactly do *you* know all this?"

"I do not *know* Colonel, my visions and dreams meld into something like knowledge, almost akin to memories, although I have no true memory of ever seeing these creatures before, however I know what they are. I know the Jed'dak are a race of mercenaries for hire from somewhere beyond this little solar system." She gestured to the thing lying on the sand nearby, "I know that that creature's kind are utterly, remorselessly, evil."

"If there is such a thing as '*evil*,' Madam," Jahns snorted. "Tell me, please; how long have you been having these visions?"

I saw that glint of ferociousness return to her eyes for a moment, then it was gone. "Since Ananthor and then the Athenaeum, the tomb on Mr Ransom's land, though truly I think I have always had them, I just did not allow myself to remember them."

"Ranolph, what she is telling you is true," exclaimed Dr Spender. "I too saw things at Ananthor and in the Tomb, incredible things, and since then, my dreams have been haunted by strange visions. Revelations."

"Stuff of nonsense!" Jahns cursed loudly and stalked off back towards our airship, leaving us looking at each other.

Aelita smiled at me and said, "I am so sorry Edwin, for not taking you into my confidence, I feel I should have told everyone, but I feared you would all think me insane."

I could no more chastise her than I could have my own sweet Nelly. I tried to assure her that she had no need to apologise, but the words faltered, and so I was about to give up when Sergeant Smith appeared at my shoulder.

"Sir, we have found others. Bodies that is."

"Dear God, what is this place!?"

"I have no idea, dear boy," replied Dr Spender.

We picked our way through the debris to what appeared to be another half-destroyed contraption, a sphere-like contrivance partially buried in the red sand, somewhat like a giant Bohnenberger's machine, constructed of endless gimbals, cogs and gears, encased in a chiliagon skin of some brass-like material.

Through the ruptured shell, we could see into the very heart of the machine. There were two crew members, this time, both human, both female and both long dead. Each wore a pair of goggles and some kind of respirator. One was dressed as if for riding out on a summer's day, the other in what a highborn lady would wear for a Sunday afternoon's stroll in the park, her long dark tresses spilling down over a lacy high collar. They sat reposed in what appeared to be the kind of seat a good barber would place you in, almost as if relaxed, unaware of the terrible fate that overtook them. Even in death, they were still holding hands. There was something so heart-wrenchingly sad about that gentle act of human compassion in the face of whatever doom befell them.

Then I noticed, in the arm of the finely dressed woman, a bundle of swaddling clothes in a blanket. In shock, I think I stopped breathing for a moment: a child, an infant. With a small shift of my position, I could make out the profile of a tiny face cradled into its mother's side. I gulped and began coughing as I turned away.

"Ho, dear God." I heard the tremor in Patty's voice. Aelita gasped.

Dr Spender patted me on the back until I had caught my breath. "There, there, my boy. Quite a shock, quite a shock."

Patty turned to us. "This is no war machine. They do not even have a gun for self-defence. Just three innocents." She paused as if fighting the urge to cry out. "What is this place, father? It is no battlefield, it is a graveyard, an elephant's boneyard of fallen ships and contraptions."

"A necropolis of war machines? I have not an inkling, my dear. Other than to observe that these craft and machines seem to have little in common with each other, as if they…" He paused, checking himself from speaking too freely.

"Go on, please, Dr Spender." Implored Aelita.

"*And they gathered them together to the place which in Hebrew is called Har-Magedon,*" Dr Spender intoned solemnly. "It is as if they came from different places, worlds, possibly even times, and were collected here."

"Collected by whom?"

"I have no idea; I am just ruminating on an impression. Maybe it is not that they are being collected per se, merely that they have fallen threw into this place, gathering here as do the odd socks and shirts studs do in the bottom draw of a tallboy."

We stood gazing forlornly at the sight before us. Each of us lost in contemplation of this strange place and of such a waste of life. Who were these ladies? What great misadventure had brought them here, to such an awful end? Confronted with this tragedy, my mind slipped back into thoughts of Nelly and my own loss. I tried to pull myself together and was just about to suggest that we should give these poor souls a decent Christian burial when a shot rang out.

The Colonel began shouting in a commanding manner at something.

By the time we reached him, it was plain that it had been he that had fired the shot to warn someone, as he was now threatening to fire again. His men immediately took up positions and began to close in on where Jahns' pistol was pointing. Jahns threats continued in a foul-mouthed tirade as he strode forward and fired again. He was shooting at the remains of an odd-looking flying machine of some kind. Long and angular with two wings and a tailplane, but no propeller just bulges under each wing. One wing was severely damaged, the other though you could see a propeller-like apparatus inside the housing. The skin of the craft looked as if it were made of a light metal, and from under the wings protruded what I took for gun barrels.

I was distracted trying to identify the red, white and blue concentric circle motif on the machine's main body, when, from behind the craft, stumbled a hunched figure. A man swathed in tatters and rags, he discarded a crudely made weapon and raised his arms in surrender.

Jahns continued to shout threats and orders until two of his men rushed the fellow and, none too gently, wrestled him to the ground. As Jahns strode forward, we followed on his heels, intrigued to know who this poor wretch was.

They hoisted the chap back on to his feet, and Jahns tugged roughly at the swathes of fabric that covered his face. Eventually, exposing goggles and a leather helmet with a facemask attached, the kind of thing a high altitude daedalist would wear. Jahns brutally tore them off the fellow's head and threw them aside. He was a youngish man, I would think no more than in his early twenties, fair-haired and hazel-eyed, but in such a dirty, dishevelled state that it made the ladies gasp. He had about him the clear indications of utter exhaustion with sunken eyes and an ashen pallor to his skin. All energy spent, he sagged like a rag doll in the arms of the two soldiers.

Jahns was having none of this, he dragged the young man's head up and slapped him cruelly across the face, demanding to know who he was.

The young man seemed to regain himself a little and replied, "Isambard Tonnison-Berregnog, the third. Captain, in His Majesty's Air Battalion Royal Engineers." He coughed several times. "I demand to be treated as a prisoner of war, under the Hague Convention!"

"War! What bloody war?" Demanded the Colonel angrily. "What on earth are you blithering about man?" The young man began to recite his name and rank again.

Jahns seemed outraged and lifted his balled fist to strike the Captain, but Patty stepped forward and grasped his forearm. "No, Colonel. This is not how you treat people." Then she added pointedly, "Or maybe Mr Franklin was right in what he said."

434

I had not thought the Colonel's face could turn any deeper red than it had that time Adam had berated him, but I was mistaken. He looked so angrily back at her, his eyes bulged, and his whiskers bristled, he reminded me of a boiler ready to explode. He shook off her grip, irritably.

Oblivious to it all the young Captain continued to recite his mantra, but a few new words abruptly caught my attention, "...*his* Britannic Majesty's Air Battalion of the Royal Engineers, The Royal Flying Corps." He paused and began again, "I demand to...."

"Balderdash!" Roared Jahns. The Captain began again. "For God's sake, shut up, man! The war has been over for twenty–five years."

The Captain sighed resignedly and shook his head slowly. "I won't fall for your tricks. You're trying to confuse me. I know you're damned Colluders."

"What in God's name, are you talking about, man?!"

Dr Spender put his hand on the Colonel's shoulder. "Ranolph, if I may. Please?"

The Colonel huffed loudly. "Go ahead, the boy is obviously deranged."

Dr Spender waved the soldiers to back away from the young man. "Captain Berregnog. I think you have come further than you may realise, but I assure you we are not the enemy, you are not being taken prisoner." The Captain began to wearily repeat his mantra again, but when he had finished, Dr Spender just said,

"Thank you, Captain. It will be noted accordingly." He seemed relieved by the response. "Now as I said, regardless of the rough handling by my friend the Colonel here, we are not your enemy, and we are not taking you prisoner, and so you are free to go. If you so wish."

"Then you will shoot me in the back as I walk away. I know that."

Dr Spender smiled kindly, "I can assure you no one will harm you. This is merely a misunderstanding. I think you have come further than you have any idea of, and though we can offer you assistance, we have no intention of harming you."

The young man looked confused. "Who are you people then?"

"Maybe you could answer that question first. After all, you could be one of these 'Colluders,' yourself, attempting to trick us into helping you. Or frankly some mad man or dangerous criminal in the grip of a delusion wondering this wasteland looking for the foolish to take him in."

"I gave you my name and rank. That's all I have to tell you."

"True. But please could you explain some things to me?"

The Captain stiffened. "I will tell you nothing," he said resolutely.

"Nothing?" Dr Spender replied, "But I only wish to know the most common knowledge."

"Why?"

"Because then I will know if you are indeed someone we can trust or, as the Colonel suspects, you are simply mad."

"This is a waste of time," growled the Colonel. "His making this nonsense up. Earth invaded! Utter poppycock!"

"What year is this?"

"What kind of question is *that?*" The Captain sneered. "I haven't lost my mind."

"One you should answer," growled the Colonel.

"It's 1920, of course."

"Who are you at war with, Captain?"

"Them."

"And who are they, exactly?"

He sighed, "Them." He pointed to the wreck of the great Aresian barge surrounded by a jumble of entwined war machines. "The Invaders, the Martians, of course."

"Balderdash!?" The Colonel roared.

The Captain looked shocked. "They came back."

"What do you mean, *'they came back'?*" asked Dr Spender softly.

The Captain eyed him suspiciously. "I don't know what you're playing at..."

"Just humour me, please."

"The Invaders, they came back, but this time we were ready for them. Well, at least we were. We gave them a good thrashing this time on our home pitch. The Frenchies just rolled over, but the Yanks have taken the brunt of it this time."

"How long have you been at war?"

"This is ridiculous. Are you trying some kind of mind game on me? I demand…"

"Answer the question boy," snarled Jahns. "Or so help me, assurances or not, I *will* bloody shoot you right where you stand."

The Captain stiffened. "June 1914, of course, that's when the second wave of cylinders arrived."

"Cylinders?"

"Like the last time, they came in huge cylinders, like huge teardrops from space."

"Oh, really Octavius," muttered the Colonel.

Dr Spender did not react, "How old are you, Captain?"

"19, Sir."

"And who is on the Throne of England?"

"The Emperor, King Edward, of course."

"I have heard enough of this bloody claptrap. He is raving. Too much dust in your head, me laddo." The Colonel waved him away. "Go on lad, off you go. Bugger off!"

"I…" the Captain was obviously confused as the Colonel stalked away.

"Forgive him, he has had a tiring day," apologised Dr Spender.

"Yes, being such an obnoxious bombastic old fart-bag must be tiring," added Patty under her breath.

"Tell me, Captain; how did you get here? Do you remember?"

That question obviously struck a deep nerve. The young man's chin quivered, and he gulped air. I listened closely as he mumbled and rambled through his tale, picking out what little sense I could make of it. His squadron had been over an area called the *'Morbihan coast'* escorting aerostat bombers searching for a new cylinder that had come down the night before, when the enemy ambushed them. Evidently, these *'Invaders'* have a new type of flying ship, exceptionally fast, faster than anything the *'Yanks'* (The Americans who also appeared to be involved in the war) have.

"*'Foo Fighters'* we call them, they look like balls of light. They just ripped us up. Three of us went down before we even realised, they were on us. They don't use guns or heat rays, they just ram right through you, and then you're a ball of flames." Tears began to leave streaks in the dirt on his cheeks. "I had this one on my tale. I couldn't shake him. I dived and rolled, but they are too fast, I couldn't outrun him or outmanoeuvre him, so I went for the dive. The Wingco briefed us that they aren't so good in a dive, so I went for it." He shook his head. "I don't remember anything else. I woke up here. Still sitting in the old crate," he gestured towards the aircraft that he had been hiding behind. "She's all bust-up, and I'm not ground crew, just a flyboy."

"How long ago was that? How long have you been here?"

"A few days, a week maybe. I don't know." He seemed to have relaxed sufficiently to feel brave enough to ask, "Where am I? Sir? You said I'm a long way from where I think I am.Where am I? What the hell is this place?Is this Africa?"

"That is what *we* would like to know," chirped Patty.

He began to ramble incomprehensibly for a few moments before saying quite clearly, "…and then those things attacked me."

"What '*things*'?"

"This place is infested with them. Like big monkey things, baboons, but scaly, with wings. Nasty brutes."

"Anemoi? But they are virtually extinct," queried Patty. "Anyway, they live in galleries and cliff faces, not in a place like this."

"Whatever they are, they are far from extinct. I have seen hundreds of them here. They scavenge the dead bodies. They even took Wells, my co-pilot." He exhibited his right forearm that was bound in bloody rags, dirty and dried brown with age. "I tried to stop them, but one took a good-sized chunk out of me."

I had begun to have an awful feeling about all this and wanted to be out of the place as soon as possible. "I think we should take him to the Professor," I said as authoritatively as I could manage. "He should hear this, first-hand."

Dr Spender readily agreed. He ordered the Sergeants to escort the Captain to the airship. The young Captain refused, saying that if he were not a prisoner, then why were we treating him as such?

I had no answer and looked to Dr Spender. "Young man, it is a matter of trust. All we require of you is to come with us to our airship and tell your story to the leader of our expedition. Once you have done so, if you wish, you will be free to go."

"And if I don't want to go with you?" he said obviously suspicious of our motivations.

"Ah, there. He never said you had a choice, lad." I had not noticed that the Colonel had returned and was standing behind me.

Sergeant Smith pointedly placed the barrel of his rifle between the Captains shoulder blades. "Do as the Colonel and the nice gentlemen ask, there's a good lad." The Captain nodded dejectedly.

We all turned back towards the *Seren Bore*, or as it was now, the *Haul Du*.

We had not gone more than a few steps when suddenly the Captain exclaimed, "Dear God! What on earth are you?" I suddenly realised Aelita and her maid had been hanging back from our confrontation with the Captain, now they were face to face with him. "That's a bloody machine!" He gestured wildly at the automaton, then his eyes alighted on Aelita. "Why is your skin painted?"

"Mind your manners. *Sir*," growled Sergeant Smith and roughly prodded him in the back with his rifle.

Aelita did not react, but with great dignity ignored his outburst and merely stepped aside. Taking Patty's hand, she fell in beside us. The young Captain gawped at them and kept asking, "Who the Hell are you people?"

I too had a thousand questions running through my head. His story was preposterous, there had not been a ship or craft from Earth in twenty-five years, our years, almost fifty of theirs. Then there was his bizarre story, a war with alien Invaders? A second Invasion? When was the first? As I pondered his ramblings a

441

chilling thought occurred to me; was that why the old Empires never came back, was that why we lost contact with Earth? The Aresians invaded Earth! It was utterly unbelievable, were it not for the fact we too had no idea where we were, and we were surrounded by the debris of war machines the likes of which we could barely have imagined.

We would have to let the Professor try and make some sense of this, and, though I felt that Dr Spender already had some idea of what was going on, though I already somewhat dreaded whatever explanation he may come up with. His reference to the field of Megiddo had left a chill in my spine.

We had only managed to pick our way through a few dozen yards or so when I began to notice that the sand and shale beneath my feet was getting softer. I was just about to remark on that fact when the Captain, who had constantly been muttering to himself in a low voice, suddenly became anxious and demanded loudly; "Where are you taking me?" As if we had not already explained to him.

Dr Spender calmly pointed to our airship and tried to explain that we were merely explorers and as lost as he was, but it was to no avail. He began to repeat, "No, no, no...! You're going to take me back to the Tower! Aren't you?" On Jahns' orders, the Sergeants took hold of him, but he managed to wiggle free.

Dr Spender was still trying to pacify him when suddenly the ground shook and began to subside beneath our feet. A choking and blinding cloud of dust arose. Terrified, I scrambled backwards struggling to pull my filter mask on. It was as if the very gates of hell were opening below us, a chasm swallowing everything above it.

Dwelling on it now, I had heard of these sudden collapses before but never experienced one. Below the layers of regolith and sand, a rill, formed by ancient water erosion through the basalt, was collapsing. From as narrow as drainpipes to sizable enough to fit two Asterion locomotives through with room to spare, they crisscross the planet in a vast matrix. Long since dried out by the Aresian's draining them for their canals, an infinite number of these tunnels remain. Now, below our feet, the roof of one was giving way.

Hands grabbed me and pulled me away from the edge. It was the Colonel and his men. Shaken but fascinated, we stood on the edge and stared into the pit opening before us. Then, with mounting horror, I noticed something was thrashing about in the cascading sand.

In the bottom of the rill was a nest of !D'ols, those horrific Aresian red worms. Masses of them, each a dozen feet long writhing amidst the debris like salmon fighting their way up a weir. I stood mesmerized by their struggles.

Then it dawned on me that the walls of the pit seemed to be moving in opposition to the sandslide, revolving around the edge of the pit, and I realised, with utter horror, they were not walls, but the bodies of three or four gigantic adults.

The dust cloud had cleared enough for us to see the ladies and Dr Spender, who was now being carried by Aelita's maid, on the other side of the widening gulf. The Colonel shouted to them to get to the ship as fast as they could, but they protested not wishing to leave us behind. We waved them on saying we would find a way.

In alarm, I looked about for the Captain, but he was nowhere to be seen. "Gone," said the Colonel. "Ran for it, I suspect."

Trepidatiously we all glanced again into the pit.

The adult red worms were beginning to free themselves from the debris and had begun clambering out of the nest. Hundreds of robust legs, beset with razor-sharp claws, scrabbled their way over the rubble and sand, up towards the surface. Each one's head was easily as big as the Professor's Emancipator.

The Colonel fired a couple of rounds at the nearest one, but his bullets ricocheted harmlessly off its gleaming red carapace. "Damn!" He seized my right arm and dragged me along with him. We had to go a few yards back on ourselves, for safety's sake, before we could even begin to circle the skylight that had formed in the rill.

Running on the sand and loose shale was exhausting enough, but circumnavigating the hole meant an arduous scramble through the wreckage of the battlefield, clambering over smashed war machine after war machine. I had to dispense with my sling, because it made it impossible to clamber over the debris and ended up knocking my injured arm several times, stumbling and falling flat on my face twice. Even in my panic-driven haste, I noticed several more corpses, human and others, amidst the heaps of tangled machinery. The dead left to rot in their engines where they had fallen, others were torn and strewn about as if had at by wild dogs, or worse. This place was not a battlefield or mausoleum, it was a charnel house.

There was no sign of the young Captain.

We were in sight of the *Haul Du* when I heard Sergeant Smith curse loudly. I cast a glance and found myself transfixed by a mixture of revulsion and fascination. The biggest of the worms was entirely out of the pit. Greater than I had realised, like a colossal red centipede, with frightening speed it scurried in front of us, blocking our path to the ship. More than a hundred feet long and so utterly nightmarish that there are hardly words to describe it. It eyed us eagerly and, lifting a good third of its body length like a cobra ready to strike, it gave out a hideous screech and vibrated the plates of its carapace; a soul-chilling cacophony.

I froze to the spot. It extended the hood about its head and we could clearly see the pouches beneath swell with venomous rheum. Our bullets were futile against even the armour of its underbelly. In that instant, I believed we were undoubtedly dead.

Though our bullets were ineffective against the creature's armour, the shells of our airship's Picaro were not. The first ripped several plates off the monster's right side. The immense !D'ol, however, seemed only to be enraged further. It twisted about furiously to strike at its attacker, but the gunners on the Picaro's had their range. The next shell tore half the carapace off the worm's skull; the following blew the creature's head apart. It fell quickly, its decapitated body writhing wildly amidst the wrecks.

As if in elation, the Cogswaines aboard the *Haul Du* released their excess steam and fired. In fact, I think Captain Llewellyn brought every weapon he had to bear upon the other monstrosities as they crawled from the pit. Outmatched, the red worms rapidly scurried back into their nest.

Wasting no time, the Colonel and his men, half led, half dragged me back to the safety of the ship.

Excerpt from;
Diary of Aelita Fontenelli (Mrs).
Sunday, September,44th. MY.26

Dear Diary.

I do not even know where to begin. Frankly, I embarked upon this adventure as a way of escaping my situation, if not permanently then but for a short while, a few weeks maybe. Time enough, I believed, for me to make the decisions I have been putting off for so long. I hoped I would be of some fair use to the expedition and that time away from Giovanni would possibly make me understand what value there is to my place in this world.

Absence, it is said, makes the heart grow fonder. However, I have not experienced such emotions. More truly, the exact opposite. With every moment I have spent absent from that dreadful birdcage of a house, and with every mile I have travelled away from Giovanni's suffocating control, I have felt more and more alive. It has now been fifteen days since I threw out Dr Hammond's horrid little tablets, and it feels to me as if I have awoken from some dreamlike state. More so than that; it is as if I have regained my own mind.

Ursula, bless her, does her best to keep my feet on the ground with her stoic pragmatism, but I am no longer a child and no longer willing to be treated as one.

Today I have had wondrous news and find myself so excited I could burst, for the first time in my life, I truly look to the future gleefully.

Now firstly, this morning we awoke to find ourselves surrounded by the eerie saffron haze of the dust that still hung in the air after the storm. I must admit I found it genuinely disquieting. The miasma seemed to play with my perceptions, causing me the sensation of sound without hearing. As if there were thousands of voices crying out in anguish. Voices that were just below the level one needs to be able to hear, yet I found the more I concentrated upon them, the more indistinct they grew.

And then there is poor Edwin. He is such a kind, gentle soul, and his beloved Nelly was a charming and beautiful young woman. I can feel the intensity of his pain, he carries it like a mantle about his shoulders, though he tries so bravely to preserve that Stoical stiff upper lip that Tharsian men seem so determined to maintain, even so beneath it, he is entirely devastated by his loss. Patty remarked to me that she heard him sobbing again last night when she passed his cabin door.

I have prayed both morning and night to the Blessed Virgin that she may bring some peace for him, the Professor and their family. I am bereft for a brother I never had, a figment of my childish imagination, and far more so when I focus on the loss of my family, but that is softened by time. I cannot honestly imagine what it is to lose such a cherished loved one in such an awful manner. What it must be to love and be loved like that? My

marriage appears to be little more than a sham in comparison.
What terrible burden it is that Edwin and the Professor carry in
their hearts.

Tired of being cooped up in the ship, we eagerly took up
Patty's idea to don our filter masks and take a turn around the
weather deck. We had almost exhausted the novelty of stretching
our legs and amusing ourselves with fruitless squinting into the
brume. Dr Spender had suggested we should retire back inside
for some tea and to prepare to attend our usual little Sunday
service when the hulking remains of an enormous airship
loomed into sight.

For all his shortcomings, Giovani had thankfully never been
one to indulge in that most voyeuristic of societal pastimes; that
of calamity tourism. So, I have never had the experience of
witnessing such a disturbing scene as that awe-inspiring colossus
thrusting out of the sands. As we passed the wreckage, I felt an
intensity of foreboding of a kind I have never felt before.
Something about that hulk had felt dreadfully wrong to me, as if
either we or it, should not be there.

Edwin told us that, if his memory served him well, it was
possibly a very famous ship, lost under mysterious
circumstances. He would make a note of its location, once we
could confirm our own, and pass it on to the authorities in due
course.

After I had taken elevenses with Patty, Dr Spender and Edwin, I retired to my cabin to change into something more befitting of attending Mr Holley's customary religious service.

Additional note added sometime later before these extracts were first published.

James Ransom

(I presume it is unnecessary to explain that, at this point, I remained a Roman Catholic. Though such issues of religion had already been challenged and were about to be ultimately confronted. Nevertheless, I felt my faith was at least one thing I could cleave to that had not failed me, as yet.)

As Ursula helped me change, she was declaring her scepticism of human religions, of course, a sentient android like her was in a unique position to question our human belief in a God. Ursula had never been like any other android I have ever encountered, and I enjoyed the conversations we had when she challenged the tenets of my faith in such a bluff manner. We were discussing Theophilos' question that if 'all men' are made in 'God's image' then what about those born blind or crippled or without a limb, and what of the Aresians? Undoubtedly, the God of the Christians does not look anything like a red-skinned Aresian? Like me.

I cannot even remember clearly when she had come into my service. I believed that Giovanni had brought her for me as a

450

wedding gift, or had someone else? She seemed to have always been with me. She was forthright, insightful, and compassionate. I suppose I, not encountering androids before, had simply accepted it as normal. In truth she was anything but, for behind that now fractured but still inscrutable alabaster mask, a mind worked. A mind equal to, if not better than, any human, unhampered as it was by human frailties and conceits. There! I still find myself thinking in terms of being 'human,' which, of course, I am not.

The Ship's Surgeon, Mr Holley, though only a Lay Preacher of the breakaway Martian Redemptionist Church, had been kind enough to go out of his way to make me feel completely comfortable in attendance of his gatherings. Although, of course, he could not hear my confession, he had offered his ear, and guidance, in complete confidentiality should I wish to divest myself of some of my disquiets. Although it was a genuinely benevolent offer, I could not dare to speak of the anxieties that had begun to plague me outside of the sanctity of the confessional.

My preparations though were in vain, as there was such a commotion on the decks that I abandoned my intentions and hurried to join the others to view the spectacle that was causing such uproar.

It is beyond my linguistic abilities to accurately describe the spectacle revealed before us in words that could possibly convey

451

the immensity of the scene. It was as if I were beholding the aftermath of the Armageddon.

My horror grew greater as I recognised so many things from my dreams and the visions I had at the Athenaeum and since. The others were so excited by the sight of the battlefield that they wished to stop and go down to investigate. I do not understand why I agreed to join them in their escapade, as I found the atmosphere of the place nauseating. However, I did. I could claim some compulsion beyond my ability to resist, or some lofty need to understand. In all probability, it was merely morbid curiosity that drove me to join their amble amid that carnage.

I know that as I expected, my experience of the battlefield was different from the others. They simply saw copious wreckages and a few scattered bodies of creatures they could hardly imagine. I though saw so much worse. As if I were wearing one of those stereoscopes, we used to amuse ourselves within the parlour. I could see two distinctly different images as if overlaid upon each other, one was a cold, dead graveyard of metal, possibly the evidence of my own eyes, but my mind's eye saw replayed around me the burning horror of those lost battles. Machines roared, and weapons flared about me, and I could see that beneath the windblown saffron sand lay innumerable dead. I stood frozen to the spot as I witnessed a great trireme do battle with monstrous tripodic machines, cannons and heat rays flashed and tore at each other until, enveloped in a great fireball, all fell together into the embrace of the red sands. All around me

452

ghostly forms of so many other creatures I could not name, let alone recognise, fought to the death, some with their bare hands and teeth. I had never seen such violence, and yet it had the unreal quality of a jittery aeroscope recording.

I tried concentrating on what I could truly see with my eyes, forcing my mind to close off those phantom images before the ghosts saw me.

Edwin called us to see something he had discovered, and we climbed up on to one of the crashed craft to view what he had found. I recognised them immediately from my vision at Ananthor and my dreams since. They were Jed'dak. Dr Spender and I tried to explain to the Colonel that they were a sentient reptilian warrior race used as mercenaries by my people, but he was in a childish, irascible mood and impossible to reason with.

I was so angry with the old bombast that I, for a moment, stopped consciously closing my mind to whatever it was that was pervading my thoughts and memories.

Suddenly I had a clear recollection of being led by the hand, my father's hand, through endless ranks of these fearsome warriors. An honour guard, in their finery, all at attention, as we strolled purposefully through a great plaza towards a vast palace. I was a small child and extremely excited by something, a promise. I was going to meet someone important, and I had to be on my very best behaviour.

Raised voices broke my reverie, and when Ursula and I found the others, the Colonel and Dr Spender were arguing loudly.

They had discovered a strange silver disklike craft, looking a little like an upturned saucer, by which lay another fallen creature. On first sight of the craft alone, I had an awful, sickening sense of dread in the pit of my stomach. Dr Spender knew the name of the vile creature that lay on the sand, a frog-headed monstrosity I instinctually knew to be evil.

Even in death, it radiated a dreadful aura of malevolence, affecting all around it. Dr Spender had identified the creature from one of my drawings, as a Y'ha-nth'lei, but that only sparked another angry exchange with the Colonel. I could not stand by and allow him to harangue the old gentleman in such a way. Edwin tried to intercede, but he stumbled over his words and lost his momentum, and I feared, that by the look on her face, Patty was about to punch the Colonel squarely on the nose. Stealing myself, I stepped forward and confronted him, much as I have grown used to confronting Giovanni's asperities over these last few years. In as calm and level tone as I could affect, I explained that it was I that had told Dr Spender of these creatures, as I had been learning of them through my visions and dreams. I, with Dr Spender's help, had been drawing and naming the images that had revealed themselves to me at Ananthor and at the Athenaeum. I tried to make the Colonel understand that it was as if recollections so long subsumed into dreams were reasserting themselves into knowledge. Now, as they were coalescing in my mind, they are allowing me to remember them clearly. I told him what I knew of the Y'ha-nth'lei, and that they came from far beyond this little solar system, and that they were truly evil, nevertheless he was in no mind to listen and only angrily ridiculed my warnings. Even going as far as dismissing my concepts of good and evil as superstitious nonsense. I, like all the rest of our group, am very aware of his reputation and his undoubted bravery, but he is such a pompous vulgarian, his manner often bordering upon loutish. His frequently discourteous conduct towards Dr Spender and Edwin irks me the most. I feel that if I had not for so long suffered at the changeable whims of Giovanni's l'oscurità dell'animas, the Colonel's outburst would have floored me. However, I am more resilient than even I ever suspected. I merely held his gaze until he stalked off grumbling like an irritated bear.

I tried to apologise to Edwin and the others for not sharing these insights with them before, but the shouts of the Colonel's soldiers called our attention away, and we all hurried to see what they had discovered next.

Amidst the strange contraptions and machines, they had discovered one even stranger than most; a spherical contrivance of countless ornate brass rings, within which sat the remains of two Tellurian women, one clutching a dead baby to her bosom. I had to turn away quickly as I was again assailed with sensations emanating from the scene. I could feel their desperation and their fears. These sisters, escaping from drudgery and stifling conventions, were still holding hands even as they faced their oblivion, but oh what adventures they had had. They did not

455

belong here, this was a mistake, a tiny miscalculation, and nevertheless, they had faced their deaths proudly, with dignity and in freedom. I heard, as clear as if she spoke directly to me, the voice of one of them, the younger, issuing her challenge, not to me, but into the face of the very doom that was overtaking her, "Better to die with the taste of freedom on your lips than to wither a little every day, without ever knowing what it is to be free."

It is as if I was experiencing the past and the present at the same time, innumerable pasts and a myriad of presents, all playing out in my head. Was this what Dr Hammond's foul medicines really were for? To stifle these senses of mine. Did Giovanni know, even before I did?

I could not clearly see that, but a dreadful sense of conviction was growing inside of me.

I had to shut everything out as I could still hear the child's wailing, and it tore at my soul. The others were distraught too. Though he held himself well, I saw tears in Edwin's eyes. I felt so overcome I feared I would faint. Ursula guided me to sit upon a small boulder, so I might compose myself, and it was while I was sitting upon that rock that the most singular of my revelations occurred.

The world around me changed completely, not the demi delusion I had experienced earlier, but entirely, as if I were not just viewing another reality but bodily transported there.

I found myself in a garden, like some tropical arboretum. Bright sunlight filtered down from the crystal roof through a canopy of waxy broadleaved boughs. High above me, small exotic birds called as they darted from branch to branch. I was standing upon a raised wooden walkway that meandered through this artificial jungle over languid waters teeming with colourful fish. I gazed about myself incredulously at the reality of it all. Soft voices and happy sounds carried on the warm air that circulated about me. Somewhere they were serving tea, I could hear the tinkle of crockery and polite chatter.

With a startle, I remembered the place; the Tropical Conservatory in Xanthe. Giovanni took me there once when we were first courting. Upon reflection, it was where I first imagined I was in love with him. He was the first man to show me any interest, any kindness, and he seemed so proper and gracious to me. A respected gentleman of letters, a powerful personality with, what he excused himself by; an 'artistic temperament.' Little more than a dizzy headed child, I mistook his boorish self-importance for panache and savoir-faire. However, all that came later, on that day, I was a little girl in love, spellbound by the attention of my suitor and entranced by this beautiful place.

I wandered onwards, towards the sounds. A small, bug-eyed black dog scurried by me pursued by a little laughing boy in a sailor suit. I rounded a corner and, as I half-remembered half expected to find, there was a little tea shop. Merely a gazebo with a stall purveying refreshments to the tourists. It was so utterly charming. A few people in their very finest clothes sat around at the half dozen tiny wrought iron tables taking tea and nibbling delicate fancies in the depths of this magical imitation rainforest.

The boy returned cradling the wiggling pug, to join his parents at one of the tables, they had with them a small girl too, such a pretty little thing, she looked so like her mother. It was then I realised I was looking at Nelly and Edwin and their children. I fought the sudden urge to call out, to announce myself, but the children were much younger than they were when I met them, though it was undeniably them, happily enjoying their day.

A soldier sat at another table, resplendent in his dress uniform, he was earnestly reading to his lady. I could not hear the words, but the sounds had the rhythm of poetry. I knew him as well, though I had only seen him like this clearly once before. The scars were gone, and he too was much younger, but it was most definitely Mr Franklin. How strikingly handsome he had been. It was with no surprise that the eyes of the young woman never left his. Excitedly I looked about at the other patrons; Patty was there, engrossed in what looked like a novel, 'Mary, a Fiction' (an odd name for a book). She sat smoking a narrow cigar with one long booted leg propped on another chair. She was wearing one of those strange little Electrophone listening sets and humming along to the music.

Charity, at another table, was explaining something animatedly to an older couple that seemed to be greatly enthralled by her tale.

Strangely, I was unaware of the other goings-on about me until I heard my name spoken. It was Giovanni's voice. A chill ran down my spine as I involuntarily turned in recognition. It was him, but not the man I left behind in Tharsis, this was a younger man, less rotund than he had grown in the last few years, smartly dressed and almost relaxed in his manner. Never a particularly handsome man he looked quite dashing in a linen suit and boater. Then I saw her, well myself, much younger, far less full of frame, almost undernourished and skittish, like one of those little greyhounds Giovanni's mother used to breed. I was not wrapped up to hide my skin colour behind layers of lacy vails and a large hat, as it seemed I always was, yet no one seemed to be surprised at my presence.

I recalled that day. It was the first place Giovanni took me when we were courting. I had never been before, though I heard tales and I so wanted to see it. It was every bit as wonderful as I had imagined. However, the almost uncomfortable humidity of the faux jungle led me to brave removing my hat, something that my chaperone, Sister Emica, warned me against. I was a wilful child and emboldened by Giovanni's attentions, I removed my disguise. For that is what it was. I looked for Sister Emica's presence in this illusion or memory or whatever it was. She had always been so kind, one of the very few of the Nuns that had shown anything more than cold indifference towards me. I could not see her, however behind us, to the side, watching everything carefully was Ursula. Her perfect impassive alabaster face unblemished.

It was on that day, though I was little more than a child, that I made the decision that if Giovanni's intentions were anything more than that of a kindly uncle figure, I would readily accept his troth. Anything, if it would get me out of that cold, damp cloister, and away from the Sisters and the mind-numbing routine of their austere existence. It was not unusual for a man of his status to take a young wife (He is twenty-five years older than me). Nevertheless, he was wealthy, of great renowned, and he appeared, at least to me then, 'interesting.' Dear Lord, above, how I craved interesting.

A sudden wave of passions overtook me, as if, all at once, I could feel every emotion I had ever felt for Giovanni. All the love and all the despair, the happiness and the anger, the warm desire that had grown stone cold, the hopelessness that had grown into dispisement, everything. I wanted to shout out to her, to that younger me, to warn her not to fall for his ruse, he was nothing more than an accumulator of exotic things, and she would become merely another exhibit in his cabinet of curiosities, the living museum he kept to honour his dead first wife. His most outlandish chattel; a living relic of a lost people. Exhibited like a zoo animal for the amusement of his guests. The sentiments in me changed, suddenly I wanted to stalk across the deck and slap, no punch, him as hard as I could on that Roman beak of a nose of his. I would then scold my younger self like an outraged mother, sending her scurrying back to the comforting safety of the Nun's with a flea in her ear.

A hand touched my arm, and I jumped in surprise.

Besides me stood a tall woman, dressed elegantly in pale ivory silk and lace. The colour contrasting vividly against the deep crimson of her skin. It now seems ridiculous to think one of my own race would appear so alien to me. My eyes had become so used to viewing the world through the looking glass of Tellurian normality that I have forgotten completely; this is what every one of them who looks upon me sees.

With a kindly smile, she apologised for startling me, and then, as if clarifying some perfectly normal situation, she explained that no one could see or hear us. I asked if it were she that had created this illusion, had she read my memories. The words hardly formed on my tongue before she answered it, explaining that 'mining' such happy memories is a pleasant thing to do, as if it were no more than rifling through the pages of a picture book.

Incredulously, I inquired how she could do such an extraordinary thing? She smiled again, as if understanding my shock, though her kaleidoscopic eyes sparkled mischievously. She told me there were lots of names given to such abilities. Nevertheless, there is nothing magical about it. Adding that, though I had no idea, I too have such abilities, it was purely that I had never been given the training required to employ them.

Sensing my confoundment, she apologised if she had upset me with this diorama. She merely thought I would enjoy seeing my companions in happier times. I agreed it was a wonderful thing. Though she explained, of course, they were never here together like this, but like me, they all have fond memories of this place. Even Mr Franklin, though, she added, he still does not believe he remembers any of it.

As I gazed upon her, somewhere in the back of my mind, some recollection stirred. Though I could not grasp it clearly.

Delightedly she noticed the refreshments being served, and taking my elbow gently, guided me to one of the little tables, while all the time wittering on about nothing of consequence. How she loved afternoon tea. How she believed it was one of the few truly civilised things that sets the British apart from all the other Tellurian Empires. Though she admitted a predilection for French pâtisseries. Although, like myself, she had to avoid most of their food as she found all that garlic disagreed with her terribly. How delightfully pretty and polite the young woman that served us was! How beautiful the Conservatory was! She marvelled that such a lovely place existed, remarking that "these Tellurians" are such paradoxical creatures.

Words failed me, as I struggled to make sense of it all. I believe I managed to mumble polite responses. Finally, gathering my wits enough to think clearly, I asked her who she was? The question rudely blurting out of me.

Those incredible eyes considered me over the rim of her teacup for a long moment before she set it down carefully. "Éspênié, my dear, do you not recognise me? I am your grandmother."

I do not know which struck me the deepest; the secret name that only Gethen had ever called me, or the revelation this was my grandmother, which, with the certainty of something I knew and knew that I had forgotten, was true. A thousand questions flooded out of me, the most immediate of them was whether my father and mother were still alive?

"Nikaïné, your mother, often thinks of you. I promise you will see her very soon." Her tone changed though when I asked again about my father. She would only say that he was very well, but 'away with the fleet,' as the British say. Sensing there was far more to that remark, I probed what fleet and where, but instead she hushed me quiet, insisting that we did not have much time left to talk.

Her tone grew deeply earnest. "Soon you will be presented with the most momentous decision of your life. You must choose wisely, as wisely as you possibly can. You will be called upon to make a decision that will not be presented honestly, but deceptively couched in emotive terms and deliberate misrepresentations. Do not be fooled by flattery or appeals to your vanity either," she cautioned. "The choice, as it will be presented to you, may seem immediate and personal. However, it will have far wider consequences, not just for yourself and your friends."

I asked who would put such a decision to me and why?

She replied with no hint of irony, "The Devil. At least a man with the silver tongue of the Devil himself."

"Evil?"

"No. Forgive me, I have spoken out of turn. Not truly evil, more; desperate. He is a desperate man driven by his passions. He carries a deep, deep, pain, a wound, for which he intends to make the universe pay amends for."

Confoundedly, like Edwin, I stumbled over my words. I told her I would make whatever choice she directed me to. I was not sure, but it merely sounded like the right thing to say.

She smiled and reassuringly patted my hand. However, she would not tell me what choice to make. She explained, "Ultimately, in the grand opera of the universe, whatever you or I choose will probably make little or no difference to the final outcome. Nothing we do does. However, so many lives, especially those of your friends, will depend on your choice."

I begged for some morsel of guidance. She regarded me carefully and added that I must never lose sight of the fact I came on this expedition for a number of reasons. I should not overlook a single one of them.

Terror gripped me, what if I made the wrong decision? How would I know?

She directed my attention to where little James Ransom was standing at the edge of the decking, dropping small pebbles into the water below. Watching patiently as the ripples spread out across the surface.

"We can only guess at the future," she explained. "He is aware of his actions. He knows the drop of the pebble will create ripples, but because of the different sizes and shapes of the pebbles themselves, the flow of the water, the warm breeze on the surface, the koi moving in the depths, each time a stone hits the water the resulting ripples are different. They travel differently, some further, some less, some even intersect with the hardly perceptible dying ripples of the previous stones, reflected off the objects in the water. And it is that unpredictability that he finds so fascinating to watch. The choice of where, when and how hard to drop the pebble though is his and his alone."

I asked if that was what she was doing? Watching to see if I make the right choice? Was this some form of test?

A look of sadness came over her, and she turned away as if trying to control her emotions. After a long deep breath, she said that she knew I would make the right choice as it was what I was chosen for. "Sometimes, the greatest choices we have to make are not surrounded by portents or fanfares. They seem small, personal, even apparently inconsequential, at the time. We cannot predict with any certainty the future, that is why we can have no real guide to the ultimate consequences of our actions."

I asked why then was she telling me all this? She replied that it was so I would be aware of the gravity of the choice I was about to make. That was all she could say.

It was then that something grasped me, and I asked pointedly; "If someone chose me, then who was it? Who chose to leave me behind? To abandon me here?" Angrily a lifetime of hurt flowed out of me, and I raged at her. "I was left here, a child without a family. A freak to be gawped at. The symbol of a defeated enemy that ran away like cowards. To be spat at in the street. To grow up in fear of everyone, everything. Beaten, abused. I was only a small child. How could they choose to do that? Condemn me to this? For what?"

She looked up at me with eyes brimming with tears, and in a softly breaking voice, she told me it was she who had made that choice. Though she loved me very much and it had broken her heart. Nevertheless, ultimately, it had been her choice.

I stood dumbfounded, as if thunderstruck, shaking like a leaf.

One day, she promised, I would understand why and what pain it caused her. Wearily she stood up saying she must be gone, and that I must return to my friends.

Overcome with remorse for my outburst, I pleaded with her not to go. I begged her profusely to forgive my behaviour. I had so many questions. She smiled kindly and took me in her arms.

The instant we touched, my senses were flooded with the scent of exotic flowers, and I knew who she was, and what she was.

I remembered as a small child sitting on her lap babbling excitedly to her while she wove g'quaneth flowers into my hair, in the vastness of an ancient throne room. I remember her showing me an entire universe laid out before me. I remembered seeing her behind the eyes of the monster that saved us all at Ransom's Farm, hers was the infinite, almost elemental, mind behind those strange eyes.

"Grandmother," I said in reverence. "What do I call you?"

"Oh, my sweet Éspênié. You may call me Oyârsa."

The real world, if that is what it is, impinged upon my senses through the auspices of Ursula lifting me to my feet and walking me back to join the others.

Patty hurriedly explained that the Colonel's men had discovered someone hiding amidst the wreckage and were escorting him back to our ship. Still a little discombobulated by the experience of my vision, I barely registered the young man's presence as we re-joined the expedition members.

Patty had only just about finished her rough explanation of what had transpired while I was indisposed when chaos broke loose, and we found ourselves running for our lives.

Extracts from

Beresford's History of the Martian Colonies.

Vol 2.3rd Edition. Milton and Dante.

Chapter 7. The Second War of the Sirenuim Planes.

Cont.

With the element of surprise in their favour, and using their new Damocles class dreadnaughts, Tharsis' forces struck out from bases in eastern Icaria at the pro-Zephyrian communities in southern Gorgonum and the military bases belonging to Zephyria and Thyle on the border of Phaetontis, destroying them all in a matter of days.

Tharsis was later accused in the broadsheets of several nations of indiscriminate use of aerial bursting incendiary bombs against the pro-Zephyrian settler communities in southern Gorgonum and ignoring attempts to surrender by both combatants and non-combatants.

Whether, due to a miscalculation on the Zephyrians behalf, or simply underestimation due to a lack of military intelligence, the Zephyrians were utterly unprepared for the overwhelming ferocity of the assault. The Tharsian forces swept all before them.

In truth, the Zephyrian ambitions in Sirenum Plains ended in the short, but brutal, air battle known as the Battle of Gaugamela.

A planned surprise assault by air and ground forces on Sirenia's second city, Red Cliffs, had been uncovered by Tharsian intelligence operatives within the Utopian Embassy in Zephyr.

Grasping their best chance for a second decisive victory, Tharsian forces moved two batteries of heavy anti-aerostat guns into Véres Mezők province, supported by elements of the Tharsian Marine Corps and Olympian Highlanders. A new aircraft landing strip was created five miles north of the city with a flight of Red Marley fighter aircraft, and several of their new Triplane Bombardiers – the first aeroplanes designed specifically for strategic aerial bombardment. The Tharsian Air Admiralty deployed three of its brand-new Damocles class dreadnaughts to finish the task. It was no jest that the whole plan was designated under the code name; 'Overkill.'

The joint 'sursaut' by a combined strike force of Zephyrian air and newly formed Thylian Desantniki forces resulted in one of the most comprehensive defeats Tharsis ever inflicted upon either nation. Those detachments of the Thylian Mechanised Regiment, and the Zephyrian Foreign Legionnaires, deployed in the attack, though they fought bravely, were ruthlessly and methodically annihilated. The Zephyrian Air Arm lost every aircraft and aerostat they deployed and, in a highly criticised decision that would cost Grand Admiral Wladislaw Lach-Szyrama his reputation and position, they also lost the twenty-five aircraft and six aerostats he deployed in a desperate attempt to salvage the situation on the ground.

Major General Sir Robert Diogenes Braine. Has since been accused of handing over Zephyrian and Thylian prisoners to the Sirenuim Free Settlers Militia to dispose of as they saw fit. When challenged on the point by a journalist, he is quoted as laughingly remarking, *"Nonsense, mercenaries and traitors the lot,"* and went on to quote the American General, Sherman; *"The only good one is a dead one."*

In less than three weeks, most of the territory of what once had been Sirenuim, including the greater parts of the forest of the Gorgonum Chaos, were now under Tharsis' control. In all but name, Sirenuim ceased to exist as an independent state and would become a newly annexed, and swiftly absorbed, territory of Tharsis. This territory was to become the

Tharsian's staging post for their campaign in Phaetontis.

Lenora Flammarion.

To Mrs. Gertrude Leverkus,

Founder and Headmistress,

The School for Ragged and Orphaned Children.

Xanthe Province.

Tharsis.

The following incomplete letter was discovered amongst the personal effect of the late Mrs Gertrude Leverkus, the founder and headmistress of The School for Ragged and Orphaned Children, in Xanthe Province. Written by my Aunt Lenora, it would appear to have begun as a formal tender of resignation from her post at the school however appears to have digressed somewhat.

We have considered carefully before including this in the documentations we are presenting to the public nonetheless, upon reflection, my sister and I decided to include it as we feel the tone and content of the letter goes to speak clearly of the state of my aunt's mind.

Only one page has been discovered, though we believe it safe to assume it was addressed to Mrs Leverkus personally. Mrs Leverkus had been very gracious to Lenora in the past and had even been a guest at our grandfather's house several times.

James Ransom

...is broken. Haunted as I am by her every picture, every object she has touched, her scent lingers here in our home, like a ghost. I am bereft, my soul is rent. Inconsolable, I find I can no longer even tolerate the intensity of the feeble daylight. And what of my father and her gutless stammering fool of a husband? Nothing! NOTHING! As my beautiful Sister, his Wife, his Daughter, lies in a casket in a bare iceroom far from her home. Torn from the bosom of her family and discarded like a piece of unwanted meat. Should that they have returned like men and faced the

472

responsibility for what they have brought upon us, their family, but NO. They continue to pursue their childish adventures regardless. More concerned with their self-indulgent fantasies than the lives and deaths of those that they leave behind them. Those they profess to love? COWARDS! Are all such men nothing but spoilt cowardly children? I have nothing but utter contempt for them, for all such boys masquerading as men, let alone gentlemen. My heart screams to avenge my Sister, my beautiful Eleanor, but what can I do? Take up arms myself? No. Thankfully the Merciful Lord, whose righteousness confounds all the vagaries of such human pretensions of justice, has placed into my hands the tools of true retribution. I shall avenge myself on all those who conspired to murder my Sister. Let the earth itself tremble, so that they may hide and run. Mr Uwharrie has made a promise to me, and he is a God-fearing man true to his oath, he knows the depth of my pain, he understands my desires, but he has warned me severely of the repercussions of such activities. I shall wear this crape for eternity, to mourn the loss of my beloved Eleanor and my own soul. Should they judge me with the bloodied hands of Queen Grouch herself, I shall stand proudly and gladly take such punishments as they see fit to mete out. No, this appalling affront, this gaping wound that will never heal, can only be salved in the bile of bloody reprisal. I am set upon this course as determinedly, and single-minded as our spineless, heedless, menfolk are set upon theirs. I know there is no way back from this path, though it were through no cause of my own, those whose true task it is will not return, if ever. Thus I shall shoulder this mantle. I must travel this course alone even if it leads unto the shadow of the gallows. And should, with God's good graces, this trail of misery lead me to the very murderer himself, this 'Captain Everheart,' I shall fall upon him with all the rage of a raven black harpy and tear his eyes out with my bare hands or die, willingly, in the attempt.

~~*Pray for me.*~~

Pray for my beloved Eleanor.

"The human soul isn't sold once
but rather slowly and methodically and piece by piece."

JAKE TAPPER

THE HELLFIRE CLUB

LE VOYAGE DU SORCIER.

The following excerpts are from a letter obtained by myself at auction from the estate of Jonathan E. Hoag, Esq. publisher. The provenance was established by means of handwriting comparisons with official documents. It was written by the Illusionist and Stage Entertainer Gabriel Wellington-Welles and appears to have been in reply to an enquiry by Mr Hoag's publishing House, Astrophobos Press. Known widely by the stage name "Jeteur de Sort," and in other circles as "La Grande Bête."

James Ransom.

(Translated from Zephyrian French.)

I was born in the Atelier de Travail de Sainte Peter, in Zephyr, opposite the Pénitencier Central, both institutions my parents fervently believed would be left back in France. My earliest memories are of death. You see, due to the situation of our dormitory windows, we, the younger children, would eagerly behold the rigmarole surrounding the executions in the prison yard we overlooked. For some, what I witnessed as little more than a babe, would have been the stuff of nightmares. Held aloft to the window by my workhouse siblings, I eagerly watched men & women, children even, dragged screaming or stumbling stupefied to meet their brutal punishments. Hacking off of hands, ears, noses, tongues, blindings, brandings & the like for the guileless felons, guillotine for murderers, traitors & anarchists, far worse still for the spies. All for the amusement of the taunting mob charged a few centimes upon entry.

475

The judgment of the Republic of Zephyria was harsh, & behind those walls, medieval in its cruelty.

At night I would lay awake in my cot listening to the wailing of the wandering spirits. Some, often the guilty, full of rage or remorse, others, the innocent& the imbecilic, crying out in confusion& fear. I never thought to question the other boys to whether or not they could hear what I heard, or, later, see the things I could see.

My mother & father were both in their pauper's graves by the time I was five years old. At seven, I was moved into the workhouse proper& put to work. There I toiled all the daylight hours, fetching& carrying for the men working in the yards crushing stone for gravel, bone for fertilizer, limestone for quicklime. Crushing, always crushing. The hammering went on all day, every day, except, of course, Dimanche, Sunday.

Sunday, we were washed, brutally scrubbed& filed into the Chapleur to sit on the arse numbing pews in the cold for hours, to listen to the interminable droning on of that dullard Pasteur Chevrolet & the berating sermons of the sadistic Monsieur Jenkett, the Maître Surveillant.

It was on one of those Sundays, unusually warm even for a summer's day, that I first noticed the others in the Chapleur. Semi-translucent shadows that crowded at the edges of the dark recesses. Watching. I thought they were merely drawn to the ceremony, ghosts still attending upon their reverential duties, but it soon became apparent to me, they were not watching the Pasteur, they were watching me. Intently.

From then on, I became aware of them, everywhere, all about me. My fantÔmes, as I called them. They were silent back then.

At the age of twelve, I was apprenticed out to a local Cordonnier. This meant that though I worked long, long hours in his workshop, I returned every night to the workhouse dormitory to sleep. The Cordonnier was a malicious man with a vicious temper, given to drinking cheap cognac& beating upon all those in his household, from his wife down to the miserable nameless mangy mutt he kept to guard the shop. As to what he thought was worth anyone's trouble to steal, I never knew. I learnt to take my beatings in turn, though I was already hardened by much worse that I had experienced during my upbringing in the workhouse.

It was a wretched life. It became quickly evident that even the promise of learning a trade was lost to me, as the Cordonnier had no intention of teaching me a thing. I swiftly became resigned to such a meagre existence. Only the workhouse profited from the charge they levied for my labour.

I was trapped in that existence for two years until one cold, wet morning, I arrived at the Cordonnier's home, as usual ahead of the Rappeur, to find nothing but a burnt-out shell. Gutted by fire in the night, the Cordonnier was dead, his family& the dog, all perished in the flames.

The Cordonnier was deceased, yes, but not gone. His stupefied spirit was there still, stumbling about his ruined workshop, bemoaning his death& cursing the dog. The dog's spirit was there too, but in death, it was no thin flea-bitten cur but as big& dangerous as Fenrisúlfr himself. From the Cordonnier's wild mutterings, I learnt that the dog had finally snapped& ripped into him, tearing a chunk out of his inner thigh, and savaging him to death. In the struggle, an oil lamp had been dashed to the floor. The conflagration claimed them both & everyone else in the Cordonnier's home.

I learnt a lot that morning. The dead talked if you have the ear to listen& they are as aware as you or I. I learnt that some that died, like the Cordonnier& his dog, remained trapped, at least for a while, whilst others, like the Cordonnier's benighted wife& children, passed on to that other place swiftly. I also learnt that when you see the dead's souls clearly, you see them for what they really were in life. The Cordonnier, in life, had been a big man, flabby fat, with big hands& a booming voice, an angry bear of a man. In death his spirit, though recognisable as him, was weak& gnarled, rat-like& rotting from within, his skin was as old shoe leather, flaking& cracked.

Unthinkingly, I hurried back towards the only place I knew as home. I got almost to the steps of the Atelier de Travail. We were not allowed to enter through the front doors, but I had to pass by that grand sweep of marble steps, to the alleyway down the side. I stood for a moment, looking at those polished stone risers that I had spent countless hours of my life scrubbing until my knuckles bled. I understood I could not go back. If I had no employment, I would be put to work in the yards crushing, endlessly crushing. I would either end up coughing up my bloody lungs or go mad from the incessant hammering.

I fled. I had a few centimes from tips I had pocketed from deliveries to the Cordonnier's customers in the better parts of town.

Just a few, as he had demanded every penny as his, but I was careful& took my portion before I ever returned.

I ran away from the workhouse. I had no plan, nor the first idea what I would do, but I intended never to return.

I survived on the streets of the city for several months. Making a living from thieving& robbing the unsuspecting. I fell in& out with several gangs& learnt to survive on my wits. I made a semi-decent pickpocket& was lithe& fast enough to make a good dipper. When I could, like so many of my kind, I sold myself. I was born male, of course, but light boned& fragile of frame, efféminé, as some cruelly denounced me, through their jealousy of my beautiful youth.

I learnt that unless you were content to sleep in the gutter, prey for whatever stalks the city's backstreets at night, one must do whatever it takes to pay the rent. In fact, I was doing rather well. I know that is not what you expect to hear, but it is true, that is until I was caught.

I was within sight of the Cathédrale de Sainte Pierre one Sunday afternoon. Patrolling the edge of the mass of gentry that moved like a heard of finely dressed cattle through the rues& boulevards of the Old Imperial quarter, when an opportunity caught my eye. A top-hatted gentleman in a long, elegant coat. An open pocket stuffed with something tempting. A wallet perhaps? I tried my luck.

Almost as my fingers touched the leather case, a hand closed around my wrist, the grip was vice-like.

My struggles were pointless. I was hauled around& up like a rag doll. Another hand clasped my throat. Leather cased fingers, as long and strong as a raven's talons, locked under my jaw. I found myself eye to eye with my captor. Eyes as black as jet regarded me over the rims of the tinted spectacles perched upon the bridge of her aquiline nose. I thought I was assuredly dead, such a lady of substance could clout a ragamuffin like me a fatal blow in the street& think no more of it than to be careful not to trip on my jittering corpse as she strolled on.

But those eyes, those deep penetrating eyes, that looked right into my soul, were not of my potential killer but my saviour, or should I say, future tormentor.

The self-styled Jeteur de Sort, "La Grande Bête," was a woman of great reputation& even greater abilities. Stage magician& mesmerist, she was famed throughout Mars for her incredible magic shows that could pack theatres to the rafters night after night. Of course, of which as a destitute child, I knew nothing. She was also famed in the salons& private drawing rooms of the rich& powerful as the Mystic, Medium& Soothsayer, the Seigneuresse Jean Wellington-Welles, which, of course, was yet another non-de-plume. She courted scandal& scorned accepted sensibilities. She would swap her persona at will, from male to female, dress as she pleased& openly take lovers of either sex, sometimes both, from all stations of society.

Welles, originally a Thaumasian, was rich, urbane, and relished wearing men's apparel. She was fated by the most powerful in Zephyria &was possibly the cruellest, most petty-minded person I had ever known, the Cordonnier included.

The night before our encounter she had returned from Tharsis, from a performance for the British Prince& was full of self-importance& pomposity. Upon reflection, I believe that buoyed her mood to a point where my unfortunate rendezvous with her on that morning was received with equanimity rather than her usual casual brutality.

She never let slip that vice-like grip for ten years. I was her captive, then her plaything, abused, tortured& tormented for her amusement, then her famulus, then her acolyte& finally her theurgist. I procured other victims for her, poisoned & murdered for her, lied, stole, whored& debased myself at her whim, all this until finally she had moulded me into what she wanted; a facsimile of herself.

I stood on stage in front of witless thousands& fooled them with pretentious sleight of hand, smoke& mirrors. But occasionally she would have us perform real aeaeae on stage, even dangerous summonings, dressed up in the mockery of theatrics enough to absolutely confound the audience. In the private salons of the wealthy, we would carry out séances& summoning's, a mixture of theatre, fakery& chilling reality.

Slowly she shared her knowledge, introducing me to her hidden world. She too had seen the dead from a young age& had been warped by the experience. They had not merely watched her, they had tormented her continually until she had sought the aid of an excommunicated Eridanian Mystagogue, Jedidiah Orne. Orne was deeply learned in the mystery religions of the Ancient Hellenes& Parthians & initiated her into his sect& unlocked her powers, as she set about unlocking mine.

As her acolyte& apprentice, I learnt from my mistress everything I needed to one day assume her mantle of power. I learnt of the ancient mystery religions, of powerful spells& what she believed

481

naïvely, was the most hidden occult knowledge that even the wisest knew nothing of. She touched upon horrors so awful they would have shattered lesser, possibly saner, minds. I was desperately hungry to learn everything I could, but as I grew more knowledgeable& more confident, so she grew more suspicious. I was young, attractive & accommodating to the rich, both them & their wives. Welles had instructed me in every aspect of my deportment, from the accents I adopted to the very tone of my voice, from the knives& forks on the table setting to the banal intricacies of mannerly small talk and the arts of the bedroom. I became as courteous, superficially charming& urbane as Welles herself, but, of course, younger& much more attractive to all. She had never been a beauty& the ravages of her early life were deeply etched into her countenance, it conspired with her long black hair, gleaming coal-black eyes& prominent nose to give her the aspect of a raven.

Her cruelty unlocked something in me that seemed to know no bounds. As I grew as strong as her, my thirst for knowledge led me to seek out other sources of learning, books& teachings. It even led me towards other masters.

One day, before a matinée performance, Welles confronted me to accuse me of stealing one of her beloved books. "*Von Unaussprechlichen Kulten*," by von Junzt, a handwritten 1838 edition, incredibly valuable& incredibly rare.

I had stolen it, of course, that& many others from her hidden library, but, fearing her rage, I denied it vigorously. Welles grew furious& in that little dressing room, attacked me, initially with her talons& anything to hand, & then, after I fended her off easily, with a terrible curse. I could not let her complete her words, my wardings& passes were useless to protect me from such a spell, as she knew my true name, but I also had learnt, from one absinth filled sex& drinking session, hers. In desperation I struck back, reciting a half-understood incantation from the very book she accused me of stealing. At that moment there was both the satisfaction of vindication& shock in those jet-black eyes. That was the last time I saw her. The spell worked& she was gone instantly, sucked into the corposant light that flared in a dark corner of the room, never to return. I hoped.

Thence, I stepped into her shoes, on stage I became Jeteur de Sort, "Le Grand Bête." In the salons, I remained as she had always portrayed me, her loyal child, Gabriel. Where had my mother gone? Travelling, of course, seeking new knowledge in far off places. Soon they forgot even to ask& eventually, sometimes with a little help from myself, they forgot she ever existed, there had only ever been me.

Those were good times, my salad years, as the English say. I must admit I revelled in it. I practised my arts more& more daringly, even on stage. I summoned the spirits before audiences of thousands, I mesmerised entire auditoriums. Necromancy came easily to me. I dragged the eidolon from their restful sleep& harried them with frivolities to amuse the unwashed rubes that crowded the theatres with their grubby faces& grasping desires. "Where did Mama hide her jewellery?" "Did your motherlove you best?" "Is there anyone here called Mary?" The dead talked to me, even those that did not wish to, & from them, I learnt many secrets, secrets they had taken to their graves, that aided my cause.

My wealth& fame grew exponentially. I acquired a beautiful wife, daughter of a wealthy Zephyrian politician& heiress to a vast fortune from her late mother's side. She fell entirely under my mesmeric control. Several beautiful mistresses& catamites, I kept in luxury& shared with only those who could aid my station. Loose pillow talk, blackmail, rumour, sex, everything Welles taught me to use I used to create a wall of invulnerability about myself.

You may, of course, at this juncture be a little confused as to my gender. This is often the preoccupation of the narrow-minded hoi polloi.

Welles taught me that all Sorcerers must jealously guard their real identity& their true natures. She insisted that, on stage, I would play her beautiful, loving daughter& assistant. In other places, I would be her devoted son& heir. I enjoyed the game& played it well. It was easy for me with my looks. As a child thrown into the workyards of the Atelier de Travail amidst men segregated from their women, my existence had been a nightmare. More than the Sight, my appearance had been my true curse, a cruel jest by God or the Devil himself. I was not alone in this torment, this was the fate of most of the boys in the yards, but I was especially singled out. A favourite cast from one to another to sate their depravities. All the while, my fantômes had stood by silently observing.

When Welles had caught me, my body was wracked with disease, but she had had plans for me& so she did one thing I will remain indebted to her for, she cured me, with the very best doctors& her strange little potions, she saved my life, but only for her own amusement.

All I had learnt throughout the sordid ordeals of my childhood I put to good use amongst the bourgeoisie of Zephyria, especially with those that Welles wished me to bed or compromise.

I admit, once free of her control, I grew decadent& debauched, bloated with power. In doing so, I grew careless. I made many enemies, especially amongst others of the Craft, & of course, I inherited Welles' old adversaries, among them the lunatic cultists of Ramié's Voynich Society& the slavering fanatics of the Ordo Venatores. I considered none worthy of any great concern.

As I grew in standing, I seldom performed on stage, though I still enjoyed private audiences& then only to the most important dignitaries& in the most prestigious settings.

All went well until one evening. I had entertained several heads of state at a private audience at Le Palais de l'Opéra when I retired to my quarters to discover a man standing in the middle of my dressing room. This may seem a trivial thing to you, to find a fellow in your dressing room is nothing unusual in the semi-public shambles of the back rooms of any theatre, but as my wealth& power had grown so had my paranoia. I would suppose that at the root of my concern was that I always feared Welles would someday find her way back from whatever Hell I had consigned her to. My room was locked soundly, the door guarded by two robust men in my employ & warded to the very best of my considerable abilities. The opera house itself was awash with uniformed militia& the armed guards of the dignitaries, securing every entrance& exit. Therefore, I was confounded to be confronted by this intruder.

He was tall, well dressed in a rather old-fashioned manner, with long jet-black hair & a strange, fixed grin on his face, at first, I thought it a mask. I would learn that it really was. Behind his little darkly tinted spectacles he had the yellow goatlike eyes of a demon.

If the Christians are right& there is truly a single manifestation of all the evil in the universe, then that is whom I found standing in my room, Satan himself. This strange grinning demon introduced himself formally as Indrid Cold.

I would like to tell you that I sent him packing with a flea in his ear, but, of course, that would be a lie. I was far too fearful. Though his manner was cultured& his language measured, he radiated evil as a boiler radiates heat into a room. I was not left in any doubt that whatever he wanted from me, I would have to give unreservedly or pay a terrible price.

Since that day, I have been in his service, or more appropriately, his enthrallment. I once believed Welles to have been a frightening woman of infinite power, but she was little more than a bumbling fishwife chanting cantrips over a cauldron compared to Indrid Cold. Cold claimed he has walked the passages of the void between the infinite universes & I have learnt not to doubt him at all. I have seen him do such wonders. He is truly a Prince of Hell. His powers are extraordinary& he has taught me much.

He set me to an undertaking that I have embarked on willingly. I dispensed with my stage career, my home in Ville d'Ys& my doting, little doe-eyed wife.

The poor thing's sensibilities were not up to the stresses of her father's untimely death, though not 'untimely' for me I may add, in fact exceptionally fortuitous. Melancholia& a fugue took hold of her. Then came the lurid phantasms that plagued her& so with deep despondency, I packed her off to Dr Seward's asylum. Seward, such an accommodating man, always so eager to please. As you can understand, a tragedy, such a terrible loss, though it left me rather well compensated for my trouble.

Why did I not dispense with her altogether? Do not assume any sentimentality or fondness for her by my actions. She served her usefulness as far as access to her father's wealth& social position. My intentions had been that one day I would have her released into my care long enough to provide me with the legitimate heir that I required& then, once a son was born, fearing that the stress of it all may cause a relapse into madness, I would be publicly heartbroken to have to have the poor confused creature returned to the asylum. Where she would spend the rest of her days writing me her incessant entreaties to rescue her. I used them mainly for firelighters, a pity to waste such good bond.

I hear the little mouse is to be freed soon. For sport, I shall encourage her dear Mama& Papa to visit upon her regularly.

I retired from public life, liquidated all my assets & I brought a splendid rambling country pile, Dashwood House. As directed by my new Aresian Master, I set about building a temple to worship the Great Old Gods of the Malacandrians, those that had held sway here for eternity & still remain. From lists of names Cold provided, I drew together worshipers from all over the world, greedy, dissolute, ruthless men& women, lured in with promises of riches& power beyond the dreams of avarice. As Cold revealed the true powers of the Malacandrian Gods to me, I revealed them to my eager flock.

I created the sect as per his instructions, drawing in converts& initiates with promises of whatever their putrid hearts & fetid desires craved. All the while being careful to create a select coven of only the most trusted & influential. I used the knowledge of the traditions of the Ancient Greeks& Egyptians, which Welles had taught me. Adopting& adapting rites& ceremonies as I saw fit. I understood clearly that all the posing about in robes, all the orgies, the midnight ceremonies& bloody sacrifices, were purely stage dressing for Cold's real purpose, whatever that was. Through these adherents, he built a spider's web of influence& venality within the governments& power brokers of Mars. Men& woman of little moral fibre& an endless hunger for power made easy converts to our new religion.

Cold had many tasks he wished these ready recruits to carry out, things that served his greater purpose. He never revealed himself to them, all the while watching but never taking part. I was his vassal, the conduit for his commands. Those that willingly did as I bade them were handsomely rewarded; wealth poured into their hands, opponents were silently eliminated, obstacles to their desires vanished. Though those that failed his commands, died, often in the most horrific manner, sometimes by my own hand upon the high altar.

I served him through a combination of appetite, fear& self-preservation, hungry to learn more& grow in my own power, but never genuinely terrified of him until he showed how ruthless he really was. One of the chief adherents, one of the earliest recruits to our ranks of worshipers, Windlestraw Volpone, had run into a major conflict with the burgers of Chalon. They were thwarting his plans by refusing to ratify licences he had drawn up with their pre-revolutionary predecessors. Plans, I believe, that had emanated from Cold himself. Cold's revenge was truly horrific. As Cold's appointed High Priest, the Hierophant of our now not-so-little cult. I officiated at the rites that brought a terrible madness down upon a city full of people. A murderous lunacy that consumed them& their entire city. Indrid Cold was merciless beyond anything I had ever known& I had found my true master in him. Utterly enthralled, I threw myself at his feet in adoration. Though you may be shocked, I shall admit to becoming truly aroused in the presence of such pitiless supremacy. The Malacandrian's culture was far superior to our human pretentions to civilization, to them Christian notions of mercy, charity &kindness, that impede human destiny were anathema, the nauseating joke at the heart of a sick, weak people. Theirs was a true civilization, one of courage, loyalty, obedience, strength &purity, one that the Spartans themselves would have understood. Humanity's greed, avarice& indolence disgusted them, but most of all they despised humanity's weakness. What a true master I had found.

Cold's capabilities& knowledge were beyond anything I could have envisioned. I witnessed him summon nameless horrors from the Avitchi, the Endless Darkness, &bend time& reality at will. He taught me little more than I ever needed to serve him in my role as Hierophant, but even that was by far more than anything I had learnt before. The Gods he served were the Ancient Gods of Mars.

Destroyers not creators, their worship entails a surrender of one's paltry grasp on rationality to comprehend even the concept of their existence outside of time& materiality.

I readily surrendered to them whatever they demanded& saw success after success, but the maelstrom surrounding our workings in the new temple spread far& wide as if tainting everything& everyone in the vicinity. Together we had unstitched a tiny part of reality& suddenly all was unravelling about us. The whole region around the temple, house& grounds began to slide into the Amen, as the tide erodes a chalky promontory.

It was then that Indrid's brother, Lanulos, first appeared, he& his henchmen, the creature Everheart& that reanimated corpse they called Knapp. I thought I would be put to death, flung into the abyss or fed to some otherworldly horror for my perceived failures, but Lanulos was magnanimous, even amused. He ordered me to seal the rift we had created, which, with his directions, I did. Though resealing the fissure cost dearly, my corax were eager to sacrifice their lives for a glimpse of eternity& the hollow promises I made them.

Everheart acted as Lanulos' formalist, an overseer sent to correct mistakes, punish vacillators& deal with the unworthy. I never knew precisely what his nature was, but the enchantments& glamours about him were so strong that it made me truly fear whatever it contained. It is said that *"One should not step too close to inspect the craftsmanship of the tiger's cage,"* but I had learnt enough to recognise great binding spells when I sense them. At first, I believed Everheart was an Anakim, bound into the form of some unfortunate human curcurbite by Lanulos himself, but I learnt later he was something

490

else, something far more dangerous. It was truly an act of unimaginable power, to bind such a creature& to set it to errands at one's whim.

With order restored, Lanulos instructed me that the temple was to be fully completed& furnished accordingly, that I was not to attempt to commune with the Gods themselves& anything more than showy ceremonies& minor summoning's to terrify the doubtful was forbidden. Lanulos set me to recruit as many new converts as possible from lists he provided & to inculcate in them loyalty by feeding their greed& ultimately controlling them by instilling abject fear in their souls. To these ends, I was allowed to have access to vast wealth& to recruit my own agathion, famulus& miles, but all under the constant watchful eyes of Everheart& the revenant, Knapp.

I was sent to travel extensively, recruiting new converts from the lists that Lanulos provided me. I also was tasked, by Cold, to seek out lost Malacandrian sculptures& effigies. One of the first recruits to my inner coven had been the industrialist Eleuthère De Maurier, a man whom I had previously encountered at a private auction house a year or two before I met Cold. We shared similar somatic proclivities, but, in truth, the inducements of the flesh held no sway with Eleuthère, neither did hunger for money or power, he had as much of both as he wished. What drove him was his obsession with collecting Aresian artefacts. The acquisition of which he believed would be a key to some lost esoteric wisdom of the Aresians. He thought that it held the key to eternal life, to which ends he had gained knowledge of the whereabouts of objects that even Cold had no knowledge of. Welles had built up a small but significant collection of statuettes which I happily used as bargaining chips to obtain De Maurier's favours. It had been easy to recruit Eleuthère into our new cult being as he was already obsessed with the Aresians, especially the Malacandian's& their mysterious religion. Now with his aid& my own theatrical flair, I created the role of Madame Camarilla, the buyer for a wealthy collector of ancient religious objet-d'art, but, like some lower-ranking devil, what I truly sought were the souls of the depraved& the iniquitous.

It was then that Eleuthère, in an unguarded moment drunk on absinth& opium, told me of an important untouched tomb he believed buried on a pissenlit farmer's land in Tremorfa County, in western Tharsis. He believed it to be connected with the Royal House of Aldébaran, possibly a family tomb. He claimed to have known of its existence for a decade& by process of vigorous acquisition, narrowed it down to one particular farm. He had been trying to purchase the land or drive the farmer off it, for a couple of years, but the farmer was intractable.

Eleuthère was a pleonexic little man, still playing his cards close to his sweaty chest. He simply did not have any idea what powers he was playing with. I informed Cold immediately, I believed the ludicrous little pilgarlic certainly doomed.

I was not to be present when Cold visited upon Eleuthère, though, of course, it fell to me to deal with the aftermath. There was no corpse, only a mess of bloody offal and that filthy merkin he wore on his head. I believed from the carnage left behind, that Cold must have done something terrible to him; I did not understand exactly what, until much later.

Over the following months, I busied myself recruiting new converts amongst the powerful across the various republics& building Madame Camarilla's reputation as a buyer. My new contacts in the Sirenuim Resistance provided me with a stream of artefacts, effigies& statues, even whole sections of frescos& bass-relief carvings. I was preparing to travel to the wilds of Cydonia, the eastern province of Eden, to inspect the fascinating discoveries of an expedition the Madame had funded, when I learnt of several significant acquisitions coming on to the market from a looted temple somewhere in the south of Sirenuim. The looters of the Resistance were prepared to dismantle an entire temple& sell it to me piece by piece. So, with Cold's blessing, I brought everything they had to offer. In Janvier of 26 N.R, (January M.Y.26) I made a somewhat perilous journey to Sothis in southern Sirenuim to view one particular piece that the Resistance fighters had to offer me. This was unusual, as in most circumstances I habitually brought directly from the sellers or from either drawings& descriptions& the occasional Maddox-type photographical image.

This item, a was assured, was different. Even amongst these hardened warriors, there was great trepidation, even fear, around it. I was told that no matter how the lithographer had tried, he could not make a clear image of this particular statue. So, with my interest aroused& in hopes of obtaining something that would truly please my master, on one dark& stormy night in a half burnt-out warehouse in the back streets of Sothis. I finally came face to face with Aradia, the Queen of Qadath.

I must tell you honestly that I had begun to dream of her almost as soon as I first learnt of her existence. Dreams of astonishing strange lands where I walked in cities of indescribable design. I meandered through foreboding forests were horrors beyond imagining hunted the night.

In a vast frozen wasteland, upon a mountain so high it reached beyond the skies unto the void, I roamed through a vast empty castle& the deserted city within. Nothing more than an insignificant insect drifting through a city built by giants.

There she first came to me, the enigmatic, alabaster skinned Queen of that nameless City of Ice, beautiful beyond words yet utterly terrifying. In those dreams, she called to me, enticed me with her body& promised me unimaginable power, beyond even that of the brothers. I had fallen under her spell long before I saw her effigy in that shabby warehouse, yet she was as every bit as beautiful as in my dreams. I could hardly contain my excitement, both emotional& physical. The sight of this meagre effigy alone aroused in me such desires that I could barely control myself in the contemplation of the day I will truly meet her. I would have willingly paid whatever price they demanded but, in truth, they were so in awe of her beauty that they all but gave her to me, so long as I promised to take her there& then.

It took some time to arrange for further transportation back to the temple I had created for her.

The major problems for me were that this was not some small piece of objet d'art to be wrapped in oilskins& dropped in the bottom of some beer barrel or smuggled in the packing straw of a crate of porcelain. This was a lifelike carving in Martian onyx-marble of Aradia, the Queen of Qadath, Malacandians' mother Goddess, weighing five or six hundred kilos. It exuded power because of the otherworldly nature of the relationship between her& her image. I tried several times to arrange further passage for her, but the ignorant's minds are weak, easily toyed with& susceptible to silly fancies. Hardened blackmarketeers were unnerved by her presence. One smuggler Captain claimed the presence of her on his ship drove his crewmen to suicide& mutiny, another dared to claim she visited him in his dreams, referring to her as a disgusting monster. I stabbed him in the eye for the insult, right there in front of his crew, though he survived, I let it stand as a warning to his brethren.

Hence moving her had to be done in stages, short journeys & regular handovers. Horses found the power emanating from her disquieting. In dreams, I begged her to help me, but she only laughed& teased me in her coquettish, erotic manner.

We had reached Szélanya in the south of the Gorgonum Chaos, where I was negotiating passage across the border into Tharsis when I received a summons from Indrid Cold. My presence was required in Zephyr. Therefore, I had to let my Queen travel the last stages of the journey on her own. It had taken a month to get her that far. In dreams, she was not pleased, but I had no choice but to obey my master. I feared for her safety&

Editor's Note.

The rest of the letter has been lost, or, as yet, has not been made available to purchase from the late Mr Hoag's estate, at this time of publishing.

James Ransom.

"Lingering on

heart in a silent sea

adrift"

BRYAN JONES

The Flammarion Expedition Journal of L. Edwin Ransom.
Day fifteen. 44th. 9th. 26.
Sunday.

Cont.

Though I was severely shaken by our misadventure on the
ground, the Professor summoned the Colonel and me immediately
to his cabin and requested a briefing. Dr Spender was already
present. I explained the events as best as I could, under the
circumstances, but Dr Spender had already told him of the young
Captain and his story. The Professor seemed to be unusually
willing to accept Jahns' argument that the young Captain was
simply a mad man and to discount his claim that the Aresians had
invaded Earth. I told him of the strange 'empyreans' we had
discovered amidst the wreckages. Dr Spender though preferred to
dwell more upon the nature of the very place itself, but thankfully,
like Colonel Jahns, the Professor was not in the mood for an
elongated discourse on the subject, but more interested in getting
to a point at which we could utilise our navigation instruments.

He then brought to our attention that there was a floating rock
quite a way in the distance. One supposed another fragment of
Phrike, the lost moon of Mars. It appeared to be out over what
maybe the epicentre of this field of destruction. We then traipsed
off to the flight deck to view it from the ships most powerful

telescope. There was indeed such a splinter, and it was of immense size, almost that of our own Pegasus Rock, which we all believed was the largest piece known, and upon it arose a featureless tower of some white material. The Professor proposed that, as we were 'flying blind,' so to speak, we should take the time to investigate the Tower. It may hold a clue to the nature of this place and possibly our location geographically.

Excerpt from;
Memoirs of Aelita, Lady Sydeian.
The Athenaeum of Harendrimar Tai.

It was not until we were safely aboard the airship that my senses ultimately returned to me. Patty, noticing how befuddled I was, sat me down in the wardroom and gave me a glass of strong drink. "G and T" she called it, and then stood over me like a nurse while I drank it, she then quaffed her own in two large gulps and refilled our glasses. I had never tasted anything like it before. That little weasel Dr Hammond, and Giovanni, forbade me anything more than a very occasional small glass of red wine, as they insisted it may have had 'adverse' effects when mixed with my medication. Maybe they both feared alcohol would have the same effects upon my temperament that it did on Giovanni's. Fortunately, the only effects it had on me though was to relax me thoroughly, and make me ever so slightly squiffy, whether that was adverse or not. Almost everything took on a mirthful hue, and we sat together giggling like a pair of loons, largely at the Colonel's expense (though mercifully he was not present) and our own rather graceless headlong flight to safety. Patty had ripped her breaches climbing over the rail, and I had broken the heel of my boot, lost my footing and almost ended up falling out the other side in the scramble to get Dr Spender on to the platform of the landing hoist.

Thankfully, by the time Edwin joined us, we had regained enough composure to engage in relatively decorous conversation.

We talked of the young pilot they had discovered and some of the very odd things he had said. Patty filled in the details, adding that the young man's story seemed most compelling, though it was bizarre, even insane, she was sure that he believed what he was saying. We agreed that though it may all have sounded fantastical, who are we that find ourselves sitting in an airship above a place that does not exist on any known map, to be rushing to such judgement?

It was then that I first heard of the floating rock at the centre of this field of destruction. I do not feel that anyone was hiding the fact from me, I simply had not been paying attention to what the others had been discussing before we went down. Now my curiosity was piqued, so much so that I almost confided in Edwin and Patty why I was sure we must go there. Nevertheless, controlling my excitement, I simply agreed the Professor was right to insist we investigate it. Something from the vision of my grandmother had left me with a sense of certainty that the answer I sought, possibly the solution we all sought, lay in that tower. I quickly understood from their reaction I may have come across a little more emphatic than I intended. However, neither of them queried me on it.

Not long afterwards, with barely enough time to clear my head a little, change my attire and borrow a pair of Patty's Hessian boots, I found myself, along with the others on the alarmingly unsafe airboat they call the 'dory.' My mind was awash with strange fancies and trepidations; nevertheless, I steeled myself, as I knew I had to face whatever lay in wait for me inside that enigmatic tower.

The Flammarion Expedition Journal of L. Edwin Ransom.
Day fifteen. 44th. 9th. 26.
Sunday.

Cont.

Captain Llewellyn informed us that at this speed we would arrive at the tower in about forty minutes and so I took my leave to freshen up a bit, change my clothes and take some tea. Dr Spender wished to remain to talk with the Professor, and the Colonel went in search of something stronger to drink. I arrived in the wardroom seeking tea to discover Patty and Aelita already having elevenses. I joined them. The ladies were concerned for the safety of the young English Captain we had encountered amidst the wreckage. I could only tell them that I believed he ran off as soon as the sand started to subside. Both ladies were intrigued by the Captain's bizarre claims. I feared that Aelita may have been upset by the suggestion that Aresian forces had attacked Earth, and so I assured them that I believed the young man had been mistaken or delusional. I focused on his claim that he came from Earth in 1920 and had mysteriously suddenly been transported here, they agreed that it all made no more sense to them than it did to me. Desperately changing the subject, I encouraged them to speculate on the empyreans we had discovered, when we were hurriedly summoned to the flight deck.

The Professor wished us to witness a quite spine-chilling sight. Below us, amidst the wreckage, were swarms of creatures moving as if disturbed by the passing of our shadow.

Anemoi, thousands of them. Though they looked almost nothing like the illustrations in the books of my childhood or the stuffed ones displayed in the Tharsis Museum of Natural History, thanks to Sir John's seminar, I recognised them immediately. Fearsome baboon-like creatures with scaly skin and bat-like wings, brandishing rudimentary weaponry. I was taken aback by their size, easily that of a well-built farming lad of twelve or so. I was also surprised that though parts of their bodies were covered with coarse reddish-brown fur and dark leathery scales, they still wore hides and rags as clothing, a few even wore crudely made armour. Some leapt and capered from wreck to wreck gesticulating aggressively, others loosed arrows, launched spears or threw rocks.

They moved as a mass, a murmuration, flowing in our wake, gathering more and more as we went. Mr Charles estimated there was several thousand, and we agreed it was easily that or more. Patty explained that she was both excited that the Anemoi were obviously not virtually extinct as many thought them to be, and shocked at how fiercely hostile they were.

Dr Spender remarked that their hostility to our kind was probably a prudent reaction. They had everything to fear from mankind, after all the British Government, like others, had declared them vermin and placed a bounty on the heads of every one of them; male, female and young alike.

Colonel Jahns commented they were every bit as savage, but much more intelligent, than they seem, and powerful. An adolescent male, he remarked, is strong enough to rip a man apart limb from limb. Some hunters had made a great fortune slaughtering them he added caustically. His tone left no doubt as to who he was alluding to.

Below us some of the Anemoi launched themselves off high points in a vain attempt to reach our ship; however, their wings were inadequate for proper flight, and mostly they just glided back to the ground. A couple managed to catch the wind or thermal updrafts and flew higher, only to be shot down by the Colonel's men. Patty demanded that the Professor order the soldiers to hold their fire. The Professor agreed, telling the Colonel his men should only shoot if the creatures got too close.

Finally, as we drew nearer, we turned our attention to the rock that loomed before us.

It was roughly an inverted cone shape. Its flat top easily equal in area to the Pegasus Rock, which at a smidgen over 160 square acres, is considered the largest piece of the third moon we know of. There were, of course, those wild explorer's tales of whole floating cities out over the remoter reaches of the Seas of Sand, but they were probably more to do with wishful thinking and too much brandy than reality. Though Pegasus is a colossal piece of rock, the science behind the signum petram's existence defied Tellurian scientists' understanding for years. Unlike 'Our Rock,' as most of the denizens of Tharsis refer proprietarily to Pegasus, the top of this one was not a hotchpotch of buildings, landing strips and mooring gantries, but mostly covered with an ancient-looking dense forest of broad-leafed red wood trees which gave way in places to a thick undergrowth of blood-red zizany. Untouched by the impact of Tellurian colonisation, it appeared to be as I would have imagined places like the crimson forests of Gorgonum may have looked like to the earliest explorers; eerily beautiful, but utterly alien.

At the centre of the forest stood a huge white tower. I say 'stood,' but it was built like it ~~had grown~~ it had been moulded out of the ground, as a potter would mould a tall pot from a lump of clay. It appeared to be constructed, or should I say grown, of that strange mucilage, amalgamated with crystalline materials, that the buildings of Ananthor were constructed of.

As we approached our conversation turned to the height of the spire, Captain Llewellyn and the Professor agreed on two hundred feet, give or take, to the point at which it began to seamlessly taper towards the sky, another fifty feet or more.

"Utterly beautiful," murmured Dr Spender.

"But, how the hell do we get into it?" growled the Colonel. "Blast our way in?"

Our ship gained height, and we began to make a wide orbit of the tower. "There!" Mr Charles pointed out a wide door-like opening in the tower's fabric, about fifty feet below where it began to taper. From that portal jutted out a broad flat slab, obviously a viewing or landing platform. The Professor asked the Captain if we could come alongside it.

Captain Llewellyn huffed and puffed hesitantly about the idea, blustering about wind speeds, proximity to the construction and other factors. Finally, he suggested it would be safer, all told, to use the ship's dory to ferry anyone over, the landing area was big enough for it to set down safely and the ship could stay close, but at a safe distance.

I do not think I was alone in not relishing the idea of a journey, no matter how short, in the dory. Low sided, flat bottomed and notoriously unstable it was little more than a glorified larger version of the ship's bl'oats, but if we were to investigate the tower, then it would have to be endured. Though I felt I had had my quota of excitement and adventure for the day, this strange pale obelisk intrigued me greatly.

While the ship manoeuvred into place and the crew readied the dory, our little team of would-be adventurers, armed ourselves and wrapped up well. As with our landing earlier in the day, the Colonel and his men went first, flying the dory over to the platform and ensuring it was secure before the rest of us joined them. The Professor, Dr Spender, Patty, Aelita and I, along with her automaton maid, were next to brave the unsteady airboat. It was only a short hop, no more than a hundred yards, but we were all glad of the safe hands of the Sergeants as they greeted us upon our arrival.

Beyond the landing-place, set back in the darkness, was a doorless arch. After aiding us to disembark, the Colonel and his men, with weapons ready, quickly pushed on into the interior of the building. The rest of us following nervously.

This level appeared nothing more than a large featureless semi-circular room, the interior made of the same pale mucilage as the exterior. Across from where we entered, there was another doorway and, without pausing, I hurried through the space to keep pace with the soldiers. It was only Patty crying out my name that stopped me.

I turned about to discover Dr Spender and Aelita standing motionless in the middle of the room. Their eyes rolled upwards and their faces set in the same thunderstruck expressions, as if both were caught in some joint paroxysm. The Professor summoned the Colonel and his men back, we could not continue with two of our number stricken like this.

We were about to debate what we should do when suddenly as if let go by some unseen force, Dr Spender collapsed. Luckily, Patty and I were near enough to catch him before he fell to the floor.

Instantly Aelita too snapped out of her reverie. "He is here. Upstairs. Quickly!"

A dozen questions were on all our lips, but Aelita spoke so forcefully that all of us, even the Colonel, obeyed instinctively.

Patty wanted to take her father back to the airship, but he steadfastly refused, saying he must see what is upstairs.

I wanted to ask of whom Aelita spoke; Du Maurier or Everheart? But words failed me, so I took Dr Spender's elbow, and *between Patty and I, we half carried him across the room and through the doorway. There was a stairwell beyond that spiralled upwards.*

Even if we had, for a moment entertained the thought that the good Doctor could have managed the climb, with no balustrade it would have been foolishly precarious for us to try to aid him. In the face of his determination, Patty was trying to make her father understand that it would not only be dangerous for him but for those aiding him, when Aelita's maid stepped forward, swept the Doctor into her arms and began to march resolutely up the steps.

"There is a time for everything."

GRETTIR'S SAGA.

c.1400AD

THE RAGNARÖK FIELD

The Field Journal of Octavius Spender, Dr
44th of Sept 0026.

It has been a most singular day, one of great surprises, but I
cannot say I was utterly shocked at our discoveries in the
Ragnarök Field, as I came to call it. It only serves to confirm my
own suspicions. I cannot name them with anything as
grandiose as theories, at this point because I have never had the
evidence of anything other than my own eyes to substantiate
what I speculated is indeed happening. Now we have
eyewitnesses, not just the Captain and crew of some merchant
airship, but men of good standing like Professor James
Flammarion, Colonel Carter Jahns, Captain Llewelyn and dare I
say, myself.

The bodies of those alien creatures, those Empyreans, we
found amongst their war-torn wreckage, proved the truth of
what men like Edward Hoy-Castle have contended for decades,

there are undeniably other races that, if not originating here on Mars, certainly were present here.

Races with technologies not only unknown to us but radically different from anything we have known to be in the hands of the Aresians.

Then there is the issue of the young Captain. If not, as the Colonel contended, merely a madman, he claimed to be from Earth. Earth in 1920, an Earth invaded by Aresians, or was it some other Empyrean race, but then again that was thirty Earth years or more ago. However, is that our past, or some other possible past? He talked of an even earlier invasion attempt, was that why we lost all contact with Earth? Was that where the Armada I witnessed went? Not to fight a few desperate colonialists but to strike at the cradle of mankind. Did they not simply abandon us but were we lost in a fight for their very existence.

For now, I shall take refuge, as James has, in the Colonel's assertion of the preposterousness of such an idea, for to entertain it would call the very meaning of our endeavour into question.

James has decided that we should investigate the tower, I am overjoyed. Now that I was becoming aware of what the real questions were if there was anything that could hold a clue to why this whole area exists then that mysterious spire would be it.

To be honest, I did hope for some further revelations somewhat like those in the Tomb on Edwin's farmstead, nonetheless, as wise men say; one should be careful what you wish for.

Almost as soon as I stepped foot onto the landing platform of the tower, my perceptions were assailed.

I found myself not in that place, but another, an ancient tower made of roughly hewn stone, more like a ruin that one would expect to find in some remote marcher county in England. A dank, dark pile, where the lime plaster was flaking from the crumbling ashlar of the walls, and the heavy boards that made up the floor were pitted and rotting. I looked about me, but my companions did not seem to notice. I took my daughter's hand to steady myself as the room whirled. Everything faded, my companions, becoming translucent shades, their voices echoing into the darkness, and I was alone. Though part of my mind still sensed Patty's warm hand in mine, I could not see or hear her. I closed my eyes desperately trying to focus my mind, though when I opened them again, I was somewhere else, somewhere out in the wilderness.

I watched from an unknown vantage point as three young men, clambered up a ridge. They wore uniforms I recognised,

British Army, but their insignias were different as if they had been hurriedly replaced. On closer inspection, I recognised one of them immediately, my old friend and comrade; Chetwynd Griffith-Jones. My God, I thought absently, how young he was! It was only then that I realised one of those young soldiers was me. The other was our Sergeant, Windy Wyndham.

I watched in fascination as the young men crawled to the top of the embankment to peer over the ridge. I felt a pang of dread in the bottom of my stomach as I knew what they would behold. There, spread out across the plain below, was the vast armada of the Aresians. Hundreds of huge aerobarges, and all about them, like bees buzzing around flowers, were thousands of other craft. On the sands below, an army of tens of thousands mustered, in preparedness for some terrible assault.

With the vantage point of God himself, I now saw everything. Many of those soldiers were not Aresians at all, but Jed'dak warriors like those we had come upon earlier amidst the field of wreckage, and other even more exotic creatures. Had I seen them? Had I forgotten? Or had I disbelieved the evidence of my own eyes?

The two young officers threw down their field glasses and frantically scribbled in their note pads. Chetwynd handed Sergeant Wyndham a hurriedly scrawled dispatch and sent him scrambling back down the ridge to where we had hidden the bicycles. He would ride to the nearest Optical Telegraph Troop outpost and get the warning to the defenders at Tyrrhena Mons.

He never did though. I would learn much later that when he reached the outpost, the yellow Aresians had already overrun it and they killed him on the spot.

Chetwynd and I did our best to record as much as we saw, but scouts from the armada were getting too close for comfort, and we had to get off the ridge before they discovered us. I watched as Chetwynd and my younger self ran back to our bicycles and fled.

Nonetheless, my consciousness remained. Time passed strangely. Was this the same day or another, I did not know, but as I watched, the skies parted and a gigantic aethervolt ship descended into the midst of the armada. This was no nondescript dreadnaught, but some great Imperial looking flagship.

I was then amongst them, those Captains, Generals and Warlords of the Aresian races, and others, some of terrifying aspect. I moved like a phantom spirit. I witnessed the angry heated exchanges between them. I could not understand a word, but I did not need to. Many seemed disbelieving and furious as if betrayed, but all acquiesced before the authority of whoever was on the ship.

Though I tried to see inside that tremendous vessel, my awareness could not penetrate the peculiar aura about it.

Then something even more incredible happened; one by one each ship, each barge, appeared to create a distortion about it and then vanished into thin air. Not like some stage magician's trick, but as if they engaged some technology far beyond my understanding and passed out of this reality. I watched as the soldiers on the ground erected strange doorway like apertures that flashed like shimmering mirrors and, to my amazement, into which they marched in good order only to vanish like the ships.

I was barely able to comprehend what I saw when suddenly everything changed. I was in some great hall, a vast audience chamber, full of yellow-skinned Aresians, in their finest robes, the great and the mighty, High Priests, Princesses and Generals. I recognised the place immediately though I have only seen it in near ruins; the Proibön Saludik, the Palace of the Empress of Malacand in the now-abandoned Imperial City of Lunismar. In this astoundingly magnificent palace, this nucleus of absolute power, upon a great levitated throne, sat a corpulent old woman, pulling at her clothes and jewellery. As she rent the ornaments from her gown, casting them angrily at those about her, she howled in bitter despair. Around her, the courtiers milled shamefaced and confused, as they evaded the flying baubles. I could sense their ire; it was almost palpable. Nonetheless, there was a cowed resignation to their expressions, as if they knew they had no choice but to accept their own impotence.

I could sense, though not feel, I could hear their words though not recognise them, but I could comprehend their thoughts. The emotion they felt was betrayal, the sensation was powerlessness, and one of the few words that I could hear and understand, thought and spoken in reverence, fear and anger was: Oyarsa. Who or what this 'Oyarsa' was I could not grasp, though it seemed to have the same connotation as 'God' does in the minds of Tellurian men.

Time moved on, and soon, beyond that palace, there was fighting between those who saw themselves loyal to the Empress and those who would obey the Oyarsa. A brutal pogrom, as the Malacandian loyalists turned against all others in their domain, and even against their own kind, the Aküirr Hros'sa, those we Tellurians call the Kitreenoh Aresians. I watched as their ancient Empire, wracked with desperation, fatally wounded itself, before the onward march of its greatest foe; us, the Tellurians.

I witnessed such horrors perpetrated by those that saw themselves no longer as Aresians but as Malacandrians. Then like, Aaron and the Israelites, out of panic, they abandoned their religion and turned to worshiping strange Gods. Their civil war became nothing more than a senseless slaughter of innocents as they clambered over piles of dead in desperation to achieve some gain that they could never attain. Only to be betrayed in the end by the hand of their own Empress. Driven to the edge of madness by despondency at what her people had become, she thrust a poisoned misericorde deep into her own heart, forever sealing her Empire's doom.

Other kingdoms distanced themselves from this insanity, disavowing their ancient pacts and treaties. Whatever this 'Oyarsa' was, its commands unbound them of their oaths. I watched as Malacandria's allies melted away, whole cities, nations even, obnubilated and placed themselves beyond the reach of the rapacious Earthmen.

The remains of the Malacandrian Empire were left to convulse and die in the red Martian sands, picked over and divvied up by the Tellurians, as vultures and wild dogs pick at the carcass of some once great beast.

Then, whatever it was that allowed me to see these awful things, showed me one last horror. A strange altar, dedicated to an obscene God. At the foot of which a young Kitreenoh noblewoman, dagger in hand, offered her newly born twins. I thought as some dreadful sacrifice, but no. As she beseeched that nameless God, she laid out her two tiny infants upon the cold dais, but the blade was for herself. As the young woman plunged the dagger into her own heart, an attendant struck her head from her shoulders. What hopeless lunacy led her to commit such an act, I have no idea, but I have had once before seen a similar ritual, enacted by two Nipponese officers after their men had been wiped out in an Aresian ambush. 'Harakiri,' I believe it is called, to me it was merely a ridiculous waste of human life.

Amber robed priests cast the body of the young woman into the votive flames of a great brazier and swept the blood-splattered babes away into the dark secret sanctuaries beyond the altar.

Then I had a startling sensation like one might get when falling asleep, and suddenly I was awake. What had felt like an age must have been but a heartbeat in reality. Parthena's concerned face hovered over me. Apparently, I had collapsed again. Once back on my feet, I insisted they did not fuss about me, as I indeed felt much better than I had for some time. Though I could not even begin to explain what I had experienced, I looked about at the featureless pale walls and floor to assure myself that I had definitely returned to the place from which I had started.

Excerpt from;
Memoirs of Aelita, Lady Sydeian.
The Athenaeum of Harendrimar Tai.

As I followed the others through the short narrow passage that appeared to lead from the landing platform to the inner tower, I found myself clutching tightly to the rosary Father Ignacio had given me years ago. I had no idea why I had brought it with me, or even how it had ended up in the little pocket of my spencer jacket. Nevertheless, my fingers had found it and instinctively wrapped themselves about its comforting worn contours.

I cannot say what I was expecting to find in that tower; still, I was initially taken aback by the unexpected vastness of the space and its absolute emptiness. I have only been in such places in my dreams, the Ananthor of my vision and the white city of my nightmares. The walls and floor were of that strange opalescent crystalline material that looks more as if it were grown, or secreted than constructed.

The others took little time to gape about themselves as they hurried across the cavernous chamber towards the opposite doorway. I tried to follow; however, my eyes were drawn to a figure standing off to the right-hand side. A hooded and robed figure that none of the others reacted to, as if they could not see.

This time I recognised her straightaway as she drew back the limousine, my grandmother. Now there was no pretence of the genteel clothes of an elderly Tharsian lady. She wore sumptuous robes and a mantle of a colour I can still not name. Her hair was iron grey and tied into a psyche knot, much as I too often prefer it. As a child I had seen pictures of Aresian noblewomen with their hair done up so and some part of me had always felt it was a subtle link to my origins, no matter how tenuous, one that even Giovanni overlooked, believing it to be just a manifestation of childish interest in following the vagaries of decadent lady's fashion.

As I perceived my grandmother clearly, the rest of the room seemed to slow to a serenely unhurried pace, their movements flowing at a glacial pace. I tried to move towards her, though I was as trapped as the others. She held up her hand to beckon me, and suddenly I was free. I hurried to her, confused by the desire to throw myself at her feet, or into her arms, and break down into a sobbing wretch. Instead, she just took my hands firmly and looked into my eyes, as if gazing into my soul. I imagined this would be what it will feel like at the end of days, the final judgement; there will be no justifying or excuses because the archangels will simply investigate our hearts and see the truth of us.

She smiled kindly, nonetheless a dreadful sense of certainty settled upon me. I begged to know if this was the time, if this was where I must make the choice, she had warned me of. Her only reply was, "He awaits."

I know it was unseemly, and I was instantly ashamed of my loss of restraint; at that moment I felt so frightened that I began to beg her again to tell me what choice I was to make.

She stroked the side of my face to comfort me. I do not know if she actually spoke the words or if I only heard them inside my head. She bade me to "remember," and, in that instant, I did. As one who is about to die reviews their entire lifetime in a flash, I recalled everything. My earliest experiences, every encounter, every emotion, everything in exquisitely painful, glorious, heart-rending detail.

Then with the suddenness of Pandora's Box slamming shut, she was gone. As my mind returned to reality, I was overcome by a dreadful awareness. "He is here," the words blurted unbidden from my mouth and, with alarming resolve and no regard for anything, I found myself striding towards the far doorway and the staircase beyond.

If this was a test, then I resolved to face it.

The Flammarion Expedition Journal of L. Edwin Ransom.
Day fifteen. 44th. 9th. 26.
Sunday.

Cont.

Our assent seemed to take forever as if some mischievous force were adding steps as we climbed. As I imagine it would feel running up one of those moving staircases in Alba's Central Station, but regardless, we trudged on up.

Just before the point of exhaustion, we reached a small landing. After a moment to capture our breath and composure, we stepped through the open aperture into another impossibly large circular room. It has since occurred to me that, as with the strange saucer-like craft I had seen earlier. It must have been the glaring featurelessness of those chambers that fooled the senses into assuming they were so much bigger than they could conceivably be.

The Colonel and his men fanned out into the space. In the middle of the room was a raised dais upon which there was a seat. A thing I can only describe as a hybrid of a huge barber's chair and an elaborate padded throne, above which hung some strange contraption of brass, rods, gears and articulated piping. A helmetlike object hung precariously from the apparatus as if someone had tried to wrench it free of its tethering.

As we all approached the dais, our eyes were immediately drawn to a figure lying prone on the floor beside it. Its white robes and flowing white hair stained with the deep crimson of blood.

Patty rushed forward, but the Colonel caught her and held her back. Though she snarled at him like an angry prattan, he held her firm, cautioning her to be careful. She was about to furiously break free of his grip when her father placed his hand on her arm and agreed with the Colonel. It was obviously dangerous and possibly a trap.

The Professor, Sergeant Kline and I carefully moved closer to examine the body. It appeared to be a woman, her milk white skin almost as wan as the walls and floor. A White Martian. I had only heard fanciful tales of such people. She had been savagely murdered, the red splash incongruously bright against her skin and the cloth of her robes.

Her left arm was outstretched, long fingers reaching desperately for an odd wooden polygon, inlaid with exquisite fretwork. As if, in her dying moments, that was the most important thing in the world to her.

Sergeant Kline was more practised in dealing with such things than the Professor, or I, and far less squeamish, examined the body for signs of life. Presently he shook his head solemnly.

I turned away, and out of pure curiosity picked up the polygon, it was an icosikaitera, a form with twenty-four sides, about double the size of a cricket ball. Beautifully carved from, what I assumed by its colour and weight, was Martian Red Wood of the highest quality, and inlaid in gold with an intricate geometric pattern. I was still puzzling over the object, how solid it felt, and how light it was when I heard the Colonel utter an oath.

The soldiers snapped to; their rifles levelled at a man standing opposite us. How he had entered without us seeing him, I had no idea. Maybe he was always there? Perhaps in our rush, we simply did not notice him. I had once seen an illusionist on stage use the simple trick of motionlessness to make a few gullible souls think him invisible, but this was no stage act. The others were so flummoxed it took them a good few moment seven to realise he was there.

He moved slowly forward; his hands open to show no signs of threatening behaviour. He was taller than average, about 6 ft, slim, and dressed in old-fashioned tailcoat, waistcoat and high-waisted trousers. His thick black hair was perfectly combed and lacquered. The skin looked waxen, and he wore a chilling vulpine grin that lent his face a masklike appearance. His eyes were hidden behind small round tinted spectacles.

We were so utterly startled by his appearance, as if out of thin air.

"Who the hell are you, Sir?" Demanded the Colonel pistol in hand.

The Cheshire grin on his face took on a mocking aspect, as the stranger bowed extravagantly. "I am Lanulos Malacandi."

As soon as I heard the name, the man Adam had named as the architect of his torment and the monster that had so cruelly twisted the mind of poor Barnsby Monck, I found myself stepping forward to challenge the scoundrel. I denounced him as a cad. The others looked to me as if I had gone mad, and in an attempt to prove I had not gone completely insane, I demanded he show us all his eyes. If, as Adam had assured me, this Lanulos was an Aresian, then his eyes would betray is true nature immediately.

I hoped it would put him on the back foot in some small way, but instead, he laughed at me.

"Ahh, the irksome Mr Ransom. Congratulations, you have become a lightning conductor for minor annoyances. Who would have thought that a mumbling, dirt grubber, like you, a dandelion farmer no less, could cause such consternation?" With a dramatic flourish, he snatched the spectacles off of his nose and, wide-eyed, glared around the room. "There, is that what you wanted them all to see?" His eyes sparkled like amber in strong sunlight, the pupils though were strangely lozenge-shaped, caprine, like that of a goat.

Only Patty and the Colonel reacted at all. Which, by his manner, was not at all what he expected.

Emboldened and determined to press home my advantage. "Take the mask off!" I blurted as commandingly as I could manage.

He rounded on me, "Why Edwin. Why do you not share with your friends here how you have come by to know such things? Hmm?"

In the full glare of his strange gaze, I hesitated. He knew I had said too much. How on earth could I explain what I knew without bringing Adam into it? And then the questions would come in an avalanche. It would put Adam in such a spot and force me to betray my word. I found myself biting my tongue, something I used

524

to do as a child when I needed to concentrate and compose myself.
Forcing myself to breathe through my nose.

As it was though, Colonel Jahns had heard enough of Lanulos'
grandstanding. He stepped forward pistol raised and demanded
that if Lanulos was wearing a mask he must remove it or, he
threatened, he would shoot him dead right there and then, and
remove it from his corpse. I have never been so glad of the old
Colonel's blunt manner.

"Oh, so predictable, Colonel." Lanulos laughed. "Better than
you have tried."

The Colonel growled an obscenity and levelled his pistol.

Lanulos held his hands up again in a placating manner, "This
might be distasteful for the ladies," he warned in a most
condescending tone. The Colonel's curt rejoinder hurried him on.
With his eyes on Jahns the whole time, he reached behind his right
ear and began to wrench off his black wig in bloody handfuls.
Lastly, he thrust his fingers through the skin under his jawline and
pulled the entire mask off. It was horrific, utterly sickening, but
none of us could drag our eyes away from the spectacle of this man
peeling his own face off. I had to keep reminding myself it was only
a mask. For a moment, he held it out towards the Colonel almost
triumphantly before discarding the bloody mess on the floor, where
it landed with a revolting splat. He produced a handkerchief from
a wide-rimmed cuff and wiped away the last of the gore.

His skin underneath was the colour of turmeric, with a smooth,
clear complexion, the features fine, balanced, noble even. But

525

those eyes now burnt with an intensity that I can only believe was fuelled with hatred. He combed his fingers through his long golden hair and straightened himself up. "I am the Dat'or Lanulos Malacandi, of Konöm Malacand. My mother was Aleriel, First Jed'darra, daughter of Jairus, the last Gre'tik Jireg, Empress of Malacandria."

The Colonel lurched forward angrily, but Dr Spender cut him off, "Your Imperial Highness," and bowed courteously.

I had no idea what to do. I could certainly not genuflect to this monster. I looked to the Professor, but he merely inclined his head, a short nod of acknowledgement.

Lanulos' eyes turned to the Professor. "Well, Professor Flammarion, I must say I am disappointed in you. Did you not come looking for me? Well, here I am. I am your vindication." He bowed extravagantly again. "I thought you would be delighted to see me." His tone was stingingly sarcastic. "After all, am I not living proof that everything your fellows and your Government assumed were just the ramblings of an old fool sent mad through grief is most evidentially true?"

I watched the Professor's face as a look of puzzlement came over it. "Your Highness, may I speak candidly."

"Oh, please do."

"You are correct, I set out to discover the last of the Aresians, but I feel, with all due respect, that perhaps you are not whom I sought." He paused, leaving the words hanging in the air. "The Malacandrian Empire was a spent force; it had almost ceased to

exist as a political entity even before the last Aresian war. That is why there were no representatives of your grandmother, the Empress of Malacand, at the signing of the treaty of Thoris Major, she was already dead by her own hand. The Autarch of Ma'alefa'ak gifted all Malacandrian lands south of the Phlegethon Canal and north of Ogygisto the new Republics. I fear that you, like so many of our own people since UDI, are little more than an orphaned atheling, an inheritor of a hollow crown."

I have never doubted my father-in-law's astuteness, but at that moment, I wanted to cry, "Well said!" and applaud wildly. Instead, I managed little more than a satisfied "humph."

Lanulos' eyes flickered, whatever answer he was expecting that was obviously not it. "It was not hers to cede to anyone," he said matter-of-factly. He then theatrically intoned; "'For God's sake, let us sit upon the ground, and tell sad stories of the death of kings. How some have been deposed, some slain in war. Some haunted by the ghosts they have deposed; some poisoned by their wives: some sleeping killed. All murdered: for within the hollow crown, that rounds the mortal temples of a king, Death keeps his court.' I have a fondness for your theatre and playwrights, especially Shakespeare. It is one of the few elements of your Tellurian culture that we Malacandrians could accept as having any value at all."

I had regained some composure and could not listen to his blethering any longer. I demanded to know who killed the woman lying on the floor?

527

"Well, you surely have more courage than your spluttering would suggest, Mr Wansom. W..w..w...your friend Mr Franklin did."

At that, my anger boiled over. "LIAR!" I roared, "You lie, Sir..." but then my words failed me, and the frustration made it impossible for me to denounce him for the scoundrel he was.

He mocked me. "Oh, forgive me I have not the time or patience to wait for you to spit out your w..w..words finally. Yes, dear Ed w..win, your friend Franklin killed her. You wish to know why?" He laughed. "I shall tell you; That is no 'woman,' it was a Thern. One of the Ahsprohs, a Galedön." He threw his arms up expansively. "The Guardian of this place."

"Balderdash, Sir! Up to a few days ago, Mr Franklin was with us, and now he is far from here." The Professor dismissed his claim.

He laughed again, mockingly. "Oh, do not be so easily confused, dear Professor. The Thern has actually been dead for quite some time. Much, much longer than it would appear."

"And what exactly is 'this place'?" asked Dr Spender.

"Now, finally, an intelligent question, from the good Doctor." He stepped closer.

"Move no further, I do not care what or who you are, Sir, take one more step closer, and I will shoot you down like a mangy dog," snarled the Colonel.

"Oops! Silly me! Of course, Colonel." Lanulos smiled and theatrically stepped back. "Is that better?" The Colonel just glared

back at him. *"Though if I were you, I would not go discharging that weapon in here."* He slowly cast his eyes up towards the ceiling.

I believe due to the bright glare of the room, none of us had noticed how the ceiling stretched far away into the vaulting above. However, now, with our eyes adjusted as it were, our gaze was drawn upwards, we beheld a single moving mass in the shadows, like a seething nest of bats. Several hundred pairs of pale green eyes glowered down at us. *"They are Ambau, you Tellurians call them all 'Anemoi,' that is because you are so busy killing them, you cannot tell one from another. These are much more aggressive. One shot and they will fall on you like rain. I am afraid they are not very house trained either. They have a tendency to bite. A lot."*

"That will not save you from my first bullet," growled the Colonel.

"Possibly, but will it be worth it to see your friends eaten alive?"

"Was it you that brought us here?" The Professor's tone was stern and irritated. *"What is it you want from us?"*

"So many questions! What, why, but never how. Dear Professor Flammarion, I did not bring you here, and I want nothing from you. Our encounter is merely due to an unfortunate oversight, admittedly on my part. An accident. An annoyance really, a minor one at that. Inconvenient, yes, but one learns to take advantage even of mistakes."

"What is this place?" Patty asked.

"Ahh, have you not worked out even that? Hmm? What about your father? Hmm, Doctor?"

Dr Spender cleared his throat. "Your Highness, I would suppose this is some dumping ground for things that get lost..." he looked uncomfortable. "That is, lost in time or space. Maybe it is not that they are being deposited here deliberately, merely that they have fallen threw into this place, gathering here as do the odd socks and lost studs do in the bottom draw of a tallboy or the space between the sideboard and the wall."

"Well done," Lanulos clapped his hands. "Exactly. But what of this?" He threw his arms wide, indicating the building itself.

Dr Spender took his spectacles off and rubbed his nose thoughtfully. "I do not know, some node or transmitter, perhaps?"

"Well done, I..."

"So, what are you doing here? And why did you murder this woman?" Aelita stepped forward.

Something changed in Lanulos' expression, for a moment he looked like a naughty schoolboy caught in mid-act. He bowed again, extravagantly. "Madam."

"I asked you a question." Her tone was brusque, her expression grim.

"If you please." Lanulos appeared to regain himself. "I did not murder this woman. Franklin killed her."

"Why?"

"Because I sent him here to. Because this place is as the good doctor says, a node. A lynchpin, in a vast charade your friends here could never hope to comprehend. Imagine; this is one of the tethering rings of a curtain, which I am in the process of unravelling."

"And what pray tell is behind that curtain?" asked the Professor scornfully.

"Another world, other worlds." Dr Spender interjected.

"Let me just say, to extend my metaphor; I intend to bring that curtain down, along with it the house as well."

"So why tell us this?"

"Because the opportunity arose, thanks to your bumbling friend and his newfound companion. Where is he by the way?" He theatrically looked about.

"Not here," said Aelita coldly. "What opportunity?"

"You coming here, without your tütan, your guardian. Madam, I came to offer you a choice."

Aelita recoiled visibly. "I want nothing you could ever possibly offer."

He feigned a disappointed look, "At least, do me the honour of hearing me out?"

"Aelita, do not trust him," I warned.

She smiled sweetly at me. "I have no intention of trusting him." Then she nodded, "Say what you want, but first, these creatures of yours, send them away."

"I am afraid I cannot, but so long as I am unharmed, they will not attack. To that I can give my yulön, they would call it 'my oath,' as a Prince."

"Say what you wish and let us be gone then."

Lanulos chuckled, "You are forthright, even more so than I expected."

"Get on with it, you damned Spooker," snarled the Colonel.

"Hear that?" Lanulos cast his glance at the Colonel and then back to Aelita. "That is what we all are to them; 'Spookers.' You have always known this world you live in is wrong for you, have you not? It has always felt wrong. Sometimes it has felt like a cage, sometimes a fantasy, sometimes a dream, most often a nightmare. As if you were trapped on a stage on the wrong side of the curtain." He paused as if looking for some confirmation in her expression. I saw none. "Sometimes though, occasionally in your dreams or daydreams, you have caught glimpses behind that curtain, beyond the veil. Did they beat such things out of you in that convent? Or drug you, or simply tell you that you were mad?" Aelita did not respond, though her jaw clenched visibly. "You are not mad. I can show you everything beyond that curtain is real. Those 'dreams' are memories. Those 'visions' are true sight. Your powers are manifesting in ways these Tellurians cannot understand, in ways you will never know if you stay with them. Look at how they have treated you; the Nuns with their rosaries and their beatings, then Fontenelli, that sick, sad collector of curiosities. He kept you drugged, displaying you like an exhibit in

one of their freak shows. What have Tellurians done for you?
Shunned you, brutalised you, abused you, thrown horseshit at you
in the streets, paraded you like an aberration for others to gawp at.
They deprived you of your very own nature."

He paused again, but this time she replied, "Do not try your
trickery on me. I can hear your voice in my head. Say what it is
you want out loud and speak in English."

I must admit I was agog at her. This was no longer the sweet
shy lady who I first met only a dozen days ago.

Lanulos looked startled at the rebuff. "Madam, Forgive my
impertinence. You are much…"

"Stronger than you thought I would be."

He bowed reverently. "Madam, you have been told lies all your
life. You were not orphaned; you were given as a hostage. Your
mother and father are not dead, they abandoned, forsook, you, to
this world, to be trapped the other side of the veil they helped
create."

"You are a liar," she hissed venomously.

"I can prove it to you." He stepped forward and held out his
hand. "Your mother is a Jireg in her own right, a Queen. Come
with me, and I will show you. Everything I say is true. I will take
you to her."

Finally, Aelita's expression began to crumble, her chin
quivered, and tears appeared in her eyes. "It is not true. It is not
true. Why are you lying to me?"

"Do not believe him, Aelita." Patty reached for her hand. *"He is evil."*

Aelita answered softly without looking at Patty, "I know what he is."

"Ha!" Lanulos rounded on Patty. "Evil, am I? You idiots! Your kind invaded my home, my world, lied, tricked, stole, spread diseases, polluted our lands with your filthy animals and plants, gouged at the very heart of our planet, murdered tens of millions of my kind, all in the name of your Empires and your God. Your kind are nothing but thieves and murderers, the apologists and handmaidens of misery, an infection, a cankerous disease. And I? I am evil?" he laughed bitterly.

"Why are you telling me these lies?" demanded Aelita.

"I am not lying to you."

"What has my husband got to do with this?"

Lanulos looked confused. "Nothing, he is a nothing."

"You said you came because my guardian was not with me."

Lanulos snorted loudly. "Sydeian. I meant Sydeian. He is the Tütan, that they appointed when you were handed over as a hostage."

"Who? Who 'appointed' him?"

Lanulos looked suddenly satisfied as if he knew he had achieved something he intended. "Your father the H'nak'rapunt Esenale, he appointed Sydeian, as your Tütan. Come with me; I can prove everything I say, I will show you such wonders, worlds beyond your wildest imaginings, everything you have..."

Suddenly the Anemoi above us began to panic and take fright, screeching wildly as they crawled and flew higher up into the darkness.

At that same moment, a breathless crewman burst into the room. "Sirs! You must come! Now! There are three things heading right this way. Bloody huge monsters! You have to come now!"

Lanulos looked unnerved, he turned back to Aelita, thrusting his hand out to her. "Come! Come with me. I will show you such wonders; it is all true..."

Aelita suddenly smiled; it was the coldest smile I have ever seen on a woman's face. Then she said something in what I believe was Aresian.

Whatever it was she said, it visibly shocked him. Suddenly he lurched towards me to snatch the icosikaitera from my grasp. I, reacting more out of instinct than intent, lobbed it across the room with a good underarm. Too good in fact, as unfortunately, it shattered into a thousand tiny versions of itself against the far wall. Lanulos bared a mouthful of vicious-looking teeth at me and screamed some Aresian obscenity into my face.

To my eternal credit, my tongue for once did not fail me, and I replied with all the élan of Sir John himself; "Sorry, old chap, I do not speak Aresian." Lanulos turned and fled towards a portal that opened to receive him in the blank wall.

Heedless of the threat to us, the Colonel took a good shot or two at Lanulos as he fled. I would attest in a Court of Law that his aim was true, but it did not seem even to slow the fleeing scoundrel. I have no idea what came over me, but I found myself, pistol in hand, along with the Colonel and two of his men racing after Lanulos. Beyond the hidden doorway, a steep, narrow winding staircase led up and finally out on to a gantry. We reached it just in time to see Lanulos take off in a beautiful ornate looking flier, which resembled a cross between a dragonfly and a box kite.

Regardless of the subtle aesthetics of the craft, we fired our guns at it in desperation, but our pot-shots were pointless.

With no time to waste, even to stop and reload, we turned and ran back down the stairwell and raced after the others. With too many of us for one journey, the Colonel unceremoniously thrust me over the gunwale of the dory and ordered us to go.

The Colonel and his men shoved us off and stood back to watch us safely clear. I shall never forget the look of resolute determination on his face. As we pulled away, he and his men saluted us briskly and then turned and ran back into the tower. I am sure I shall never see them or the likes of them again.

As soon as we were on the Haul Du, we begged Mr Charles to send the dory back, even the Professor tried to order him to do so, but he insisted there was no time. Three dreadnaughts were heading our way. We had to leave immediately.

Alerted to how imminent the danger was, we rushed to the starboard, just as the strange 'dreadnaughts' broke through a bank of clouds and hoved into sight. They were immense Aresian Nautiluses. At about two miles out, one peeled off to chase

Lanulos' flier. The others unfurled what appeared to be gigantic wing-like sails.

"Nautiluses do not have sails." There was no hint of surprise in Dr Spender's voice.

The Haul Du seemed to take an age to get underway, or maybe it was just that those behemoths were closing so fast.

Dr Spender was right, they were no natural nautiluses, in fact, they were strange hybrids; part living creature, part warship. I gawped at these marvellous machines like an astounded schoolboy. They were the most enormous and beautiful ships I have ever seen, even bigger than the Dreadnought Daedalus. The configuration was practically mindboggling; the body of the vessel was made up of the great swirling shell of the vast living creature, across the surface of which rainbow colours pulsated endlessly. Above the enormous eyes, upon the hood, stood tiers of ornate decking, which also appeared to be built directly into the immense shell of the beast. Countless tentacles, some at least a hundred foot or more, both organic and metallic stretched out before it as if reaching for us, its prey. Either side and above and below, fin-like crimson sails, emblazoned with some heraldic crest, unfurled, these were mounted upon massive articulated arms that moved more like wings than sails. Even from where we stood, we could hear the distinctive rhythmic throbbing of their engines.

It was a sound that once heard, is never forgotten. "My God! They're Aethervolt ships."

At about three-quarters of a mile out the creatures swiftly retracted their tentacles, gun ports upon the upper decks opened, and they unleashed a barrage of fire at the tower. Blinding balls of light trailing smoke and flame behind them exploded the upper portion of the building into a million pieces. The creatures roared triumphantly and unleashed another salvo of rockets.

I heard Aelita gasped the Colonel's name and crossed herself.

The mass of fleeing Anemoi did not escape the warship's attention either. A ray of light and heat flashed out from the second Nautilus cutting through their flock, reducing dozens of the poor creatures to ash in mid-air, and sending so many others crashing like flaming meteors to the ground far below.

Our ship's engines were at full power now, but we were in no way at any safe distance. We all stood helpless and open-mouthed as the lead warship rounded the flying rock and fired two rockets after us. The burning fireballs drew alarmingly close, only to past our stern by a few yards. When I remembered to breathe again, I heard Dr Spender remark that those shots were so wide of the mark that they could have only been warning shots.

"At this range, they would have had to work hard to miss us," observed Mr Charles.

The second warship gave out a terrific roar, released a cloud of black smoke, and rammed its prow straight through the remains of the tower, utterly destroying it.

Aelita gasped and buried her face in my shoulder. I tried to console her, but the words would not form properly, so I just held her while she sobbed.

Patty exclaimed. "We have to go back! We have to go back for the soldiers."

I have only seen such a dour expression once before on the Professor's face, and that was when he told me of Nelly's murder. "I am so sorry Miss Spender, but there is very little chance that they could have escaped alive, and I cannot risk our lives and those of every one of the crew to search for the bodies of dead men."

"But..." Patty turned fully to face him. "But if there is even the slightest iota of a chance..."

"I regret to say this, though Ranolph and I have had our ups and downs over the decades, he and I have always remained firm friends, even from childhood, he would not countenance us jeopardising our lives, even if there was anything more than the remotest chance that he might have survived."

"I agree," added Dr Spender. "But old Iron Guts has been declared dead numerous times, and he has always turned up like a bad penny. I would not wish to bet on this being his last hurrah."

"But what of the soldiers? Those men have families and..."

"Miss Spender, they are serving soldiers of the Tharsian Army, following the orders of their superior officer, so please concede them the dignity of that. As for Ranolph, he has always put his men first. That is why they are so resolutely loyal to him. If at the

remotest chance, there was a possibility to escape, he would have seen to it they did, even before his own safety."

The thunderous roar of the nautiluses took our attention back to the attack on the tower. Now all three released a broadside into the shattered stump as if intent at erasing every sign of its existence.

It was then that something hit us, it felt like a sudden colossal wave striking a ship at sea, not that I have been to sea, but I imagine it a similar sensation. It seemed not to just physically rock our airship, but to pass through our bodies as well, leaving us all nauseous and disorientated.

The Professor and Mr Charles immediately turned and headed off towards the companionway to the upper decks, Mr Charles calling out to jolly the crew along to their tasks as they went. Dr Spender and Aelita both felt faint; I imagined from the exertion and the shock. Patty, and Aelita's automaton, began to help Dr Spender to his cabin, while I escorted Aelita to the wardroom. She had accepted my suggestion of some tea to calm our nerves. It was the disbelieving cry from one of the crews that brought us all rushing back to the viewing point. The young crewman whose watch it had been stood gaping open-mouthed.

"What is it, Mr Potter?" asked the Professor.

"Report, man," Mr Charles demanded.

"They're gone, Sir." Potter pointed. "Look."

I think we all took a moment to actually realise what we were looking at. Potter was right; the aethervolt warships were gone.

540

Patty, now beside me, uttered an oath that made the young crewman raise his eyebrows in surprise. "For once, my dear child," added Dr Spender, "I concur."

The ships had indeed disappeared, but so had the floating rock, and below us, where there had been an endless sea of shattered machines and burnt-out craft stretching as far as the eye could see, was now nothing more than a featureless landscape of red sand dunes.

"Impossible!" The Professor took the field glasses off Mr Potter and scoured the horizon. "Impossible."

"Obviously not, James, dear chap," said Dr Spender. "Obviously not."

I have never seen the Professor lost for words nor so utterly perplexed but, as always, his instincts were sound. "Mr Charles, tell Captain Llewellyn to get us out of here as fast as physically possible, do not spare the engines." He then addressed us, "I shall be in my cabin." At that, he walked off a little unsteadily.

Aelita and I retreated to the wardroom in search of something stronger than tea, only to be joined a few minutes later by Patty and her father. We tried to make some sense of what had occurred, but it all seemed too fantastical for words. We had no possible rationalisation for the disappearance of the tower and all, other than to reassure each other that we were not mad, nor hallucinating, unless, of course, we were all subject to the same visions. We compared our observations and notional theories, but we had no real explanation for what appeared to be an affront to reality, or at least our grasp upon it.

Dr Spender seemed unusually quiet for a man of such cerebral activity; he contributed hardly more than a few points of interpretation. I felt it would be impertinent to attempt to draw conclusions from him until he was ready to share them.

I wondered openly what had happened to the Captain we had encountered, he ran off, and so must have disappeared along with everything else.

Dr Spender put down his glass. "I have been thinking about what that young officer said, and I cannot discount it as the ravings of a madman as easily as Jahns or James have done. An attack upon Earth, by whom he meant, I do not think is clear, makes me wonder. Forgive me, Aelita my dear, but on Earth 'alien' and 'Martian' are synonymous, to the point of meaningless. So that does not help us clarify that point, but the suggestion of an assault upon Earth, by forces unknown, causing them to abandon us, does make perfect sense. As for the Aresian forces to strike at Earth also makes perfect sense, until you contemplate, they must have had that ability for hundreds if not thousands of years. Besides, they had us over a barrel here, we were all but defeated. Why commit forces to attack Earth when they could have wiped us out here, with minimal effort. No, that does not make sense. Added to that his obvious shock at seeing you, not because you were some enemy alien, but because of the colour of your skin. Which makes me believe he had never seen your kind before. Then there was his

542

assertion that the year was 1920, that by my reckoning is over thirty years ago. He was claiming to be a man from the past. Even if he were alive in 1920, on Earth, he would be almost fifty years old, if he just arrived here as he claimed. It makes no sense at all."

Finally, our conversation turned to the man in the tower; Lanulos. Patty asked me how I knew he was wearing a mask, and how did I know he was an Aresian? I felt I owed it to her to answer as honestly as I could, but I could not answer with complete candour. I told them that Barnsby Monck had spoken of him back in Mefitis, which, to a degree, was true. I then changed the direction of the conversation by giving them a potted and highly edited, account of my encounter with Barnsby Monck and his wife. Thus, they all understood that when Lanulos announced himself, and I saw his face. I just reacted, probably through outrage. Though, I had no idea that behind the mask was an Aresian. It was sufficient to throw them off the scent long enough for me to ask Aelita precisely what she said to Lanulos that so obviously shook him. Patty added that she did not think Aelita could speak the Aresian language so beautifully.

Aelita put her brandy snifter down carefully and composed herself before explaining that as far as she was aware, she could not speak Aresian, or at least, had always believed she could not remember how to, until that moment. She could only recollect tiny snatches of words from her childhood, and that she thinks and dreams in English, and has done so since being very young.

Patty asked Aelita if she knew what it was she said to Lanulos? Could she remember or was it like some mesmeric trance?

Aelita looked uncomfortable, so Patty and I apologised immediately and withdrew our questions. Nonetheless, she waved our apologies away, "I said; 'My grandmother sends her regards'."

It was such a curious thing to say, but it seemed to shake him to his rotten core. Patty asked what it meant, and Aelita explained she has been seeing her grandmother in her dreams. However, she had no idea why it occurred to her to say that to him there and then.

I would never dare to suggest that Aelita would be telling anything but the truth; nonetheless, there was obviously more to her tale than she was willing to share with us at that point.

A steward came to summon me to the Captain's salon. I found myself heavy-footed, dreading what new misfortune might be about to be revealed. A deep sense of guilt washed over me as I abruptly realised, I had not thought of my dear Nelly since we had come upon the field of destruction this morning. What kind of wretched man had I become that she could so easily slip from my mind. The yoke of despair had resettled firmly upon my shoulders by the time I reached the Captain's quarters.

Captain Llewellyn and the Professor were pawing over a heap of maps and charts. The news though was at least better than I expected. The ship's compasses were working again, and now as darkness was approaching, we could take exact bearings from the stars. The problem was that these new bearings placed us in southern Lybia, an area known as "Homokóra-tenger," the Hourglass Sea. Roughly, six and a half thousand miles from Mefitis and way further off course than any logical deductions could account for. I reminded them that, for myself at least, it would appear that since the last storm, 'logic' did not appear to hold sway out here.

Mr Charles joined us. He had double-checked the readings carefully and could confirm our location. We were indeed in southern Lybia, about a hundred and fifty-five miles southeast of the city of Altoura. He had ordered the ship to come to, so that we could have time to decide our heading.

Lybia! How did we end up in Lybia? I was both astounded and alarmed. Firstly, I must admit I have no first-hand knowledge of Lybia, all that I know of the place is a patch of mustard yellow on the map and what I have read in the papers over the years. I must admit that I have never been an avid reader of the political pages. What I do know is Lybia is no friend to Tharsis, careful to never side militarily with our enemies during conflicts but had allied themselves economically with Utopia and Zephyria. It had been an Austro-Hungarian colony, but since independence from the old Empire, their nation has become increasingly insular. The Professor remarked that he had visited Altoura several years past with Professor Lambertini, on a lecture tour for the School of Martian Sciences. He had found it an extraordinary place indeed. Everyone seemed to be nervous about what his or her neighbour might think of them, or worse, might say of them. He remembered how vociferously Lambertini had railed against the intricate Byzantine bureaucracy of the place, and the fact he felt every single official he encountered shook his hand with one hand and robbed his pocket with the other. The Professor told us that he returned home early because Alexa, who had come along to visit the famous palace complex of Stel Harrat, the great 'star city' of Prince Altfoura, that Hamilton had written so eloquently about, but she became distressed by the presence of soldiers and fighting machines on every street corner, and hussars patrolling every boulevard and park. There were even chary looking soldiers in the vestibule of the hotel. The whole city had a pervading sense of paranoia.

Captain Llewellyn agreed, adding observations from his own experiences. He had had several 'run-ins' with the authorities in Lybia over the years. He found Lybian officials to be one sort or another, either jumped up, narrow-minded, petty rule mongers or as bent as 'a five-bob-note' (He actually used a somewhat more colourful idiom).

We rapidly agreed that this was no place to linger if we headed East-North-East we could be over the border into southern Amenthes within five hours, though it would take us over the Bradbury mountains of southern Lybia, which, Mr Charles warned, is a pirate hot spot and renowned for the unpredictable weather around Mount Őrület.

Captain Llewellyn laughed at that, commenting, "After today? If anyone is foolish enough to try to interfere with us, then I will relish the prospect."

The Professor glanced up at the Captain from the charts over the rims of his pince-nez spectacles. I expected him to say something admonishing of such talk, but instead, he softly murmured. "I agree. Amenthes it is."

"Witchcraft to the ignorant…Simple science to the learned."

LEIGH BRACKETT
THE SORCERER OF RHIANNON.

DAY SIXTEEN

<u>DASHWOOD HOUSE</u>

Charity Bryant-Drake.
Notes to self.   45/9/26.

The Story of Two Queens.

Cont.

Our journey to the town of Medmenham in the border county of Wharton was uneventful, though uncomfortable, especially for myself being a woman upon a vehicle designed for, and solely crewed by, males. Living even for only a day and a half in such close proximity to so many men and boys, left me desirous of returning to the space of the Seren Bore, which was palatial in comparison especially as I found myself inconvenienced by that most female of exacerbations. And how I missed Patty, her warm arms, good nature, and wry wit.

Medmenham lies so close to the border that without a good map, you would be hard-pressed not to stray into Ophyr, or, more worryingly, across into southwestern Elysium. The land through which we journeyed was a mix of rough uninhabited chaparral and broken fell lands, untouched by Tellurian or Aresian hands, consisting of coarse red grass prairies and great forests of native crimson leaved trees and shrubs. In places, the rough ochre sandy soil gave way to endless fields of rock-strewn savannah, desolate astroblemes and saffron-coloured dunes. Out here only the hardiest creatures survive.

Nevertheless, here and there were pockets of intrepid, green-leafed plants that had self-seeded into the wilderness, but without tending, they struggle to subsist. Only a handful of Tellurian crops flourish here; apart from Edwin's beloved dandelions and numerous species of cacti grown for their fruit, the most abundant produce is hemp, cultivated for its abundant uses, everything from the clothes on our backs to the fuels in our engines. It was extensively planted by the early settlers to form barriers to hold back the sands and out-compete the native red zizany. We passed the remnants of some of those early boundary plantations, left untended the hemp had grown into impenetrable swathes of woodland-like groves.

Just after dawn we were forced to change direction to avoid a vast herd of wild Martian blue cattle, lounging in and around a lake that had formed in a crater. Giant tardigrades, huge, ugly, pale blue armour-plated creatures the size of hippopotamuses but with no faces and too many legs. Sir John was excited to see them, lamenting that he did not have time to "bag one for the pot."

Naïvely, I asked why we could not just push through the herd? Afterall they seemed quite placid; would they not move out of the way?

Mr Cotton laughed and replied, "Slow steppers, Ma'am. They are the stubbornest and slowest creatures in the world. They won't move for nothing. Unless you make them angry and then, well, then all those legs can move them at quite a pace. I saw a herd take exception and charge a locomotive once, almost derailed the thing. Smashed the big ol' cowcatcher right off the front of it, then all got up and meandered off, all kinda nonchalant. If they took a mind to, they could bang us up real bad." He winked, "Best, we go around them."

Later, at my request, we stopped at a small crater in which nestled a tiny lake, in the midst of which, upon a small island, one single courageous Terran tree had taken root some time ago. A willow, grown huge with age and plentiful water, dominated the scene.

Once I had seen to my ablutions, I took time to sit for a while on the edge of the lake and gaze at that old tree.

I found my thoughts dwelling on poor Aelita's dilemma. Though she is a woman, and to all intents and purposes, she is, yet she feels incomplete. It is a strange quandary, she is confident that her gender is what she would have chosen it to be, but the fact that she now knows there was a choice that was denied her by circumstance, forces upon her anxieties I can hardly imagine. Though Patty talked to me of a similar feeling of incompleteness in her soul, I doubt either of us can truly understand what it is to know that you have been denied such a choice, and left trapped in a body that is physically incomplete. Like a caterpillar driven by desire and need, but unable to fully metamorphosis.

My uncle Victor was an apiarist and passionate lepidopterist. He bred butterflies and moths for University collections. I can remember him showing me a tragic misfortune; a large exotic caterpillar trapped in its chrysalis unable to become a beautiful butterfly. Dead, of course. To him, it was just nature, but to me, as a small girl, it was heart-breaking.

I resolved never to think of these monthly inconveniences again as some curse upon womankind for the fallibilities of Eve. Though I have throughout my life been a tomboy, to the eternal irritation of my mother, and though my preferences for career and companionship have led me towards a lifestyle that may never result in me having children, regardless of what society's self-appointed sentinels have bemoaned, I have always been happy within my own skin.

I shudder to think of what misery my life would have been if my parents had been the type to force their child to kowtow to those antiquated social conventions that so many of my school companions have blithely condemned themselves to. I think I would have gone as mad as Bertha Rochester herself, locked away in some attic, screaming at the walls. For dear Aelita to be imprisoned in a loveless sham of a marriage with that pompous old buffoon, displayed as Sir John does his hunting trophies, whilst sensing without knowing, that she was trapped physically in some transitional stage, must have been unbearable.

I regarded the tree again.

Like me, its seeds supplanted from another world, millions of miles away. We were both born here, with our roots deep in its red soil, but we are still both, in essence, aliens to this unforgiving land, as alien as Aelita is in the civilisation that happenstance has imprisoned her in.

And I fear this world is far more alien to all of us than we ever imagined.

Sir John, Red and I spent quite a while mulling over which course of action would gain us the clearest understanding of what this Dashwood House place was, and who would be there. I needed to know what to expect before I took a course of action that might put them all in jeopardy.

Having the others along to help me was far preferable than doing it alone. Still, it meant I had the added concern of their safety, especially as they insisted on being involved, even in the face of the imminent threat of danger.

We mulled over several ideas but found ourselves dismissing each as either too dangerous or simply unworkable. Red's suggestion was the most elegant; some of us pose as the carmen and deliver the statue. At worst we might only get to see the gatehouse and those that come down to collect the crate, at best we might get a good look around the place and be able to size up its security.

If Everheart or De Maurier are there, Karl, Red, Sir John and I will return later to deal with them. If there is no sign of them or anything untoward, we return to the caterpillar and decide what to do based on what we have seen. Whatever, I knew we were going to have to pay a call on the house and crack a few heads to see who is willing to talk.

"Not much of a plan really," Sir John said, lighting another little cigar.

"Simplicity is best. Keep it simple and keep it malleable."

"You were wasted in the Army, old boy."

Sir John's remark raised both mine and the Sergeant Major's hackles. "What do you mean by that?"

He caught something in my tone and apologised, "Sorry, old chap. I simply meant you are too free-thinking for the regular army. I cannot for the life of me imagine you blindly following anyone's orders. Yes, Saar. No, Saar! Your skills would have been better suited for something like the Pioneers or the Tharsis Rangers, where the ability to think for yourself is more an asset than a hindrance."

Just when I was finally beginning to find his company a little less than nauseating, he reinforced all the previous annoyances. Now he was probing for casual information of my background. I ignored the baited hook and asked him straightforwardly if he had any serious objections to the plan.

He exhaled a ring of smoke. "What if it all turns really nasty?"

"Then we do what we have to do. I came here for answers, and I expect to get them."

"So, exactly what is it you are expecting to find?"

"Nothing pleasant," I admitted.

He then insisted we needed an alternative plan if things went awry. After a couple of hours or more our strategy came to this; we would leave the caterpillar outside of Medmenham, on the pretext it had broken down, and hire a waggon from the town to deliver the thing in the crate. I had Barebones and

Cotton draw up a map of what they knew of the area and the estate.

While we were delivering the statue, the caterpillar would make its way to about half a mile south of the estate to a small hemp forest where it would be in readiness for our escape. If all went smoothly, we would make the delivery and rendezvous with them. If it went badly, half a mile or so is not too great a distance to cover in a hurry.

Charity took me aside. She had had a thought that she wanted to share with me. What if, by some strange quirk of fate, someone recognised me?

I asked whom? How? She looked me in the eyes intently. "Apart from Karl, we are all pretty nondescript really; put us in a working fellow's togs, and we blend in easily enough, even Sir John, so long as he does not open his mouth, but you, my dear Adam," she patted my shoulder as if to emphasize her point.

She was right. "I stick out like a sore thumb." If these people had been alerted to a possible threat then my description would be simplicity itself; a tall, well-built man with a face like a ripped rag doll, poorly repaired by an overly enthusiastic child. I do not exactly blend into a crowd easily. I asked her what she was suggesting.

She proposed that she go in my place. She knew De Maurier by sight and Everheart, but they have never seen her. If they have a description of her, then it is going to be something along the lines of "A plumpish, carroty headed girl with freckles." She gave an ironic chuckle at her own remark, something that made me realise there was some sting underlying it. "A wig and a bit of powder, some soot and they will easily overlook me." As if to convince me, she added, "I am a journalist. I have even done a little private investigation work in the past. I am trained to be observant. I am good at it."

She was right, of course. My physiognomy would draw too much attention even if they were not actively looking for me and trying to hide my face would just draw even more interest.

Karl and I would travel with them as close to the estate as we all felt safe, and then head off on foot. While the others delivered the statue, we would see how good the estate's security was, and if we could get close enough, we would have a look around the house itself.

Sir John asked me exactly how I intended to stop Barebones and Cotton 'hightailing' it as soon as we were off their machine. That was easy, because Mr Barebones, well Cotton, has to be there for the transaction no doubt and to be paid. A group of unknowns cannot just role up to the gatehouse with the crate. The people at Dashwood House would be expecting to see Barebones.

Unfortunately, when we informed Barebones and Cotton of our plan, Cotton just laughed. "Why Sirs, this old girl has but one pilot, and that's me. I have never taught a single one of these fine young men to drive my ship. Without me, she goes nowhere."

Sir John looked to Isaiah, but he only shrugged expressively, "There's no way I could drive this thing even if he had taught me." There was no reason to doubt the veracity of what he claimed, and it made complete sense when you considered their arrangement.

It was then that Charity observed. "At the handover from the Queen of the Skies, both of you had to oversee the transaction. Because, as you said to me, Isaiah is the brains of this company, you are just playing the part of what they expect. You would both go to deliver this thing, would you not?"

Isaiah's eyes narrowed as he pursed his lips. Then he begrudgingly nodded in agreement.

"I do not see how that helps us," said Sir John.

"Because we do not need Cotton, do we, but we need Isaiah."

"Ma'am, they will be expecting Omari, not me on my own."

"Well, then, we will give them what they expect." She looked very pleased with herself. "I may have a way for Mr Barebones and Isaiah to come with us to the House, and Omari to remain to pilot the Oruga."

"I would really like to know how you propose to do that," laughed Sir John. "Apart from chopping him in two."

With a plea to wait, Charity rushed off, only to return moments later with her carpetbag. She began to rummage through it excitedly while explaining. "Before I left, I thought these things might come in useful. You see, I know you gentlemen have a tendency to charge in where angels fear to tread, while I, on the other hand, being merely a frail and delicate girl," she sneered. "I would rather use my wits." She looked up at Sir John. "Most men seeing a woman pass by them, only notice what?"

I could see him struggle to catch an immediate offhand quip before it escaped his mouth. He thought better of it and raised his hands and eyebrows theatrically.

Charity turned to me, "Adam, please describe Captain Rambeau."

"Curly dark auburn hair, tall for a woman..." I got her point immediately.

Out of her carpetbag, she pulled another smaller bag from which she produced a couple of hairpieces. "Most men are blithely unobservant. When men describe a woman, they have met in passing, they almost always focus on her hair colour. They will remember that more often than the colour of the clothes she wears or her build."

"Yes, so what has that to do with our problem?" Sir John seemed irritated.

"Bear with me, please. If you were searching for a woman in a crowded place, what things would you look for first?"

"Hair colour, clothes, hat."

Charity looked pleased. "Therefore, if you were searching for me, and I put this on," she flourished a black wig at him, "put on flatter shoes and changed my clothes, you would overlook me."

"I suppose, at first, I might. Until I looked harder."

"But you would be still searching for a woman. What if I dressed as a man, in a bowler and frock coat and put this on?" she produced a dark false beard.

Sir John laughed, but I could see by his eyes he grasped what she was saying. "If I were searching for a woman in a crowd, if you did it well, worked on your walk a bit, then I probably would not give you a second glance."

Charity seemed satisfied. "Isaiah, when was the last time you delivered to Dashwood House?"

"About three months ago, Ma'am."

"Do you hang around to pass the time of day, or is it always a fairly quick handover?"

Cotton looked suspicious, but answered truthfully, "They're a glum lot, and it's a business transaction, Ma'am. We deliver the goods, get paid and leave."

Charity looked at me as if challenging me to follow her reasoning.

"What Charity is suggesting is that someone accompanies Isaiah posing as Mr Barebones."

"Ha, and who the hell is going to do that?" Sir John chuckled. "This is not a minstrelsy, where you can just blackface up one of us and..." I think it dawned on him as he spoke.

All eyes turned to Red, who was gently shaking his head. "No," he said adamantly.

"Take no notice of John," sneered Charity. "I fear his mouth often works independently of his brain. Red, there is no one else that could do it. You are about the same height, I can work the beard into your whiskers, with his hat on and an immensikoff. You will easily pass for him."

Red sighed resignedly. "That is a maybe Miss, but I cannot do his funny accent. As soon as I open my mouth, they will know I am not him."

"Then don't speak," growled Mr Cotton. "Anyways, I don't believe I've ever passed more than three words with them at the gates in all the time we have delivered to them. They ain't exactly chatty folks."

"I will do all the talking," assured Isaiah.

"Oh, this is going to be amusing," Sir John dumped himself heavily onto one of the chairs, crossing his arms and ankles. "Red masquerading as Cotton, masquerading as Isaiah Barebones. What on Earth could go wrong?"

"On Mars? Everything," quipped Charity. It was a customary sardonic riposte, but it hung in the air for a little too long for all our comfort.

We reached the outskirts of Medmenham, by about 2 PM, and stopped in a shallow crater on the lee side of a dragon fruit orchard. The massive thickets of cacti afforded more than enough cover to hide the 'hunkered down' vehicle from casual notice.

Charity did an excellent job in turning Red into the fictitious Mr Barebones. She had managed to seamlessly weave the tight curls of his muttons into the false patriarch beard, and with Omari Cotton's battered topper and a huge coachman's coat, padded out with some carefully located chair stuffing, he looked fairly convincing to my eye. The others agreed, even Cotton was grudgingly appreciative, "I guess, in a bad light, with one eye closed and a squint, he could pass for my little brother."

Red protested, he felt ridiculous and reminded us all should he be availed upon to speak; the game would be up. He could in no way pass for the man they expected.

"They are expecting a large Negro man, with a big beard and a top hat, and that's what they will get. Just throw out the occasional 'ya-all' and 'mam', and you will be fine," joked Sir John.

Charity shot him a look that said more than I could have put into words easily. I am aware he was trying to alleviate the situation, but his sense of humour, for want of a better word, was grinding on my nerves, not only mine but the Sergeant Major's. Although Howe and the Hopeforth boys seemed to find him immensely droll, they were the only ones appreciative of Sir John's jests.

"Yeah, and all you white folks look much the same to me to," growled Cotton.

"It is only a part, a role to play," interjected Charity. "Who of us ever looked too closely at the last carman or drayman we saw or even the last messenger that brought us the post? It was six months before my step-father noticed that their upstairs maid, that they had employed since she was thirteen, had left to get married and my mother had taken on another girl."

Medmenham is a dour little community grown up to service the hemp industry. Most work there is either tending the vast plantations or in the cluster of the processing manufactories on the edge of town. Hard work and subsistence living were about all such places offered its inhabitants. On the town's high street, little more than a dirt track a bit wider than the rest, existed barely a handful of independent businesses, the others were truck shops owned by the same men who owned the fields and manufactories.

Of the few grubby people, we found abroad, most had the weary downcast gaze and sloped shoulders of indentured servitude.

Our basic plan went well. Red, Howe and I hired a waggon from the only independent livery. A down-at-heal establishment, fronted by a cluttered and grubby tack shop. Mr Wainhouse, the proprietor, was the living embodiment of his business;

antiquated, grimy, and afflicted with an air of age-worn weariness. Unfortunately, he also reeked of the dwelling he inhabited, but much more intensely. He was brusque initially, almost to the point of impoliteness, but immediately became compliant when he noticed our Mr Barebones stalking about outside his window edgily puffing on his cigar and impatiently looking at his pocket watch.

Red played the part well. As I asked him to, three minutes after we entered the shop, Red shoved open the front door, gestured aggressively to me and whispered conspiratorially in my ear. Then with a stern glare at the livery owner over the rim of his tinted spectacles, he slammed the door closed behind him. The livery owner looked like he was going to pass out through fear.

Howe, whose father had been a drayman, knew what we were looking for. We hired a ladder waggon with two sturdy drays, and five nags for an excellent price, along with a load of old tools, grain sacks and other tat that Sir John insisted on and left as quickly as we could.

We spent the short trip back to the caterpillar congratulating Red on his performance. The livery owner had unquestioningly taken him for Barebones.

Upon our return, we loaded the crate on to the ladder waggon. Darra was to drive. Isaiah would ride shotgun. Charity and the Hopeforth brothers would ride in back. Sir John, Karl,

Red and myself would ride along until we got near to the estate, where Karl and I would leave them.

Even as he stashed almost every weapon we had under the old grain sacks, tools and smaller crates on the waggon floor, Sir John was still arguing we should leave someone to watch Cotton to make sure the caterpillar did not take off and leave us high and dry. Isaiah, who was sitting on the guard's seat, wrapped in a heavy coat and cradling a shotgun that Red had unloaded, turned to us, "I assure you, Sir, Omari won't leave me behind, and neither will my crew." The young man had a certitude about him that was admirable. I wondered just how strong were the bonds that held these fellows together. Brothers in arms or something even more potent?

With a "humpf!" Sir John jumped down and stalked over to where Cotton was standing, by the main loading bay ramp. Although almost half a foot taller and far broader, I saw the nervousness in Cotton's manner as Sir John spoke to him quietly.

Sir John turned away to hold out his hand to Charity as she stepped down from the ramp, and together they returned to the waggon.

I should not have enquired, but I felt I needed to know. I pulled Sir John aside; "What did you say to him?"

"I just reminded him that if he is not where we told him to be, then when I catch up with him, I shall deliver him young Isaiah's head in a basket." He looked at me brazenly. "Do not go getting

all bleary-eyed on me, Sir. A couple of days ago you would have shot them all, one by one, solely to prove a point. Or were you bluffing? Because if that was your poker face, old chap, I am certainly never going to play against you."

"Best that you don't," growled the Sergeant Major. For the first time, I saw a glimmer of uncertainty in Sir John Sydeian's eyes.

I do not know who John Sydeian is and that uncertainty concerns me. Captain Rambeau linked him with Percy Greg, the Inspector I found dead in the Citadel's Clock Tower. And, as things have transpired, I am more and more confident that she was right; it is all an act. He is some kind of agent or spy, but for whom, I have no idea. The Tharsis Bureau of State Internal Security, as Captain Rambeau suspects or someone else? There was no coincidence in him putting us on that particular aerostat, carrying that particular cargo.

Percy Greg was not killed investigating Du Maurier; he was killed investigating Lanulos. What was the connection there? The thought made my blood run cold. Someone somewhere is pulling strings to place us in the right places at the right times, and, if Sydeian is not the puppeteer than he is close to them. Colonel Carter Jahns perhaps, or the people old Colonel Blowhard works for, or maybe worse?

I must fight the Sergeant Major's continued urgings to put a bullet between Sydeian's eyes and be done with it.

The Story of Two Queens.

Cont.

We set off for the Dashwood estate just after noon, across rough uncultivated country. Tossed about in the back of that old wagon I quickly regretted even the little I had managed to eat at lunch. It seemed that Howe was determined to hit every rut he could find. Things got only a bit better when we reached the road. After about half an hour the rough terrain gave way to endless hemp fields, the main agronomic crop in north-eastern Tharsis. We travelled in silence, punctuated only by Howe's verbal instructions to the drays.

I found myself wondering where Patty and her father were now, how far had the Seren Bore got them. They should be easily beyond the reach of Tharsis' power, probably somewhere in the Republic of Chryse by now. I missed her terribly. It is so strange that you can know someone your whole life and when they are gone not miss them for an iota, and then you can know someone for an instant and miss them as if they were your entire world. I wondered if she had yet lost her temper and thumped that old buffoon Jahns on the nose, as she kept threatening to do. I prayed that they were all safe. I also said a quiet prayer for our own safety.

Adam and Karl rode on ahead, only to return with occasional directions, until after what seemed like half a lifetime – probably no more than an hour and three quarters – we reached a branch in the road. Sir John gave the signal to stop. I took the opportunity to dash off into the waist-high sedge to be sick, while the others clambered off the wagon and tried to rub and stomp feeling back into their legs and behinds.

Adam and Karl returned. They had reconnoitred the area ahead. The gatehouse to Dashwood House was about a mile down the side road. A couple of rough-looking types manned it, but the rest of the perimeter was porous to say the least, in some places it looked as if you could step over the ruined wall. They decided to return on foot, so they handed over their horses to Sir John and I.

We quickly went over the arrangements again as we all checked our timepieces. I tried to throw off the deepening dread that had begun to settle upon my stomach. Something I could see paralleled on the faces of the others.

If all went uneventfully, we would rendezvous back at that point in an hour. Adam was explicit that we were not to wait a moment longer than that. If we ran into any difficulties at the house, then we were to head straight to the Oruga. He and Karl would catch up, as and when they could. Adam seemed more concerned about our safety than his own.

They then took their rifles and equipment and headed off into the tall rows of hemp. As we sat patiently watching them disappear into the waving greenery, I had the dreadful thought we might never see them again. I heard Red mumble a prayer under his breath as we watched them go, and Isaiah crossed himself.

Sir John held us at the turning for five excruciating minutes before we too set off.

I have not been in a saddle for a couple of years, and even back then I was never particularly enamoured with the experience. I prefer monocycles, but riding was much preferable to being bounced about on the cart for another fifteen minutes.

The gatehouse loomed into sight. It was a grand affair, more martial than domestic. I had expected the usual small lodge and pillared wrought iron gate with possibly a heraldic beast or two surmounting the pillar capitals. This was more like a barbican to a fortification, replete with a short drawbridge over a shallow ditch, raised iron portcullis and iron-bound doors. It was no rich man's folly either. The squat two-story towers that flanked the entrance looked far more functional than aesthetic.

Two armed roughs cradling rifles sauntered out to meet us before we could reach the edge of the drawbridge. They eyed us all suspiciously, as they asked a few perfunctory questions. They got well-rehearsed answers from Isaiah. He told them we were expected, and they should let someone in charge know we had arrived.

One of the guard's interest was piqued. He insisted on checking what was in the crate.

I found myself holding my breath as my hand slid inside my coat towards the grip of my father's Eliminator pistol. I could see Sir John's hand slowly travelling up the length of the stock of the rifle slung across the pommel of his saddle towards the finger lever.

That was when to all our surprise, Red spoke up. In a perfect impression of Mr Cotton's baritone rumble, he growled, "I wouldn't be doin' that if I were you, son. Anyways, once we have our dues, you can look on it as much as you like. Until then, no one's goin' to be touching it. You get my drift, boy?"

I almost laughed with delight.

The guard's face was a picture of chastened confusion; he had no idea how to react in the glare of our Mr Barebones' icy glower. The guard's companion muttered something and went back across the drawbridge where another couple of men had appeared. He spoke to them and disappeared through a small doorway, only to re-emerge a few moments later and beckon us forward.

The guards directed us through the gateway and into a small, cobbled courtyard, bordered on one side by stables and a wagon house on the other. There we were ordered to wait.

The impressive impact of the barbican was lost now we were inside. The buildings were shabby and uncared for. Windows were broken, doors and shutters scarcely hung on rusted hinges. Around the filthy yard were dotted numerous piles of dung and straw that had been mucked out of the stables, and then abandoned.

The roughs that made up the guard detail were as crude as their environment, dirty, unkempt, mean-looking men. I counted nine in all, including the two we had first met. All were heavily armed with a bewildering array of weaponry. Most of them just stood about, hunched in heavy coats, smoking clay pipes and glowering at us from under the brims of bowlers and flat caps.

I caught the tail end of a whispered conversation started between Sir John, Red and Howe. It appeared that the guard's demeanour irked them, and, to my horror, they were wagering on how many they could 'take down' (I believe they meant, kill) before the guards understood what hit them. Howe patted the shotgun on his lap and chuckled a rather derogatory remark about the lineages of the guardsmen, their mother's morality and their ability to fight.

Red reminded him of my presence and told him he could say what he wanted of the men but leave their poor unfortunate mothers out of it. Howe laughed uproariously, which seemed to unsettle the guards even more. They took it as a challenge and grew more hostile looking.

After several strained minutes, one of the guards seemed to muster enough courage to make a provocative remark about Isaiah to one of his fellows at a volume deliberately loud enough for everyone to hear. It elicited some nervous laughter in reply. Red with deliberate casualness cracked open the short four-barrelled boarding gun that Mr Barebones favoured, made a show of inspecting it before snapping it shut noisily and glared at the guard who had spoken.

Mercifully, before things could get any edgier, a hunting break rushed into the yard carrying four passengers. As soon as the wild-eyed horses came to a stop, two men, wearing monastic style white hooded robes, leapt out and set themselves as sentries either side of the carriage's step. One of the hooded sentries reverentially helped the first passenger dismount.

She was a portly woman dressed in elaborate silk robes and a turban, and little red silk slippers. With the hooded attendant's aid, she excitedly tiptoed across the yard towards us, making high pitched childish noises of delight. A thin, swarthy-skinned man with greasy looking hair and a craggy face closely followed her. He had hard eyes that darted about constantly.

"Oh, hello! Hellooo! Finally, she is here!" By the time the woman had reached our wagon, I had realised that behind the cosmetics, painted nails and demeanour, 'she' was, in fact, a man. Though one affecting an extravagantly effete manner. "Ooh, I am sooo excited." He exclaimed shrilly as he clapped his hands. "Merci, thank you so much." There was a strong Gallic accent to that high-pitched whine of a voice. However, the effect was that it sounded more Music Hall than real.

The other man asked a few questions of Isaiah, who told him the Oruga had broken down, so we had had to hire a wagon for the last leg of the journey. Apart from that, no trouble at all.

The turbaned man, shushed him quiet, dismissing him with a waved hand and a casual comment. "All is well. She is here now. Please, I must see her." He made to mount our wagon, throwing out a hand to be aided up on to the backboard. Sir John nodded to the Hopeforth boys who hoisted the fat man's considerable bulk up onto the wagon. "Open." He waved his hands excitedly. "Hurry. Open it up! I must see her."

The Hopeforth brothers looked confusedly at each other. Howe puffed loudly, climbed over the back of the driver's seat, snatched up a crowbar from the wagon's floor and began to pry open the crate. With the twin's help, and to the excited squeals of the fat man, they had the lid off the container in a moment.

The fat man fell to his doughy knees beside the open crate and began to hurriedly pull out handfuls of the wood-wool packing. As soon as he had sight of the statue itself, he began running his hands over it and cooing like a lovesick pigeon. I have never seen a man touching an effigy like that, there was something distasteful about it, disgusting even, something erotic as if he were caressing a lover.

The hard-faced man cleared his throat and asked formally if everything was in order, addressing the other as 'Madam Camarilla.'

Camarilla's podgy hands stopped exploring the more intimate recesses of the statue's anatomy as if snapped out of his erotic mania. With surprising agility, he leapt back to his feet, almost losing his turban in the process, as it slipped back off the bald plate under it. "Yes. Yes, Monsieur Swearengin, all is perfect." His face and jowls now flushed with colour beneath all that powder and rouge.

My stomach rolled at that name. Swearengin was the Antiquities dealer Isaiah, and Omari Cotton had dealt with before. I swallowed hard against the sickening dread that if Red's disguise did not hold up, we would have to fight our way out of this yard through eleven or more armed guards. To my relief, Swearengin looked our Mr Barebones in the eye and smirked, "Right then." He produced a wad of big white Tharsian ten-pound notes from his inner pocket and began thumbing through them. "We'll unload it, and you can be on your way."

He turned and gestured to the roughs who were lounging around.

I was about to say that they would need more than a few men to lift the crate when Camarilla cried out in his whining voice. "No! No! Is not good enough." He waved the men back, "Dirty rubes! You will not touch her. Away!" It was overly exaggerated as if he were constantly play-acting a role. I wondered whether we were supposed to mistake this Pantomime Dame performance as actually being a woman? "I will not have this." He turned to Isaiah and Red, "You will take her up to the house, on this...errmm...cart. N'est-ce pas?"

'Thank you, Ma'am, but we were only paid to deliver the crate," replied Isaiah.

"Nonsense! Monsieur Swearengin will pay you whatever it requires." Camarilla said emphatically, then dismounted with the aid of his two hooded attendants. "Allez! Allez!"

We all glanced at Sir John at the same time for some indication of what we should do. He only shrugged in reply. I stared at him harder, trying to convey my disbelief, but when he caught my eye, he merely grinned and winked conspiratorially. He is sometimes the most exasperating man I have ever known. At that point, I could have left him to it, turned and ridden away, which I would have happily done if it were not that I would have abandoned the others.

Camarilla and Swearengin had remounted the hunting break and signalled us to follow. Camarilla waving his pallid chubby arm and shouting, "Allez! Allez!" over his shoulder at us.

Sir John pulled close to the cart and said quietly, "Well. Maybe it will get us a good look inside. If we go into the house, have a jolly good look around, okay? Entrances, exits, staircases etcetera. Charity, see if you recognise anyone." He winked again before he made a few clicks to his horse and rode on.

Red turned to me when I drew near to the wagon and said, "Miss, if you do not mind, if we have to shoot anyone, I am going to start with that sodding flouncing windbag first." I replied that if it came to that, I was thinking of taking a few pot-shots at Sir John myself.

Red laughed, "That's the particular sodding flouncing windbag I meant, Miss." Whether Sir John heard us or not, and I sincerely doubt he did not, he chose to ignore the jibe.

We followed the hunting-break out of the yard and down a narrow track. It took us through a little grove of long uncared for ornamental trees, and out on to what had obviously once been beautiful gardens. All had the look of a place still inhabited, but untended, as if the attention of those that dwelt here lay in such other directions that they cared little for their immediate surroundings.

Dashwood House soon loomed into our view. My stepfather would have described it scathingly as yet another imposing anachronistic pre-revolutionary testament to failed imperial colonial aspirations. More mockery than 'mock.' A late Georgian neo-Gothic miscreation in Martian red sandstone, replete with spires, turrets and ostentatious crenellations. I almost expected to find some Clara Reeve inspired heroine swooned upon the steps of the colonnaded portico. If anyone were indeed about nefarious business, then this was the ideal theatrical staging for it.

Howe pulled the horses to a stop behind the hunting-break at the foot of the portico's steps. For a man of his bulk Camarilla was nimbler than expected. He leapt down from his carriage unaided and began to shout in French for "assistance!" The big front doors of the house were thrown open by more guards, and out spilt a dozen, or more, men in monastic robes of different colours, mostly taupe but also grey and black. The door attendants, like Camarilla's bodyguards, wore their white robes with all the lacklustre insouciance of men required to wear a uniform they disparaged.

I tensed as the gaggle of men approached us, but they were all unarmed and far more interested in the crate than us. Camarilla shouted orders to them in Zephyrian French as they clambered on to our wagon and began to strain at the chest. Whomever these men were, they were not used to hard manual work. Hoods were quickly pushed back, and robes opened as they strained to move the box. I noticed they were mostly older men, well-groomed and well-dressed under their robes. Their soft, manicured hands and even softer lifestyles had not prepared them for such hard work, but for what they lacked in strength and experience they made up for in enthusiasm.

Compared to the efficiency of the smugglers we had seen at work, the antics of these old duffers, goaded on by Camarilla's hysterical invectives, was almost comical. After one fellow had broken several fingers when the weight of the crate slipped and crushed his hands, and another grey-haired old dolt had stumbled off the back of the wagon, Sir John intervened. Howe, Red and the Hopeforth twins got the crate moving, while Sir John organised Camarilla's geriatric minions into some kind of team of bearers. Between them all, they got the crate off the wagon and, like some strange funeral procession, headed up the steps. Camarilla flamboyantly led the parade into the great house, with Isaiah, myself and Swearengin bringing up the rear. I noticed how uneasy Swearengin became as we passed under the portico and through the enormous, ornate front doors. His eyes darted everywhere, and he took to mopping his brow with the crumpled bandanna from around his neck.

Beyond the front doors, we passed through a small vestibule with a polished marble floor and wood-panelled walls. No expense had been spared even on such a functional space. The walls were bedecked with heavily framed paintings and objet d'art. Most of the excess space was taken up by two enormous prattans, frozen in deathly heraldic poses, positioned either side of the opposite doorway. Beyond which, we entered a sizeable galleried hall, the ornate painted ceiling of the main space three floors above our heads. I had never seen a room like it. It was a bizarre, cluttered mixture of picture gallery, trophy room, museum and drawing-room. Comfortable seating vied for space with glass cabinets full of curiosities and dead animals, along with suits of armour and weapons of all sorts. The floor was covered with richly patterned rugs and carpets that spoke of wild tales and desert fantasies. I could imagine Ali Baba himself flying away on such carpets to ancient Zerzura. The whole impression was of both opulence and sad neglect; two of the glass cases were severely cracked, the carpets were dirty and threadbare in places, the furniture was tired and worn. Objects that had once graced the walls or held pride of place were stacked unceremoniously in corners gathering thick layers of dust.

The room as full of people, at least fifty men and women. All dressed in a similar array of monkish style habits of the same dull colours, except for a few men robed in cardinal red, who held back as the crowd gathered about our cortège. Their cold eyes and contemptuous expressions gave off an air of haughty disdain for the whole proceedings. I tried not to stare at them, though I immediately recognised the sneering vulpine visage of Windlestraw Volpone, from the caricatures of him in the press, he really did resemble a white-whiskered fox. The other two looked familiar though I racked my mind to put names to them. Later I concluded the shorter of the three was Efram Edgars, and the other may have been the infamous traitor Rollo Lenox.

Two taupe robed women rushed forward and reverentially draped Camarilla in a lavish turmeric coloured robe embellished with gold embroidery and jewels. As he took on the mantle, the white-robed guards began to push back the crowd until they had made a space for the crate to be set down.

The box arrived on the floor with a thud that provoked shrieked abuse from Camarilla who rushed forward and slapped everyone aside. Realising he could not lift the resealed lid, he demanded Howe pry it open again. Howe looked uncomfortable at the thought. Sir John stepped forward, took the crowbar from Howe, and quickly had the lid off.

Camarilla fell upon the statue, tossing handfuls of the wadding aside in his excitement. The robed onlookers crowded in, cooing and gasping like thrilled children at a magic show.

Camarilla began raving incomprehensibly, whipping his audience into hysteria.

Isaiah touched my arm and whispered, "I think we should leave."

I readily agreed and motioned to the others, but before we could back away, Camarilla addressed Howe and Sir John. "Lift her! Allez! Get her out of this thing. Free her! Quickly, quickly!"

The expression that crossed both their faces at the idea of touching the sculpture was priceless, but they resolutely stepped forward and began to crack open the sides of the box. With the Hopeforth boys' help, they did short work of disassembling the wooden panels. Camarilla gave out another excited cry, "Allez!" At that, the crowd surged forward, almost fighting to get their hands on the effigy to lift it upright. The crowd gasped as the statue was revealed in all its horrendous glory.

What I had seen of it in the crate had been disturbing, but now, fully revealed, it was utterly abhorrent.

I have seen pictures of some horrible pieces of pre-conquest Martian temple 'art,' in the museums and university collections that my stepfather curated, but this thing was vile beyond words. I do not think it was just the horrific subject, but the strange white alabaster like material from which it was fashioned retained a level of incredible detail. To my uneducated eyes, it resembled more of a cast than a carving, or worse, as if the monster itself had been frozen in some way. Apart from the lack of colour, it looked real, almost alive, so much so I found myself avoiding the intensity of its deathly pale gaze.

Isaiah beside me spoke quietly in my ear, "They are welcome to it, Miss. That thing makes me feel sick in my stomach just looking at it." I found myself gripping his hand in mine for reassurance.

I looked to Sir John who nodded to Red. Red gestured with his head, and we all made our way quietly back towards the doorway where Swearengin lurked. He looked even more uncomfortable now than earlier. Playing his part well, Red demanded payment, another twenty pounds for haulage, as he called it. It was a ridiculously exorbitant sum, but Sweargin seemed as eager to pay us and be done, as we were to make our getaway.

The rest of us filed past into the vestibule where the mighty forms of the stuffed prattans were almost reassuring in comparison to the proximity to that horror. Business done, Red and Isaiah turned to join us, but as they did Camarilla came rushing after them.

My hand instinctively found the grip of my father's gun, but Camarilla was not hostile. Like an excited child, he begged us not to leave. He wanted us to stay and toast the arrival of the goddess. Red tried to refuse politely. However, Camarilla was having nothing of it. He claimed he wanted us to remain so he could thank us. Bizarrely his childish persistence was almost charming, but a stern look at Sir John seemed, this time, to convey my concerns.

Sir John gave Red a barely discernible shake of his head. Red firmed his resolve, politely making the excuse that the Oruga needed repairs and they had to get back to it with enough daylight to get the work completed. Nonetheless, Camarilla would hear none of it; he called for drinks and almost dragged Red back into the main hall. "Just one salute!"

Sir John and I managed to get to all of our team warning them not to drink anything before the liberally filled champaign flutes arrived. The whole proceeding now took on an even more curious tone, more like a weird cocktail party, people laughed and drank and chattered as if this were all perfectly normal. We accepted our glasses and stood in an awkward huddle looking about nervously. Red demanded we leave as soon as possible; he hated this place, and the false beard was itching "like a bugger." The Hopeforth boys kept looking to me anxiously. Sir John laughed saying he had been trapped in worse parties and launched into a risqué tale of some "bash" he had been at. I was so angry with him; I could have screamed.

Howe, whom I supposed had never been to anything more than rough Saturday night revelries, looked utterly bemused. The delicate champaign flute looked incongruous in his huge, bandaged fist. He moved forward as if about to say something to me when a woman in black robes intercepted him. Her manner was not so much flirtatious as lewd. She must have been in her fifties at least, but with a good body, which Howe and I saw quite a lot of as her robe parted a little too much. She was naked beneath it. Her hands were all over Howe exploring him like Camarilla with the statue. The big man's embarrassment would have been amusing under other circumstances. To try to save him from this indignity, I stepped forward and grabbed the woman's wrist before her hand reached his nether regions. I growled, "Leave my husband alone." I pulled her off him and pushed her away.

She came back at me like a snarling animal. "What a pity to waste such a fine big ox on a fat mewing quim like you." She spat at me and swaggered off into the crowd.

"Nice lady," commented Red. "My mum always said rich people have such fine manners."

"It is the breeding, or rather the inbreeding, that does it," Sir John replied.

That awful feeling of dread in my stomach was growing by the moment. "We need to get out of here," I said as categorically as I could, without taking my eyes off the strumpet that had accosted Howe. "Now."

At that Camarilla, who had climbed on to a stool, began clanging a handbell, summoning everyone to gather around him. Bell in one hand and champaign bottle in the other he made some barely comprehensible speech about what a joyous day this was. I must admit I was too busy trying to get Sir John and Red to listen to my warnings than to pay any real attention to precisely what he said. Finally, he ended with a salute, "Welcome, the Queen of Qadath!"

As the crowd echoed his words, I felt an icy chill run down my spine. Praying the others felt as uncomfortable as I did. I turned and walked steadily and as purposefully as I could towards the doors. One of the guards hesitated for a moment before opening the door into the vestibule. It was not until I was almost at the front door that I looked to see who had followed me. Isaiah and the Hopeforth boys were right on my heels, but Red, Sir John and Howe had been ensnared in conversation with Camarilla.

Every sinew in my body now wanted to be out of that place, but still, I stepped back into the doorway to discover what was going on. Red was explaining that Howe is his own man and not indentured to him. If he wanted to accept another offer of employment, that would be his choice.

"Ahh, so you will let him stay if he wishes too. N'est-ce pas?" Camarilla looked delighted.

Red's persona of Mr Barebones was perfectly played, even down to the "silly accent" he had been so concerned by. He shrugged his padded shoulders, "Why, of course. He's free to do anything he wishes."

Camarilla then boldly approached Howe, "You are a fine figure of a man, Mr Darra. I shall be honoured if you would accept my hospitality, and my offer of employment. Yes? I shall treble anything you earn from these...erm...fellows," he cast about expansively. "You shall want for nothing, here in my home."

My heart stopped. Howe was obviously as surprised as we were. "An' what is it you'd would be wantin' me to do, Mad'am?"

"Oh." There was a long pause, almost as if Camarilla had not thought through that part of the offer. "You shall be my personal attendant, erm...valet, my manservant."

One of the women on the edge of the crowd sniggered. Camarilla shot her a glance and made a hissing sound through his teeth. She visibly quelled and quickly disappeared into the throng.

Howe scratched under his wild red beard as if honestly considering the offer. "I'm really sorry, Mad'am. It's a grand offer, so it is. But the wife and I," he gestured towards me, "we hav' two weans to support. An' there's me poor mam, bless her heart, she's not at all well these days. We beneedin' to get back to them."

I stood open-mouthed. Darra Howe had proved himself not half the dim-witted dolt we had all taken him for.

I realised the crowd fallen silent and all eyes were on us. Camarilla's face visibly reddened, and his eyes narrowed wrathfully. "Comment osez-vousm' insulter!?" Gesticulating wildly, he screamed, "Sortes! Aller! Go. Get out!"

We did not need any further encouragement. With Camarilla's hysterical tirade of abuse ringing in our ears, we fled the house, back to our wagon and made as quick a departure as we could.

It was only once we were on the wagon and away from the house that suddenly Sir John burst into laughter. Immediately we all started giggling like fools, only the Hopeforth boys appeared not to understand why. We had just about regained our composure when we reached the yard before the gatehouse.

That is when all sense of absurdity died in my breast.

"Shite!" hissed Red through clenched teeth.

The yard was empty, but for one lone figure, standing casually in the middle of it, smoking a long cigar. It was Lucius Everheart. He was unusually tall, thin to the point of wraithlike, but immaculately turned out, in a long black coat, a heavily brocaded waistcoat, and a wide-brimmed hat. On his hips, he openly wore a pair of revolvers and a big sheath knife. He looked every bit as formidable as I expected.

"What do we do?" whispered Red.

"Keep moving," replied Sir John. "The gate is still open. Do not stop unless he..."

Just then, Everheart stepped forward and raised his right hand to halt us. Howe pulled the horses to a stop. I did my best to play it all as if bored and disinterested, but inside me, my stomach churned nervously. I thanked the Lord, there was a wagon between him and me, though little use that might be. As far as I knew, he had never laid eyes on me, but when face to face with such a monster reason escapes you. I had only seen him once from a distance in Tremorfa Township, and I could not imagine he saw me.

Nevertheless, someone had ransacked my hotel room; did he know who I was? Would he recognise me? I became aware that my hands were shaking with fear.

Everheart drew nearer. He wore small round glasses, tinted against the sunlight, and a fulsome horseshoe moustache, his skin though had a pallid, unhealthy complexion, as if he had suffered pox as a child. He tipped his hat towards me. "Ma'am." I did my best to acknowledge him without speaking. His gaze though turned to search the other's faces.

"Is there a problem?" Sir John managed to sound both disinterested and mildly put out.

Everheart turned to look up at him. "Don't I know you?"

Sir John replied without missing a heartbeat. "I do not think so, Sir. I mean no disrespect, but I would remember you for sure."

Everheart seemed to ponder that reply before turning back to the wagon. "What's in back?"

"Sorry?" Red replied, dropping his assumed accent.

"What have you got in the back of the buckboard?"

"Stuff, Sir. Flotsam really," answered Red.

"Show me."

My heart sank into my boots.

It was at that exact moment chaos burst into the yard. Several wild-eyed horses came charging across the courtyard with a couple of white-robed attendants in full pursuit. One crazed animal careered towards us, realised Everheart was in its path, quickly changed direction, and made a break for the open gate. With lightning speed, Everheart seized its reigns as it flew past, almost hauling it off its feet. The enraged animal retaliated by frantically thrashing about, kicking and biting.

More guards came running to help, but few seemed to have the foggiest idea of how to control the distraught animals. I noticed Sir John niftily, but quite subtly, turn his horse's flank to guide another charging beast in Everheart's direction. The horses collided, reigns entangled, and they began to fight.

Seizing the opportunity for what it was, Red slapped Howe's shoulder, and we fled as fast as we could.

We reached our rendezvous point in short time, in fact, such a short time that I was aware of how easily any pursuit could have caught up with us. We had arranged to wait there for Adam and Karl, but as Isaiah reminded us, Adam's instructions had been that if there had been any problems, we were to head straight for the Oruga. Then began a hurried debate as to whether what had occurred constituted enough reason to run for the caterpillar or not.

With mounting panic rising in my breast, and after reminding them that I had had Everheart and his thugs chasing me before, I found myself rather forcefully arguing that we get the hell out of there before he came after us. I was becoming rather infuriated with Sir John's laissez-faire attitude; he simply would not take any of what happened back at Dashwood House seriously. Suddenly the hemp stands beside the road burst apart.

It was Adam and Karl. They ran straight to us and clambered into the back of the wagon, shouting, "Go, go, go!"

At Sir John's direction, Howe swung the wagon off the road and headed across the fields, in the rough direction of our meeting place, as fast as the drays could pull. My riding abilities had been barely adequate for our hurried departure from Dashwood House, now, at this pace, over rough ground, all pretence at any riding proficiency deserted me. I resorted to just hanging on to the saddle of my galloping animal for dear life.

For my part, it was a blind heedless headlong charge, but by the time my senses had started to return to me, we had already reached the Oruga.

Adam and Karl were in no mood for lengthy explanations. They shouted orders like Sergeant Majors on a parade ground. The drays were set loose from the wagon as we emptied it of anything useful, before abandoning it. The riding horses were manhandled on board in good time, the ramps taken up, and the Oruga was underway in moments.

After about an hour at the caterpillar's top speed, we had reached a soft-edged canal and waded down the shallow slope. Adam ordered Mr Cotton to stop the machine.

I do not know what was more concerning, our panicked flight or the sudden stillness. Now stopped, the Oruga gently sank another foot or two into the thick mud of the canal bottom, as we watched the water lap over the top of the pilot's dome.

Desperate for information and to impart our own, we gathered under the eerie green light that the dome threw about the room beneath. Mr Cotton furnished us all with a bottle of rye whiskey, and we shared our tales. I reported what we saw and did, with the others chipping in, mostly superfluous details. Adam asked if we had seen D Maurier, but I could not confirm he was there, though there were obviously more than the three red monks I had been able to take a good look at. Though when we got to our confrontation with Everheart, Adam already knew, as it was, he and Karl that let the horses out of the stables and spooked them. Unfortunately, one of the stable hands got in the way. Adam added coldly that it would probably be put down to a tragic accident of being trampled by a horse.

I began to explain to them what we discovered after we left the others at the crossroads.

Karl and I headed westwards following the rough map Isaiah had drawn. It took us about ten minutes to reach the boundary of the estate, and then we followed it for almost quarter of a mile until the rag-stone wall fell into such disrepair that we could easily step through the gap.

Beyond the wall, the once well-tended grounds, once a pastiche of monastic gardens, were now abandoned to chaos. The hardy remnants of the green Terran domestics clung on against the choking rampant swathes of blood-red zizany. We pushed on, past broken-down greenhouses, overrun vegetable patches, fenced off animal enclosures, and chicken coops abandoned to time, eventually we found a well-worn path through a tiny vineyard, down past some kennels and into the rose gardens at the rear of the main house.

We did not have the time to follow it any further, though we could see it led off towards a copse of trees in a dell. There was some kind of folly down there amongst the trees.

Sydeian observed, "Every bizarre sect needs a temple. After all, it adds some legitimacy to them. I would wager that the sculpture is meant as a centrepiece there. If there is going to be festivities tonight, it will be going on in the temple. Some sort of consecration rite or some such."

"You sound like you know an awful lot about these things." I challenged. "Are you talking from experience?"

"Oh, dear boy, I have done a bit of the old trouser rolling and bedsheet wearing in my time. Nothing as sinister as this though I am afraid." He chuckled to himself, "Though I did have some fun with a dissenting Agapemonite sect in Hellas for a while. Those ladies were very thorough in their search for a Messiah, I can assure you. Mr Howe, would have gone down a treat with them!"

I ignored him and continued.

We reached the House itself unnoticed. Most of the building around the back is derelict. Windows boarded and stone crumbling. Eventually, we found a way in, through a broken back door, but decided not to venture too deeply inside. What we did see of the interior was in a disgusting state with rubbish piled everywhere.

Outside the back doors to what was evidently a kitchen, we found a big pile of old packing crates and boxes from all over. All addressed to Tonto-Jitterman. A lot of old furniture and household bric-a-brac was also dumped outside as if making space for something more substantial.

About a dozen yards from the back of the house was another cobbled yard, surrounded by more large kennels. I think they had once been for a pack of hunting hounds. There were no dogs to be seen now; the only occupants were two dead men. They appeared to have been starved to death.

We checked the other kennels, but they were empty, though they are keeping something in those cages. There was a great deal of fresh mess and gnawed bones. Whatever it is, it is a hell of a lot bigger than any dog. There were paw prints bigger than my hand.

I let that sink in.

"Prattans," ventured Sir John. "What idiot would try to keep prattans? There is a stuffed pair in the hallway."

"I admitted I am no big game hunter or ranger, but what made those prints must be huge, and I think they are feeding it on humans."

They all looked at each other, horrified.

I let Karl continue in his matter-of-fact manner. "Near the kennel yard, there is an ornamental pond with a fountain. It was full of skulls. Human and large animals. I counted thirty-six human craniums at least."

In some way, I hoped that information, put so bluntly, would put them off from following me into the next stage of this operation, and for a moment I thought I had achieved my aim.

"I have no idea what you have gotten us into old chap, but this really is not a nest of vipers, more like a nest of red worms." Sir John remarked. "God alone knows what is going on here."

Charity Bryant-Drake.
45/9/26. Monday.

The Story of Two Queens.

Cont.

Adam's findings only confirmed my darkest fears. There was something very very wrong with this place.

What we saw inside the house confirmed my suspicions. I explained that 'Lady Camarilla' was, in fact, a man, and that that man may also be this mysterious Tonto-Jitterman. Also, how he tried to convince Howe to stay and when Howe refused, he became furious.

Isaiah remarked he had seen that look on some men's faces before. When I asked what he meant, he said, "It's like a hunger, like something inside them is so hungry it shows itself. Like a starving dog looking in a butcher's window. On the streets you learn first to avoid that look, then later, depending on what line of work you're in, you learn to read it, and use it against them."

"Salivating," said Sir John. "I would venture that if you had stayed for dinner, old chap," he grinned and winked at Howe across the room, "You would have been the main course."

Howe looked shaken.

Adam asked me if there were any faces that I had recognised amongst those 'guests' in the house.

I had seen several that looked familiar, especially amongst the few we had seen dressed more like cardinals than monks but putting names to them was not as easy as I thought it would be, on the whole, they kept their distance from us. I definitely recognised The White Fox, Windlestraw Volpone, and I was, by then, sure the two with him were Efram Edgars and Rollo Lenox. I noticed just before we left, a tall, swarthy, Spanish looking man, I believe it was the Saltmaster, Guillermo D Sampo, but I never saw a sign of D Maurier.

Adam questioned me thoroughly on my assertion that the elderly Spaniard was D Sampo. I admitted I could not swear to it, but it looked a lot like him from images I have seen. I wanted to ask what interest he had in D Sampo in particular, but he deftly changed the subject. "No sign of D Maurier, but we know Everheart is there."

He turned to me, "What is this place, do you think?"

I found myself groping for a definition; finally, I settled on agreeing with Sir John. It is possibly a cult. Some occultist group venerating, well Lord knows what, probably that thing in the crate, the thing Camarilla called "the Queen of Qadath," in some perverse hodgepodge of misunderstood Aresian religion and ancient Tellurian mysticism."

Adam's face hardened at those words.

"So it was that thing Lady Niketa was warning you about," Sir John interjected. "A lot of bizarre secret societies sprang up amongst the Red Bookers and their kind during the Viceroy Prince's tenure of Office. He was into that kind of thing. But nothing like this, this is more akin to that murderous Thuggee cult."

I did not know whether that was helpful or not; either way, I shot him a glance that stopped him in mid breath. I carried on; "I have heard of people, the debauched rich mainly, who get into this kind of thing. Something like Madam Niketa's group, but creepier, more dangerous. One lot I heard of in Hellas were trying to recreate the religion of the Aresians. Or, at least, a perverted version of it. There was a raid on a house in Peneios City where they were all found to be out of their heads on God knows what. All dressed up in robes and painting themselves Red and Yellow."

"I never read about that one," laughed Sir John. "Though who knows with those Hellaens."*

"And you will not. It was quashed. There were a couple of politicians, a judge and some senior Army officers arrested. Therefore, it never got to the broadsheets, but we journalists are terrible gossips."

*Editor's Note.

Although it would be more correct to refer to a citizen of Hellas as a 'Hellene,' the predominate American English-speaking population always preferred 'Hellaen.' Possibly to differentiate themselves from the Greeks.

James Ransom.

Just then, David, one of the Hopeforth twins, spoke up to tell us of the strange fellow he noticed watching from one of the alcoves behind the upper balcony. Both Adam and Sir John beat me to the questioning. David blushed and nervously stumbled over his words like Edwin, but his eyesight was good, and he had called his brother's attention to it as well. They described the man as having a face like one of those ugly ventriloquist dolls, both saw him, and both were very unnerved by him.

Adam said nothing but immediately started collecting his gear. Sir John and I tried to reason with him, but all he would say was he was going back to the house, and he aimed to go alone.

That was it. I had had enough of all this leonine masculine nonsense. I stood up and put myself between Adam and the doorway. "Enough, Adam." I shouted, "Enough!" he stopped immediately, looking down on me as if he had never seen me before. "This is not your private war. Nor is it some boys own adventure out of those penny dreadfuls you boys read. In fact, it is more his fight than yours," I gestured towards Karl standing impassively by the door. "It was his mistress that was murdered, and he was almost destroyed defending her." Adam's eyes flickered toward Karl. "We all came here looking for D Maurier and Everheart. Now we have found one of them. I have no idea of what other compulsions drive you, but, in all honesty, I do not care." That, I admit, was a lie for effect. "We came here to kill Everheart, and that is what we shall see done. All of us. Edwin is my friend too, and I will not be left here like some little frail, left in safety while you big tough men folk go a-hunting."

Sir John moved to say something, but I cut him off. "Shut up, John." He closed his mouth in surprise. "I want to see justice for Eleanor, for Edwin and those poor little children, even for the Professor, damn it, even for my stepfather. I know, every bit as well as you do, that out here justice only comes from either a rope over a tree bough or out of the barrel of a gun. Believe me, if I have Everheart or D Maurier, or in fact any of those scrubs poncing about in scarlet bedsheets back there, in my sights I will pull the trigger as easily as I would swot a gnat, but I will take a lot more pleasure in it."

In an almost defeated whisper, he replied, "It is going to be dangerous."

"Dear God! Do you not think I noticed that when those brigands and a bloody air-galleon attacked us? Or when people were trying to blow my head off in Alba's Train Station?" My stepfather has always chided me for resorting to sarcasm when I get frustrated in an argument. Still, I have always considered it a perfectly legitimate way of getting my point into thick heads. "Do not mistake me for some simpering debutant. I can use a gun as well as any man." I pulled out the Odic pistol Aelita had given me. "And I have had a lot of practice lately."

"Well said, Miss," said Red.

"Damn right, old girl," chimed Sir John.

"Quite a speech, Ma'am." Omari Cotton grinned. "Quite a speech."

"Miss Bryant-Drake is correct, Sir," said Karl.

Adam turned to the room. "Mr Cotton, as soon as it gets dark, take us back on to the bank. As I promised, once we are gone, you are free to leave. I suggest you get as far away as you possibly can. Anyone who wishes to accompany Karl and me back to the house be ready to leave as soon as we get on to dry land. Anyone that does not, well I hope Mr Cotton and Mr Barebones will agree to..."

"We can always use extra hands," Isaiah commented. "You are welcome to work your passage back to civilisation or stay on if you wish."

I understood the comments were directed at the Hopeforth boys and Howe, rather than myself, so I kept my mouth tightly closed this time.

David spoke up for himself and his brother, "Mrs Ransom was a wonderful lady, more like an aunt to us than an employer, and we have known her most of our lives. She used to play hide and seek with all us kids in the garden of the big house when we were small, and she helped nurse Eli when he had diphtheria. That's why he doesn't say much these days. The Ransoms have always treated us like family. That murderer stole her away from all of us." His brother nodded tearfully.

Howe coughed and looked uncomfortable as he shifted from toe to heel and back. "Ah, well, I'd be still chokin' me lights up in Mefitis, that's if I'd had ever got meself past th' damned gaugers, if ya hadn't given me a chance. Besides, it just wouldn't be right would it to turn down a lady's invitation to a célidhe."

Letter from Charity Bryant-Drake to Parthena Scáthach Spender

Delivered by hand.

I have trusted this letter to a friend, Mr I. H. Barebones. He will not require payment, as I have already remunerated him.

Dearest Patty,

Dearest love forgive me for leaving you to come on this ludicrous adventure. I pray you and your father are well and safe. Oh, how I miss you so.

More by luck than judgment, we have come upon the vile man who murdered poor Eleanor Ransom. He is at a manor called Dashwood House, near Medmenham in Wharton County. It is a strange place inhabited by an exceptionally peculiar man known as Camarilla and his sizable retinue. They masquerade as some form of a religious sect. Our considered opinion though is they maybe occultists. I have actually laid eyes upon the 'White Fox' himself, Windlestraw Volpone, as well as Efram Edgars, the traitor Rollo Lenox and, possibly, the Saltmaster, D Sampo. All here parading about in scarlet robes. I believe D Maurier is involved as well. Mr Franklin insists upon returning to the house tonight to confront Everheart and God help those foolish enough to get in his way.

Although Mr Franklin did his level best to dissuade me, I have insisted on accompanying him. Do not be angry with me, my love, but I must go. There is truth to be told, and I must report that truth. The people of Tharsis, the whole of Mars, must know who these people are and what they are up to here.

Forgive my handwriting, but I am shaking like a leaf in the coldest of breezes. I have tried so hard to appear as brave as Mr Franklin and Sir John, or should I say, more rightly, foolhardy, but I disappoint myself. I am utterly terrified. More so than I have ever been in my life. More so than at the incident in Alba Central Station or at Edwin's Farm.

I promise I shall be careful. It is not us four alone. We, of course, have the redoubtable Sergeant Rawlings, but now Karl, Mr Ransom's automaton, and two sons of the Ransom's gang-master Mr Hopeforth. Even Howe, the engine stoker that was so rude to Aelita, has reformed and is proving himself a stalwart chap. We could not leave him to suffocate in that dreadful place.

Mr Franklin instructed us to try to sleep for a while, but I cannot quell the butterflies in my stomach.

I promise I will be most careful.

One day this will all be over, and you can take me sandflier racing on the Maraldi Sea as you promised.

Remember, I love you and long for your embrace.

Your Charity

PS

Oh, how I wish I could speak to you. To tell you how much I love you.

Charity.

PPS

I have entrusted my journal notes to Mr Barebones. For safekeeping. Should I be indisposed he will pass them on to you. The key is in my heart.

C

Extracts from

Beresford's History of the Martian Colonies.
2nd Edition. Milton and Dante.

Appendix A. Tale of Rollo-Lennox.

Not all those that sided with the British Empire
against the Secessionists did so openly. Many kept
their affiliations close to their chests; some though
practised their treachery with relish, in the mistaken
belief that regardless of whoever won, their part in the
revolution would never come to light. Such a man was
Alfred Ernest Rollo-Lennox.

Rollo-Lennox claimed to be nothing more than an
occasional entrepreneur and philanthropist, living on a
minor investment annuity and a stipend from a small
inheritance. His main business interests, as listed in
the Red Books, were the theatre and a part share in a
family-owned haberdashery business. He was
considered a minor impresario by the theatrical
community. He had a personal desire for the theatrical
life, considering himself somewhat the dramaturge and
up-and-coming thespian. The closest he got to
dramatic acting though were the few gullible young

actresses, actors, and desperate theatre managers he conned and bedded.

Rollo-Lennox's real profession was spy. His affable, bumbling manner, often hysterically inept attempts at the theatrical arts, predilection for drink, and eye for the ladies, made a perfect cover for a man of low morality and even lower cunning. This role as the buffoon would prove, in fact, Rollo-Lennox to be one of the greatest actors of his time.

In Alba, penniless and down on his luck, he was enlisted by the British Government's Colonial Secret Police to befriend and gather information on suspected Secessionist sympathisers close to the Viceroy Prince. He did so with aplomb, selling out enemy and friend alike. He wheedled his way into all echelons of Tharsis society through his contacts in the theatre and a nodding acquaintance with the Viceroy Prince himself.

Unfortunately for him, or perhaps, fortunately, his subterfuge came to the attention of other interested parties. In short time Rollo-Lennox was gathering information for the British Colonial Government, the French Deuxième Bureau, the infamous 2nd Bureau, and the equally ruthless Austro-Hungarian Kundschaftsbüro. By 1898 Alfred Rollo-Lennox had become quite an independent merchant, selling information, often the very same information, to all sides.

With the assassination of the Viceroy Prince, Rollo-Lennox's game became far more complex. He was directed by the Kundschaftsbüro and the 2nd Bureau to make contacts within the Tharsian Secessionists, with the aim to funnel money, weapons and supplies to them, in return for strategic information on the British. The British, in turn, wanted him to infiltrate the higher levels of the Secessionists with the aim of breaking their cell structure open. The Austro-Hungarian's Geheime Staatspolizei were paying him to report on British troop movements and capabilities.

Rollo-Lennox was without a doubt a superb actor, but then again not actually much good as a spy. His initial successes had caused suspicion amongst the real pro-Secessionist factions and they, believing him more an inept blabbermouth than an agent of the Crown, kept him at a distance. Though, he did manage to enmesh a few less careful would-be Red Handers in his deadly games.

Put into such a difficult situation, Rollo-Lennox relied upon his own ingenuity. Initially, he creatively embellished the information he was supplying depending to whom he was selling, but that led eventually, of course, to a point where he was fabricating most of the information he was passing to all sides. This though was in no way as harmless as it might seem, as to gain credence and tinge the lies with a little truth, he implicated all sorts of demonstrably innocent people, at all levels, in his web of deceit.

Rollo-Lennox made a great deal of money out of the whole enterprise; accordingly, as long as the political status quo remained, he was safe. Unfortunately, the Long Intake of Breath had to end; consequently, so did Rollo-Lennox's luck.

With the success of the Secessionist revolution, large amounts of secret documents from all the colonial powers, fell into the Secessionist hands, along with numerous agents who changed sides. In truth, the British Directorate of Military Intelligence was fully aware of the extent of Rollo-Lennox's activities. It had been using him to feed false information to their rival organisations for years.

Regrettably, for Rollo-Lennox, the new administrations did not take such a laissez-faire attitude to his treachery. He instantly became a wanted man across several nations, with a substantial price on his head. Narrowly escaping the clutches of the Tharsis Secessionists, Rollo-Lennox famously escaped on an airship out of Alba, posing as an old matron, and fled to the fledgeling Zephyrian Republic.

Tried and sentenced to death in absentia, his sensational trial led to his name becoming synonymous in Tharsis with treachery, to the point that almost all references to him have gained the prefix *"The Traitor."* The new Government of the Tharsian Republic placed a 10,000-guinea price on his head that remains uncollected.

Written statement submitted by Sergeant
Fredrick Rawlings Jr, Tharsis Olympian
Regiment of Highlanders (Rtd) to the office
of The High Sheriff of Tharsis, Alyaksandr
Bogdanov. Regarding the prosecution of
Gabriel Wellington-Welles, also known as
Jeteur de Sort, also known as 'Madame'
Camarilla, also known as 'Prior' Jeramiah
Tonto-Jitterman. This statement focuses on
the events of the night of 45th September
M.Y. 26.

My solicitor instructs me to make clear
that we had no intent to harm anyone. Other
than the criminal people that we, as
citizens of Tharsis, were legally duty-bound
to attempt to apprehend; Lucius Everheart,
who was a murderer, Eleuthère Du Maurier and
the traitor Rollo-Lennox. We set forth with
no ill intentions towards anyone.

My orders from Colonel Jahns were to
consider Mr Franklin's directions as if they
were from himself. During the time I knew
him, Mr Franklin showed himself to have
excellent military acumen.

The crew of the walking machine took us back up on to the riverbank just after dark. We armed ourselves with what was available and considering carefully that we had several mile's journey across rough territory to get back to the manor house. We had only five horses for the eight of us.

Sydeian used the flying apparatus he had brought with him. Mr Howe had been lugging several kit bags full of the man's flying gear around since he joined us in Mefitis. Sydeian was flying ahead and would meet us at the crossroads.

Mr Franklin and the Ransom's overseer, the automaton known as Karl, said they could keep up on foot so long as we kept things down to a trot. An automaton is a machine, and he could quite easily outdistance us. Mr Franklin though is not, and it seemed madness that any man would even consider running that distance at night, over rough farm tracks, and beside horses. We could not use the lanterns or the torches for fear of announcing ourselves. Saying that though, it was a very clear starlit night, Demos was high in the night sky, and Phobos was about

as bright as I have ever seen it. Sydeian
called it a "*Hunter's Moon*." I recall Miss
Bryant-Drake wondering aloud if we would end
up the hunters or the hunted.

We met up with Sydeian at the crossroads
near the manor house, without incident, at
around about 9.30 PM. I was astonished that
Mr Franklin seemed no worse for wear after
running all that way.

Although we had discussed the plan before
leaving the Oruga, Sydeian still wanted to
argue the toss over details, even at that
point. The plan, as far as it went, was to
enter the grounds of the Manor, via the
broken-down perimeter wall. Then we would
break into two groups; Sydeian, Mr Howe and
the Hopeforth boys would go around the front
of the house. Mr Franklin, the automaton
Karl, myself and Miss Bryant-Drake would
find a way into the house from the rear.

At precisely 10.30 pm Sydeian, Mr Howe and
the Hopeforth boys were to shoot a few
windows out of the front of the house.
Drawing everyone's attention, but if things
got too hot, they were to run.

Our intention was to have entered into the house by that time, and soon as the balloon went up, we were to crash the party and lay hands upon Rollo-Lennox and Everheart.

Miss Bryant-Drake, wanted us to capture several others, if they were in the house, including the man called Camarilla. I now know to be the defendant, Gabriel Wellington-Welles. I believe Mr Franklin agreed, but I think it was quite obvious it was highly unlikely in the chaos of what was going to happen.

We made our way along the perimeter wall of the estate until we come to an area where it was so tumbled down, we could easily step over the rubble. There we tied off the horses. It took us another ten minutes running through the overgrown gardens to get to the mansion itself.

After we separated into two groups. I voiced to Mr Franklin that I was not too sure of how reliable Sydeian would be. In fact, after his poor showing at the Ransom's Farm, I had thought him a foofool. Miss Bryant-Drake agreed wholeheartedly. Mr Franklin said he had some reservations, but

we needed every hand we could call on, and
Sydeian had a reputation as an excellent
shot. Having a *"bird in the air,"* as he put
it, would be quite an asset when we needed
to make a getaway.

Apart from one or two chinks of light in
the upstairs windows, the house looked
deserted. Mr Franklin led us towards the
back.

We were expecting to find a way into the
building, but instead, we stumbled into the
end of a procession. All robed, cowled and
lantern carrying they were. Winding their
way from the rear of the house. They moved
in a strange swaying, almost shambling
motion, and I shall remember their weird
murmuring to the end of my days. It was the
uncanniest thing I have ever heard.

Miss Bryant-Drake said they reminded her of
sleepwalkers. She suggested we tag on to the
end of the parade, but the path was guarded
every couple of yards by armed men wearing
white robes who would tip us as soon as they
saw us. Instead, Mr Franklin took us back,
and we made our way around the back of the
kennels, which stank like the outflow from a

knacker's yard, so we could skirt the edge of the rose garden. The procession was heading towards a brightly lit building within a grove of trees. It was white marble and surrounded by colonnades and ornate stonework. Mr Franklin sent Karl to apprise the others of the change of circumstances.

It was impossible to discuss our actions even in hushed tones as we were by far too close for comfort. Mr Franklin led us around the edge of the tree line until the bulk of the building sheltered us from the glare of the gaslights and any unwanted attention.

It was precisely 10.15PM by then. We hunkered down to wait for the others to join us. Mr Franklin whispered to us that as soon as the others arrived, we were going in. He emphasised again that, no matter what happens, we must only shoot in defence of ourselves.

It was then that this strange music started up, the murmuring had been eerie, but this was even more unnatural. I do not know if you can call music ugly, but that is the best word I can think of for it. There was also an awful caterwauling that I cannot imagine was singing, at least not by any human being, more like the wailing of something in terrible pain.

Karl returned with Howe and the Hopeforth boys. They said Sir John had disappeared off to see something and said he would be along as soon as he could. It was the first time I ever heard Mr Franklin curse so bitterly.

There was no time to rethink as that was when the screaming started. It was coming from within the temple, a cacophony of voices screaming in agony or terror.

With a quick shout to Mr Howe and the Hopeforth boys to stay outside to cover our retreat, Mr Franklin was up and running towards the front of the building. We followed.

As soon as we emerged into the pools of light around the front of the building, the white-robed guards attacked us. Together we fought our way into the portico at the entrance. Probably thanks to the element of surprise, Karl managed to get to the front door before the guards within could slam it in our faces.

That is when the first shots were fired; by
the guards in the vestibule of the temple.
We defended ourselves but at no time did I,
or any of the others to my knowledge, fire
upon an unarmed person, or anyone running
away.

There was a short exchange of gunfire in
the vestibule, but we still had the element
of surprise on our side. Mr Franklin and
Karl were formidable fighters, Miss Bryant-
Drake and myself were relegated to all but
bystanders, as they ploughed through the
guards towards the main chamber.

I hung back with the lady, as Mr Franklin
had ordered me earlier to consider Miss
Bryant-Drake's safety as my only priority.
Which was more than difficult as she aimed
to be in the thick of it.

The doors to the main chamber were shut,
and beyond them, the screaming continued. I
did not have time to consider what on earth
was going on beyond them if I had I might
have dragged Miss Bryant-Drake out of there
and run. The doors were impressive looking
but quite flimsy. Mr Franklin and Karl had
no trouble in shouldering them open.

Though the pause must have only been for a moment. I can remember precisely the sight that greeted us upon opening those doors and will do so for the rest of my days.

It is hard to describe what I saw without sounding insane. Though I swear upon my oath as a loyal soldier of the Republic, and in the knowledge that I must accept that no one who was not with us that night will believe me, I testify to the truth of this statement.

The main chamber was a big circular sunken room, in which there must have been at least two hundred people crowded into it. They were naked, men and women, young and old, writhing on the floor, screaming and clawing at each other like wild animals. Stalking amongst them were figures in red robes who were laying about with hammers, striking at the heads of those thrashing upon the floor. It was a sickening orgy of violence and bloodshed.

In the centre of it all, there was a raised platform upon which now stood the statue that we had delivered earlier in the day. Its white alabaster now covered with gore.

One of the red-robed men was in mid-action of smearing handfuls of blood and brain matter onto the idol.

The room froze upon our entry.

In front of the statue stood the person I can now identify as Gabriel Wellington-Welles, his arms held wide as if beseeching it. I swear the statue seemed bigger than when we delivered it, and I swear it was moving. That thing was somehow alive.

Welles stopped and turned to face us. He was wearing a crown on his head made of bones, and he was naked underneath his yellow robes, which were covered in blood. Welles looked so insane he barely seemed human. Frothing at the mouth, he pointed at us and screamed out some tirade of incomprehensible gibberish. That is when Karl shot both him and the red robed man beside him.

That broke whatever spell, for want of a better word, that was over the people on the floor because they suddenly snapped out of their frenzy, and, those that could, upped and fled. They rushed at us, a wave of bloody, naked flesh, screaming now in panic

and fear. I had to pull Miss Bryant-Drake
out of the path of the stampede as they
escaped screaming into the night.

In the chaos, the red robed men flung
themselves at us. I shot one who came at me
with a hammer. Miss Bryant-Drake shot
another. With Mr Franklin and Karl, we
forced the rest back into the chamber. There
was a dozen more of them at least, mainly
older men, but they attacked us in the most
feverish manner. Even when beaten down they
jumped up and attacked again like rabid
dogs. We had no choice but to defend
ourselves as best as we could. Some managed
to slip past, for we were in no mind to
pursue them.

A scream of warning from Miss Bryant-Drake
called our attention back to the gore-
splattered thing on the platform. The
statue, for that is what we had taken it to
be, was no longer a frozen image, it was
moving, no longer imperceptibly, it breathed
heavily, its strange yellow eyes opened, and
it began to move.

It was no trick of the light or illusion,
the statue, the monstrosity, somehow came

alive. Strange colours pulsated across its skin, like a kraken. It took a halting step forward as if roused from a deep stupor and made a terrifying noise. I can only describe it as somewhere between a roar and a screech. A penetrating noise that shook our minds and rattled the teeth in my head.

Mr Franklin, possessed of more bravery than any man I have ever known, stepped forward to the top of the steps down to the sunken floor, levelled his boarding gun, and blasted the monstrosity. It staggered back at the impact. Then roared angrily and sauntered forward. In terror, we fired upon it with everything we had. Our bullets though had little effect as it just kept coming.

The slavering monstrosity was halfway across the body strewn floor, coming right at us and nothing we did even faltered it. It no longer looked, or moved like a statue come alive, it was disgustingly real and was intent on killing us.

Miss Bryant-Drake had run out of ammunition for her revolver, so she drew the Odic pistol Madam Fontenelli had given her and blasted the creature. The blast must have hurt it badly, though I saw no wound, it screamed in pain. Mr Franklin seeing the creature's reaction threw down the weapon he was using and drew his own Odic.

The screaming monster staggered away. Mr Franklin pursued it, relentlessly firing, again and again, intent on killing the thing. Suddenly there was an empty clack that reverberated around the hall like a latch being dropped. The charges in Mr Franklin's Odic had ran out. The monster turned on him, splayed its tentacles in an enormous arch, revealing a huge venomous looking black beak, roared triumphantly, and lurched to the attack.

Suddenly there appeared an Aresian woman between them. I never saw where she came from, she may have been in the room all along, but I had not seen her. It was if she sprang out of thin air. For a moment I thought it was Mrs Fontenelli, all dressed up in traditional Aresian robes. I have only ever seen one other Aresian lady in my life, and they stand like a real woman should stand, you know, tall and proud. Mrs

Fontenelli, stands like that, regal. Like a Queen. This lady was older than Mrs Fontenelli but still very beautiful. She held out a hand to hold back the monster and then turned to us and commanded us to go.

We did not wait to be told again. As we ran for the door, the monster spewed forth a disgusting cloud of stinking black gas that billowed across the room after us. We fled into the vestibule for fear of being suffocated by the noxious brume.

I never laid eyes on Mr Welles again. I believed him dead, as I had seen him shot in the chest and fall off the platform. I do not know who the Aresian lady was, nor what happened to her.

THE FOLLOWING SECTION WAS REDACTED FROM THE FINAL DRAFT SUBMITTED TO THE COURT.

Miss Bryant-Drake screamed for us to wait for the lady, but Mr Franklin slammed the doors shut hard behind us. Miss Bryant-Drake tried to open them again, but they were shut firm.

I think that that was the point at which our ears had stopped ringing enough for us to become aware of the gunfire outside.

Outside was a scene of slaughter, as terrible as what we had left behind. The whole area was littered with white-robed and naked dead, all shot down. In the air above them slowly rotating was Sydeian in his flying apparatus. Like the Angel of Death himself. He had a machine operated gun that sprayed bullets at anything that dare move. It was like a little version of the steam-cannons on the airship. A beam of red light emanated from his helmet, and everywhere it passed the dreadful spew of bullets followed.

Mr Franklin marched out into the open, and the red light instantly fell upon him. He levelled the boarding gun at Sydeian, one-handed. The Automaton and I followed him. For a moment, we all stood like that, weapons pointed at each other, unmoving. Miss Bryant-Drake then rushed out and shouted up at Sydeian, in some very colourful language, to stop. Sydeian did not answer. He just released a plume of smoke

from his engine, then whirled around, and
flew away.

Charity Bryant-Drake.

45/9/26.

The Story of Two Queens.

Cont.

I cannot expunge the indelible stain on my psyche left there by what I witnessed when Adam and Karl burst open the doors into that chamber. Nor will I ever forget the other horrific events of that night.

I believed that by our intervention, those poor people there, trapped by some kind of dark mesmerism, were freed to escape. Only to suffer the terrible fate of fleeing heedlessly into the midst of a gun battle. Though I know that there was nothing I could have done to avert it, I find it difficult to countenance my part in their fate.

I also have to contend with the fact, that, in that chamber, I witnessed the impossible, not once but twice. I have always prided myself on being a rational person. Though I have seen some unusual, strange even, events, I have always kept the healthy scepticism that my mother and stepfather taught me. Nothing is truly impossible, and that which presents itself as seemingly inexplicable may be all but mundane in the future.

Now though, after that evening, I found my grasp on the certainty of material reality weakened.

Amidst all the unspeakable horror, I witnessed, with my own eyes, the effigy of that hideous fell beast come alive as if awakened from some deathly stupor. The very thought that my hands once touched it, no matter how fleetingly, impelled me to squeamishly scour my palms against my clothes. Its strange, lozenge-shaped, amber eyes with their sha-shaped irises opened and gazed about the room. When it fell upon me, the intensity of that gaze was unbearable, as if all the evil in the universe were focused into one glare. Then it sauntered forward, its pendulous breasts and disgusting distended pudenda flapping as it moved. We fired everything we had at it, but still it came on, oblivious to the rain of lead we showered upon it. Its appendages writhed and lashed, as kaleidoscopic, mesmerising, colours pulsated across its skin.

Adam strode forward and fired the heavy gun he carried fully into its face, but the creature, the monster, barely shuddered.

I realised I was pulling the trigger of an empty pistol. In panic, I drew Aelita's Odic gun from my pouch, and out of sheer desperation, with little idea of what I was doing, pointed it and pulled the trigger. The blast hit the monster with a spine-shaking thump. It screamed. It screamed like something truly hurt it for the first time. It staggered back a few paces. Instantly I understood that no matter how invulnerable, or impossible, it seemed, this was a living creature, and it could be hurt. Adam drew his Odic, and we both blasted the beast several times.

I felt we had it on the run, we were driving it back when my charges ran out. I fumbled helplessly at the mechanism unable to recall even the simple instructions Sir John had given me. Finally, I managed to flip the cover open only for the hot empty cartridge to fly up and hit me on the bridge of the nose completely stunning me for a moment. It was then I heard the same empty 'clack' sound from Adam's Odic.

I looked up as the creature lunged to attack. Adam leapt back out of reach of its tentacles. It roared triumphantly, drew itself to its full height (somehow far bigger than the statue we had delivered) and sauntered forward.

Then, I have no idea how or where she came from, there appeared as if out of thin air, a red-skinned Aresian woman in billowing robes, standing between Adam and the monster. She raised her hand to the creature, and it stopped in its tracks. When she turned to Adam, I saw her face. It was almost the face of Aelita Fontenelli, but older, fiercer, framed with flowing white tresses. The expression on her face and tone of her voice broached no argument; she ordered us to leave immediately.

I was too shocked to take my eyes off her, heedless of what my feet were doing as Red hauled me backwards towards the doors. The monster lunged forward again, but the woman raised both hands and sent it skidding back across the bloody floor. In its frustration, it drew itself up again, splayed its tentacles into an enormous arc, and spewed forth a black cloud of noxious gases.

Once safe in the vestibule, Adam slammed the doors to the chamber behind us. I insisted that we must go back to save the woman, but Adam regarded me with the queerest expression and said, "I do not think the Lady came through a door, least not one like these." I wanted to know what he meant, what was he saying to me, but there was no time, my questions would have to wait.

Outside the temple was another shocking scene of devastation, resembling a battlefield. Sir John, Howe and the Hopeforth boys had fought a pitched battle with Camarilla's guards and hirelings. Into that brutal melee, the naked attendees had rushed, only to be cut down in the crossfire. There were dead and wounded everywhere.

I have never been so frightened or felt so alive, I was shaking with fear and exhilaration, my senses felt as if they were strung out like catgut on a violin. The horror of it all only came crashing down on me later, when I had time to think.

The images of that night haunt me, none more than the terrifying sight of Sir John in his flying contraption, hanging in mid-air, like some awful vengeful angel. A deathly red light emitting from his helm. I think he had become so focused that he must have not realised who we were, for as we emerged from the temple porchway, that terrible beam fell on us.

Adam strode forward into plain sight and levelled his big boarding gun at Sir John. For a moment I thought they were going to fire on each other, so I rushed forward waving my arms and shouting to them both not to shoot. Sir John must have realised who we were, as he turned and flew off over the rooftops of the house.

Howe and the Hopeforth boys immediately appeared from their positions. The big man was shaking like a leaf, he had a wound in his upper arm and a nasty gash on his face, blood was dripping through his big ginger beard making him look like some wild-eyed sky pirate. The young Hopeforth boys were both unscathed save for a few minor scratches.

Howe quickly explained that when the trouble started a dozen white-robed guards came running to the temple. At first, they were able to hold them at bay, but then a lot more heavily armed ones turned up, and it was all they could do to keep their heads down. Sir John appeared, and all hell broke loose. Then all these naked people came screaming out of the temple right into the middle of it. The guards did not seem to care who they were shooting. Neither did Sir John, remarked David Hopeforth coldly.

A dozen confused thoughts raced through my mind; we should help the injured and the dying, we had to send for the local Constable, we should go back to help the woman in the temple. Adam was trying to convince me that we had to just get away as quickly as we could when suddenly the few undamaged gas lamps hanging about the temple's frontage died, plunging everything into darkness.

My protestations were cut off by a dreadful noise. A sound which shall haunt my nightmares for the rest of my days; a deep guttural snarl, that reverberated through all of us. It was as if the ground itself shuddered in fear. Howe exclaimed an expletive, but his words were silenced immediately as the rumble came again.

A hand grasped my wrist, and Red thrust the now reloaded Odic back into my hand. I did not even realise he had taken it from me. "Do not hesitate, Miss." He said softly.

Something was moving around us, just on the edge of the impenetrable darkness, something very big. Adam stood poised with his boarding-gun, his eyes darting hither and thither, intently scrutinising every tiny movement in the shadows. Slowly he reached out with one hand and tapped Red's shoulder.

Once he had his attention, Adam slowly raised one, two, three fingers.

I made to ask but was waved into silence by Red. Adam pointed to the pistol in my hand, and I immediately understood why. I hugged it like an evil babe.

It felt like a lifetime passed as we stood crowded back-to-back peering into the shadows, awaiting whatever was out there, circling us. My eyes were rapidly adjusting to the limited light. It was the clearest of night skies, and both moons were still bright. As we waited in silence, I found myself holding my breath until I was almost dizzy.

After what seemed an age, Adam gestured to Karl and Red, a lot of quick hand movements that appeared to be towards the house. I suddenly understood and was about to protest when that terrible snarl came again. This time there was a human scream and an awful crunching sound, like bones being smashed by a machine.

Red whispered to Adam, "They are not interested in dead bodies."

"I did not think they would be."

Darra mumbled another obscenity.

"Mr Howe," hissed Red. "There is a lady present!"

I was stifling a nervous laugh at the irony of it when I suddenly saw one of the creatures as it slunk between pools of shadow.

I gaped open-mouthed in horror of it. It moved. No. It flowed like liquid, effortlessly, like warm molasses. A huge creature as tall as a man at the shoulder. Its grotesque head, with upwardly thrusting tusks and exposed sabre-like canines, hung low before it, the long neck covered in a dark leonine main. It resembled some horrific amalgam of a lion and a crocodile with far too many legs. As it passed through the pool of moonlight, I could see how its massive muscular shoulders bunched and flexed like cables beneath its reptilian skin. It had immensely powerful haunches, but no tail to speak of. For a second the moonlight caught in its eyes giving them a terrible eerie yellow glow, and I knew this was no simple beast, those eyes were full of malevolence, almost otherworldly, and then it was gone.

I could not contain myself, "What in hell's name is that?"

"A banth." It was Sir John. "There is at least four of them out there." He had divested himself of his flying apparatus and Gatling gun and somehow managed to get back to us.

"You did not mention them in your talk," I recalled the seminar he gave.

"Because, dear lady, they are extinct."

"That did not look very 'extinct to me'," remarked Red.

Another snarl issued from the darkness to our flank, we whirled about nervously. "Yes, it would appear they are not as extinct as people thought."

"Tell me they aren't half as nasty as they look," asked Howe.

"No, sorry to say, old boy, their reputation is worse, far worse."

"Why do they not attack?" asked Red nervously.

"Far too cunning for that. They are not mindless beasts; they are waiting for us to make a mistake. Then they will come at us all in one attack." He chuckled as if it were amusing, "I have never heard of anyone keeping them in captivity. Not even the Malacandrians."

"I count three of them," said Karl.

"They are all males. There will be a fourth, a female, she will be bigger than the males, but she will hang back and let them soften us up."

I gasped, "Bigger!?"

"Are we just going to stand here and wait to get eaten?" asked Howe. "Or worse?" he gestured behind us.

Adam whispered instructions; he and Karl would hold the beasts off while the rest made a run for the back of the house. Once there, we would cover their retreat. We began to check our firearms.

"You know that as soon as we move, they will attack," observed Sir John matter-of-factly.

"That is what I am banking on," replied Adam.

"Very well, old sport. Just remember they are notoriously hard to kill. Skin like armour plate. Underbelly and throat are the weak spots if I remember rightly."

"Could do with that rotation gun of yours right now," observed Red.

"Yes, sorry about that old chap. Out of ammunition, you know, and I just could not get the old bucket back into the air. Fuel line is blocked, and she is leaking coolant. Another minute or two in the air and she would probably have blown my arse off!" He laughed heartily. "Still, it looks like this is going to be fun."

For a moment, we all looked at him in disbelief. It was a second too long. Karl shouted a warning and thrust me out of the way. One of the banth sprang out of the shadows towards us. Adam stepped into its path and fired his boarding gun into its face. It collapsed only feet from me with the sound of a tree falling. Its face a bloody mess of pulped fur, bone and teeth. I stared awestruck at a paw at least twice the size of my open palm, with talons four inches long, that came to rest only an inch from my feet.

Adam shoved me roughly, "Run!" I ran. Blindly and without a thought, I did not stop or look back until we reached the rear of the house.

Behind me, Adam and Karl were firing into the darkness around them. The flare from their guns was blinding, making it almost impossible to make out anything more than the occasional glimpses of the massive creatures circling them.

Sir John rallied us. I screamed in frustration that I could not see anything clearly enough to shoot at, but he laughed that it did not matter so long as we did not shoot Adam or Karl. Eli Hopeforth handed me a repeating rifle, and I blasted away wildly at shadows until I ran out of ammunition.

Adam and Karl had almost made it to us when one of the banths came flying out of the darkness at them. It hit the ground short and, with impossible agility for a creature that size, sprang to the attack again. We all shouted a warning. Adam and Karl flung themselves to the ground. The banth sailed over them and landed only feet from us. So close, I could have touched it with my outstretched arm. Instead, out of pure instinct driven by nothing more than terror, I fired the Odic pistol at it. The weird thump of the discharge was almost satisfying. The blast tore through the beast's shoulder as if some unseen thing had taken a massive bite out of it. The banth screamed in agony and fled towards the shadows. I fired after it.

Adam and Karl leapt back to their feet and ran to join us. I noticed the first one that Adam felled was gone.

We had taken refuge behind the crumbling remains of an old privy, with our backs to a broken but barricaded door. Karl strode past us and effortlessly shouldered the door open. We bundled in as quickly as we could. The door had one good bolt, but that was not going to be much use, so we braced it with an old table and some discarded timber that came to hand.

Karl quickly found a pair of oil lamps and lit them, revealing a disused, cobwebby scullery or domestic's kitchen. It looked like it had been rapidly abandoned, crockery was piled up on the drainer, mould covered the plates on the side, and had not been revisited for decades. A startled rat ran for cover. "Is this how you got in last time?" I asked. Karl answered no, but it was how they left.

Something massive and snarling angrily thudded against the barricaded door. "May I suggest we get a move on, chaps? That is not going to keep that old Cheshire moggy out for long."

"They would never fit through that doorway," I said incredulously. Another enormous blow shook the wall.

"I don't want to stay here to find out, Miss." Howe, gun levelled, was backing away from the door, nervously.

"This way." Adam took a lamp and headed across the room and out of the kitchen. I followed closely. "Where are we going?" I asked, "If Everheart was still here, he will be long gone by now."

Adam paused to look at me. His face a fearful mask in the yellow glow of the lamp. "I doubt that. He is here somewhere waiting for us. Men like him do not run."

I tried to argue further, but Sir John concurred, "He is right. The bugger will be here somewhere."

It took us an age fumbling in the dark to find our way through the maze of corridors and rooms full of books and miscellany, beds, piles of discarded clothes and rubbish. We picked our way carefully past the body of a young man in a Footman's uniform sprawled on the servant's stairs, someone had beaten him to death with a poker. For some reason, I know not why, I took the poker. The cold iron comfortingly heavy in my hand.

We discovered bloody, naked adherents, hiding in rooms and corners, still hysterical with fear. They had obviously managed to find other ways back into the house. Some begged us to spare them, others begged us to take them with us, some just screamed hysterically. I am deeply ashamed to say; we closed the doors and left them to whatever fate awaited them.

Finally, we passed through the armoury, with its walls bedecked with antique weapons, shields, suits of chainmail and banners from Earth's ancient past, made even eerier by the flickering light of our oil lamps, and into the well-lit grand hall.

Of course, Adam was right.

Lucious Everheart stood in the middle of the room awaiting us. The centre had been cleared since we saw it that afternoon, all the furniture and the object-d-art had been pushed to the edges of the room.

Everheart stood isolated in the middle of the space, one man alone, but his presence, like the foul-smelling cigar he smoked, filled the room.

We spread out, but he hardly reacted other than to puff casually on the cigar.

Someone began clapping, a slow derisive clap. Upon the balcony overlooking the room stood a man in a crimson robe. I gasped; it felt like we had come face-to-face with another monster like that in the temple. He was taller than I expected, but it was undoubtedly Eleuthère D Maurier himself. His clothes beneath the robes were business-like but a couple of decades out of fashion, his black hair lacquered to his perspiring forehead. His greasy skin had the waxy sallow look of the consumptive. His aquiline nose was pinched at the tip by a pair of darkly tinted spectacles, and below his exaggerated handlebar moustache, his thin-lipped mouth was wet with drool, which he dabbed absently at with a handkerchief. "Bienvenue, Monsieur Franklin, and you brought your little friends with you."

"D Maurier," his name blurted out of me as if I were spitting poison.

He grinned widely, his face distorting strangely to show a mouthful of bloody teeth. Stepping forward, he leaned casually on the balustrade. "Ah, oui moi. Mademoiselle Bryant-Drake. Here I am. Did you not expect me?" His every word dripped with condescending self-satisfaction. Whatever was going on, D Maurier believed he had us right where he wanted us, and I feared he was correct. "I must admit Monsieur Franklin; you have done rather well, so much destruction! But we know you were more than capable of that, did we not? What with destroying your old ami Lloyd. Trashing our little experiment in Mefitis. Tell me, did you really kiss her before you killed her? How romantique of you! Monck told us everything, such a little chatterbox, but ne t'inquiètes pas, your secret is safe. Capitaine Everheart silenced him for good. Then you storming poor Gabriel's little celebration party! Honte à voustous! He has worked so long, so diligemment, for this night. He must be so upset if he is still alive. Is he still alive?"

Adam did not reply.

"I shot him," said Karl flatly.

"Mon Dieu! Behold, the Man Engine speaks!" He clapped his hands, "Wonderful." He paused, sighing theatrically. "But why are you here? The trail of breadcrumbs I left was for Ransom, not you. The cowardly little runt has not even the gall to attempt to avenge his own wife's murder."

"It was you that ordered Everheart to murder Eleanor Ransom." It was the only thing I could think to say.

"I can see why you are such a fine journalist Miss Bryant-Drake; nothing gets past you." He sneered. "How else were we going to lure Ransom and his father-in-law back? Though I must say, I am disappointed in them."

"What have you done all this for?"

"Charity. May I call you Charity? You know what it is for, simple vengeance. I cannot allow your kind to defy me with impunity. Not that dirty little dandelion grubber, nor your high-handed stepfather with all his haughty condescension."

I knew he was baiting me, but all I could think to say was, "We have come to take you back to answer for what you have done."

He laughed uproariously and slapped the handrail loudly. "Oh, dear, dear Charity. You have no idea, do you? None of you is getting out of here alive." He dabbed at the bloody foam at the corner of his leering mouth. "Well, it has been lovely to meet you all, but, unfortunately, all good things must come to an end.

You have of course met mon serviture Capitaine Everheart here." With that, he stepped back into the shadows.

Everheart took one last long drag on the cigar and tossed it away. Suddenly he snatched for the revolvers on his hips, but Adam, Karl and Sir John were faster. The deafening blast from their guns propelled Everheart across the room like a rag doll, crashing him into a glass-fronted display cabinet full of china, which collapsed upon him.

Was that it? I realised I was not breathing and gulped air as I gaped at the body of Everheart. As easy as that?

Adam though seemed trepidatious. He was eyeing the corpse suspiciously and carefully reloading his boarding gun. I was about to insist we pursue D Maurier before he could escape when I heard a gasp from Howe, and the look on his face told me there was something very wrong.

The cabinet tottered and then crashed to one side as Everheart slowly climbed back to his feet. His hat was gone, and his waistcoat ripped to tatters, but there was no blood. Where his wounds should have been, he just dripped a thick aureolin coloured mucus.

Adam took two quick steps forward and fired the boarding gun at the closest of ranges into Everheart's face. Everheart crashed back into the stack of cabinets in a shower of shattered bric-a-brac. Karl and Sir John rushed to back him up, but all they could do was watch in horror as Everheart slowly began to get up again.

I stood paralysed by indecision. The Odic was in my hand, but I did not dare fire it with Adam and the others in the way. Everheart let out a terrifying inhuman noise and lunged towards Adam, who met him head-on with the brass-bound butt of the boarding gun. There was a sickening crunch of metal on bone, and Everheart went back down to the floor. The others took their chance to open fire, but it was like fighting the thing in the temple; their gunfire appeared little more than an annoyance to whatever Everheart was.

Everheart sprang up again, dodging another hammer blow from Adam's gun butt. Instantly they were at each other's throats in a ferocious struggle. They grappled and clawed at each other like wild animals. Suddenly Everheart gained the advantage and threw Adam to the floor. He roared again and snatching up the remains of an oak built china cabinet, as if it were little more than a cardboard box, smashed it down upon Adam before he could get up. As Adam faltered, Everheart began to rain blows upon him.

Snapped out of my revelry, and seeing my opportunity, I aimed my Odic to fire, but Karl stepped in the way. Swinging his own gun like a club, he slammed Everheart across the head, staggering him, and then with his great metal fists beat him to the floor.

Everheart threw himself around Karl's legs and began to claw himself up. I could not believe what I was witnessing. Karl fought so hard we could hear the grinding metal of the gears and cogs in his arms, but still, somehow Everheart overpowered him.

I pleaded desperately for Adam to get up, but it was too late. Everheart's hands wrapped around Karl's neck as Karl's wrapped about his. I could see Karl's brass fingers imbedded in Everheart's throat almost to the bone: mucus flowed from the gaping holes, but still, Everheart's grip tightened. There was a shocking metallic crack, and instantly Everheart changed his grip, then, with a screech of triumph and rending metal, he tore Karl's head off his shoulders and threw it across the room.

I screamed. Of all the horror of that evening, all the shocking things I had witnessed, this was the worst. Everheart drove his hands into the gaping hole and ripped Karl's chest open, wrenching gears and pistons apart until he tore free Karl's machine heart and threw it to the floor.

Something cold came over me, an icy rage. I have never wished someone dead, so profoundly, or so emphatically. I took my chance and shot Everheart. The green flare struck him in the shoulder, and he screeched like a scalded cat. The clothing was destroyed, the flesh beneath it instantaneously burnt black. Cursing with every obscenity I knew, I stepped forward and fired again, this time taking better aim to hit him in the chest, then, as he staggered backwards, in the head. He fell.

A hand gently rested on mine and lowered the gun. It was Adam, bloodied and battered but still alive.

As he turned back, Everheart began again to get up. This time he was agonisingly slow. His face was just a charred mess, his body broken, but he was still dragging himself back to his feet.

Sir John snatched the poker from my other hand and threw it to Adam. "Use this." There was a momentary look of confusion on Adam's face as he weighed the poker thoughtfully.

"Don't think, man! Hit him with it."

Everheart was almost on his feet as Adam stepped forward and with a double-handed swing, struck him across the head. This time Everheart went down instantly, but Adam was not going to stop. With almost workmanlike efficacy, he battered Everheart until there was no sign of movement.

"The heart," ordered Sir John. "Drive it through its heart."

Adam did not hesitate, with all the force he could muster, he drove the iron poker through Everheart's chest, pinning him to the floor.

None of us dared take our eyes off Everheart's body. I prayed he had to be dead. Dear God! He must be. I must have said it aloud because Red added, "Amen."

Howe swore loudly. Everheart's body was moving again. I could not tolerate looking, but I could not avert my eyes. It was not the movement of someone trying to get up, his body began shaking and then with a long sigh it began to change, his skin began to crinkle up and became brittle looking. The corpse becoming nothing more than a dried husk.

A voice cried out in anguish from the balcony above the hall, it was D Maurier, now flanked by two white-robed henchmen. He gripped the balustrade and howled wretchedly. "No! NO! What have you done?" he glared down at Adam. "What have you done?" his face twisted with anxiety. "YOU!" he pointed at Sir John, "You cannot interfere. Damn you!" He then began to cry out in the same strange gibberish that Camarilla used.

Adam drew his Odic pistol and fired, but one of D Maurier's attendants hauled him out of the way of the blast that exploded the thick handrail into dust. The henchmen fired a few Parthian shots down at us before fleeing after their master. We returned fire wildly as Adam and Red ran for the staircase, but by the time they had reached the first landing, Eleuthère D Maurier and his men were gone.

Though it aggrieved me awfully to do so, I had to insist they let him go. The ground floor of the house was a maze of rooms and passages, undoubtedly so were the upper floors, they could spend a lifetime searching for him, and I was sure, he probably had a dozen hidey-holes and secret escape routes. Frustratedly, they return down the stairs like two sulking children.

Out of morbid fascination, and a need to know for sure, I viewed Everheart's body carefully. It no longer resembled a corpse, more like the empty husk left behind when an insect or snake sheds its skin, wrapped in human clothes. I prodded it with the toe of my boot, and it was hollow as if what had been inside had gone. Or, as it occurred to me, worse still, released.

Written statement submitted by Sergeant Fredrick Rawlings Jr, Tharsis Olympian Regiment of Highlanders (Rtd) to the office of The High Sheriff of Tharsis, Alyaksandr Bogdanov. Regarding the prosecution of Gabriel Wellington-Welles, also known as Jeteur de Sort, also known as 'Madame' Camarilla, also known as 'Prior' Jeramiah Tonto-Jitterman. This statement focuses on the events of the night of 45th September M.Y. 26.

Cont.

After the fight in the hall, we knew we had to get away from the house as soon as possible. Though it took time to gather our wits. The Zephyrian had escaped.

As far as we knew, the banths were still patrolling outside. Sydeian assured us that in open country they would make short work of us. Which was stating the damned obvious as far as I could see.

The Hopeforth boys helped Miss Bryant-Drake in the sombre collection of the pieces of the automaton. She was intent on taking it with us. Mr Franklin, Sydeian, Howe and I toured the great hall's ground floor windows to try to get a glimpse of the creatures.

It was as we were doing so Howe discovered a fat, elderly man hiding in a corner behind an upturned chaise longue. Though dressed, he had divested himself of his robes and was little more than a gibbering wreck. Howe dragged him to his feet and demanded to know who he was. A gun pressed to his temple calmed his ravings enough for us to make sense of his claim to be just a servant, an Orderly to some Colonel or something. He pleaded his innocence and miserably begged us not to harm him.

Sydeian swore loudly, marched over, and roughly dragged the sobbing wretch out into the middle of the room and announced him as Alfred Ernest Rollo-Lennox, famed traitor to everyone.

Miss Bryant-Drake was aghast.

Lennox immediately stopped play-acting and began to try to bargain for his freedom. At first, he insisted we should let him go as he was *protected* by someone called *Jeteur de Sort.* After Mr Franklin told him that we had no idea who *de Sort* was, and if he had been in the temple, he was undoubtedly dead; either beaten to death, shot or eaten by that monstrosity. Lennox changed tack; he offered us all very substantial sums of money to let him go, even more, if we would get him away from this place. Sydeian ordered him to shut up, but he continued to plead, so he struck Lennox aside the head with his gun, knocking him to the floor.

Miss Bryant-Drake was outraged at that and went to Lennox's aid.

Mr Franklin told us all that Lennox was our prisoner and must be treated properly, at least until we could hand him over to the authorities. He then ordered me to bind Lennox to a chair and gag him.

Myself, I would have shot him on the spot, but Miss Bryant-Drake pointed out that Lennox was one of the most wanted men on Mars and whoever brought him to justice would be seen as a hero.

Sydeian remarked acidly that Lennox would make quite a trophy or an excellent bargaining chip.

Mr Franklin remarked that it might come to that.

Sydeian demanded to know what the plan was as it would be impossible to make a run for it cross-country dragging that tub of lard behind us.

Miss Bryant-Drake suggested he should carry Lennox; in the bitterest tone I had ever heard from her.

At that, we went back to looking out the windows for the banths.

From the front windows, we could see one of them laying, apparently asleep, on the moonlit driveway. We watched it for a while, but it did not move. Sydeian cracked a windowpane and, while we stood ready to slam the shutters, took a shot at the reclining creature. It still did not react. Mr Franklin then fired his Odic at the banth. It blew a hole through its shoulder, the size of a cannonball. We looked on in amazement; it was like Everheart's body, it was nothing more than a hollow shell as if someone had made a perfect copy out of papier-mâché.

We had to move. There was a hell of a lot of open countryside and hemp fields between the Oruga and us, assuming, of course, the

Oruga was still waiting for us, and it was getting darker. Demos would soon follow its brother over the horizon, and the rest of the night would be pitch black.

We fell into debating what to do. Could we risk that all the banths had somehow turned into these strange husks? Moreover, what of that thing in the temple? To get to the horses quickest, we would have to go out through the back, and around the temple. None of us wanted to go back and pick our way through that slaughter. Sydeian threw his question into the pot again, how could we take off across country dragging a prisoner with us?

Finally, Howe offered to go, collect the horses and meet us at the gatehouse. The Hopeforth boys volunteered to go with him. We were still arguing the merits of that plan, as we had no idea where the Zephyrian had gone, nor how many of the guards were still around, let alone the thing in the temple when Miss Bryant-Drake hushed us into silence.

There came a familiar noise from outside; the sound of a chugging, clanking, hissing steam engine made rhythmic by the thump, thump, thump beat of the piston-driven feet.

We rushed to the windows, hardly believing our luck. We could hear it clearly, but we could not see it at all until its big gas headlights came on illuminating the entire front of the house and it finally shimmered into vision. The massive machine released a plume of smoke and came to a shuddering halt at the bottom of the portico.

So that was the trick Omari Cotton alluded to the previous day; The man that had built it had indeed been a genius. The Oruga could turn invisible to the naked eye.

The side loading door dropped open, and Isaiah Barebones appeared with a stentorian in his hand and began calling out our names.

We were all too relieved to think clearly, or at least to think about Lennox, our prisoner. I began to help Miss Bryant-Drake with the remains of the automaton, but Mr Franklin intervened. He gave me orders to guard Lennox. I think he did not trust Howe and the Hopeforth boys to be able to protect the prisoner from Sydeian, who had been arguing from the moment we found him that someone should "put a bullet in the white-livered bastard and be done with it."

Somewhat annoyed by Mr Franklin's remarks Sydeian and Howe went off to retrieve his flying equipment.

So, while the others made sure the dash to the Oruga was safe, the Hopeforth boys and I were set to guard the prisoner.

As soon as the others were gone, I sent the boys on an errand to raid a cabinet of drinks we had passed outside the armoury for whatever they could find, as we were all sick of drinking that cheap whiskey Barebones keeps.

I could not allow any opportunity for Lennox to escape or bribe his way out. Once he was on the Oruga, Lord knows what would have happened, and then there was the question of how we would hand him over to the authorities. We were part of a crew that had already disobeyed a direct order from the War Office. We had no idea if warrants had already been issued for our arrest.

Once the lads were out of the way, I executed the traitor Rollo-Lennox. I shot him once in the heart and once between the eyes. Before doing so, I informed him who I was and that as a Sergeant in the Olympian Highlander Regiment of Foot it was my duty to carry out the sentence passed down on him by the High Court in his absentia.

So, I did what had to be done; I, and I alone, executed the traitor Rollo-Lennox. I have lost too many people; both of my brothers, several good friends and innumerable comrades because of men like him.

The Flammarion Expedition Journal of L. Edwin Ransom.
Day fifteen. 44th. 9th. 26.
Sunday.

Cont.

*After the exceedingly strange events of the day and the sad loss
of the Colonel and his men, I think we all had too much turmoil
going on inside us to be able to make even the mildest of
conversation. Instead, we shuffled about like automatons making
polite noises, but at a loss to put anything into words.*

*I can barely remember anything until I found myself picking
aimlessly at my dinner, or what was a very late luncheon. I think
we all hardly ate a thing. Subsequently, we found ourselves sitting
in the wardroom each lost in our own thoughts. After a while,
Aelita excused herself, saying she needed to retire early, as the day
had been exhausting. With deep understanding, we all murmured
our wishes for a goodnight; though personally, I feared her sleep
would be no more restful than the one that awaited me.*

*I had been trying to divert myself by reading one of the books
from the wardroom's little library, a whaling adventure by an
American called Melville, but was having little success. It was an
avoidance strategy to put off going back to my cabin as it would
mean being alone with the dark thoughts inside my head. I gave up
reading, and taking off my spectacles, stretched out in the wingback and rested my eyes.*

*Dr Spender, Patty and the Professor had been playing a half-
hearted game of cribbage at the table. After a few moments, Dr
Spender, probably believing that I had dropped off, changed the*

subject of their conversation from the card game to the events in the tower. "May I ask why you did not for a moment believe that fellow Lanulos? It was as if you did not even entertain the thought for a moment that what he said contained any modicum of truth at all. Though, essentially, he was accurate in observing that he is indeed living proof that your theories are correct; there are Aresians still here on Mars."

The Professor thought on that for so long I was almost compelled to raise an eyelid to observe his reaction. "I agree," he conceded, "to some degree, the man's presence proves that other Aresians do indeed remain here. However, whether or not that alone can be taken as proof that elements of their wider civilisation endure, I doubt, as his presence could as easily be explained as analogous to Mrs Fontanelle's unfortunate situation. As to my initial response to him, my 'gut reaction' so to speak, was that I took the man for a fraud. There was something very wrong in his manner. I found his whole demeanour to be erroneous. Edwin's strident reaction only served to enforce my initial response. That that Lanulos fellow should appear in the disguise of a Human was, I feel, significant. His cocky manner and the use of a mask smacked of dissimulation. It seemed nothing but an attempt to frustrate our endeavours at discovering the truth of the Martian's disappearance. I saw him as nothing more than a liar, a confidence trickster, playing some game of half-truths, like a penny-ha'penny stage conjurer, a leftover from a lost Empire, hiding in plain sight. Also, any man, Tellurian or Aresian who would be a party to the murder of an unarmed woman, for whatever reason, and be so callously brazen about it, was not someone from whom we would seek aid, let alone trust with all our fates.

"His attempt to enmesh Mr Franklin in a crime he could not have committed and to persuade Aelita to go with him was more than enough proof for me that his singular aim is to thwart us, shake our resolve and stop us going any further."

Patty interjected, "Is it not obvious? The reason for murdering that poor woman was to stop us learning whatever truth it was she had to tell. She was the true emissary of whoever brought us to that place."

"You think that we were brought to that place deliberately? But by whom?"

"Whosoever was upon those terrifying ships," Patty answered emphatically.

"If they were 'ships' in any sense," mused the Professor. They appeared to be half-living aethervolt spacecraft. Have you even heard of anything like them before? Because I have not."

Dr Spender fell silent for a moment. "I mentioned to you before about the visions I had in the Tomb at Edwin's farm. I believe those visions real; the evidence of the creatures we found in the wreckage of those war machines this morning bears testimony to that. In those visions, I did see strange, nigh on bizarre, aethervolt ships in flight. Some resembled those we saw today; some were even more outlandish."

"More outlandish?" repeated the Professor incredulously.

"Indeed. Though what really fascinates me is that the sigils emblazoned upon the sails of those crafts were familiar."

"I know. They appeared very similar to the drawings of the nobori upon the ships you witnessed amassing to assault Tyrrhena Mons."

"You have an excellent eye for detail, my friend. Parthena and I took time to double-check, as I feared the excitement might have clouded my own recollections, but I dare say those nobori were identical."

Patty concurred. "I think, Professor that the Aresians you seek, found us."

The Professor sighed loudly. "Then, Octavius, what in Hell's name is going on? If those were the Aresians we seek, then why bring us to that place only to chase us off with gunfire? Why did they destroy the tower? I feel like we are being toyed with, in some bizarre game of Blindman's Buff."

"You might be right, though I fear some of what that cad said may have been true. As possibly some of what that young Captain we encountered before him, told us, the very best deceptions are liberally seasoned with truths."

"What do you mean? In what possible way could any of that be true?"

"Lanulos talked of unravelling some form of curtain between worlds. The Captain claimed to be from the past, possibly a past alternate to ours." He paused as if to let our minds catch up. "I

think that there may indeed be some truth in the idea of some form of veil between distinct realities, something of which we are totally unaware."

"Octavius, it is more likely they were in cohoots, and it is all part of the deception they were playing on us."

"True, but James, if that was the physical scale of their deception, at what point does it stop being an artifice and become a reality?"

At that moment, a crewman burst into the wardroom, loud enough to startle me out of my not so feigned doze. "Sir! Sirs and Madam. The Captain believes you would wish to see this."

"What is it, man?" There was a note of irritation tinged with dread in the Professor's voice, but the crewman was already gone.

We rushed after him, out on to the deck. A steward pointed us forward, and we followed the gawking and pointing crewmembers.

The evening panoramic was utterly breathtaking. There was a spectacular sunset behind us, the sky, flecked with a few wispy cirrus clouds, was ablaze with countless rainbow hues. Below us, the land was a patchwork of forbidding ancient, red-leafed forests on the higher grounds that gave way to swathes of saffron shall and sand dunes stretching off towards the foothills of the Bradbury Mountain range. All cut in sharp relief by the sunlight against the deep azure of the eastern horizon and the distant, brooding presence of Mount Őrület itself.

Patty grasped my arm and pointed to our portside. In the distance, possibly a mile or two from us was what I first took to be a great airship, a glowing galleon in full sail, but it was no ship.

Sailing majestically on the airstream was a vast Aresian Man-of-War, its huge lucent gas envelope illuminated fantastically by the dying sun's rays. Below the hull of the creature, for want of a better word, its trailing tentacles glittered dazzlingly, like a festoon of mirrored ribbons miles long, reflecting the blazing colours of the sunset.

As my mind grappled with the fabulous yet terrifying beauty of the sight, I realised there was not one but a dozen or more, strung out towards the horizon for as far as my eyes could see. A magnificent silent armada of creatures, soaring through the sky towards the same far mountain range we sought.

The End of Second Collection

Notes on Language.

Astute readers may notice what might appear odd usages and spellings of words in Tharsian English, these may or may not appear to be idiosyncratic to individual writers, this is not because of any lack of education on the writer's part or spelling mistakes – which we have endeavoured to address throughout the texts.

As with all colonial communities, the parent language usage almost immediately began to change when in isolation from its root form. Idioms in everyday use amongst the working and lower classes rapidly entered universal use, such as *'smole'* for a type of peculiar smile, and divergences in the spelling of even common words occurred.

We have not removed or changed the more easily comprehensible instances when they have occurred. Examples include my grandfather's use of *'expectatious'* and Adam Franklin's spelling of *'waggon.'*

The Secessionist amongst the patrician class and intelligentsia were the original prime instigators in these changes, as a reaction to a letter to the broadsheet newspapers from the ex-British Governor-General, Sir Oswald Carfax in 1895, decrying the lamentable misuse and falling standards of The Queen's English across the British colony and suggesting a linguistical standards authority be created to address the issue. In reaction, the Secessionists often adopted archaic words, new words, idioms and idiosyncratic spellings in their written communications with each other. With the advent of Independence, English, used at all levels of Tharsian society, rapidly changed.